Praise for Deidre Knight's Midnight Warriors Series

Parallel Seduction

"Never a dull moment." —*Romantic Times*

"Filled with heart-pounding action, plot twists, passion, and great steamy romance."
—Fresh Fiction

"Gives . . . readers a taste of everything they could possibly want in a highly sensual, action-packed tale. . . . A poignant, everlasting love story." —Kwips and Kritiques

"[The] spiciest installment of Deidre Knight's Midnight Warriors series."
—Wantz Upon a Time Book Reviews

"Beyond amazing." —Single Titles

Parallel Heat

"Twists and turns abound. Reuniting with characters from the first book is only part of the fun that awaits you in this sensually intriguing look at what is, what might be, and what could have been." —Romance Junkies

"Knight's unique perspective and clever plotting make this story and this series something to savor!" —*Romantic Times*

continued . . .

"[Deidre Knight] has cleverly created some great and complex characters. Everyone seems to be hiding something, whether it's intentional or not . . . in this fantastic paranormal series."

—Fresh Fiction

"A riveting novel . . . a must-read."

—Romance Reviews Today

"A hot romance." —Romance: B(u)y the Book

"A combination of fine characterizations, great pacing, action-packed plotting, and a truly imaginative take on the dizzying intricacies of alternate realities makes for a very worthy sequel."

—BookLoons

"Richly layered with mood, atmosphere, and vibrant details. This unique world . . . will capture the hearts of fans." —Romance Divas

Parallel Attraction

"From a fantastic and riveting new voice in paranormal fiction comes a thrilling debut novel of danger and passion, and a love that will cross all boundaries of time and space."

—Karen Marie Moning, *New York Times* bestselling author of *Spell of the Highlander*

"A unique plot, with twists and turns that leave you guessing . . . a fantastic paranormal tale of the redeeming power of love."

—Susan Kearney, *USA Today* bestselling author

"Not a book to start at bedtime, as you won't want to stop reading once you start."

—Romance Reviews Today

"At times humorous, at others heart-wrenching, but always compelling, Deidre Knight offers readers a fresh, wonderfully creative glimpse at the complexity of human decisions. What a page-turner!"

—Gena Showalter, author of
The Pleasure Slave

"An intriguing paranormal romance with compelling characters, complex world building, fascinating alternate realities, and riveting love scenes."

—Catherine Spangler, author of
Shadow Fires

"This book swept me off my feet. A fantastically original, smart, and sexy adventure."

—Susan Grant, bestselling author of
Your Planet or Mine?

"An intriguing new voice in paranormal fiction has arrived! This novel is chock-full of passion, betrayal, and redemption, and will certainly leave you wanting more!" —*Romantic Times*

"One compelling and absolutely phenomenal read! Intensely erotic, passionate, and riveting."

—Paranormal Romance Writers

"[A] wonderfully gripping mystery. . . . The world Deidre Knight created is fascinating. . . . *Parallel Attraction* is flat-out incredible!"

—Reader to Reader Reviews

"Ms. Knight is coming onto the paranormal scene with guns blazing."

—Once Upon a Romance Review

Also by Deidre Knight

Parallel Attraction
Parallel Heat
Parallel Seduction

PARALLEL DESIRE

A Novel of the Midnight Warriors

Deidre Knight

A SIGNET ECLIPSE BOOK

SIGNET ECLIPSE
Published by New American Library, a division of
Penguin Group (USA) Inc., 375 Hudson Street,
New York, New York 10014, USA
Penguin Group (Canada), 90 Eglinton Avenue East, Suite 700, Toronto,
Ontario M4P 2Y3, Canada (a division of Pearson Penguin Canada Inc.)
Penguin Books Ltd., 80 Strand, London WC2R 0RL, England
Penguin Ireland, 25 St. Stephen's Green, Dublin 2,
Ireland (a division of Penguin Books Ltd.)
Penguin Group (Australia), 250 Camberwell Road, Camberwell, Victoria 3124,
Australia (a division of Pearson Australia Group Pty. Ltd.)
Penguin Books India Pvt. Ltd., 11 Community Centre, Panchsheel Park,
New Delhi - 110 017, India
Penguin Group (NZ), 67 Apollo Drive, Rosedale, North Shore 0632,
New Zealand (a division of Pearson New Zealand Ltd.)
Penguin Books (South Africa) (Pty.) Ltd., 24 Sturdee Avenue,
Rosebank, Johannesburg 2196, South Africa

Penguin Books Ltd., Registered Offices:
80 Strand, London WC2R 0RL, England

First published by Signet Eclipse, an imprint of New American Library,
a division of Penguin Group (USA) Inc.

First Printing, December 2007
10 9 8 7 6 5 4 3 2 1

Printed in the United States of America

This one is for my soul mate and best friend, Judson Knight, who is Jared, Marco, Scott, and Jake all rolled into one—well, with a little bit of Chris Harper in the mix, too. I love you very much, doll!

ACKNOWLEDGMENTS

As always, I have so many people to thank and am afraid I might leave someone out. No wonder I actually thought, "Maybe I can just forget the acknowledgments this time?" But how could I, when I have so many wonderful supporters and team members?

First off, thanks go to my family, for their willingness to share me with my crazy writing obsession. To my kids, I promise that I will one day cook again, and to my hubby, I promise that I will get off my writerly duff and start walking more often. I PROMISE. Grin.

Major shout-outs to my talented and wonderful editor, Anne Bohner, as well as Liza Schwartz for all they do for me. The entire team at NAL is truly the best, and I greatly appreciate the support I receive from everyone there, especially Kara Welsh and Claire Zion. Thanks for believing in my stories and in me!

To my fellow TKA gang, Elaine Spencer, Nephele Tempest, Jamie Acres, Kerensa Wilson, Julie Ramsey, megathanks. You really kept me sane on this one. And of course, big thanks to my agent, Pamela Harty, for being so terrific and supportive. Likewise, I am eternally grateful to Jana Hanson and Rae Monet for all the work you do behind the scenes. Also, I'd like to send a special hug and kiss to my Girl Everything, Kim Acres, because I couldn't do it all without you.

My Knights of the Round Table, you women and friends are amazing! What a gift you've been in my life. Big smooches and thanks for always making me smile.

Brian Stark, you're a Web god. Thanks for being so innovative and bringing your talents to my sites!

Angela Zoltners, I couldn't do this without you, dear friend. Thank you, thank you.

Marley Gibson, thanks for the great name loan. I heart you.

Prologue

A Future

No one was coming. The thought sounded hollow and round, like one of the cruelest bullets in the humans' arsenal. There wasn't a soul who could help his wife; no one at all.

Vainly he searched the battlefield for a healer, but they'd been tapped dry by the day's carnage; to the very last man and woman they were spent. The medics were knee-deep in loss and bloodshed, unable to hike the long distance to the wind-battered tent where Hope lay dying as she labored in vain to deliver their baby girl. Human or hybrid, the doctors couldn't say for sure what their child would be, yet Scott Dillon knew one fact for certain: Precious Leisa would be *theirs*. It was the only thing he needed to know about their daughter, born of love in a time of hardship and turmoil—born to them against all odds, including Hope's fragile health.

He could picture the tufts of light blond hair atop Leisa's head, silvery gold, just like Hope's, and he could already feel her nestling close beneath his chin on cold nights like this one. In a cruel world made so much crueler by the years of endless fighting, their tiny child would smell of innocence. And perfection . . . of a love that defied battle lines as well as the lines that separated species.

Yes, by All, she would be theirs.

But only if he could get someone—hell, anyone—to deliver their baby girl on the night of this Armageddon.

With the night-vision goggles fixed over his eyes, he scanned the perimeter of the battlefield but still found no one who could help. He'd hiked more than an hour, beyond the defenses of the day's skirmish and onto the next plateau. Blood, bodies, death. There wasn't a soldier he recognized who might help them, just devastating loss in every direction.

Falling to his knees, he lifted his hands in supplication. "Lord of All, please save my wife . . . our baby girl. Help them, I beg of you." Bowing his head, he reached with every particle of his being, every molecule of his essence and lifelong faith in the One who governed their destinies.

Help them. Take me, but spare them, please!

A rustling of wind caused him to adjust his night-vision goggles and glance up toward the tree line along the ridge. There, kneeling and bent over a fallen soldier, he glimpsed Rory Devlin, one of their strongest and best healers. How he'd missed the man before, he had no idea, but like a gift from above, Rory glowed bright green with energy through his goggles. Without another breath or thought, Scott took off running, sprinting with all his might toward that one gifted healer gleaming out of the darkness, the answer to his prayer.

Time. Just give me one more breath of it, he begged, stretching his shaking legs as long as they would go.

By the time they reached her, almost another hour had passed. An hour of heartrending, unstoppable moments that Scott Dillon counted off with every passing step. An hour of hiking and dragging their drained bodies over rough terrain, forcing themselves onward. Sighting Rory on the ridge had been a miracle, and for the first time in his quest, he'd allowed himself to truly believe that Hope and Leisa might have a fighting chance for survival.

Arriving back at their shabby encampment, he led the way into their battered tent, but none of his worst imaginings could have prepared him for what he saw: the love of his life, still and motionless. Rory followed quickly on his heels, gasping in shock, but Scott could only stare in mute horror, unable to process the unholy image before him.

"Hope," he whispered, falling to her side. "Sweetheart . . . love." Only then did he see the swelling bruise along her neck, the purpling outline of fingers around the pale and delicate column of her throat.

Her lovely gray eyes were closed, one hand crumpled across her forehead, the other cupping her full belly in a protective gesture.

"Gods in heaven!" Rory hissed behind him, but Scott could only laugh. Insane—hideous, wrong—but he couldn't seem to stop himself.

Rory grasped his shoulder. "Dillon—"

"Shut the fuck up!" he screamed, pressing his face against Hope's. She'd wake up; hell, of course she would. It was some kind of sick joke. What else could it be?

Nuzzling her, he whispered, "Sweetheart, knock it off. What're you trying to do to me, huh? Stop this right now!"

Rory tugged at his elbow, but Scott shook him off like he would a rabid dog. "Get the hell outta here!"

"Let me lay hands on her," Rory tried lamely, but Scott's tears blinded him senseless.

"Get out!" Scott screamed, and Rory backed out of the tent, leaving him alone with Hope.

Burying his face against hers, he kept murmuring to her, reaching for their bond. Anything just to wake her up.

"So it comes to this," a chilling voice spoke into the quiet.

Scott jerked his head sideways and saw a giant of a human in the far corner of the tent, sneering, the scent of Hope's death all over him.

For a long, distended moment Scott kept his face

against Hope's cool one, time playing out, playing him for the ultimate fool. Until he lunged upward, slamming to his feet and to his fighting senses.

Without a thought or any rational process, he lunged toward the human stranger, both hands about the giant's throat as he tackled him to the ground, all awareness dimming. Struggling, he had the much larger man pinned beneath him almost instantaneously.

Scott sucked at the air all about him, gasping. "How could you . . . fucking . . . do—"

His opponent cut him off. "You know how!"

The stranger's human stench was unmistakable as he writhed within Scott's grasp, gurgling and laughing up into his face as they grappled, fought. His enemy had the weight and size advantage, but Scott had the advantage of hatred and fury, pinning the bastard beneath him, both hands stifling breath from the man's throat. Just as this enemy had stolen life from Hope's body.

The human actually half smiled up at him, smirking even as his life was being choked away. As if he knew a secret—as if he knew *why*. Why he'd killed Scott's wife and unborn baby.

And something about that sneer unlocked the berserker within Scott Dillon, caused him to delve deep within his nature as an Antousian shifter, taker of life and being. With one last glance toward Hope, her body lifeless—Leisa lifeless within her, too—Scott waged war upon the human. Probing deep within the stranger, into the marrow of his being, he determined to kill. *To take.* To murder, as his soul mate had been murdered at this dark man's hand.

Scott Dillon became everything he'd always sworn he would never be—something clicked inside him, something driven and dark. He would leave his own mortal body and take possession of his enemy's, thereby snuffing out the other man. He would abandon himself so he could choke out every bit of identity that the killer had ever known. He'd always reviled this about his kind, this ability to harvest another living being's body, forcing that person into oblivion. But blinded by grief and fury, it seemed right somehow. Seemed the only possible ending to the life-and-death battle that he waged against the human who writhed beneath him.

"You'll pay." Scott clenched his hands about the human's throat, eyeing him hard with his gazing ability. Searching him totally with his Antousian's gift of stealing everything. A life, a body, an identity. Images invaded Scott's mind, flashes of a dusty road, a military installation, a corporate-looking office, a bar. A slashing staccato of mental photographs that he couldn't string together, not when his rational mind had deserted him so completely.

"Why would you kill them?" Scott demanded, tightening his grasp around the man's throat.

The human slugged at Scott's chest weakly, his eyes shutting, but said nothing.

This killer would pay, totally.

"You are ours," Scott hissed into the darkness of the tent. "You belong to Hope Dillon. Leisa Dillon. And me." He was crazed, unaware of his wife's lifeless body, of anything that smacked of goodness. He didn't give a hell's virgin for his soul, not then. Not for eternity. "You are *mine*," he swore.

And I am yours, he thought, feeling his own body blend with that of the murderous human's. *We are one.*

Kelsey Bennett pushed her way past the gathered soldiers outside Scott and Hope's tent, ignoring the protests of several who tried to stop her. "Careful, my lady!" some called out. "A killer's in there."

One of the burliest soldiers grabbed hold of her arm, pulling her back. "My queen," the lumbering man implored her, "he's a madman."

She shook off his grasp, striding into the tent and shoving her way past the several officers who had guns drawn and aimed at the intruder. She'd mentally prepared herself for the sight of Hope's dead body, but despite that fact, finding her friend lifeless—and held by a stranger—drove the very breath from her lungs.

A large man lay behind Hope, holding her against his chest, rocking her. He stared at some unseen sight on the far side of the tent, singing a quiet song in Antousian under his breath—a song she'd recently overheard Scott teaching Hope, a lullaby from his childhood.

She heard the weapons around her engaging, safeties dislodging, as she moved ahead of the gathered soldiers and stared down at the large man who cradled Hope within his arms. On the far side of the tent lay Scott Dillon's lifeless body, but she couldn't bring herself to do more than barely glance at it.

She didn't even know why she was here; everything within her said this tent was an incendiary point of danger. Still, she'd jolted awake from her disturbing, vivid dream, absolutely compelled to come. After leaving the tent, Jared still asleep inside, she'd heard the news—that Hope had been murdered, and that Scott Dillon was dead at the hands of her killer.

Still, that wasn't what her dream had shown her, and she'd learned that her intuitive visions were always significant. The most important ones were infused with a particular smell, a palpable feeling—just like the dream that had called her out of deep sleep and into this tent.

Dropping to her knees, she took Hope's cool hand within hers, bowing her head. The man holding her flinched, then wrapped both arms about Hope's body more tightly—as if he thought Kelsey would try to take her from him. For long moments she knelt beside her dead friend, praying and listening to the mournful Antousian song the man sang.

She was supposed to believe he'd killed Hope, but because of her dream she knew better. Casting another glance at Scott's lifeless body on the other side of the tent she finally spoke. "You're going to have to let her go."

"I can't leave her here, not like this," was the man's answer, his voice a deep gravelly sound.

"The fighting's going to start again in just a few more hours. We don't have long to give her the burial she deserves."

He moaned softly. "I'm never burying her."

"If you don't, then the wolves will get her. That's not what you want."

He rocked her harder in his arms, slipping one large hand over her full belly. "I'll stay with them. From now on, I'll stay."

Kelsey looked up and for the first time saw the brilliant, almost eerie green eyes he now possessed. *"Scott,"* she answered meaningfully, "you are going to have to let them go."

His eyes slid shut. "They think I killed her."

"Of course you didn't—you could never hurt Hope or Leisa."

"They don't understand what I did." He trembled all over, burying his face against the disheveled blond hair atop Hope's head.

Kelsey slid forward on her knees, lifting her fingertips to Dillon's forehead, stroking his temple with a soothing gesture. "They've forgotten who you are, Scott, and what you can do. You were distraught—"

"I had to stop him; he couldn't do this again."

"I know." She kept her hand atop his head. "I know, Scott. I saw it all in my dream."

"They're going to kill me." Tears welled in his green eyes; he looked like a stranger, but his soul was that of her husband's lifelong best friend—and one of her closest friends, as well.

"I won't let that happen—neither will Jared."

"How do you know who I am?" He jerked back angrily, fixing Kelsey with a furious stare. "You don't know that I won't kill you, too."

Ignoring him, she bent down and kissed Hope's cool cheek. "Scott, we'll get you through this. Just do what I say, and I will help you out of this, okay? They're going to listen to me—they *have* to listen to me."

"Leave us here." Scott shoved her hand away, sending Kelsey sprawling backward.

The soldiers behind her took several steps closer; she tossed a glare over her shoulder. "Back down! Ease down, right now, Lieutenant," she said to the leader of the small knot of fighters. He searched her face, and she gave a brisk nod, whispering again, "Back down."

The gathered soldiers lowered their weapons, and their leader gave an unconvinced nod. She turned back to face Dillon, to the man he had become, that he was, after seizing his enemy's body. He appeared to be a stranger, but she recognized his soul and spirit thanks to her dream vision.

Shaking, he tightened his hold on Hope. "I'm as dead as she is."

"That's not true." Kelsey shook her head.

"I don't even have a name now."

"You're still Scott Dillon."

One of the soldiers tossed a wallet in her direction and it landed beside her knee. "Found this in his jacket. Says he's Jakob Tierny."

Kelsey flipped open the wallet and examined the driver's license inside. Only a few other slips of paper, a lined photograph, and a computer chip were crammed within. She studied the man in the license photo, but he had almost no resemblance to the one huddling in front of her. The green eyes in the ID were the same electric hue, but they were hollow and empty. Chilling. The eyes gazing at her right now were filled with heartbreak and weariness. They did not belong to the man in the license photo.

She extended the ID to Scott. "Take a look. This is the man you killed. Can't you see what's wrong with him? You have to see the soullessness in his eyes."

Scott examined the photograph, staring at it for many minutes before slowly handing it back to her. "From this day forward, call me Jakob Tierny."

"I don't understand."

"Scott Dillon is dead," he pronounced, slowly releasing his hold on Hope. With a quick glance at his former body, crumpled on the floor of the tent, he said, "Everything inside of me is dead. I'm a killer, just like the man whose body I stole. So from now on, I will become him."

"You took his body, but you're not him," Kelsey tried to argue, but he only shook his head.

"Scott is dead." He bent low, nuzzling Hope's cheek. "Scott is dead. And I am Jakob."

Chapter One

Present Day

Jake stared at the cell phone cradled in his palm and deliberated whether he should actually make the call he had planned. The last time he'd phoned Hope, it hadn't gone so well, a result he'd come to expect after about, oh, twenty or so calls like the one he was currently contemplating. Of course things would be awkward between them, he told himself. Of course their relationship would be strained. After all, she had once been his wife, many years before. Not many—five, he corrected himself, although each one of those calendar rotations had felt like an eternity. Days had given way to months had dissolved into years, a blur of body-numbing grief that had finally bled into one long march of pointless time.

And that sensation of timelessness and pain had only grown more muddied now that he was stranded ten years in the past, where everything he'd ever known had been altered. He was a stranger living in the wrong time and dimension, and although he rejoiced that Hope would now live, it was slowly killing him that she was joined with his younger self.

He'd thought he could handle it, knowing that the two of them would have the happily-ever-after that he'd been denied with her. But with every passing day, another chamber of his heart went dead cold.

In his future, she was dead, murdered by the man

whose body and identity he'd chosen to seize in a murderous act of his own. At least he had been justified, acting in a moment of blind fury and grief. And that grief hadn't stopped dogging him since that day five years earlier, when Hope and their unborn baby daughter, Leisa, had been ripped right out of his arms. And now, after all that he'd once endured, it was happening again: Hope was alive and well in this world, sure, but she might as well be dead. Dead to him.

Just as dead as the man he'd once been—Scott Dillon.

Every part of his soul that answered to that name had died long ago, too. All that remained in its place was a shell, a hulking hollow of the man he'd once been. Staring down at the cell phone clutched in his hand like a lifeline, he realized that he couldn't possibly stop himself. It was inevitable: He had no choice but to try reaching out to Hope once again.

Hitting speed dial, he lifted the cell to his ear and held his breath. She answered after six rings, sounding slightly winded, and his nasty streak of jealousy kicked right in. What the hell had she been doing before he called?

"What's going on . . . Jake?" She always stumbled over his assumed name; then again, he couldn't imagine that she would want to call him Scott, either.

For a moment, he let silence grow between them, listening to the sound of her soft inhalations across the line. "I needed to hear your voice," he admitted at last. "That's all."

He could practically sense her urge to groan aloud. He'd been calling her far too often lately, more frequently with every passing month since he'd last seen her back in December. It was May now, and not one of those months had dampened his love for her—or the ache lodged deep inside his chest.

"Jake, this has to stop. You know it does." Her voice was gentle, tender. Loving, even.

"I can't seem to help myself, sweetheart."

"But you're going to have to, Jakob." Her tone was

firm, insistent. "You're killing yourself like this, and we don't want that."

"We?" he mimicked distastefully. Yeah, he had no doubt that his calls were bugging the shit out of his younger self.

"*I* don't want it, Jake. I want you to start living again, to figure out what you need . . . here, now. Not keep mourning me forever like you've been. It's time to let go."

"What's *he* doing?" *Making love to you, kissing you from navel to collarbone?* No wonder she sounded so breathless, he thought, muttering a quiet curse.

"Scott's not here right now," she told him, her tone more clipped than usual.

He buried his head in one hand, staring at the floor beneath his cowboy boots. The dismal room he'd been calling home lately, with its torn mattress and lopsided dresser, only made his mental state more dark and oppressive.

"What if I can't stop?" he whispered into the phone. "What if it's not possible?"

"It's *not* what *I* want, Jake. Don't make me start screening your calls." She attempted a laugh, but he knew her too damned well. The jocular note was entirely false. "I love you, Jake, and I always will. But I really just want you to let this go."

"*This* . . . or you?"

"Our past. I want you to move on."

"Where am I supposed to move on to? Huh?" He felt tears sting his eyes; he'd been caught in an impossible triangle with his younger self and his one-time wife for five months now, and he wasn't even treading water. He was sinking fast. He guessed that Hope could read that in him; no wonder she was getting more forceful.

"You should go back to the main base in Wyoming."

"And if Scott returns? I can't be in the same place as he is, not if I don't want to obliterate us." He laughed mirthlessly. "You of all people know that I can't occupy the same space and time as my younger self. Not unless I want to destroy us both. The universe just isn't going to tolerate that kind of displacement."

"Scott and I are staying here at Warren Air Force Base indefinitely," she told him. "Working with the Joint Alien Task Force. So it's safe for you to go back, and you should. Make a life for yourself with your own people." How easily she dispensed her advice, how simple she made it all sound.

"Are you happy?" he asked, a stab of pain digging into his chest.

She hesitated, blew out a sigh. "How do you want me to answer that?"

"I want to know it was worth it, everything I gave up. Everything I've lost with you. I need to know that you're happy with him. . . ." He paused. "And that he's happy."

"You remember what we shared in your past," she admitted in a thick voice. "You already know what it's like."

"Oh, gods," he half moaned, shaking his head. "Look, I gotta go."

"Jake, please—"

He cut her off, positioning his finger over the END button. "Gotta . . . go," he repeated, realizing that what he needed was to get shit faced and lose himself in a bottle. But he didn't tell her that. "You take care, sweetheart," he said in a choked voice, and quickly disconnected the line.

Some guys just ought to know when to stay down. When the jaw took a certain kind of hit, when the guy clubbing him had all the advantage, well, hell, that was the time you should just play possum. Of course Jake Tierny wasn't one of those guys, and Shelby would have been disappointed if he had been. Still, she winced watching him flip backward over the pool table, his long, lean legs buckling over his head.

"Hey, hey," she tried to intervene, peering across the table at her fallen friend. "Enough's enough, no?" She looked up at the red-faced hitter, who tossed her a glare, then revved his fist up once again, ready to deliver another blow.

"He had it coming, okay? He brought this shit down."

"I'm sure that's true." She pressed her eyes closed, not wanting to see yet another fist pummel into Tierny's already bruised face. "But surely a guy's paid his price after, oh, an hour's bout or so?"

"An *hour*?" The jerk straddled his awkwardly crumpled opponent on the far side of the pool table. "Hell, we ain't been at this but five minutes."

A gathered group of onlookers parted for her, an assortment of potbellied men with alcohol-reddened faces who'd been cheering the whole thing on. A few of the fools even hung their heads shamefully. "Sorry, ma'am," one of them muttered, cigarette dangling from his lower lip.

She squeezed through the pack, rolling her eyes in disgust at the lot of them. Men could behave like such overgrown children when it came to their egos and territory. She stepped carefully past a splintered pool stick, tempted to pinch her nostrils shut. The nauseating scent of aggression permeated the bar, nastying up the place with its twin odors of sour alcohol and day-old sweat.

She dropped to the floor, squatting beside Jake. "What have we here?" She chuckled, balancing her hands on both knees as she bent closer to examine Jake's injuries. Her patient squinted up at her, lifting a broken beer bottle in a toast. Then all of a sudden Shelby was being airlifted, Jake's assailant having slid his pair of beefy hands beneath her armpits. She flailed with her sandals, one of them flying like a dagger at the far wall, clattering as it bounced off the vinyl-paneled surface.

"You. Let. Me. *Go!*" She writhed her hips, bicycling

her legs until she finally managed to kick her attacker. He dropped her with a painful thud onto the cement floor of the pool hall, climbing past her to get at Jake.

Huffing like he'd just run five miles, the human took advantage of Tierny's prone, drunken position. He snatched Jake's broken beer bottle right out of his hand, drawing instant blood with a slice to Jake's forehead.

Shelby had truly, finally, and completely had enough.

She grabbed the brown bottle out of the attacking redneck's hand, gesturing toward him with its sharp edge. "Do that again, and you'll lose half that pretty face of yours. Okay? This is just retarded, so stop it already."

"He came in here looking for a *man.* You don't come in *our* bar, in *our* town, pulling shit like that." His overbite seemed to get worse, his mouth turning down at its edges until bloody spittle shot toward her. "It just don't go over, not around here."

Shelby thought fast. "He's looking for his missing twin brother." She worked her face into a mask of semigrief, weaving her hands together in front of her chest as if she might break into prayer at any moment. "Gone so many months now. So very many." She shook her head wistfully, raking her eyes over Jake meaningfully. "It's terrible when someone you care about vanishes without a word."

The attacker tugged his T-shirt down over a beer belly that protruded like a swollen upper lip. "I don't care who the hell he's looking for, not after what he called me. Y'all heard it." Thrusting his chest out and preening like a *flkiisii*, the fool gestured at his pals, who'd closed a small perimeter around her and Jake.

Uh-oh. Warning bells chimed like midday mess call inside her mind.

"Yeah? What did that boy say, now?"

"Called me something I can't repeat, using that funny language of his." The surly redneck pointed his forefinger at her, wielding it like the stubby barrel of a sawed-off shotgun. "Couldn't pronounce it."

"Called him a *slav'nrksai.*" Jake struggled to sit up, temporarily bobbing out of his drunken haze.

Just freaking brilliant. Here the guy was lost in South Texas, in some after-hours honky-tonk, calling this dude by a particularly obscene Refarian expletive. Perfect. Perfectly perfect.

"Jakob Tierny," she announced in her loudest, most annoyed voice. "You don't have a fuck's clue what you're doing, now, do ya, boy?"

Closing one drunken, long-lashed green eye, Jake stared up at her with the other, wrestling to untangle his legs. "I'm all right." His voice was a slur.

"Yeah—and that's why I told you that you needed a guide here in Texas." She gestured at his assailant, who looked ready to pounce on Jake again without the slightest provocation. "I did warn you about needing some qualified help."

More than four months had passed since last December, when Jake had hauled ass out of their compound—without her offered guidance. And, man, had she ever offered it, practically insisting that he cart her along with him on this crazy-assed odyssey of his. But the stubborn fool had snuck off base in the middle of the night, leaving her with a packed bag—and a few shattered fantasies about what might have happened between them on the open road. She'd realized it wasn't personal, not for a loner like Tierny, and had finally managed to put the whole dang thing out of her mind.

Besides, from the look of things right now, he hadn't stopped grieving the loss of Hope Harper, not for one day since his hasty departure. He might have come down this way with the thinly veiled excuse that he was searching for the real Jake Tierny, in order to stop him from killing Hope a second time, but it was more than obvious that he was lost in a haze of drunken grief. He couldn't be with Hope, so chasing Tierny was obviously the next best thing.

Knowing that Jake was still in love with Hope had made it obvious she should just forget him completely.

That was, until their commander had asked her to go after him. She'd do anything her king requested, including following Tierny into the deepest bowels of Texas, and so she'd complied. Her mandate was to bring Jake back to their camp, and so she was here to follow through. She'd die before disobeying Jared Bennett. And she might die, actually, right here in this hellhole of a dive, if she couldn't disentangle Tierny from Redneck Man in five seconds flat. In fact, it sure looked like dying was the major part of Jake's plan.

"So, Bruiser, you drive a truck?" she called over her shoulder, lifting her shirt sleeve to Jake's bloodied cheek. *"You freak,"* she added under her breath, scowling down at her crumpled comrade. "Told you. *Told* you not to try this alone."

Jake laughed up at her, blood gurgling from between his swollen and bruised lips.

She blotted at his mouth with her sleeve. "This ain't funny. You're in a shit storm now 'cause you didn't listen."

"You're that pretty little medic with a southern accent," he announced wondrously, both eyes rolling back in his head.

She just clucked her tongue. "That I am, boy. That I am."

"He's about to kick my freaking ass." He managed to focus his gaze again, leveling her with his startlingly beautiful green eyes.

"He's already done that, but I'm getting you out of here before he finishes the job."

With a one-eyed squint, Jake studied his human opponent. "I'm not done with him yet."

"Jakob," Shelby said with an intense, meaningful glare, "say you're sorry. Just go on, now."

"All right." Jake wrestled to sit up straight, his legs finding a semblance of the floor, his back pressed up against the wall. "I never called anyone a *slav'nrksai*"—he kicked Redneck Guy in the shin—"especially not your mother. I don't need that word for someone like your mama."

Shelby barely heard the roar before she saw the pale human's fist rip into Jake's jaw like a ball-peen hammer bludgeoning a melon. "Oh, no." She ducked out of the way at the very last minute.

Some aliens just never learned, especially the green-eyed, wickedly handsome kind.

Jake's head cracked back against the wall, and hard, but not before she managed to half whisper, "Lieutenant, good thing I came after your ass."

"Holy hell, that hurts." Jake moaned, ducking away from the medic's efforts at working on his bruises. His first thought was that he hadn't managed to get himself killed in that bar, not like he'd wanted to after that pointless call with Hope. Moaning, he tried to force her from his thoughts, glancing about him in an effort to figure out where he'd passed out.

Obviously, he'd slept the damn brawl off, but somehow—some way—he seemed to have wound up in a motel room. Not his own room, in the center of what passed for a town around here, but one off a local highway. He could tell that much because of the occasional sounds of trucks and other vehicles busting past their thin door, the way it rattled with the roadside vibrations. Somewhere else around here he had his own room, a dingy bit of a place where he'd been keeping his pack and measly belongings while he trailed the real Jake Tierny around half of Texas.

"Holy hell?" Shelby repeated, bending over him until her long blond hair tickled his throat. "You done become a real Texan, boy. Haven't you?"

Jake growled up at her, ducking away from the damp cloth she was working over his bruises, and spit at her in low Refarian. If the dainty little medic was going to accuse him of going native, well, by All, he'd fight her fair. He was no more Texan than she was, what with that pretty little accent of hers, fake through and through.

The both of them had been raised on a planet far, far away—so far away that they'd learned English in their own separate manners. Shelby Tyler had apparently done so right here in Texas a few years back. Jake, on the other hand, had learned the language on the endless transport from Refaria to Earth, the computerized dialect and linguistic files training him. He'd always prided himself on his accentless English, that it could belong only in the United States—not Great Britain or elsewhere on the planet. He and his fellow aliens hadn't made their home in London or Sydney, and his bland accent reflected that fact.

But not Shelby; no, her version of English, from the very first time he'd met up with her five months ago on the base back in Wyoming, had been heavily infused with a southern accent. Quite Texan, he'd later realized as they'd kept talking—and that fact had been confirmed once he'd ventured down to this part of the United States. Hers was an authentic drawl bought by time in the trenches. His questions as to how, precisely, she'd earned that time, well, he figured they'd be answered eventually. She'd told him vaguely that she'd been posted to their Texas facility prior to its decimation by their enemies—and while that explained some aspects of her acquired Texan nature, it hardly explained it all. This woman had passed plenty of time among the locals, not something any of the soldiers at the Texas facility would or should have ever done.

"Who are you, Shelby Tyler?" he asked softly, staring up into her clear blue eyes, finally letting her blot at his bruised jaw without ducking away. For a long moment she seemed arrested by his question, staring back at him wordlessly, hand frozen midair.

"You know exactly who I am." Her words were careful, precise. No more Texas accent, not this time.

"I don't know *meshdki* about you, Medic Tyler. So start talking."

"And if I don't?"

He propped his head along one elbow, giving her a smile. He hoped it looked wicked, seductive, even though he felt too battered at the moment to really mean it. "Well, I'll have to extract that information."

"Don't even try and go that devilish, charming route with me, Lieutenant. Seen it all from you before."

He narrowed his eyes, studying the pretty blond medic. In their few interactions he had no memory of having been either devilish *or* charming. Maybe there was something between them that he couldn't recall?

"Say what you mean, Shelby Tyler."

She removed the damp cloth from his face, making a great show of folding it first in half, then over again. "I know all your moves, sir; that's what I'm saying. Gone a few rounds with you down in the medical center and come out on the . . . Well, the winning side, I'd say. You'd say different, no doubt."

"Are you talking about when you stitched up my belly?" He remembered how she'd tended him after his fight with the Antousians months back.

"Not your belly. Good lord, more than that. I mean when I was your night nurse, sir. Took care of you after your legs were shot out from under you at Warren."

Jake's eyes slid shut. "Oh. Him."

"Yeah, him—your younger self, that's who."

"You're talking about Scott Dillon. He's the one you tended to after Warren, not me." He shifted on the mattress, fighting a wave of nausea. "I'm not him, and I keep telling all of you that." *After all, Hope certainly knows that's true*, he wanted to add.

Shelby sidled closer, wedging her hip right up against his as she leaned down over him. "Um, then, who are you, sir? I mean, really? You're him, come back from ten years in the future; of course you are."

Jake turned away from her, putting his face to the wall. "Go away, Shelby Tyler." He groaned, working a hand at his temple; it throbbed with a hangover from last night's drinking and last night's brawl. "Honestly, just get away while you still can."

"You denying it?" She pressed her face into the

small space between the wall and his body. He couldn't avoid her, not like this—especially not with her wide blue eyes peering right into his own so openly.

He burrowed his face into the flimsy pillow. "You took care of that knife wound of mine, end of story. Now, go away."

"Our king charged me with a duty—to bring you back with me to Wyoming."

He had to hand it to the woman: She was persistent if nothing else. "Tell him I wasn't willing."

"I can't do that, now, can I? We're talking about Commander Bennett. Imagine me reporting something like that back to our king? No way, no how. You're coming, too."

Jake rolled onto his back, shoving Shelby back across the bed. "Look, Nurse Tyler, clearly there are a few things you don't understand right now. One"—he raised his index finger—"I'm not Scott Dillon, not anymore. I don't have his body, or the exact memories your Lieutenant Dillon has . . . or that his wife does either." Jake battled a spasm of intense, choking pain for a moment.

"And two?" Shelby prompted, blue eyes alert and waiting.

"Two, is that my business down here isn't finished. I have to find Jake Tierny, the one who murdered Hope in the future, and stop him from killing her again—in this timeline."

She nodded thoughtfully, but still he knew that some kind of snappy retort would be forthcoming. The only surprise was that it took about fifteen seconds, not two. "So, sir, you were what? Just renting that body back in Wyoming? The one that still belongs to Scott Dillon? That wasn't you?"

He flopped back against the pillow, staring at the ceiling. "Where is this going?"

"I'm just trying to be clear on why you won't go by your proper name, that's all, sir."

Jake bolted upright in bed, clasping Shelby's arm

tightly. His fury always simmered just beneath the surface, ever since the day of Hope's murder at the hands of the real Jake Tierny. "I died when I took his body," he snarled. "Don't ever ask about it again. Do you understand?"

She met his steely gaze with an unwavering, purposed one of her own. Never flinching, never backing down. "Understood, sir."

"And don't call me *sir*. Not for the reasons you're doing it."

"You weren't still serving our king in the future?"

Of course he'd been; and he'd been a lieutenant, too—but she was trying to make him into Scott Dillon, someone he'd long ago ceased to be. "Call me Jakob. Or Jake. Either one, and I'll answer."

She chewed on her lip, glancing down at where he still clasped her arm. He released her, holding a palm up to indicate his desistence.

"I've got some aspirin for you," she volunteered, popping to her feet. In a few seconds, three tablets were extended toward him in the center of her palm, and a bottle of water was held out with her other.

"You take nursing pretty seriously, huh?" He downed the medication, tossing his head back.

"Very seriously. But there's one thing I'm even more serious about, and that's following my king's directives."

Jake lifted an eyebrow. "That again?"

"If you aren't going to come back with me, I need to know what to tell him. I know you, sir, and I also know how you love Jared Bennett. I can't imagine you'd want to hurt him or defy him—not at all."

And of course she had him strung up like a roped calf. He sat up in bed, leaning his back against the wall. "What did Jared say exactly?"

Shelby walked across the room to a desk and pulled a chair out, then dropped into it right beside his bed. "Well"—she drew in a breath, and he guessed it was because she wouldn't stop talking anytime soon and needed to store up—"our lord has been increasing with his intuitive abilities since our queen became pregnant. They're tuned to each other, their respective gifts heightening." She sucked in another breath and dove back in. "Anyway, he's been plagued by bad visions concerning you, quite frankly, sir—uh, Jakob."

"Bad visions, huh?" He rolled his head against the wall and wished like hell that the aspirin would start their work. "That's pretty general, Medic Tyler."

"Call me Shelby."

"Shelby, why should bad visions concern me? My whole damned life is a bad vision at this point."

There was a long, heavy silence, so profound it caused Jake to open his eyes again. "He's foreseen your death, Jakob," she told him softly, her gaze never wavering from his face. "Here in Texas. It's why he wants you back."

Jake returned her stare for several silent moments, then sat up in bed. "All right, fair enough. But before you insist that I return with you, there are a few things I need to show you first."

Shelby stared at the battered wallet and other documents that Jake had spread across his desk. They'd left her motel room, riding in his mud-encrusted pickup to his place on the far side of town. If you could call Hell's Creek a town. More like an opportunity—or a state of mind—but surely not a real town, not from what she'd seen so far. It was a windy dust bowl dotted by sagging double-wides, abandoned storefronts, and a main street that consisted mostly of rolling tumbleweeds. Unless you counted the bars; too many bars for so few people, at least by her reckoning.

During their short drive, he'd made it pretty clear that there was something she had to understand about his situation down here in south Texas. One thing was obvious: He had no intention of obeying their king's directive to return to the main base.

"So what is all this?" She reached for the wallet, but he caught her hand roughly.

"Before you open that, I need to explain." He bent

down slightly, lowering his hefty shoulders in order to meet her gaze head-on. "You should understand what you're seeing."

After months alone, Jake was clearly relieved—more than he'd ever willingly admit—to debrief her on his activities. "Go on."

His bright green eyes narrowed with an almost predatory glint, and he gave a brisk nod, turning toward the desk. He jabbed a finger at the wallet. "I took this off of Tierny the night he killed my wife."

"Hope." No way would she let him objectify the situation. She'd been through enough grief and loss to last more than three lifetimes, and understood the temptation to depersonalize. "You took it from Tierny the night he killed *Hope*," she clarified.

"Yes." He leaned a little closer, his large shoulder brushing against hers as he bent to open the wallet. "The night of Hope's murder, this was all that remained of the man who did the deed. This wallet and"—he braced both hands on the desk, slowly rotating his head until their gazes locked—"this body."

"So you killed him . . . took his form because he'd killed her?"

Jake swallowed, his Adam's apple bobbing wordlessly. Finally he whispered, "Payback."

"I understand payback, sir." He cut his eyes at her continued use of the formality, and she lifted a hand. "Jake, I'm sorry, but it's danged hard to relinquish the chain of command."

His shoulders sagged and his grip on the desk tightened. "If you need to call me *sir*, then do so, Shelby."

"I'm more comfortable that way."

"So long as you have a clear handle on the facts."

"Which are?"

"That I am not the man you're convinced I am. I changed after Hope's death, after taking this body"—he tapped his chest—"and this man's identity. You can't understand it; you're not Antousian."

She couldn't help but flinch, and she saw the instant regret in his eyes when he stood upright again, backing away slightly as he continued, "I'm sorry to remind you of my genetic heritage and am well aware of how distasteful that must be for a Refarian such as yourself."

She shook her head dramatically. "I ain't got no problem with you."

His eerie green eyes filled with unexpected amusement. "What is the deal with this accent of yours, Shelby? This way of speaking? 'I ain't'? You studied human language, the same as me, and the emphasis was on nonregional dialects."

She felt her face flush; if only the man knew. If only he could understand why she spoke the way that she did. "I perfected my English down this way, sir. That's all."

"I'm not buying it."

Shelby bent over the desk, reaching for the wallet where it rested just beneath his hand. "Give me this thing, okay? I'm ready to find out what's really going on here."

"Tactical avoidance." He chuckled, a low rumbling sound that would have turned on any woman this side of the Rio Grande, and plenty more on the other side, too.

She avoided his electric gaze, focusing on the wallet. "No, sir, but I have a mission here, and I'm keen to fulfill it."

"A woman with a purpose," he purred with a sly, seductive smile. "I like that."

Scott Dillon, through and through, no matter what name he goes by, she thought. *Ever the purveyor of his masculine charms.* Still, she was fairly certain his tone was more show than anything else; the sadness in his eyes was much too obvious to indicate otherwise.

"Give it to me." She yanked the wallet out of his grasp, but he caught her hand, and for an infinite moment nothing mattered except the touch of his swarthy skin against hers. He seemed to feel the same electric shock because he grew still, arrested, a slight scowl creasing his midnight black eyebrows.

At last she jerked the wallet to her chest, holding it there protectively. "You've got to give me a while to catch up, *Tierny*." Hell, if the guy wanted to live the role, she'd call him by whatever godsforsaken name he asked of her.

He waved his hand magnanimously. "Be my guest. I'd love to get your take on its contents."

Cradling the wallet close below her chin, her gaze never leaving Jake's, Shelby flipped it open. The first thing she saw nearly sucked the wind right out of her: a driver's license dated four years in the future, bearing the photo of a man who might have looked exactly like the one beside her. Only he didn't, not in the ways that really counted. Sure, this Jake Tierny was older than the one in the photo—a strange trick of time-traveling fate that she couldn't begin to reason out—but it was far more than that. The stranger in the photo ID had cold, lifeless eyes, the kind you wouldn't want staring back at you on the wrong end of a gun. Or alley, if it were a bad time of night or even day.

She studied the address on the ID. "He lived here, in Hell's Creek?"

"Not a man or woman I've met has ever heard of him."

"So he hasn't moved here yet—this thing's dated four years from now."

"Maybe. Or maybe there's just more to it than that."

She eyed him suspiciously, opening the billfold section of the wallet. "What's this, huh?" It was a computer chip—typical Earth-based technology, more or less state of the art down here.

Jake crossed both arms over his chest, his green eyes assuming a sly, seductive glint. Just like his younger self, he exuded sensuality without even trying. "Oh, it's nothing much." Then he laughed, a bitter, hollow sound that filled the room. "It's only the key to absolutely everything."

Chapter Two

Thea jogged onto the main hangar deck—with any luck, she'd be early for the upcoming debriefing with Jared and his other advisers. She certainly needed the extra time to gather her thoughts after receiving this latest report from her source. It had come in just an hour ago, intel from deep within their enemy's camp, information that had chilled her to the very core.

She'd worked this particular spy for the past year, milking her dry, draining her totally when it came to sensitive information. They'd traded e-mails across cyberspace, pretending they were part of a multilevel scheme for fortysomethings who wanted to keep their skin "elastic." The hoax masqueraded as a truly simple sales game, the perfect front for exchanging classified information.

It really is just that simple, Thea thought upon entering the conference room, thankful that she was the first to arrive. For every bit of subterfuge she'd ever practiced in this war, for every weapon she'd ever fired, in the end it was *all* simple. Only the consequences weren't.

Pacing around the table, Thea worked to still her thoughts. The truth was that it didn't exactly feel good knowing she was collaborating with the enemy. Who cared if her source was a spy, feeding her critical information? Who cared if that same soldier had helped her free Scott Dillon and Hope Harper back in December? She was still partnering with a full-blooded

Antousian, a member of the same race that had decimated her home world. The very same race that now sought to devour Earth without compunction. It wasn't exactly the sort of thing that helped her sleep any better at night.

She pressed her fingertips against her temple, determined to train her racing thoughts into a central point of energy. Too much was at stake this morning to do otherwise—at least according to her spy's latest transmission. A wave of panic speared through her, but she shivered, shaking it off.

She needed Marco *now*.

Reaching across the permanent bond she shared with her lifemate, she linked with him. *Where are you? I feel you getting stronger.* She could sense Marco very close by, his energy radiating in a more powerful rhythm with every one of her heartbeats.

Almost there, baby. Jared's with me. See you in two.

It had been days of barely passing each other in their quarters, with Marco on double duty guarding Jared, and with her wrapped up in . . . too many things. Too many worries about Marco and her people, fears that multiplied gravely because of her intuition, thoughts that she couldn't yet verbalize. Couldn't even *materialize*, not in her quiet time, when she tried so hard to give every sensation a physical form.

Whatever was shaping up, the information her spy was feeding her, all of it tied into her uncertainties, those black-shrouded *vosii* that haunted her meditations. With another shiver, she stared at the meeting room door, ready. Waiting. For whatever might be coming down the pike.

She told herself that her premonitions had nothing to do with Kelsey's father visiting the next day. Outsiders rarely came onto the base, not without extremely compelling reasons, and Thea wasn't convinced that Kelsey's need to see her family justified such risky measures. But she'd come to love her queen very dearly over the past months, and understood the isolation the human had been experiencing during her pregnancy.

The sound of booted footsteps moving in unison filled the corridor, a precise, familiar cadence of military order. Several high-ranking officers filed into the room. Commander Bennett swept in behind them, Marco at his side, both of their black uniforms flawless, striking. A shiver of sexual heat shot through her core as she glanced at Marco, but she suppressed it. Instead, she trained all her energy toward her cousin, focusing on giving him a crisp salute.

"At ease." Jared dropped a sheaf of papers onto the table, waving a hand to indicate his permission for them to take their seats.

Lieutenant Daniels paused, dipping into a formal half bow as he placed one fist over his heart.

"Rise, Lieutenant," Jared muttered, a look of annoyance shadowing his features. Thea fought back a smile: Her cousin's impatience with old-guard respect always amused her. He could decry it all he wanted, but he was still their king.

Marco stood, waiting patiently; only after Jared was fully settled did he slide into an adjoining chair. Jared murmured something under his breath, expressing some need that only Marco could hear. In turn, Marco issued a quiet order to the attending officers within the room, and a flurry of movement ensued. As always, Thea was awed by the balance between king and protector, the symbiotic relationship that went back at least a thousand years in their royal traditions.

Marco bent sideways, whispering something in Jared's ear. Heads inclined together, they looked shockingly alike. The same broad shoulders, the same gleaming black hair, the identical long noses. And of course they shared the same sultry-dark skin, hardly enough—in either case—to contain so much raw masculine energy within one body.

She studied the matching sweep of both men's eyebrows, the elegant arch that reached a little too dramatically into their respective hairlines. They looked alike . . . too much alike, and she couldn't imagine that the speculations weren't flying wild all over camp. Everyone had to have noticed that, somehow, some way, the two men shared a bloodline.

She was shaken from her thoughts by Jared's deep voice. "I'm told there is news from within the Antousian camp," he began, opening his handheld. Forever multitasking, he was perfectly capable of reading transmissions, following his comm, and listening to a complex conversation all at once. She'd always been too single-minded to manage that kind of juggling act.

"My source has sent a disturbing transmission, sir." Thea knew her next words would rock the gathered advisers to the core, but she barreled ahead. "I'm told that our enemies are receiving very sensitive information from high up within the American government."

Jared's black eyes fixed on her. "How high up?"

"From inside the White House, our source suspects."

Jared leaned back in his chair, forming a steeple with his fingertips. "What makes your source so sure of that fact? Couldn't it be someone within the CIA or the FBI? Not knowing your source, Lieutenant, makes it hard for me to decide what to think or even how to analyze this information."

Nevin Daniels cut in. "My lord, it's for your protection that we've set this system in place. The less you know about our spies' identities, ultimately the safer you'll be." Nevin turned to face her, black eyebrows lifting. "But, yes, we do need to know how you're so confident the leaks are coming from the White House."

Thea had to tread carefully; she wanted to assure the team that her source was reliable but also had to protect the soldier's identity.

Marco caught her eye, giving a slight nod of encouragement. *Just tell them, baby,* she heard within her spirit. *Jared's safety depends on this source—not you protecting her identity.*

She bowed her head, averting her eyes lest any of

the others realize she and Marco were communicating.

If Jared is ever captured, she reminded Marco, *knowing the source's identity could mean he'd be tortured . . . or worse.*

If Jared's ever captured, your spy would be the least of our problems . . . or his.

Marco's words caused Thea to shiver yet again, despite the heat coming off the adjoining hangar deck.

"There's been a great deal of backlash since the Antousians' defeat at Warren," she began. They'd recently quashed an attempt by their enemies to seize US missile control at Warren Air Force Base, and their enemy's casualties had been considerable. "The revenge quotient is very high right now. Apparently a plan was mentioned—one Antousian in particular was a huge proponent of it. The idea was to intercept the vice president when he visited Warren in the attack's aftermath. To intercept him and . . . replace him."

"And this plan has been carried out?" Jared's voice remained calm, but after years under his command, she could easily read the grave emotion in her leader's tone.

"The man who concocted the idea has vanished from camp," she explained, "and now very high-level intel is coming down their pipeline from the Americans. Very accurate information, as well."

Jared slid his chair back from the table and rose to his feet; placing both hands behind his back, he began to walk the room. "Kelsey's father is friends with the vice president. Knows him well from years ago here in Wyoming, as well as from his political consulting work."

Nevin raked a hand through his silvered hair. "I don't believe it wise, sir, to involve an outsider in our situation."

Everyone knew that Patrick Wells would be visiting the next day. After months of waiting, Kelsey would finally see her father for the first time since marrying Jared—and at slightly more than four months into the five-month gestational phase, her father would glimpse, firsthand, just how pregnant his only daughter truly was.

"I have to agree," Marco added. "It is risky enough that her father is coming on base at all. We can't involve him, not in any way."

"Someone in the human command's structure needs to know our latest intel," Thea argued, locking gazes with her commander and cousin. "The FBI . . . the USAF. We can't just sit on this—it's too big."

"Agreed. We bring the alien task force in on this one." Jared nodded thoughtfully, returning to his place at the table. "We'd best begin analyzing what it might mean for Earth if the *vlksai* have truly infiltrated the American government at such a sensitive level.

"Damn it, we need Jakob back in camp." Jared drummed his fingertips on the table, clearly thinking. "How is Shelby Tyler's mission faring?"

Nevin raised a quizzical eyebrow. "What was it you reported, Lieutenant Haven? That Medic Tyler located him in the midst of a . . . 'beer brawl'?"

"The retrieval is going as planned, gentlemen," Thea told them sharply, although she couldn't help but wonder if it wouldn't have been wiser to send a squadron to reclaim Scott Dillon's future self. She knew what a stubborn fool the man could be.

"With this new intelligence, I believe reinforcements are in order." Jared turned to face Marco. "I'd like you to intercept them in Texas. Get them back to base straight away."

Thea lifted an eyebrow. "For a moment, I thought you had a full battalion in mind, sir." She laughed softly despite herself. Dillon—in any form—was always quite the handful.

Jared glanced sideways at Marco, a glimmer of pride in his eyes as he studied his Madjin protector. "Marco will do. And perfectly well," he said, then tapped the classified folder open before him. "Yes, this latest report raises the ante. Makes it all the more critical that we retrieve Jake from Texas." Jared pushed back from the table. "With the threat in the White House . . . it is time."

"Time for what?" Thea stood, facing her cousin and king.

Jared reached for the briefing folder and clasped it to his chest. "Time to solidly join forces with the human realm. We have to let the task force know about this latest development, even though it means greater risk. Marco, go. Go and make sure that Jake returns. Thea, you stay here, and remain in close contact with your source. Report to me if anything—*anything*—changes in terms of current status quo."

Marco sank back into his chair at the table, trying to block the assault of emotions and anxiety that the meeting had caused. Some days were harder than others as an empath, and highly charged situations were never much fun. Back home on Refaria, his kind went insane or worse from their gift in young adulthood. Including his own mother, although she'd been a bit older before her empathy had splintered her mind. But long ago he'd mastered his ability, learned how to battle it into the background, to use it whenever safely possible—and necessary. Still, in just that brief meeting with Jared and his advisers, a slight migraine had begun squarely behind his eyes.

Being with Thea was a different matter altogether: He was so deeply attuned to his wife and mate that none of her unsettled emotions had the capacity to weaken him. But Jared had a wholly unique impact on Marco's psyche. Between his role as the man's Madjin, and—as he'd recently learned—his brother, the powerful emotions the monarch tended to exude had the capacity to drain him for days if he wasn't careful.

Reading his thoughts, Thea whispered, "You've got to tell him," and slid into the chair next to his.

"When the time is right." Marco reached for her hand, rubbing his brow with the other.

"Blocking him . . . being so connected to him without his knowing the truth about who you are . . . it's killing you! I sense it. How many more meetings can you go through and come out like you are now?"

Marco gritted his teeth. They'd been over this ground repeatedly, and somehow Thea could never get why he didn't want Jared to know. The migraine swelled harder and faster behind his eyes.

"You're the only brother Jared has."

"Half-brother," he corrected with a growl. "Not something he'll be particularly proud of, not if he learns the details about our father's affair."

"How can you be so thickheaded? If I didn't *know* you were brothers, I'd surely guess at it because the two of you are so much alike. Stubborn, proud. Sometimes to the point of stupidity."

Marco gave her a grudging grin. "I love it when you talk dirty to me."

Thea tilted her head sideways, and he could practically hear her counting to ten in his own head.

"Think about what family means to that man." She squeezed his hand tightly within her own. "He'd be furious with you for not telling him."

He jerked backward in his chair. "Tell him what? That he has a bastard for a brother? That his sworn servant—his very own Madjin protector—was given to him as . . . as what, Thea? As his bondservant? I live to serve that man." He gestured toward the closed meeting room door. "Following him is all I ever trained for. If he learns the truth"—he shook his head remorsefully—"then I am no more. All that I am crumbles to dust."

She took hold of his face, cupping it in her hands. "What are you so afraid of? Tell me. Please just tell me."

Marco pressed his eyes shut, fighting the throbbing headache that battered his senses. "That he will forbid me to serve him. That he will cast me away."

"Cast you away?" Thea cried. "What sort of man do you take him for? Don't you know him at all? His kindness and fairness?"

Marco dropped his head, burying it in his hands. "No, baby, not that he'll reject me . . . that he won't accept my service. And I have to serve him." He cut his eyes, determined to make her understand his heart. "Don't you see that if I'm not his Madjin protector, then I have nothing? I am nothing."

She pressed her face close to his, drawing in a long inhalation of his scent, then kissed him softly on the cheek. "You've sworn your life to our king, but now you need to trust him—at least just a little."

Oh, trust, such a beguiling thing, Marco thought, as the migraine reached a maddening crescendo inside his mind and spirit. Such an easy word, but with so many difficult and far-reaching complications.

"Let me think on it," he whispered, but in his heart he knew that he could never breach the barriers of class and service that Thea was suggesting.

Chapter Three

Kelsey Wells lay naked in the king-sized bed that she shared with her king-sized husband—a thought that made her giggle despite the seriousness of the day ahead. In the five months since she'd bonded with, and married, J'Areshkadau B'net D'Aravni, exiled king of Refaria, she'd often found her new lot in life more than slightly amusing. Twenty-eight years old, she was now carrying Jareshk's unborn child within her womb; and at slightly more than four months into the five-month Refarian gestational cycle, she had begun to realize that the surreal quality of her new life had only just begun.

Jared moved about their quarters, a master suite in a lodge nestled high in the Tetons of Wyoming. Today was perhaps the most important day in their shared lives—at least since that first day they'd met as teenagers some fifteen years earlier. That was if you didn't count their soul-bonding, or the creation of the unborn baby girl who kicked and moved within her belly.

Today her father would meet her alien husband for the very first time. Today she would share all the facts of this strange alien war with him as well.

"Fliishki," Jared muttered from deep within their walk-in closet.

"What's wrong?" She wrestled to sit up in bed, holding one palm against her swollen belly. *Five months, my ass*, she thought, feeling the skin across her abdomen itch and the baby give another tumultuous roll. *This baby's coming any day now.*

"It's been far too long since I've had my dress uniform on." Jared appeared in the connecting doorway to their large bath area. "It looks ill fitting on me. I've gained muscle since last I wore it." Jared grimaced, casting a glance at the floor-length mirror on the far wall. "And I dare say I've gained weight since mating with you, sweet love."

Funny, all she could think was that he looked absolutely stunning in the formal uniform of all black, what with his ebony eyes and gleaming dark head of hair. He'd grown it some since they'd mated, allowed it to fall loose about his shoulders except on days like this one. Today he'd pulled it into a short ponytail, a smooth sheen of raven black hair streaked with silver.

He tugged at the jacket in irritation, adjusting it where it fell along his hips. "Why I couldn't simply wear my usual uniform, I am not even sure."

"Because this is probably the single most important day since you landed on Earth." Kelsey propped herself against a swath of overstuffed pillows, cupping both of her hands about her stomach, needing to feel Erica's movements just beneath her fingertips. A future princess! The thought that she carried someone so powerful—possessing the ability to become a pure sphere of energy just like her father—boggled Kelsey's mind when she thought about it too hard.

"Do I seem heavier to you?" Jared tossed a vulnerable glance over his shoulder.

"And you're asking me that—right now?" She laughed, waving a hand over her large belly.

"You've never been more beautiful, whereas I am—"

"A nervous wreck about meeting my dad. Besides, how often have you been working out lately?"

He bowed his head, putting his back to her. "Daily."

"If you've gained weight, it's just like you said—it's all muscle." The fact was there wasn't one ounce of wasted weight on her husband's body. For months he'd been driving himself harder and harder, it seemed. Honing himself, making his body into a weapon in its own right. When she'd questioned him, asking why he kept pushing his physical boundaries so hard, Jared never had an answer.

But Kelsey understood his heart well enough and had intuited one simple fact, one that perhaps even her husband hadn't realized yet: He was anticipating something. Some dark thing on the horizon that he couldn't name, but nonetheless felt the need to prepare himself for, both spiritually and physically. Because just as he'd been punishing his body with relentless physical trials, he'd also spent increasing amounts of time in private meditation.

"Jared, look"—she beckoned him toward the side of their bed—"just come over here. I need to talk to you."

As he turned to face her, she saw thinly veiled anxiety in his black eyes. "We don't have much time, love. Your father arrives at eleven hundred—"

"I mean really talk to you. Okay?"

With a nervous glance at his communicator's time display, he crossed the room, settling on the bed beside her.

For long moments, he stared into her eyes, and she felt the swirling cauldron of emotions vying for control within her mate. Anxiety, anticipation, even fear for her—at least somehow.

"I'll be all right," she whispered, reaching a hand to his cheek. He was fiery warm to the touch, whereas her own hand was chilled by the early May temperature within their lodge.

Jared grimaced, bowing his head, then reached a tentative hand to her abdomen. "How fares Erica today?" She could hear the fatherly concern, the protective note in his voice.

"She's doing great. You worry about us both way too much."

He struggled with something, his almond-shaped

eyes narrowing to slits. "I have never felt so vulnerable in all my life. Not as I do now, loving you like this, Kelse. Loving our baby girl." His palm tensed against her abdomen, cupping the rounded fullness protectively.

"That doesn't mean anything bad will happen."

"I can't help but fear it." His voice was soft, electric, but he averted his gaze. None of this was about the uniform, or about meeting her father for the first time; something much bigger was going on.

"Tell me the real issue, then."

His fingertips flexed against her warm belly. "I've been plagued by bad visions lately."

"Yes, about Jake, I know." He'd had numerous dark premonitions about Scott's future self, about Texas.

Jared lifted his gaze, locking with her own. "It's more than Jakob." Again his hand tensed against her warm skin, hovering protectively over their unborn baby. "It's . . . all of us."

Kelsey's heart skipped a beat, then hammered frantically within her chest. "What are you saying?"

His long-lashed eyes drifted slowly shut. "I don't know yet. I just feel this darkness coming, something dangerous—and here we are about to step into your world, into the *human* world, more firmly than we've ever done before."

"We aren't going anywhere. My dad's coming here. Are you saying you think this meeting with him is a bad idea?" If it was, she wanted to know his premonitions now, not later, once her father had arrived.

"It's our work with the FBI, the task force, everything. I can't lay hold of it exactly, can't get a clear picture. If only I could, I'd know why I'm so anxious."

She lifted her fingertips to the scars along his cheek. "You know my dad is going to love you."

"Once he gets past the fact that I'm alien. That you're carrying an alien child, and that I've changed everything he ever knew about you."

Kelsey couldn't help smiling, and felt an answering

gyration within her belly. "You did change me. But that's a beautiful thing."

"And what about the mitres? What would he say about that?"

Kelsey pushed back against the pillows. This was familiar ground between them: Jared's fears that the operational codes to their greatest weapon, the mitres, were lodged deep within her psyche—and had been ever since he'd made a temporary link with her to keep the codes from falling into enemies' hands. His anxieties weren't entirely unfounded, either; the mitres allowed them to alter time itself, and their enemies would kill to gain control of the weapon. "My dad won't know anything about the mitres."

"I'm a father now, and if some man—an alien—had done to our daughter"—he pressed his hand firmly against her stomach—"what I did to you? I'd have his head. I'd take his life for endangering her like that."

She frowned. "Are you talking about Erica? That I'm pregnant with your child?"

"How could I ever regret anything about our baby?" He shook his head adamantly. "I'm talking about the mitres codes, that you're the only one of us who can operate the weapon."

She slid sideways on the bed. "So that's what this is really all about, huh? You still don't think I'm strong enough to handle what you put inside of me."

He reached for her, but she ducked out of his grasp. "You're the strongest woman I've ever known—of any species."

"Woman. Strongest *woman*."

Jared shook his head ruefully. "Strongest person, Kelsey. Please don't play my words against me. Don't act as my interrogator."

She glared at him and slid toward the end of the bed, planting both feet on the floor. Quickly, she moved toward their bathroom. "I'm gonna take my shower. Then we can get moving."

"If our enemies ever learned that you're the one who can control the mitres . . ." His voice trailed off.

She turned to face him, pulling her bathrobe tight over her belly. "And how would they know? They don't have a clue about the mitres—they've never even found the freaking thing. How would they figure out the truth about me?"

"You've never been to my home world, haven't seen what they did to my people."

"*Our* people, Jared," she corrected softly, planting a palm over her heart. "Your people are my people now—I'm their queen. I may not have seen the devastation, but I feel it all around me every day. I've seen what they've done here on Earth . . . the attack at Warren. Of course I understand who we're dealing with."

He raised both hands. "My point precisely. So if they ever did learn of your true identity"—he shook his head, crossing the small distance that separated them—"I couldn't live with what they might do to you."

She wrapped both arms about his torso, resting her cheek against his chest. His heart was racing frantically beneath his uniform, and all her frustration melted away completely. "Jared, I'm right here, and I'm safe. You know what's been prophesied. I'm key to this revolution, and I love that fact."

He blew out a heavy sigh, stroking her hair. "How can I argue with the Beloved of Refaria?" That's what the prophets had called her, a fact that had been confirmed by the intuitives in their midst. "I should spend all my days worshipping you and keeping you deeply satisfied."

He slipped a palm beneath her bathrobe, sliding it suggestively along her thigh, then inward, stroking the silky curls between her legs.

"Well, when you put it that way"—she tipped her face upward, kissing him full on the mouth—"I get all turned on and want to take you back to bed."

"Then we could forget everything." He sighed, drawing her mouth back to his. "The war, our enemies."

The kiss deepened between them, Kelsey's robe falling completely open. Fear clawed at the edge of her mind, but she brushed it away, losing herself in this pure moment with her mate. The need to make love with him had been overwhelming since she'd become pregnant, and now was no exception.

"Do we have time?" She panted, tugging at the zipper of his uniform pants.

Jared slid her robe to the floor. "I don't care if we do or not." He growled in her ear, working her back toward the bed. "We only have now, and I want to mate."

Fully naked, Kelsey sat on the end of the bed, opening her legs to him. She worked at his belt and the fastenings of his pants, which quickly pooled about his ankles, revealing his fully erect cock, long and thick and ready for her. She never ceased to marvel at Jared's beautiful body, the darkness of it, the exquisite lines of muscle. She circled her fingertips around his erection, taking hold of his hip with her other hand. There was a slight indentation where his hip met his muscled abdomen, and she always loved to touch that place. Valley of Kelsey, he'd jokingly named it because it turned her on so much.

A shuddered breath passed from his lips as she tightened her hold about his shaft; he slid both hands atop her head, pulling her against his abdomen. With a flick of her tongue, she laved his belly button, all the while increasing the friction of her hand against his quivering length.

Jared slid both hands along Kelsey's shoulders, then back, needing desperately—as if his very life depended upon it—to feel physically closer to her. To take her within himself and hide her there. Opening their connection, he allowed his soul to reach toward hers, the featherlight touch of their deep bond opening. Without warning, an explosion of their shared power and light jolted into him, causing him to stagger slightly.

"Easy, there," Kelsey murmured, lowering her mouth until he felt the warm wetness of her tongue encircling his hard cock.

"Didn't you . . . feel that?" Warm rays of light filtered through his mind, his spirit. It was always like this when they mated, yet something felt different this time, too.

Something dark accompanied the light.

Kelsey smiled up at him, caressing his abdomen. "I only feel you."

He returned her smile, bending to kiss her, and with every bit of strength inside of himself, he willed the darkness away.

Chapter Four

Jake stood back from the desk, gauging Shelby's reaction; he'd sprung the truth on her without any warning, prying open the surface microchip from the wallet that had belonged to Jake Tierny—the original Jake Tierny—to reveal the much tinier quantum chip hidden within.

The look of horror he'd anticipated swept across Shelby's features. "That's Antousian."

He kept his gaze on her. "You've seen one of these before?"

Shelby bent low over the desk, narrowing her pale blue eyes as she examined the chip; he swore that she blanched. "Of course." She didn't elaborate, but he heard the revulsion in her voice. "I'm a medic—I've had my share of encounters with these processors in the past."

Now it was Jake's turn to be surprised. "You've tended to Antousians before?"

She rubbed at her eyes, frowning. "There have been times back home. I did some viral work at one of the rebel outposts. It wasn't like I would turn someone away just because they were my enemy, not when they were that sick."

"Some people would."

Shelby shook her head vehemently. "Being a nurse is my calling. I'll always answer to that, no matter who the patient might be."

They exchanged a look of understanding. Even

though Jake had never identified with his native species, or even called himself Antousian, the devastation of the virus had been a horror beyond description. He would always be Refarian in his heart, even if he technically was a human-Antousian hybrid; still, he wouldn't have wished the virus on anyone. Not even a bloodthirsty race like the Antousians. "My parents were scientists, working on a cure," he explained quietly.

"I never knew that. How old were you? You must have been just a boy."

"They were killed by their own people when I was barely more than ten. The same people they'd given everything for in an effort to find a cure for this"—he jabbed his index finger at the quantum chip—"madness."

The greatest battle back on Refaria had been waged long before Shelby—or even Jake—had been born: a philosophical debate over the choice to become "enhanced," adding a microprocessor to the brain to become cybernetic. With an ever-developing landscape of intelligent machines, they'd believed it the only way to keep pace with their own creations.

And so many had become implanted. Millions and millions of Antousians had allowed themselves to become cyborgs—part living being, part computer. It had worked for a while, too—until a lethal disease had spread among them, a computer virus that killed off most of their population. Without any other recourse for survival, the Antousians had resorted to their *other* state, a formless, ghostlike existence. It had been a terrible, demonic exodus.

Until one Antousian leader had offered a way for survival: Raedus had introduced a new brand of enhancement—the possibility of assuming a host body. *Human* hosts, to be exact. How Raedus had identified the perfect genetic match, well, nobody ever disclosed that fact, but growing up, Jake had always considered his own "people" murderers. Thieves . . . body snatchers. And he'd refused to consider himself Antousian ever since.

This was ultimately what had led the Refarians to Earth: the need to protect the planet from the scourge of death and devastation that the Antousians had wrought like locusts back home.

Jake suddenly found Shelby peering up into his face, her eyes wide. "You zoning on me, Tierny?"

He gave his head a slight shake. "Talking about home never does me a lot of good."

"You miss your folks?"

He gave a mirthless laugh. "Hardly."

"But they were your parents—I don't understand." She chewed on her lip, studying him as if he were an Antousian *gorabung*.

Jake slid the quantum chip back into its protective casing. "They were killers. They assumed human hosts in order to keep battling the virus."

"That was a noble reason."

"There's never a good reason for killing—or taking a body that doesn't belong to you. Trust me"—he eyed her fiercely—"I know firsthand."

"You took Jake's body when he killed Hope, right?" Her voice was soft, sympathetic, but he sure as hell didn't want any sympathy.

"I don't talk about that," was all he said, sliding the chip back into the wallet. "In fact, the only question I'm willing to entertain right now is this: Why did Jake have this chip hidden in his wallet? He was human, totally human. How did he know about this aspect of the war? What was his part in it?"

"What do you think the answers are?"

"Hell if I know, Shelby," he snapped bitterly. "It's why I'm here, in this godsforsaken state, chasing nothing but dead ends."

"Good thing I've come, then," she said, just as she had earlier. "Cause you need someone who can help you see things straight."

"Oh, so you've got this all figured out? Already"—he snapped his fingers—"just like that?"

"You've shown me yours, now it's time I showed you mine."

He swore her blue eyes sparkled with sexual innuendo, and there was an immediate tightening in reaction all through his body. "Show me what, Shelby?" His voice sounded husky, wolfish, and he felt his cock stiffen.

She ignored his come-on, instead digging through a canvas satchel that she had slung over one arm. She produced a slim-line cell phone, declaring it "dead as a doornail" as she tossed it aside, then, after quite a while—and after plunking a variety of bizarre items (including a silver dinner fork) down on the desk—she finally retrieved a file folder. "Aha! Here we go, sir."

He took what looked to be a pretty thick dossier from her hands and flipped it open. Much to his surprise, a younger version of the human Jake Tierny stared back at him from several photographs within.

"How did you find this?" He thumbed through more pages, and yet more, seeing Tierny's name appear repeatedly. She had just given him a gold mine—leads and detailed information about his enemy.

Shelby looked pleased with herself, her eyes sparkling. "A girl has her methods."

Jake clutched her by both shoulders and, without thinking, gave her a playful kiss on the forehead. "Whatever you did"—he kissed her a second time, lingering a bit longer against her smooth skin—"thank you."

She placed a warm palm against his chest. "No, no. Thank you," she half purred, her eyes sliding shut.

Jake froze; he had Shelby practically swooning within his grasp, his lips against her face, their bodies pressed together. Damn it all, he was only a click away from tilting her head back and kissing her hard—and then doing a hell of a lot more than that with her supple little body.

Her lips parted slightly, and she kept her eyes closed, leaning into his body. The woman might as well have moaned, *oh, yes, yes, yes,* into his ear, from the look of pure ecstasy on her face. It was tempting, gods, so totally tempting, to hike that little miniskirt of hers up her thighs and take her right atop the desk.

But it had been years since he'd touched a woman other than Hope. He'd promised her that much the night of her murder, as he'd rocked and rocked her, and a part of him had been closed off ever since. It had been a pretty big vow for a guy who'd once craved and needed sex almost insatiably. Now he was pushing forty even if the body he inhabited, Jake Tierny's body, was only thirty-three, and after so many battles and so much loss, it was hard to remember the dreams and desires of his younger days.

He made a great show of releasing Shelby, holding both hands up. Slowly, her eyes opened again, and the quirky smile on her face slipped. "Good job on this information," he told her, walking with it toward the other side of the room.

"You can thank Hope for that."

He glanced up and caught her tugging at her skirt; it had hiked up a little during their almost embrace.

"Hope?" He couldn't contain the thrill that shot through him at just the mention of her name.

Shelby gestured toward the folder. "Yeah, she pulled some major strings to get that for you." Her normally bright eyes looked a little dull, but only for a beat.

"She called her brother?" Hope's twin, Chris Harper, was a special agent with the FBI.

"I wasn't supposed to tell you, but"—she gave a little shrug—"well, she had to know that I would. Wasn't that big a deal; Chris has been in and out of camp ever since you've been gone. He's working directly with Commander and Hope and . . ."

"And Scott," he finished for her, sensing her awkwardness. But he didn't volunteer exactly how much of these details he already knew, thanks to his incessant phone calls to Hope.

"They're working together on a Joint Alien Task Force, between the FBI and our people, sir," she explained, telling him what he already knew. "FBI is employing her as a special consultant because of her . . . special knowledge. That's how it's going down, sir."

Maybe Shelby would tell him more about Hope's new life; she had hardly been forthcoming during their repeated phone calls. Of course it was to protect his feelings, he knew that, but it killed him to know so little about her. "How is she?" His throat went dry with the very question. *And how is* he, *my younger self?* He didn't dare ask.

Him. Always him, the lucky, happy bastard. It was damned unfair that his younger self had won the draw in this cosmic lottery.

It was as if Shelby had heard his thoughts, his deepest fears, when she answered quietly, "They got married. A few months back."

"I'd heard that." He made a great show of studying the file as he sat down on the bed, hating himself for the bitterness that raged in his heart. Hating himself for still loving Hope, in any version he found her, when that love would bring him only more heartbreak.

"Look, you." Shelby flew across the room and planted herself right in front of him. He kept his gaze lowered but couldn't ignore the creamy pair of legs and the curvy little hips that were only a few inches in front of him. "Look up. At me, right now, soldier."

Shelby would be damned if the sad-eyed giant of a man was going to mope another moment.

With a sigh, he obeyed, lifting his gaze upward. "Yes, *Commander*?"

"You should be whooping and hollering. You just got what you've wanted for a long time now, right?" She pointed at the folder spread open across his lap. "And you've got help in your search—good help. In other words"—she curtsied significantly—"me."

"Modest help, too." His full lips quirked upward at the edges, a sure sign of life in the poor guy, and that made her smile, too.

"I'll stick with you in this fight, Tierny, but only on one condition."

His mouth settled into a frown again. "What would that be?"

"You're in a hell of a mess, son, in case you hadn't noticed. And all this pain you're in ain't getting you nowhere."

"What condition?" His voice rose, and his green eyes assumed a ferocious look that caught her off guard.

"That mean you want me to stay?"

He threw his hands in the air. "Gods, woman, no way in hell at this rate."

Meeting his stare, she bobbed her head. "Alrighty, then. I see how it is. I'll just be hitting the road here in a minute or two—"

One bearlike hand shot out, long fingers encircling her wrist. "You aren't going anywhere. Tell me that condition."

"The truth is," she said, plopping down beside him on the bed, "it's more like two or three conditions." Jake growled but said nothing more, waiting for her to elaborate. She sucked in a breath, raising a finger. "You have to accept that Hope's life here—in this time—is with Scott."

He gaped at her, his mouth falling slack. She lifted a second finger. "And you have to stop mourning a wife who died a long time ago."

Jake slammed the folder shut. "Just get out. Go back to Wyoming."

She ignored him, raising a third finger. "And you have to realize you need help. Seriously need it, if you're going to have any chance of finding this guy."

Jake's bright green eyes drifted shut. "And if I don't obey all these simple directives?"

Shelby planted a hand on his shoulder, leaning in much closer. "Then I'm leaving and taking that folder with me."

"Like hell you are." He snarled up at her, his blazing eyes assuming a severe, almost predatory gleam.

"Is it the thought of losing that folder or the idea of me leaving that's got you so worked up?"

For a long moment, he kept his forceful gaze on her, never letting it waver. There was only the sound of his heavy breathing, the image of his powerful chest rising and falling as he sucked at the air between them. He reminded her of a bear that she'd surprised once in the woods, frozen in its tracks, frightened and threatening all at once.

"Jake," she whispered softly, "just admit that you need me. And the folder."

He blinked, slowly training his gaze across the room. "I'll have the folder and send you back to Wyoming. I can't have a crazy chick like you slowing me down."

"Then I'm not leaving the folder with you." She reached for it, but Jake jerked it out of her grasp.

"No way in hell, Medic Tyler. This is mine." He waved it overhead. "I thank you for it, and now I'll thank you to leave."

"Maybe I have it set to self-destruct, huh? Maybe it's just gonna go *poof* as soon as I'm on that highway." She gave his shoulder a small shake. "Ever think of that?"

He eyed her as if she were a crazy woman. "We don't have that kind of technology. You've been watching too much human media."

"The time you came from and our time are different, parallel universes but not the same—you understand that fact."

"Your point?"

"Well, in this timeline, universe, dimension, whatever you want to call it"—she captured the folder, sniffing it distastefully, as if it were emitting some sort of poisonous gas—"we've developed new formulas for all sorts of security precautions."

He tilted his head, just studying her. "You're messing with me."

"Maybe," she demurred, "or maybe not. But if I were you, lusting after this folder like you are, I sure wouldn't bet on it."

Before she could blink, his boxy, mittlike hands were grappling her down onto the bed beside him. "Give me the folder," he cursed, pushing her onto the thin mattress. "Shelby, I fucking mean it. Give it over now."

She found herself wedged beneath his hip, his enormous body half atop her own. He pulled and jerked at the folder furiously, wrestling to get it out of her grasp; finally she simply let go, an action he clearly hadn't anticipated since it ricocheted backward, slicing him in the forehead. He cursed in low Refarian but, oddly enough, made no effort to move from his position over her. Instead, he braced his hands about both sides of her head, wincing and breathing heavily against her face. With a slow and deliberate gesture he pressed his nose against her cheek and inhaled her scent, the first of the Refarian mating rituals, and it sent a shockwave of sensation and reaction throughout her entire body.

He dragged in another long inhalation, trembling as he held her scent within his lungs, then slowly released the breath with a groan of pleasure and arousal. She couldn't help it; she just couldn't help herself at all—she arched back into the pillow beneath her head and returned the gesture, dragging the very scent of Jake Tierny deep into her being. Spirals of need and intensity crested through her, creating sudden wetness between her legs.

"Again." He growled forcefully, pushing his forehead against hers. "Take me again, Shelby."

"Just your scent, Jake. Just—"

A rumbling sound of lust and anticipation escaped his lips. "Scent me again, damn it."

She nodded, dragging at the air between them for a simple breath, much less to inhale the essence of the man. With sharp awareness, she realized that she'd slipped one hand about his neck, was clinging to him. With even more awareness, she felt a sudden hardness press into her thigh right as Jake's pupils dilated, growing large and dark within his brilliant green eyes. *Move your hand away, girl. Go on, now.*

And she really did mean to let Jake go; she truly did. But the thing was, feeling him against her, the smell of him infusing all of her senses, well, she just couldn't be the one to do the letting go. Thankfully Jake did that duty for the both of them. He lifted into a push-up, hoisting himself off of her, but then—their gazes locking, his tongue licking his lips—something snapped.

"Aw, damn it," he swore, and planted a hard, wet kiss against her lips.

Desire curled deep within Jake's belly, tightening with the same urgency that his groin had. Shelby Tyler's delicate, lithe body was the sweetest thing he'd felt beneath his own in such a long time. Too long. But this—this moment with Shelby—it felt like the old days before Hope, when he'd prowled and lusted for women, endlessly needing sex. Only those had been *human* women, he reminded himself, sliding one flat palm underneath Shelby's bottom. Just thinking of Hope sent a cascade of guilt rushing through his spirit; it was ridiculous, but he felt like he was cheating on her when he'd barely done more than scent Shelby. Still, he couldn't help remembering the thousands of times he'd become intoxicated from Hope's unique aroma, the way he'd always craved it. But those powerful memories didn't prevent him from pushing his face against Shelby's neck and inhaling once again.

She ran her fingers through the bristling hair along his nape, thrusting her hips upward against his, teasing him, begging him. He'd never been able to hold back with a beautiful, sexy woman like she was; and he'd never had an ounce of resistance when it came to aggressive, seductive women, either.

"Am I still drunk?" he murmured, kissing her on the neck. How had they gotten to this point so fast?

"No, cowboy, you're in heaven." Her hands slid low down his back, meeting the warmth of his bare skin as his T-shirt rode up—but she didn't stop. She plunged her hands lower still, cupping his bottom and pulling him hard against her own body. Bringing their groins together.

For the first time in his life, he just might have landed in the sack with a woman who was faster than he was. It was a thought that terrified him—and made him grin with wicked anticipation. Oh, yes, it had been a long damned time since he'd held a woman—so many lonely years. Surely he could indulge just this once and keep Hope out of his mind, he told himself, shoving the pangs of guilt aside.

"You're a wild little thing, aren't you, Shelby?" He sniffed of her cheek, nuzzling her.

"No wilder than you, sir." She panted softly, lowering her lashes.

He rolled with her, and she landed in a straddling position over him—almost as if they were in some defensive maneuver, a training exercise back on base. It was a fight for domination, with this intensely sexual moment their battleground. "Oh, I'd say you like your sex. And not a little bit." He watched her face turn crimson, her tongue flicking nervously over her lips. With both hands he anchored her against him, even though she began to squirm slightly. "Nothing wrong with liking sex, Shelby."

"I'm a woman, sir," she whispered huskily. "Different rules apply." Her eyes shined with vulnerability.

"Doesn't have to be that way." Her miniskirt had ridden all the way up her thighs, revealing a thatch of dark blond curls—a satiny V right between her legs, now level with his eyes. Taking his forefinger, he pushed the denim fabric higher up her leg. "We both know that's a backward way of seeing it."

She pressed her eyes shut, and he dragged her skirt higher up her creamy, satin-smooth thighs. "What, girl? No underwear?" He gave a rough chuckle, feeling his groin answer with a tightening spasm. Only the men of their species went without underwear; the women typically wore silk panties—especially if they were wearing a skirt.

"Didn't have no clean ones," she blurted, yanking

her skirt back down. But it was a tug-of-war she was going to lose, and he began peeling the material right back up her thighs.

"Don't ever play poker," he threatened seductively. She started to lift off of him, but he anchored her against his hips, hard. "Because you're a terrible liar. It turns you on to go commando, period. I bet you do it more often than not."

Her lips parted, and suddenly she bent low over him, planting both her palms squarely atop his chest. "What if I admitted that you were right? What would you say?"

"That you're a lot like me." He gazed up into her clear, vibrant blue eyes. "That you have needs just like me—and that's not something I've found too often in my life."

She sat up, locking both her thighs tighter about him. With an exaggerated roll of her eyes, she laughed. "Now look who's a liar, huh, boy? You haven't had sex since the day Hope died." She played a little rhythm on his chest with her palms, still laughing, taunting him. "You ain't so much as *touched* another woman besides Hope since that first time you made love to her."

He felt his pulse hammer, and the sound of rushing blood filled his ears. He gave his head a slight shake. "You don't know that. No way in hell you could know that. You don't have the gift of gazing."

"And I'm not an intuitive, either." She gave him a self-satisfied smile, climbing off of him. This time he did let her go, propping his head on one arm and watching her glide across the room.

"Then what in All's name *are* you, Shelby?" She gave him a faint smile in return, one tinged with something he couldn't name, but didn't reply. Again, he questioned her, only to be met with stubborn silence. "Are you an empath?" he pressed, already knowing that the gift of empathy wouldn't give her knowledge of his past actions.

"Look, Jake, we gotta make some decisions here.

You've got that folder"—she gestured toward where it lay on the floor—"and once you review its contents, we need to hit the road. So you might as well get your mind out of the gutter, Commando."

Commando. It had been Hope's teasing name for him that very first night they'd made love, that crazy drunken night when they'd gone home together from the bar. It was supposed to have been a one-night stand.

Terror chased down Jake's spine, a feeling that he could hardly acknowledge, much less name.

"Did you hear what I said, sir? We need to leave, stat."

"For where?" he asked, bending to grab the folder. "Because I'm not heading back to base—"

"Commander Bennett is expecting your return in two days, three tops. You're to meet with Chris Harper, sir."

"I d-don't understand," he barely managed to stammer. He couldn't imagine a face-to-face meeting with his brother-in-law, not after so much time. Not when he had years' worth of memories, of friendship and brotherhood and fighting, that *this* Chris couldn't begin to understand. They'd interacted briefly during the raid to rescue Hope and Scott—but Chris hadn't had a clue as to his real identity. He swallowed hard.

"Look," Shelby explained, planting one hand on her hip, "there's a lot that's gone down in your absence. I've finally got you sobered up, so now it's time you knew a few things yourself."

He ignored the way his heart tripped double time inside his chest, the almost nauseating terror choking at his throat. "Starting with?"

"Chris doesn't just have answers for you about the real Jake Tierny, sir—he needs your help. We all do."

He rose slowly to his feet, his right knee suddenly aching. An old battle injury, it kicked up whenever he least expected it. "All right, but tell me this: Why do you need my help? Why does Chris need my help? I should know that much before we go."

Shelby crossed the small distance that separated them. "I can wrap that knee for you," she volunteered without explanation, then plowed right ahead, "and I'll tell you what Commander Bennett has in mind once we're on the road."

How did she know about his knee? How did she seemingly read his mind—hell, his body, even? Yet she claimed she wasn't intuitive.

Grasping her by both upper arms, he backed her toward the door, pinning her there. "I don't go anywhere without knowing what you are, Tyler. So start talking. My knee, my sex life . . . you seem to know a great deal about me." He tightened his grip on her arms, giving her a shake. "Tell me what you are, damn it, Shelby."

She blinked back at him, hesitating, then finally whispered, "I'm the one All has sent to challenge you."

"That's not enough of an answer." Growling, he bent low, blowing a hot breath against her face. "Not enough at all, so I will repeat: What are you, Shelby Tyler? How do you know so damned much about me?"

Her eyes slid shut, and she leaned her head backward against the flimsy door. With a quiet sigh she admitted, "I'm a little intuitive, yes, but it's more than that."

"More how?"

Her clear blue eyes opened, fixing on him with a meaningful stare. Whatever she was about to say, he knew it was going to rock his world in a serious way. She drew in a slow breath, released it, then quietly admitted the one thing he never would have imagined.

"Well, Jake, it's pretty darn simple." She never took her gaze off him. "I'm a time walker."

Chapter Five

Kelsey stared into the bathroom mirror, allowing her robe to fall open. Her belly button had practically stretched to nothing, and as she stared at her stomach, she could actually watch Erica move, a bumping glide from one side of her belly to the other. Sliding her hand over the warm skin, she whispered to the baby, murmuring sweet words of comfort and welcome. That's what all the pregnancy books had told her: Always talk to your baby, even when she's still inside your stomach.

With an anxious lurch, she thought of standing before another mirror, just five months earlier. It had been before a presidential fund-raiser her father was hosting in Jackson, and he'd paid to put her up in an expensive hotel right at the base of Jackson Hole Ski Resort. The view from the swanky lodge had been fabulous, her room's windows opening to slopes already covered with fresh snow, even then, in mid-November. The bed itself was a solid wooden sleigh bed, the kind she'd not slept in since her teenage years, when she still lived in her father's home. A gas log fire roared in the hearth, and with the easy flick of a switch she could manipulate the temperature up or down. Rustic, but luxurious; she could definitely get used to that kind of life.

Little had she known that within weeks she'd become a queen.

After years of low-budget academic life, the bathroom at the hotel was a veritable palace, filled with lavender-scented bubble baths and aromatherapy shampoos.

Kelsey smiled, picturing the black cocktail dress she'd chosen to wear for the fund-raiser, a night she'd known would be special—even if it meant tolerating her father's new girlfriend—so it demanded something ultrasophisticated, not her usual faded blue jeans, knit cap, and hiking boots. After all, the president had flown all the way to their Wyoming hometown to glad-hand her father's people.

Closing her robe, she reached for the hairbrush resting on the marble counter and remembered how she'd battled her hair the night of that fund-raiser. The thick hair that spilled across her pale shoulders hadn't cooperated then, any more than it did this morning. Wetting one fingertip, she secured an errant lock that sprang loose above her left eyebrow like an unwieldy corkscrew. Her hair had always been too thick, the curls prone to tangling and difficult to manage, but at least she loved the color. It was deep auburn—not brassy or garish—just like rubies caught in sunlight, her father used to tell her when she was a little girl.

That night had seemed magical, the last time she'd seen her father before meeting Jared again and leaving everything—and everyone—she'd ever known behind. And then the evening had turned ugly; if only her dad hadn't brought his new girlfriend out from D.C. That had turned out to be the big deal, not the fund-raiser. Patrick Wells had carted his twentysomething little hottie home for one reason and one reason only: to obtain Kelsey's approval. Whether he got it or not hardly mattered in the end, since, like everything else her widowed father tackled, he had been determined to have his way.

Her thoughts drifted back to the past again as she absently brushed her hair in long strokes.

"Angel, you'll like Blaire." They'd been standing in the elevator, her father in his tuxedo, striking as always, and Kelsey glaring at her own reflection in the mirrored doors, still wishing she'd bought a new dress. "She works for CNN in their Washington bureau," he continued. "She's a real up-and-comer. A bright woman, just like you, darling."

A comer. Kelsey had a pretty good idea of *exactly* what this Blaire woman wanted to come into: her father's money. Why else would a twenty-four-year-old find her *forty-six*-year-old father of interest? He'd saved that little age-difference bombshell until moments earlier, at which point he'd decided he should warn her.

She turned to him, gazing up into his clear blue eyes, and schooled her face into the most innocent expression she could manage. "Daddy?"

He smiled back at her, his freckled face crinkling with laugh lines. "Yes, angel?"

"You do realize I turned twenty-eight three months ago, right?" she asked. "Which makes this Blaire person, what? Four years younger than me?"

His boyish grin had slipped somewhat then; he'd jingled the change in his pockets as the doors opened to the lobby, but said nothing else.

As for meeting Blaire that night, it had been . . . confusing. Although she'd grilled her endlessly, determined to unmask her evil plan to scarf up her dad's money, girlfriend had never crumbled.

"So you graduated from Georgetown last year?" Kelsey had asked while they waited in the buffet line.

Blaire brushed at her sleek blond hair, granting her an awkward smile. "I graduated *three* years ago," she corrected. "Actually."

"Oh, my mistake. I guess I figured you'd have gone for a graduate degree or a doctorate."

Blaire glanced around the darkened banquet room, laughing. "I guess I wasn't exactly a 'school' person," she said. "At least not on a long-term basis. I mean, I wanted to get out into the world. To make things happen. I can be pretty impatient that way."

Was this a subtle dig at Kelsey's many years of schooling? At her preference for study and learning over the driven social interaction her father thrived upon?

"I personally prefer to use my mind," Kelsey answered coolly, and Blaire glanced up at her, her brown eyes widening.

"Oh, believe me, I'd love to be more like you," Blaire answered sincerely. "Patrick has told me all about your maps, and how NASA came to you when you were just a freshman." Genuine admiration—almost a kind of awe—filled the small woman's voice. "You really should hear Patrick talk about you."

Patrick. Blaire's familiar, breathy use of her father's name definitely undercut her efforts at placation. Kelsey clutched her dinner plate and wondered how on earth she could make conversation with the girl for another two hours or so.

The buffet line snaked forward at that moment, and Kelsey pointed. "You need to move up," she said, but Blaire stood her ground, obviously refusing to be derailed in their conversation.

"You know, maybe it's hard for you to believe, but I really love your father, Kelsey," Blaire continued with a tentative smile. "And I'm hoping you and I can be friends."

"Sure," Kelsey said with a disaffected shrug, glancing around the room at the gathered bunches of balloons hovering over each table. "We can be friends." But everything in her was screaming *Terror alert!*

Blaire pressed the dinner plate against her chest protectively, holding it there like a china shield. "I know this is awkward," she said with a serious expression.

"My dad dates lots of women, Blaire." Kelsey laughed. *But he doesn't marry them.* That's what she wanted to add, but something about the genuinely warm expression in Blaire's brown eyes caused her to hesitate. "Lots of women who—" she tried again, and Blaire nodded, urging her to continue. "Look, you better move up," she said instead, pointing to the gap in the buffet line. Blaire turned without another word, and Kelsey found herself *wanting* to dislike her, yet somehow not quite able to. Especially as she watched the rail-thin woman slather gravy and potatoes and all manner of evil carbs onto her plate without batting an eye.

Blaire turned back to her. "Lots of women who what?" she asked, smiling. "You were about to warn me off your father, I think." Blaire watched her, waiting, and obviously didn't plan to let the almost comment go.

Kelsey shrugged. "The man has commitment issues, that's all."

Blaire still smiled, almost as if this assessment of Patrick Wells came as a surprise, but said nothing more.

Later that night, things had actually been going pretty well until she realized her father hadn't planned to stick around for more than a few hours the next day. He was determined they'd all have lunch even though Kelsey had warned him about her research trip to Mirror Lake—and he'd promised to stay long enough for them to have a visit.

"Kelsey, please." She remembered him catching her by the arm as she'd rushed to leave the bar where they were having drinks. "It's important to me that you get to know Blaire."

Kelsey walked farther down the hall, so she and her father could have more privacy. Dropping her voice low, she turned to him. "You're always dating people," she said. "What's the big deal this time?" Tears burned her eyes because, deep down, she already knew the answer that was coming.

Her father's expression grew intense, serious; he hesitated, then cleared his throat. "Because I've asked Blaire to marry me, Kelsey. She's going to be part of our family. She is a wonderful woman," he said, keeping his voice even. "You will love her, like I do."

"No, I won't love her." Her throat tightened, aching. "I can't believe you'd do this to our family." She spun away from him and began hurrying down the carpeted hallway toward the elevator.

Her father followed right behind. "I have never stopped loving your mother," he said, falling into an easy stride beside her. "But it's lonely without her. I want to have someone. A partner in life."

She rounded on him. "*I* don't have a partner in life, Daddy! *I* don't have anyone," she cried. "And I am fine with that."

Her father lifted a hand, stroking her hair. "Are you really so sure about that, angel?"

Kelsey opened her mouth, ready to retort, ready to deny—to insist that strong people stood fine on their own. But somehow, despite her ready arguments, her throat had tightened and no words had come at all.

Of course he'd been right; how well she understood that fact now, the way she'd always pined for Jared after their memories of meeting each other years before had been erased. How restless she'd been.

Kelsey gripped both hands about the sink, feeling a sudden wave of dizziness, a frequent occurrence these days. *I have no idea if he and Blaire are together anymore at all. I know nothing about his past five months.*

She couldn't help but feel guilty. And angry. That same bitter, roiling fury that had dogged her from the time her mother had died, and her father had uprooted them in a move to D.C. Staring at her full belly once again, she noticed that the skin had started to glow.

I can't get upset, not with Erica inside of me.

She loved her father so much, and yet few people had ever held the power to hurt her as deeply as he did.

Today will be different, she vowed. *Today we'll get along.*

Chapter Six

Kelsey's stomach churned with nervous anxiety, causing Erica to kick and churn in response. "You're going to meet your granddad today," Kelsey murmured, rubbing her round belly.

"I'm so happy that you'll get to share your pregnancy with him." Jared gave her a slightly wistful smile.

She slid her hand through the crook of Jared's arm, pulling him closer. "You're thinking of your own parents."

He smiled, stroking her cheek tenderly. "They would love you just like I do—and our baby? They would have showered her with royal jewels and ceremonies until"—he laughed, a distant look in his eyes—"well, until she came of age, most likely. Yes, love, I miss them and wish they could meet my family."

His mother and father had been murdered when Jared was barely more than ten years old, placing him on the throne when he was still just a child. He'd lost more than his family then; he'd lost his youth and his innocence, something Kelsey had grown to understand more deeply during this pregnancy. She missed her own mother more than she had in a long time, years really, wishing she could share all the little details of her pregnancy, her fears and hopes for baby Erica. Her disconnection from her father had made those melancholy feelings only more pronounced—the main reason Jared was willing to risk Patrick Wells's visit to the base today.

A diplomatic officer joined the two of them. "My lord, once our visitor arrives on deck, he will be escorted into the Special Planning Room in quadrant one."

"Why the last-minute switch?" Jared stiffened slightly against her, and Kelsey wondered what about this change disturbed him.

"Security precaution, per Lieutenant Daniels. Standard op, sir." The young officer's face reddened slightly, his dark brown eyes blinking nervously. Clearly it was a major assignment for the guy, and she got the idea that he hadn't spent much time in her husband's presence prior to today.

"Lieutenant Harty, what possible security precaution should dictate a move from my quarters—where we were scheduled for a late afternoon lunch—to the impersonal planning room?"

Harty gave his head a slight shake. "I'm not sure, my lord. But those were my orders."

Jared disengaged from Kelsey's grasp, slipping an arm around the officer's shoulder, walking with him and whispering something in quiet tones. A look of pride shone on Harty's face, and he nodded while punching something into his comm. Jared returned to her, grinning. "We're going to eat in the planning room."

Kelsey scrunched her nose, confused. "What did you tell him? And why did that bother you so much?"

"I told him that he was doing an excellent job, and would receive a glowing report from my staff." Jared folded both arms over his chest, glancing at the control tower. "And that he was to do everything within his power to personally impress my father-in-law. I suggested there could be a promotion in it for him if he made me look especially good today."

Kelsey slugged him playfully. "You're shameless, Your Highness."

"My pride knows no bounds."

"It's not pride." She smiled up at him. "You're just looking after me. He will love you, just like I do."

Jared stroked her cheek. "I wish I felt so confident."

They'd talked about Jared's anxieties repeatedly, his fears that her father would resent him for essentially secreting her away from the rest of her family. Not to mention the very fact of Jared's alien nature—and that he'd put Kelsey squarely in the midst of an ongoing war.

Officer Harty returned, half jogging to where they stood. "My lord, Lieutenant Daniels explained the reasoning behind the move. They wanted to perform a last-minute security sweep of the main lodge and of your quarters. He suggests that perhaps you might bring the queen's father there directly after lunch."

Something didn't feel right to Kelsey; whether it was her newly developing intuition, inherited from Jared upon their mating, or simply her gut instinct, she wasn't sure. She turned to her husband. "Is something going on here? Something more than Dad's visit?"

"Security is elevated, my lady," Harty volunteered. "We've raised the code by two levels since yesterday."

Kelsey cut her eyes at Jared. *What is going on, huh? Something you're not telling me?*

He's a human, Kelse—an outsider. We have to take precautions.

But he's my father; something more must be going on.

Jared's lips parted as if he would answer aloud, but catching himself, he spoke through their bond. *We had disturbing intel come through yesterday. We're acting on it, heightening our security alerts.*

And you were going to tell me when exactly? Kelsey planted one hand on her hip, and Harty watched them like he would a tennis match as they volleyed back and forth wordlessly.

Jared grinned at her, doing his best to look guileless as he bent to kiss her forehead. "Once you'd delivered the baby and I knew you wouldn't worry."

Harty squinted, glancing back and forth between them in confusion: Obviously their navigation between spoken and internal dialogue was difficult for an outsider to follow—much less understand.

"I expect details once my dad leaves." Kelsey stared at her husband meaningfully, widening her eyes. "There can't be secrets, not between us."

A loud horn sounded, a digital light blinking red by the main hangar door. "And that would be our guest," Jared said, drawing in a heavy breath.

Kelsey's hand swept protectively over her large belly. *Oh, Dad, please love them like I do. Please accept who I am . . . who they are.*

One of their midsized transports entered the bay, and Kelsey reached for Jared's hand. "Here we go. Showtime."

Kelsey watched as her father disembarked from the craft, flanked in front and behind by a joint force of several Refarian and USAF flight officers. Even though some of the human ranks had been coming on base for months, the sight of her father in the company of mixed human and alien forces shocked her slightly.

But clearly not so much as the entire event shocked her father, whose normally warm blue eyes had a startled expression to them, much like the time she'd announced her plans to become a geologist. Not a politician like he had always planned for her to be. Her father glanced about as if he half expected to come under attack by evil aliens, and Kelsey's anxiety doubled.

But then his gaze lighted on her, and she broke away from Jared, rushing into his arms. "Dad!" She flung her arms about his neck, her large belly bumping him squarely in the stomach before she remembered just how pregnant she really was. Some part of her mind wondered if he'd been briefed properly, or if her advanced state of pregnancy was a surprise. Still, she didn't care; it had been five long months since she'd seen him or even much of the outside world. "I'm so glad you're here," she said, burrowing her face against his shoulder.

"Whoa, whoa," he chided. "Let me get a good look at you." But she only clung to him harder, tears stinging her eyes.

"I'm pregnant," she blurted, slowly peeling away from him.

"I can see that." His mouth tightened slightly, and he kept hold of her shoulders, raking her with his parental gaze. Disapproval, shock, confusion, were obvious on his freckled face, the lines around his normally boyish eyes bracketing with tension.

"I hope they told you—I mean, well, the USAF or whoever gave you the briefing."

Her father nodded and slipped his hand atop her belly. "I just can't do this math, sweetie. . . . You're almost full term. They said you were four months pregnant." He glanced about them, blinking at the bright work lights suspended over their heads in the hangar.

"Four and a half months, actually, and that's a big part of my story—our story, Jared's and mine." Kelsey turned, searching over her shoulder for Jared, who gave her a cautious smile but still kept his distance. She waved him closer, then turned back to her father.

"That's him?"

"Of course it's him." She laughed uncomfortably because her father didn't exactly sound overjoyed to see Jared. Again she sought out Jared, who walked toward them, his gait a bit more regal than usual—an obvious defense mechanism that nearly caused her to giggle uncontrollably from nervousness.

"Sir, it's my honor to meet you." Jared extended a firm hand toward her father, inclining his head slightly out of respect.

For a beat her father hesitated, then clasped Jared's hand, giving it a stalwart shake. "I'll admit it's a strange day for me." Her father broke into a strained smile. "Normally I'd know everything about you, Bennett. As it is, I'm playing catch-up, and that's a pretty big disadvantage for any father."

"Understood completely, sir." Jared nodded thoughtfully. "I have many regrets on that point, but I hope that today will begin to remedy our situation."

Kelsey suppressed a grin, hearing Jared speak so formally with her dad, a man who—although well acquainted with the upper echelons of political society—was still, in his heart, an outdoorsman and a rancher.

"Look," she interjected, noting the many curious faces of the engineers and soldiers on the flight deck, "let's go someplace private, okay? I've got so much to tell you, Dad, but not out here where the world can see."

"The world? Sweetheart, I just took a top secret flight with a USAF escort. I don't think the world's eyes are on us right now."

He didn't laugh or smile as he said it, and she fought a flash of anger. Of course her father wouldn't make today easy for her; as much as he loved her, he'd never made much of anything comfortable, at least not when it came to the things that mattered most to her heart.

Thankfully, Jared intervened. "We have lunch waiting in one of our meeting rooms." He extended his hand, indicating the direction they would go. "If you will, sir, follow me?"

"I saw you five months ago, Kelsey, at that fundraiser." Patrick took a sip of his water. "Were you pregnant then? Were the two of you already involved?"

Jared leaned back in his seat, letting Kelsey take the lead in answering the questions. So far, he was having a hard time getting a fix on his father-in-law's mood about current events, much less his opinion.

Kelsey stared down at her plate. "Dad, you know, it's just really complicated."

"You either were or were not pregnant. That's not too complicated."

"I hadn't met up with Jared . . . again back then.

The gestational period"—Kelsey patted her belly—"it's different because of the baby I'm carrying."

Patrick scowled at each of them, his eyes, so like Kelsey's, narrowing in confusion. "I don't understand any of this. Met Jared again? I thought you only met him . . ." His words trailed off, and he gaped at his daughter as if finally hearing her words. "What kind of gestational cycle?"

"Dad, it's five months with this baby." Kelsey's voice rose slightly. "I'm almost to term, okay? Your granddaughter, Erica, will be here in a few weeks. As for Jared"—she glanced nervously in her mate's direction—"we met a long time ago. It's something that we'll have to explain over time."

But, not surprisingly, Patrick Wells seemed fixated on the health of both his daughter and his granddaughter. "Five months. You look well past eight months on a, uh, human time frame."

Kelsey leaned back in her chair, blotting at her mouth with her napkin. "That's about right, Daddy. Almost done." She laughed, a bit hysterically. "Thank God! Man, it's been really uncomfortable for the past two weeks."

"You hadn't told me that, love." Jared's black eyes narrowed in concern. "That you've been in such discomfort."

Kelsey tossed down her napkin. "Geez, just what I need, not one but two men in my life, worrying about me, hovering."

"It's an alien pregnancy, sweetie." Her father took hold of her hand. "Perhaps the first? Hell if I know the truth about that."

Kelsey avoided both of their eyes, hanging her head. "No, it's not the first. We know of others."

Patrick squeezed her hand, smiling at last. "You'll do fine, then. The baby is healthy, right? All the signs are that she's progressing okay? That you are?"

Kelsey played with her food, almost like a little girl. "Daddy, it's all fine. Me, Erica . . . don't worry. We really are okay."

"You named the baby after your mother," Patrick observed softly, not quite looking at his daughter. Jared felt a strange tightening in his chest, a painful yearning for his own mother and father spearing him to the core.

Kelsey didn't look up, didn't meet her father's stare. "She's my daughter, Mom's granddaughter . . . of course."

"Didn't Jared have someone with a name?"

A hard silence fell over the room, and Jared knew it was his responsibility to reply. "Sir, my own mother is long dead, lost in this war that—even now—we still fight. Our daughter's name was not my choice, but your own daughter's. Erica is perfect for our precious girl."

Kelsey's heart rate sped double time. "You know, Dad, I get that you don't approve of this situation or my choices, but I'm not a little girl anymore. I'm twenty-eight years old, and for once I'm doing something for me. I'm here with Jared because it's where I want to be." Her palms began to sweat where she'd planted them on the table, and it was all she could do to meet her father's heated stare straight on. "When Mom died, you never cared what I wanted. You hauled me across the country for your career and never thought twice about it. So you know what? I don't really care if you approve of my relationship with Jared or not."

Kelsey's throat constricted, and she couldn't bring words forth at all. Her father's warm eyes grew cold, angry. "How can you claim I was never there for you?"

"I didn't say that," she managed to squeeze out, hot tears filling her eyes. "But you didn't care what was good for me, or what I needed."

"You needed a father, and that's what I was."

"No! I needed my home, Daddy! I needed to be here, in Wyoming, close to the life we'd led as a family. And to my memories. Instead, you just uprooted me and went after your own dreams."

Kelsey leapt to her feet, pacing the room. She'd

never been allowed to return home throughout high school, only later—when she'd insisted on attending college out here—had she even set foot on Wyoming soil again. From that moment, she'd felt the heavy sense that something was missing. Someone more than her mother.

"I might even have found Jared sooner." She threw her hands into the air. "Who knows, Dad, but none of that matters anymore. All I have is here and right now, and you can either turn your back on me again, or you can try and understand why I love him so much." She stopped just behind Jared, planting her hands on his shoulders. Jared covered both of her hands with his own, and she longed to see his face.

Love, take it easy, he cautioned gently. *He just needs time.*

"No, he doesn't! He needs to support me," she cried aloud, not caring whether her father understood the private bond that she shared with her mate, that it allowed them to communicate privately. "So, Daddy, you still planning to marry Blaire?" She practically spit the woman's name.

Her father's reaction was surprisingly sedate. "We're making plans, yes, sweetheart."

"And you have the nerve to judge me? At least Jared's older than me, basically the right age for me, even if he is an alien! Unlike you, obviously dwelling in midlife-crisis-land, pining after some schoolgirl who barely has boobs yet."

For the first time since arriving, her dad smiled. A real, honest smile that revealed the warmth he usually displayed toward her. "You just looked so much like your mother." He reached toward her, opening his arm to draw her close. "She was a gorgeous pregnant woman, just like you."

Kelsey crumbled, her anger fading to dust as she allowed him to pull her close against his side. She buried her forehead against his short-cropped auburn hair, the tears streaming anew. "I need you to support me, Daddy. Please."

He nodded his head wordlessly, the two of them in an awkward tangle because of her position standing over him, and then he slowly disengaged, rising to his feet. He took her by both shoulders. "You've got to let me catch up here, Kelsey. Just a little bit. There's so much I'm trying to understand right now. If you love Jared"—her father paused, turning meaningfully to look at her husband—"then I accept that. I trust that and I trust you. You've always had terrific instincts."

Kelsey wiped her eyes, one hand flitting nervously to rub the strake stone she wore around her neck. It had been Jared's wedding gift, a rare Refarian jewel that possessed an almost magical power—it was hot to the touch for anyone besides the person who wore it.

Grinning, she glanced up at her father through the tears that blurred her eyes. "I want to show you something wild." She retrieved the stone from where it dangled from a necklace, hidden between her breasts. "Jared gave me this on our wedding day."

Patrick reached into his jacket pocket, retrieving a pair of reading glasses, studying the stone closely. Beneath the track lights overhead, it gleamed a particularly luminous ebony shade. "That's unlike anything I've ever seen."

"It's from Refaria, called a strake stone." Winking at Jared she added, "You should touch it."

With a tentative hand, her father reached to feel the stone, instantly jerking his hand away. "That sucker's hot!"

"I know! Crazy, isn't it? It feels perfectly normal to me, but that's because I'm wearing it."

Jared rose from his position at the table, joining them. "Sir, that was the prize jewel in my father's crown, something my people smuggled out for me. It's always been a symbol of the world we hope to one day restore."

Patrick lowered his reading glasses, tucking them back into his jacket. "And will you take Kelsey there one day, too?" he asked Jared softly. "Should I prepare myself for that sort of separation?"

Jared planted both hands behind his back. "We don't know what the future will bring. Right now, our role here is to protect your world. It's our highest calling, and now that we're working with the USAF, that role is more important than ever. Our enemies are many, their plans as nefarious as they are ambitious."

Patrick's blue eyes widened. "What sort of plans?"

Jared tilted his chin upward, smiling faintly. His next words rocked Kelsey to the very core. "Actually, sir, I was hoping you might be able to help us on that matter."

Jared had never intended to draw his father-in-law into the fray, but something about the moment—the need to gain his trust—had made the idea seem right. Perfectly right, even though it was a considerable risk to release any of their intel to an outsider. Still, this was Kelsey's father, her own flesh and blood, and using his intuitive gift, he felt certain that the man could be trusted. That he would never do anything to betray Kelsey, that much was evident from being around him, and also from reaching with his gifts to confirm what his gut instincts told him.

"I've known the vice president for more than twenty years. I find it impossible to believe that he's any kind of traitor." Patrick stared at the table between them, clearly trying to digest all that Jared had just told him.

Kelsey, for her part, seemed more angry than shaken. "This is what you were talking about earlier. The reason security is elevated."

Hell hath no fury like a woman pregnant with an alien child, Jared thought ruefully.

"We received our intel yesterday, from a very high-up source. The suspicion is that the switch has already taken place."

"What are you people, then?" Patrick fixed him with a piercing stare. "Body snatchers?"

"Not them, Dad—the Antousians," Kelsey explained impatiently, her gaze never leaving Jared. "You're saying they somehow replaced Vice President Clarke?"

"So these Antousians are body snatchers?" Patrick pressed, a look of mild horror on his face. "Like some B-grade horror movie?"

Jared rubbed his jaw. "Sadly, it's far more complex and evolved than what you're imagining, sir, but yes. The short answer is that our enemies are capable of seizing human hosts, and by some act of subterfuge we believe they may have done just this with the vice president."

Patrick reached for his water glass, his hand shaking so badly that the liquid sloshed inside of it, nearly spilling. "That puts your enemies just one step away from controlling our missiles."

"Which would be their plan, sir. I'm sure the USAF team explained the attack we diverted at Warren?"

"In vague terms, yes."

"They almost gained control of the silos then, but we were able to shut them down. It seems that in their anger, they reached a bit . . . higher."

"How can I help?" Patrick asked.

Jared hesitated, glancing cautiously at Kelsey, whose anger seemed much more muted now that she'd heard the facts. "I was hoping you might try to meet with Clarke. See how he seems to you. You've known him for many years—I believe you could tell us if he is changed at all. Different. Not that you're to say anything to him, simply to get recon as to his behavior and frame of mind."

Patrick threw his head back, releasing a deep, rumbling laugh. "In other words, you want me to join forces with you just like my daughter?"

Jared couldn't help smiling in return. "I believe your unique placement could be of great benefit."

Patrick kept smiling. "My daughter told you to do this—right?"

"No, I didn't know anything about it at all, and frankly I'm a little pissed that he didn't warn me." Kelsey wiped a hand across her brow, where a thin sheen of perspiration had broken out.

Once again, Patrick's expression grew somber. "If my friend is gone—and one of these aliens is in his place—will he ever make it back? Back to the surface or however I should think of it? Or is he—"

"I'm sorry, sir. If he's gone, well . . ." Jared's words trailed off.

Patrick fell silent, then added, "If he's gone, then our world is in serious trouble. That's the real gist of it, right?"

Jared bowed his head significantly. "Now you understand why I decided to ask for your help."

Chapter Seven

"So, cowboy, it's straight up on six o'clock, and that makes about five hours you've been sulking over there in that passenger seat." Shelby shifted, a thin sheen of sweat having formed beneath her thighs that caused them to slide against the leather seat of Jake's truck. She'd volunteered to do the driving because it made the time pass faster on the long journey home.

For hours and hours they'd been passing across Texas, through oil fields and open range, until she thought the empty terrain would never end. Especially with Jake slumped against the window, not sleeping, but hardly living, either.

She gave his arm a poke. "What? You're not going to talk to me? I know you're awake over there."

"Just watching this lovely scenery go by." He sat up straight in the seat, stretching his arms overhead. "The varied terrain, the unparalleled beauty that is northern Texas."

"You're just acting assy because I wouldn't stop at that bar."

"I wanted Tex-Mex."

"You *wanted* a beer."

She turned to smile at him, but it wasn't an expression he returned. She figured he was in a funk because he dreaded returning to camp, dreaded the possibility of seeing Hope again, and mostly dreaded having to face the facts of his existence here in *this* time. After all, he'd pretty much hightailed it away from the compound and hadn't looked back for the past four months. He'd never exactly dealt with the fact that he was marooned in this reality and that there wasn't a damn thing he could do about it, either.

She hated seeing the bleakness in his eyes, that thousand-yard stare that was especially haunting in his eerie green eyes. With a sigh, she watched another mile marker go by; they still had a good ten hours ahead of them until they got back to Jackson, and she felt it her particular duty—she was, after all, a nurse—to cheer Jake up.

Distraction was always a good tactic, so she tried again. "You haven't asked me about being a time walker. I'm sorta surprised. You're pretty direct about things, and all that. I figured you'd have grilled me by now."

He stretched his arm along the bench seat, his fingertips slightly grazing her shoulder, bare except for the halter-top strap that looped about her neck. Swallowing, she wrestled to focus her thoughts, but it was tough when every bit of her awareness had flooded to that soft place on her shoulder where Jake's rough fingertips touched her. She might as well have received a casual caress from a lightning bolt.

"Well," he answered, glancing her way, "I don't actually believe you. So my only curiosity, Shelby, would be why you needed to claim to be a time walker when there's no way in hell that you actually are."

Her rush of desire was instantly replaced with a spark of anger. She tilted her chin upward, kept her eyes on the road, and slipped into formal speech. "Well, Lieutenant, lying to a superior officer would certainly land me in the brig. Perhaps you haven't thought through that line of reasoning, at least not thoroughly."

A raspy rumble passed over his lips. "You might be under orders from our commander. In fact, you've already said as much."

"Still couldn't lie to you, sir. That's not who I am."

"So you're a time walker." He slid just a fraction

nearer, his long arm slipping closer along that damned bench seat. "The first I've ever met, Tyler. Tell me what it means."

Her whole body warmed at the physical contact with him. She couldn't decide whether this maneuver with his arm was a come-on or if he was simply opening himself physically in order to hear the truth about her gift. Her confusion on that point was more than just a little bit disconcerting; she forced her gaze onto the open ribbon of road that wound ahead of them. "You're a deeply spiritual man, sir," she answered softly. "You know what a time walker is, what it means I am."

"Deeply spiritual?" He gave a scoffing laugh. "Yeah, I worship All, and he's watched my back on plenty of occasions. But I'm not sure he's doing more than mocking me at this point."

Something in his tone frightened her, hearing him speak so caustically about the God they both believed in. "We all lose people, Scott," she murmured.

"Jake." His tone could have cut her very soul to shreds, and she winced.

"Sorry."

Her heart hammered in her chest, partly from fear and partly from emotions she wouldn't dare name. Being with Jake Tierny scared the bejesus out of her on more levels than she could count. He thought he was the only one with a past? Who'd lost someone he loved?

Don't go there, girl.

Oh, he terrified her all right, so much so that her hands had begun to sweat against the steering wheel, and they shook with slight tremors. Maybe if they had sex, then he wouldn't scare her so bad; the playing field would be more even. In fact, it was a whole, whole lot easier to just focus on the thought of them doing it. Until she was blind and senseless and didn't feel anything else; until the aching place in her chest—the one that intensified when she was around him—

went away. The place between her legs grew damp against the leather seat, and it took all her soldier's discipline not to reach for his hand and draw it right down to where she ached for him. To let him feel how he affected her.

Jake had been absolutely right: She liked sex and not a little bit. She had an intensely high libido, one that never seemed to find total satisfaction. Only once had she been with someone who'd come close to being her sexual match, and that had ended in heartbreak and disaster. So she'd tried going celibate, hoping it would tame the lust and senseless hunger inside her. It wasn't feminine; hell, it just wasn't right.

Jake's fingers slid along her bare skin, skimming upward toward her neck.

Just screw me, baby. We'll forget everything together.

Abruptly, he withdrew his hand, folding both arms over his chest. "I've read a bit about time walkers in my studies of the scriptures. It's the rarest gift that All bestows. . . . Frankly, I've always believed it pure myth that someone like you would even exist. It's said to be the highest blessing."

The man was talking scripture when she was thinking about the physical. The very, very physical. "More of a curse, really." She meant the words to stay inside her head—honest, she did—but still they slipped past her lips.

Jake threw his head back and laughed. "So that makes two of us who believe the gods have forsaken us."

That one? Well, that one she just wasn't going to touch.

He turned in his seat, fixing her with those gorgeous green eyes of his. "You don't like that?"

"Don't agree with it, that's all."

"Then what did you mean about your gift being a curse? How does time walking work? The scriptures are entirely vague on the matter."

On the radio, a Tim McGraw song came on, and

for a minute she just listened. "Live Like You're Dying"—a pretty good motto considering all the death she'd seen.

"I love this song." She reached to turn up the volume, but Jake's massive hand halted her. Their fingertips brushed together, their hands suspended in a strange dance of electricity and need.

In the silence, she could hear his breathing grow heavy, just as hers did. He seemed to be waiting on something from her, asking for something more than plain facts about her gift.

Closing her fingers around his hand—as cautious as she would be with that bear he kept reminding her of—she waited. For a reaction, for him to pull away or lash out, but he remained perfectly still beside her, frozen except for the heavy sound of his huffing breaths.

One of us has to make a move, she thought, cursing herself for being so blinded with lust for the guy that she couldn't think worth crap around him—much less control her physical reactions to his unstoppable sensuality. If she'd ever doubted he might be Scott Dillon in another body, well, his barely constrained physical presence was all the proof she'd ever need. Only one other man that she'd met in her life had ever radiated so much hunger and passion without even uttering a word, and that was absolutely Scott Dillon.

"What do you want?" Her question came out breathless, edged with frustration and emotion.

Jake took her hand, anchoring it against his thigh. "I think you know."

"You'd better tell me, just so I'm sure."

"I want to know my future. I want you to be a time walker, Shelby, to walk *me*." He slid her hand a little bit higher up his thigh. "And tell me if I succeed in killing Jakob Tierny in this timeline."

Jake's hand was practically flung back at him, if such a thing were even possible, as Shelby yanked her own out of his grasp.

"Frak me!" she cursed.

"Frak *what*?"

She shot an furious glare at him. "*Battlestar*, baby. Not that I'd expect you to know that." He didn't know what the hell she was talking about but wasn't about to reveal that fact to her. She continued ranting. "Seeing as how you don't know who the Grateful Dead are, or what your own dang tattoos mean, I'm pretty sure you wouldn't know about *Battlestar Galactica.*" She threw both hands in the air, completely releasing the steering wheel, ignoring the fact that the car veered slightly over the line. Good thing Texas was so flat.

"Well, frak you, too, sweetheart." Leaning closer to her, he sidled across the seat and allowed his words to absolutely drip with seductiveness. "I mean, who wouldn't frak you, as hot as you are. You're my very own little Texas tamale."

She stiffened, her full lips quivering slightly with emotion. "This ain't about that."

"*Ain't* about what?" he mimicked. "That southern accent of yours hits overdrive every time you're emotional or upset or"—he reached for a lock of blond hair that had come loose from her clip, stroking it between his fingertips suggestively—"turned on. Especially when you're turned on." He watched as deep color infused her face, feeling his own body flush with unstoppable heat.

"I—I thought you wanted to talk about my gift."

Trailing his fingertips across her cheek, he stroked the nape of her neck, watching a pure look of sexual satisfaction pass over her face. It might have been a long time since he'd touched a woman, but some things you just never forgot—not when you'd bedded as many women as he had over the years. With a languid gesture, he ran his fingers along the base of her scalp until her eyes slid halway shut and she squirmed slightly in the seat.

"I'm gonna have an accident if you don't cut that out."

"Pull over." He invoked his voice of authority, sounding every bit her commanding officer.

She jerked in surprise, leaning forward and out of his grasp. "Not out here—there's nowhere to stop."

"Like I care—do it, Tyler. Now. Pull over this vehicle." He turned in the seat to face her. "That's an order, Medic."

Half a mile down the road, without ever saying a word, Shelby located a dusty pull-off that led to absolutely nowhere. Perhaps a turnaround for cattlemen in the area, it wound a small distance off road and behind a copse of cactus and brush. When he realized the privacy the place would afford, he issued another order: "Park here, Shelby. This is the spot."

Once the car was parked, she turned to him, her clear blue eyes brilliant with emotion. He was tempted to soul-gaze her, to figure out what was really going on behind those gorgeous, long-lashed eyes of hers. But he knew that she'd call him down on that before he'd even get started.

"What do you have in mind, sir?" She folded both arms across her chest—both bare arms because from this angle he mostly saw skin, inches of pale, beautiful skin that had been left exposed by her halter top and miniskirt.

"Gods, you're a gorgeous woman." He rubbed his jaw, just looking at her, appreciating her pure, unspoiled beauty—possibly for the first time. He'd thought her hot as hell back in the motel, but here with the sun setting behind her, with the heat of emotion showing on her face, he could see her for what she really was: an absolutely breathtaking beauty. From her full, pouty lips to her thick, feathered eyebrows, there wasn't a single aspect of her that wasn't sensuous. Deeply, provocatively sensuous.

"This isn't about me. You wanted something; now, tell me what it is, or I'm pulling right back on that highway."

The directness of her question, the proximity of her utterly feminine body, knocked the breath out of his lungs, terrified him to the very marrow until all he could think was that he had to get away. "Bad idea, this," he grumbled. "Terrible, terrible idea."

Gods, he was suffocating. This woman was choking the life out of him, and he had to break away from her before he did what he most wanted, which was to make love to her, here in the desert without worrying who might drive by or who might see. Wanted to take her lithe little body up underneath his own massive one and brand her with his mark. To bind her to him somehow, in some way that neither time nor death could ever challenge.

Only, he of all people knew that caring for any woman was a danger because death was always a possibility. The one woman he'd ever loved had died, taking his soul with her to the grave; the last thing he needed was to fall hard for Shelby. His heart went wild inside his chest as grief and longing spun together, practically choking him.

He reached for the door handle, fumbling with it awkwardly, but all at once she was on him. Her arm braced between his body and the door.

"Not so fast, sir."

He pressed his palm against the glass, trying to find his breath. "I'm so sorry, Shelby." Damn it, he meant it, too; he never should have come on to her, not so strongly, and not when she'd been charged with the duty of bringing him back to base. This was a mission for her. For him, it was all about the ever-loving *strka* right between his legs. She deserved someone better than he, with his broken soul and wretched memories. She deserved a man who could truly open his heart.

"Sorry for what?" She purred in his ear and covered his splayed palm with her own. He could feel her energy pulse within his own body; if he'd doubted her giftedness before, all that disbelief faded away as she touched him. He could feel the power radiating all through her—something she'd obviously held back when they'd kissed earlier. "Sorry for what, cowboy?" she repeated, whispering the word right into his ear.

He pressed his forehead against the glass, keeping his back to her, wishing that he weren't awash in so many bad memories. "Please . . . just accept my apology and leave it at that."

Mirroring his own earlier gesture, she ran her fingertips along the nape of his neck, and his cock tightened in deep reaction. "I'll time walk you, Jakob." She pressed a languid kiss against his neck, stroking his sensitive skin with the tip of her tongue. "I will give you that, but there's something you have to do for me first." Her fingers, spread atop his on the glass window, trembled. "There's a promise I need, if I'm going to open my gift to you like that."

His head swam with a thousand impulses and desires; she offered him the future, she promised him her body—but what, by the gods, did she want from him in exchange? Everything inside his mind told him to leave, to just get out of the car. "Anything, say the word," he heard himself mutter, silencing the warring voices within his head.

She planted a hot, needy kiss behind his ear, stroking his jaw with her fingertips, coaxing him to finally turn and look at her. "Make love to me, Jakob—"

He cut her off with a growl, sniffing at her face in a frantic effort to scent her, but she pushed at his chest, stopping him. "There's more," she explained.

"Anything." He tugged her against his chest, not letting her keep any physical distance. "I told you *anything*, woman," he rumbled in her ear.

"All right, then." Her warm hand slid between his thighs, outlining the ridge of his erection with a rough motion. Slowly she raised her eyes until their gazes locked meaningfully. "The promise is that you let me take the lead."

He released a prayer to All, begging for mercy, because he suspected this pretty little medic had just purchased his soul.

* * *

Shelby lowered herself onto Jake, who she'd pushed onto his back right there in the front seat of the pickup. With all his stops and starts, she knew damned well that she had to take the lead—and she also knew her heart would be in far less danger this way. She couldn't help smiling at the image of Jake, so aching and ready that he didn't mind having his head mashed up against the door handle. Didn't care that his boots were braced against the driver's side window, or that his uncontainable and massive body was contorted into a ridiculous posture just so she could straddle him.

"I make the rules," she had teased him as she'd forced him onto his back.

"Why's that so important? For you to call the shots?" He sucked in a startled breath when her palms slid beneath his T-shirt, dragging it upward to reveal his rose tattoo. The one she'd first seen on his abdomen back at base when he'd been stabbed. In the fading sunset light, she could see the silvery white line of a scar alongside the red bud of the rose, and traced both marks with her fingertips.

"So your man Jake"—she caressed the stem of the rose suggestively, his abdomen muscles jerking in reaction—"must've been into the Dead. That's why he got this tattoo."

"Not . . . now. Gods in heaven, don't mention that bastard . . . now." He arched slightly beneath her, his hips riding upward.

She bent low over him, stroking the day's growth of beard that covered his jaw, that shadowed the area above his full upper lip. "Just remember, I'm a nurse. I have a pretty good idea of what it is you need."

A wicked, half-cocked grin formed on Jake's full lips. "You're going to dress up in a nurse's uniform for me? Give me medicine, huh, Shelby? I can play doctor with the best of 'em." He clasped her by the waist, tugging her forward abruptly; she landed flat atop him, both elbows sprawled on his chest. "Or are you just going to tend to my bodily comforts? Please don't spank me if I'm a bad boy."

With a raspy, sensual laugh, he leaned his head up enough to kiss her, one hand anchored behind her head so that she couldn't squirm out of his grasp. The other skimmed down her back, lifting her halter top until his flat, rough palm met her bare skin. He stroked her mouth with his tongue—he stroked her back with his fingertips, winding them lower until he found the waistband of her miniskirt. Nothing stopped him, and his large hand cupped her bottom, squeezing and urging her farther up his body until that same thick ridge along his thigh, the one she'd felt earlier, was fitting between her legs.

Good lord, he had all the control; despite his promise, he'd taken total charge over her body and over what he was doing to it. His kiss grew rougher as he thrust his tongue deeper and deeper into her mouth, battling with her. That hand on her bottom slid inward, then down between her sweaty thighs until calloused fingers were parting her legs, finding their way into the slick folds that ached for him so desperately.

"You promised," she murmured as their kiss broke briefly and they gasped for air.

He shook his head, forcing her legs wider apart, which gave her even less balance and control from her position atop him. "I promised to make love to you." A first and then a second finger pushed up inside of her, stroking the tender place behind her wet opening, rubbing and tantalizing until she buried her face against Jake's chest so he wouldn't hear her cry out.

"Let me go," she murmured weakly, enthralled and terrified all at once by the drumbeat of his heart beneath her cheek. "You promised to let me call the shots."

"Control is my sexual trademark, sweetheart. Relax, I'll give you what it is"—he tickled her lightly between her legs, grinning at her like the devil himself—"you so very clearly need."

She began to tremble against him, a swell of unexpected energy invading her body; it had to be from him. *His* energy. His power. Of course, he was an Antousian-human hybrid; sex with him would be totally different than sex with one of her species. She'd forgotten about that. Shelby began to shiver from the way his pure, unbridled energy poured into her, and from the knowledge that, in a sense, she was sleeping with her enemy.

Panting, she sat up, planting both palms against his chest. "I—I won't time walk you if you don't keep the bargain," she stammered. "Y-you won't get what you want."

All at once, Jake bolted upright in the seat, pushing at her. He seemed angry, a terrible scowl turning the corners of his lips downward. They were in an awkward, tumbling heap, and it was a battle just to get untangled, what with his rangy legs and thick torso pushing against her. Finally, she scooted back behind the wheel and reached for the door handle, staggering out onto the dusty road where they'd parked.

In the past moments the sun had almost set; all that remained were faint fingers of pink and angry red in the distant sky. She slammed the door behind her, wondering what had just transpired between the two of them; she'd wanted him—excruciatingly so. And she'd had such a brilliant plan in mind, one that he wouldn't be able to shake off or shut down from. But somehow, some way that made absolutely no sense to her, he'd wound up with every ounce of control. He'd dominated her, overpowered her.

Leaning against the closed door, she undid her hair clip since it had slipped halfway down her neck. She made a great show of sweeping the ponytail back into its flip, tugging at it, and then slowly turned to evil-eye Jake inside the truck. His response to her glare was to lift one eyebrow. She put her back to him, folding both arms angrily over her chest. Good lord, at least she could breathe again, something of an improvement.

Jake slammed his door, and then there was the

sound of his cowboy boots crunching heavily on rock and sand. She leaned back against her own door, trying to appear relaxed even though her entire body was tighter than the fists she clenched at both her sides.

Jake rounded on her, wiping his brow. "How do you know what I want? What I really want?"

"You're the one who said you wanted me to time walk you."

"Because I didn't believe you, sweetheart. It was a ruse."

She blinked, her lips parting as he loomed over her. It was the first time they'd stood so close together, and it was finally clear to her that Jake was perhaps six foot five. She tilted her head upward, meeting his stare, and said, "Whether you believe me about the time walking or not, I *do* know you want Jake Tierny dead."

His jaw ticked, something wild flashing in his eyes, visible even in the darkness. "Maybe I want you more."

She shrugged, lowering her lashes coquettishly. "Maybe you can't have me, not really."

"And if I let you have your godsforsaken control?"

She snaked her arms about his neck, leaning into his body, molding herself to him. "I'll take you places that you haven't been in a very long time—places you may never have even thought about."

His Adam's apple moved as he swallowed hard. "What do I have to do?"

"Get back in the truck, face forward, and watch."

—

Chapter Eight

"They've left Hell."

"Hell's Creek," Thea corrected him from the other end of the line. Marco just muttered back at her. The truth was that the little town where Jake had last made camp really *did* feel like hell to him, with his empathy going haywire from the onslaught of so many negative emotions and sensations.

"I just want to get out of here, baby. It doesn't feel right here."

"You're sure they're gone?" He could hear the note of wifely concern in her tone. She of all people knew the toll a place with such bad energy could take on his psyche—and on his body.

"The motel room where he's been staying was empty, and I can't get Shelby on her cell. It seems to be either missing or the battery is dead."

"Love her." Thea laughed softly. "Definitely love that woman, but I never thought she was the right choice to bring him back."

Marco smiled despite himself. Jared had been the one who insisted that Medic Tyler take the duty, speaking cryptically about something his intuitive gift had shown him. Marco sensed the same thing whenever he tried to hone in on the missing pair: They had a deeply personal synergy, even the possibility of making a love match, but only if they could get past the barriers in their respective hearts. At the moment, however, he was more annoyed with Shelby and her errant cell phone.

"You're definitely sure they're together?"

"They are." Marco had used his own intuition to determine that much, although their current location had been hazy at best.

"No luck pinpointing them with your gifts?" He could hear the concern in his mate's voice. "I don't like you roaming around off base for this long. It's not safe."

"See what you can do, baby. See if you can put me back on course; then I'll get the transport to drop in for me again."

Jake's hands clutched at the dash; he felt his flesh tingle, his groin tighten—yet all he could do was watch. Watch Shelby Tyler through the windshield as she climbed atop the hood of the truck, facing him. At first all he could see were her knees, then her pair of strappy sandals dropped onto the hood with a thud; just the sight of something so racy and feminine had nearly caused him to lose it before she'd gotten started.

The little exhibitionist! She was quite the seductive minx, he thought as she dropped low, planting both palms against the windshield, licking her lips as she stared at him through the thin sheet of glass that separated them.

"Got your full attention, soldier?" Her words were muffled, but he still understood. Swallowing hard, he nodded obediently. "Turn up the volume," she added, gesturing toward the radio where someone named Christina someone-or-other blared huskily.

Rising to her feet again, she gave him a full-on view of her shapely, sexy legs. He noted an ankle bracelet dangling low along her right foot, something he hadn't seen before. His hands itched to take that slip of gold and unfasten it, to lick and nip at her ankle with his mouth, dragging the gold chain right between her legs until its cool, metallic surface drove Shelby Tyler wild.

As the music hit its major chorus, words about "no other man," Shelby's plan hit overdrive—she was dancing, just for him, and atop the hood of the pickup no less. It was like his own personal lap dance, with the glass windshield as their chaperone. Her petite hips swung back and forth, dainty palms sliding downward along her thighs, and then piece by piece, all of her clothing began to vanish.

First, that damned miniskirt pooled about her ankles, easily kicked aside with a deft movement of Shelby's toes. She dropped low, planting a hand on the glass, making sure he could see as she reached behind her neck, licking her lips as she allowed the halter to fall away from her chest. With a tantalizing pirouette, she moved for him, gloriously naked beneath the rising moon. He couldn't help himself, couldn't hold back, he slipped a large palm between his legs and began to rub, hard. But even that wasn't enough, not watching Shelby's gyrations, so gypsylike and maddening. With a fumbling, awkward gesture he managed to unfasten his jeans, giving a jerk to the zipper until his pants fell open about his waist.

With a greedy gesture, he got his hand about his cock, rubbing in time to Shelby's frenzied dance atop the hood. Gods, he would come into his own hand if she didn't let him touch her soon. He hardly cared; it hardly mattered. . . .

Shelby! Save my scoundrel's soul!

She halted midsway, dropping to her knees as if she planned to pounce through the glass and onto his lap. Blond locks of hair swept across her eyes and she made no effort to brush them away. Jake's hand clutched and clawed at the dash; with his other, he stroked himself shamelessly. Shelby's gaze followed his gesture, a smile of vixen's approval forming on her swollen lips. *Help me, Shelby. Help . . . me.* He swallowed the words, keeping them tucked within his crazed mind, increasing the mad friction of his hand about his erection.

In reply, there was nothing, nothing but sweet

Shelby Tyler, staring at him like a tigress. Her chest rose and fell; her fingers constricted against the glass, and she mouthed just one word: *Now*.

Jake was out of the truck and upon her faster than any shape-shifter. For a moment, Shelby wondered if the guy had used his Antousian gifts of spirit-slipping because one moment he was in the car, wild-eyed and desperate as he gaped at her, the next he had her sprawled atop the hood, her ass cool in contrast to the warm metal ticking beneath her.

"Come here." Jake growled. It wasn't going to take this boy more than a minute to climb atop the hood right with her.

With a forceful pull, he dragged her across the smooth surface of the hood, positioning her right at the edge. With his massive hand he forced her legs wide apart, but she clasped him by the shoulders. "Don't forget the rules, soldier boy."

His massive chest pulled at the air between them, agitated puffing sounds escaping his lips until finally he managed, "I thought you . . . were going to dress up and . . . n-nurse me." His jeans slid down his hips, revealing that just like her, he'd gone commando.

She blinked, feeling a wash of uncontrollable emotions crest through her body. This man was excruciatingly beautiful; from his long-lashed ethereal eyes, to his rough-hewn, sculpted body, to his coarse way of needing sex . . . he overpowered her. Angling her hips, she slid backward on the hood like a little naked crab, but his beefy hands shot out, tugging her by the calves until she was right flush against him.

"Open to me," he ordered, his full lips parting slightly as he stepped up onto the front bumper. "I'm taking you here. Now."

She meant to argue, good lord, she really did. She shook her head slightly, but then the lovely giant took another step onto the front of the truck and wrapped her legs about his naked torso. Pushing his lips against the base of her throat, he sucked in a long scent of her, and his hands began to tremble where they held her by the thighs. "I'm going to do things to you that you've never even thought of, sweetheart. Now lean back."

Again she tried to protest, shaking her head weakly. She'd never intended to lose so much control, wasn't even sure how by the gods it had happened. All she knew was that, her soul be damned, the alien had her half pinned beneath his large torso, his wide, sensual hips already rocking against her. The expected satiny hardness stroked at her opening, and she gave a slight whimper. "Jake, I—I can't. . . ."

He pushed her fully onto her back, bracing both elbows about her neck. "Can't lose control? Already done that, sweet girl. Already done it."

She clutched and clawed at his shoulders, needing him, so hungry for him, but terrified out of her mind. "I want you so badly." She moaned, arching upward against him, feeling the bending metal of the hood complain slightly beneath her back. With another moan, she murmured, "There's no stopping this."

"You had no idea who you were really taking on." He laughed wolfishly in her ear, plunging deep within her, and her body convulsed in immediate reaction. "Now you do." He immediately withdrew, until only the swollen tip of his cock remained inside of her. With a small cry of frustration, she clasped his bottom in both of her greedy hands, squeezing him closer.

"Don't pull away!" She chased after his hips. "Please, Jake . . . come back."

He leaned on one elbow, suddenly languid and relaxed. "You mean like this?" he teased, sheathing himself inside of her, as deep as any man could possibly go.

She licked her lips, nodding. Panting.

"Sweetheart, you are one hell of a woman." Those were his last words before he plunged his tongue deep within her mouth, seizing her in the same way his body already had.

Jake's knee was killing him, braced as it was against the front grate of the truck, but nothing could compare to the ache between his legs, the sweet heaven of plunging deep and deeper still inside Shelby. He loved teasing her, loved shattering her sexual barriers. Nobody would ever dominate him, least of all a little slip of a Texan alien.

Thrusting, he sped their rhythm, glancing up at the moon. It was all he could do to tamp down his need to howl, to let his mating needs known to the empty world around them. Shelby leaned back, her hair spread like fairy wings about her face, all golden and shimmering beneath the moonlight; he planted kiss after kiss on her lips, teasing her hips into a faster rhythm. He'd make her come, and he'd do it repeatedly.

Wrapping both of those shapely legs about his hips, she nestled him deeper inside of her grasping warmth. It was all he could do not to fucking lose it . . . while fucking her. He laughed softly against her neck. "You'll be the death of an old man like me."

Her calves tangled about his lower back, embracing him like a strong pair of arms. "Deeper. Deeper, Jake. Please." She panted hungrily, her fingernails dragging harshly across his shoulders, scoring the flesh.

That was the moment when he almost lost control. He almost shape-shifted right there and entered her in his ethereal state. It was a sexual thrill that he and Hope had given in to hundreds of times . . . but something held him back. Shelby didn't know what all he could do, his many forms and abilities. He was alien to her, an enemy. The thought of her natural disdain for his hybrid nature only sped him into a sexual frenzy, and he pumped harder, harder, faster.

Shelby's body trembled, shattered by orgasms. In reaction, his own erection spasmed, shooting his seed up inside her. Dim thoughts hounded him about protection, but he couldn't be bothered at the moment. Jets of his warmth filled her to overflowing, slowly seeping outward, trickling along her open thighs. Still he kept pumping, riding her throaty little cries like he would a massive tidal wave.

When at last he grew slack, he buried his head against her chest. "In All's name, you've got a gift all right, and it sure as hell isn't just time walking."

"I'm . . . on top of a truck." She giggled, threading her fingers through his hair.

His breathing grew a little more even, and he rolled halfway onto his side. "Don't worry. It's a new one for me, too, sweetheart."

Her clear blue eyes fluttered open, locking on him. She gave him a half smile. "You've got one hell of a pistol on you, baby. Glad you like firing it." Her words were pure Texas drawl.

"You saying you'll be my firing range whenever I need a little practice?" He nuzzled her, tickling her behind the ear.

She ducked out of his grasp, sitting up. "Jake the Snake . . ." At least she laughed when she said it. "Think that's what I'll call you from here on out."

"Have you seen my thigh yet?"

She wrinkled her brow, then smiled devilishly. "Thought I'd seen most of you by now, honey."

He didn't reply, just rolled flat on his back and tugged his jeans halfway down his legs until *it* came into view: reason number ten thousand why he hated the body he'd stolen from Jake Tierny. "Ugly as sin, I know."

"I wasn't thinking that." Shelby reached gentle fingers to the place where his right hip met his muscular thigh.

"What *were* you thinking, then?"

In a serpentine trail, she outlined the dark green snake that coiled about his right thigh. The tattoo was grotesque, hideous, some gleaming demonic monster that had been grafted onto his body. "I was wondering why, if you think this tattoo's so horrible, you made such a point of showing it to me." She lifted her eyes briefly, then dropped her gaze again.

"Figured it's better you knew what you were getting into, that's all."

"Don't forget," she laughed, "I know you a lot better than you think I do—even though you just barely know me. Thanks to Scott's stay down in the medical area. Yep, I know your ins and outs, baby, and that's a pretty good situation for a girl like me."

"Because you have all the power."

She gave him a smug smile. "Told you, control. That's the ground rule, pistol boy."

He slid off the truck cautiously, careful with his knee. It was already aching enough after the day's long drive. "We better spend the night here. Get a few winks before we hit the road again."

Jake's big idea of catching some sleep roadside had turned out to be cuddling up under a blanket in the back of the truck. He slept the easy rest of a fallen oak, one large arm flung overhead, the other looped about her side, anchoring her against him. It was amazing, really, just how peaceful he could look when he relaxed or rested. Those demons that seemed always ready to devour him vanished. Shelby stroked her hand across his eyebrows, the place where there were normally creases that betrayed his inner turmoil.

She blew out a sigh. Her sad-eyed giant had let himself go during their lovemaking—to a point. She understood his need to be the one sexually in charge all too well, and in Jake's case, she was sure his wounded heart was calloused over from too much loss and heartbreak. And that pretty much worked for Shelby; she wasn't ready to open up to anyone, particularly not someone as emotionally dangerous—and broken—as he was. She'd already been down that road once before and was darned sure not going to make the same mistake twice. The last time she'd let her heart go, and to someone like Jake, it had practically brought the universe down on all their heads.

Beside her, Jake stirred, pinning her closer against him as he murmured in his sleep. Shelby froze: Scott Dillon had done the exact same thing while under her care as a medic, often having orgasmic dreams of being with Hope. She'd even caught him stroking himself in his sleep once, moaning and thrusting his hips.

Jake moaned like that right now. Right in her ear, a slow, hungry roll of thunder followed by a catlike sigh of pleasure that vibrated against her cheek. *He's gonna call out to Hope,* she thought, emotionally panicked.

He shifted his massive body, rolling his head to the side, "Oh, yeah, baby. Sweetness, yeah."

Shelby's eyes widened, and she was shocked to realize how deeply Jake's ongoing attachment to Hope stung. After all, they'd only just hooked up today. It shouldn't matter that she'd been so attracted to him months earlier, had thought about him way more than she should have. None of that should entitle her to feel jealous of the one woman he'd ever truly loved.

And yet she did.

Again he groaned, groping at her restlessly. "Sweetheart, come closer. Yeah, come on."

Come on, Hope. Of course—who else would he be having such lusty dreams about?

"Shelby, come on! Come on, baby doll. Shelby . . ." He kept on, groaning her name, shifting his hips aggressively, sliding his hands all over her body.

Oh. My. God. He's dreaming all about me. Full-bore panic hit her this time, and not out of feeling betrayed or cheated on. But because she realized that unlike Jake's younger self, Scott Dillon, whose dreams at the medical center had always been about Hope, Jake's dreams were populated by none other than . . . her.

Then, probably from such extensive physical exertion, Jake bolted upright, one long arm still looped about her. She avoided looking at him, even though he stared down at her with pretty obvious intent.

"I had a dream," he murmured, raking a hand through his disheveled dark brown hair.

"Whew, did you ever."

She eased out of his grasp, staring at the sky overhead. A sparkling tapestry of stars glittered above them, and some part of her wished she could see all the way across the galaxies, could make a wish on Refaria. It was a thought that saddened her deeply, made her long for her sisters, forever lost to her in the war. They'd gone missing years earlier, several seasons before she'd joined the military—in fact, their disappearance had been the driving force behind her desire to join Jared's resistance. She'd transformed from a rebellious teenager, one who ventured into militarized zones if the parties were good enough, into a committed soldier and medic.

And never once had she been able to time walk effectively enough to learn where her sisters might be. Dead, alive, murdered, or lost, she could never unravel their whereabouts. It had torn her apart, bit by godsforsaken bit, before she'd ever landed on Earth. She was the oldest, meant to protect them from the war's growing shadow, and she'd failed. Totally failed them both.

Jake rolled onto his side, leaning on his elbow, oblivious to the melancholy pall that had come over her. This was the way she often felt after having sex . . . like no matter how much she yearned for connection, there could never truly be the depth that she needed.

"So you really are a time walker?"

She nodded wordlessly, still staring straight overhead at the stars.

"Why's Jared got you in the medical complex, not spending 24-7 trying to glimpse what's coming down the line?"

It wasn't a question she was prepared to answer, at least not so early in their relationship.

Jake laughed, twirling a lock of her hair around his fingertip. "Ah, so it's not just me who's totally shut down, is it, sweetheart?"

"There are reasons that Commander doesn't expect me to do it, that's all. It's not a gift I can operate in very . . . reliably."

"Why not?"

She stared at the sky, avoiding his searching gaze. "You're not the only one who's lost people you love, Jakob. That's all."

Jake bent over her, hovering, but she shut her eyes. She didn't hear him move at first, but then there was a rustling noise, and he covered her with his jacket.

"Get some sleep. You need it. . . . Hell, we both do."

She rolled onto her side, away from him, but then his husky voice pierced the desert quiet. "Who did you lose, Shell?"

She drew her knees to her chest, feeling protective, but he would have none of it. "Damn you, woman. You want me to stop grieving, but what about you?"

"He was killed in the fire," she blurted. "At the Texas facility."

"Everyone was killed in the fire down there, far as I know—except you. And I've wondered about that, how it was you escaped."

She scurried out of his grasp, taking his jacket with her, and sat on the back end of the truck. Jake pursued her, utterly determined. "Why did you get out of there? How?" He dangled his legs off the end of the open gate. "Did you see it while time walking?"

She shook her head vehemently. "I never saw none of it."

And that's when she knew Jake really got it, the reason why she was so shut off. "My gift failed to reveal the attack," she said.

"You can't blame yourself for that. Our gifts come from All; he puts them inside of us, but that doesn't mean we see everything. You weren't supposed to see the attack."

"That's not it," she practically croaked, hot tears streaking her face. "Don't you get it? I loved someone there. I had friends there."

"And they died."

She shook her head vehemently, clutching at her throat. "We were going to be bonded," she admitted, hanging her head, "but . . . the attack."

Jake reached for her, but she shook him off, unwilling to accept his comfort—not when he didn't understand. "You don't get it. You don't realize who he was. Who Nate was."

"What was Nate's Refarian name? Maybe I knew the guy." She could tell by his expression that Jake was scrolling through men he'd known in the ranks over the years.

She lowered his jacket, turning to face him. "That's not the question you should be asking. It's not the right question at all."

"Then what is?"

"He was Antousian. My lover was an Antousian spy, Nahim Lalihim."

"For All's sake," Jake hissed, actually pulling back from her. It was a name they'd all learned in the aftermath of the Texas fire.

"And I loved him. With all my heart I loved a man who betrayed us all—and yet chose to let me live."

The images of the colossal Antousians, their massive height as they stormed the facility that day, the weapons, the smell of them in her nostrils, all the memories overcame her like acrid smoke. She coughed, rubbing at her chest, remembering. They'd entered the main engineering quadrant, not in their humanized bodies, but in their natural ones—taking the substantial size and height advantage their Antousian forms had offered.

She'd been in the hangar with Nate, trying to make plans for later that night, and they'd stormed in like a massive army of locusts. The fire, the explosions . . . She'd been temporarily blinded when a grenade exploded nearby. Nate had crawled with her toward the hangar door, dragging her. One of the Antousian soldiers, seeing Nate, had spun on him and Shelby had been sure he would be killed. That they were both as good as dead. Then, in that garbled, vibrating voice that all Antousians possessed, the man had saluted Nate, asking, "What shall I do, sir?"

In her memories she clutched at Nate, hardly able

to see, feeling hysterical as he issued an order. "I want you to get this Refarian out of danger, Lasvan," he said. "Now!"

"What's going on?" Shelby asked, shaking her head as rough Antousian hands clasped her arms, dragging her to her feet. "Nate! What's happening?"

"I'm sorry, Shelby," came his reply, only the words had the same garbled, distorted sound that his comrade possessed. Blinking, her eyes watering, she got a look at Nate as his form stretched and changed, pulled and distorted, and he loomed over her like the dreadful, monstrous Antousian that he truly was. She'd screamed until her throat went raw, his accomplice dragging her from the warehouse to safety.

"Stay here," the soldier told her with a primitive grunt, shoving her to the ground behind an Antousian transport. With a dim glance about the nighttime, she could sense dozens of air transports hovering just overhead, could hear their quietly whirring engines, and she could see a few more land vehicles all around them.

But when she looked back at the hangar and warehouse, nothing could have possibly prepared her for the giant ball of flames that fireballed out of the roof, then the answering explosions—a series of them, rending the night—until the entire facility was engulfed in a massive, incendiary blaze. As much as she should have hated him, she'd fallen to the ground, weeping for Nate and her lost friends. He'd betrayed them all; he'd never loved her—but he was dead.

Over the years she'd come to believe that in some way, some twisted, half-decent Antousian sort of way, Nate must have loved her. He would never have risked setting her free otherwise. She ran that night; ran and ran until her feet bled, until her very life force gave out, until she couldn't see anything but the exploding warehouse and hangar, filled with her closest friends.

She had kept on wandering; for months and months that was all she did. She waited tables around Houston, did housework in Galveston, kept moving, and all the while her Texas accent kept on getting thicker. It had taken a year before she'd had the nerve or the heart to seek out her own people again. She was convinced that she'd failed them by not seeing Nate's betrayal for what it was.

"I'm Antousian," Scott whispered into the darkness between them. "As you well know."

She stared into her lap. "You reckon that matters to me?" Her voice came out dull, much more muted than she meant.

Jake slid a hand about her shoulder, gently rubbing her neck. "Yeah, I do, actually. I figure it matters a whole damned lot."

She turned to him, tears blurring his moonlit image. "It's me, Jakob. Just me. Please don't make this about who or what you are."

Stricken, he turned to her, not bothering to mask the pain in his eyes. "I know what it is to lose the person you love, that's all." His voice was unnaturally quiet, edged with tightness.

"Are you feeling guilty because we just made love?" she asked gently.

He raked a hand through his hair but said nothing at first. "I'm still in love with her. I probably will be for the rest of my life. So there's not much here for you, Shelby, that's all I'm saying."

"I don't believe that. I felt your passion a little while ago."

He laughed darkly. "I'll say."

"It's been five years since you lost your family, Jake. You can't grieve them forever, dying a little more yourself every day."

"This coming from you? The woman who just told me all about the man she still loves?"

"I don't love him anymore," she said. "He betrayed me and so many of my friends. That's not love."

"All right, then, let's call it heartbreak. Something we have in common."

"You're just twisting my words around."

He gave her a bittersweet smile, one that said he was shutting down to her emotionally. "Like I said, you need some sleep. Tell you what, let's crawl inside the cab and get the heater on. That'll warm us both up."

But Shelby knew the conversation was far from over, and more than that, she knew that Jake's own demons had just been called out of the mountains. Thanks to her, and her horrible revelations about his own kind. Still, she didn't have the strength to heal him, not tonight when her own heart felt so battered itself.

Chapter Nine

Marco stared through the dusty window of Jake's pickup, worried at first that something might have happened to the couple within. Thea had helped him find them, locking in on Jake and Shelby's coordinates with her sharply honed intuitive skills. The transport had made their drop by following her specs.

Pressing his face against the glass, Marco was relieved—and a little shocked—to discover Jake and Shelby inside the truck, wildly entangled in each other's arms. Jake leaned against the far door, Shelby nestled between the large man's spread thighs. It was a Rubik's Cube of arms and legs and torsos that Marco couldn't begin to solve, not in the predawn darkness. He heightened his vision, throwing the inky landscape into hazy relief. Clearly his assigned pair were now lovers, and he tried to figure the best way to rouse them—especially without making the situation even more awkward than it already was.

He was about to rap on the window when a rush of emotion from within the cab zeroed in on him like an out-of-control missile. The shock wave was so intense, it was more like a psychic tsunami; he actually staggered backward slightly, battling his empathic gift's mad gyrations.

What is this? He wondered frantically. His gift *never* acted up when the other parties were asleep. That had never happened, at least not since he'd come of age and learned to fully master his problematic ability.

Bending over to catch his breath, he gasped as if he'd just run eight or nine miles, bracing both hands atop his knees while he tried to gain control again. The splintering migraine took no time to attack, swooping in like a vulture, clawing at his thoughts.

"Damn it all to hell." He gave his head a slight shake, thankful that everything was so dark. These headaches could be more than a little debilitating. Once, while sick with a particularly nasty one, he'd even become nauseous just from looking at a bright yellow sweater. The only trigger, ever, was intense emotion that he couldn't effectively block. In this case, what could have prepared him?

Straightening up, Marco approached the truck once again. Barricading his mind with a strong defensive barrier, he banged on the window. Loudly. Muffled shouts answered from within, and it occurred to him that if he weren't careful, he just might get himself shot. He'd been so blindsided by his empathic diffusion, he'd totally forgotten standard approach and protocol.

Dropping to the ground and shielding himself behind the truck's front bumper, he identified himself. "McKinley! It's Marco McKinley, king's Madjin."

From within the truck burst a string of Refarian expletives, punctuated by feminine laughter. "McKinley!" Tierny roared, the sound more like the explosion of a grenade than an actual spoken word.

Marco rose to his feet, inching cautiously along the edge of the truck lest he wind up with a luminator pointed at his face. He knew what an itchy trigger finger Dillon had and doubted that his future self was any less into weaponry.

"It's McKinley," he repeated, stopping just beside the rearview mirror. "Sorry I came up on you guys like that."

The heel of one large cowboy boot slammed against the window, then retracted until Jake's merciless face appeared in the window frame, all scowls and accusation.

Ah, shit. Marco braced himself for a serious dressing down, the kind Dillon occasionally delivered to the corps.

Finally, the door creaked open, Jake Tierny practically tumbling out of the cab. Seated inside the truck, Shelby raked her hands across her long, disheveled hair. As if a neatened-up ponytail could conceal the bare-skinned evidence of what the pair had been up to.

Tierny staggered a step, then regained his equilibrium, and Marco's heightened vision didn't miss Jake's unzipped pants.

"Hang on," Tierny grumbled, turning away as he yanked at his shirt and made quick work of his pants' zipper.

Shelby made no move to exit the truck, just sat staring neatly forward, both hands positioned beside her legs.

Jake faced him, hard. "Look, McKinley, you've gotta be out of your fucking mind to come up on me like that. I could have—"

He bowed his head. "I apologize, sir."

"I'm not your superior officer," Tierny practically spat.

"You're correct," Marco replied cautiously. "I don't answer within the chain of command."

"I meant"—Jake stabbed at his chest—"that I'm not an *officer* in your outfit. That's Dillon, not me. So don't bother calling me *sir*."

The man's lie lingered between them, giving off a moldy, rotting smell. Marco's empathy always reacted to dishonesty most of all. In this case, Tierny was fooling himself, trying to believe that he wasn't actually a future version of Scott Dillon. It wasn't a battle Marco planned to tackle, at least not right now.

"I understand, Tierny," he agreed, "and won't argue about your identity. I think it's enough that *you* know who you are; I can figure things out along the way. But your king has sent me for you." Marco glanced past Tierny's shoulder, studying Shelby's profile, the way she bent her head protectively. "And for Medic Tyler."

Tierny folded his bulky arms across his chest. "One soldier wasn't enough to come claim my sorry ass, huh?"

Marco forced a barrier against the Antousian's bitterness. "Our lord has an assignment for you."

"So I heard." Tierny didn't exactly sound compliant; far from it.

"You're clearly on your way back to camp . . ." Marco let the implied question dangle, hoping Tierny would take the cue.

"I had to bribe him," Shelby piped in. Her bare feet slid onto the dirt, and she made no effort to straighten her lopsided miniskirt. "Otherwise, he wasn't going nowhere."

"Don't ask what the bribe was." Tierny's rumbling laugh said it all.

Marco kept his gaze on the ground, cursing himself for the heat that rushed into his face.

Shelby planted a feisty hand on her hip, flatironing Tierny with her gaze. "Oh, puhlease! As if you needed bribing for *that*. Don't try and convince me you were just serving our planet." Shelby swung her spirited gaze toward Marco. "I didn't bribe him, not precisely. Just reminded the stupid fool that Jared Bennett is still his king, here in this time. Not much he could argue about after that."

Tierny's breathing grew heavy and intense, his chest expanding as he stared Shelby down. "You promised to time walk me."

Shelby laughed, an overly exaggerated release that nearly turned into a cough. "Now he's talking out of his ass, totally."

Marco smiled at her faintly but filed this new information away for further reflection. He had never—not once—heard that any of the time walkers still existed. Maybe a joke, or maybe a genuine slip, the idea captivated Marco nonetheless. After all, his own gift was equally rare.

Any further conversation was interrupted by the dull hum of the transport swooping low over them. Marco glanced upward, brushing at his hair as it blew in the sudden wind. "Our ride's here."

"What about my truck?" Jake sounded genuinely sorry to lose his wheels.

"Registered to you?" Marco started around the side of the car, prepared to remove any traceable documentation.

"Hell, no." Jake caught him by the arm. "Thing's clean as a whistle."

Once a soldier, always a soldier.

"Then, let's get out of here."

Shelby filed into the meeting room of the main lodge, following Jake and Marco. Several soldiers had met them in the hangar, hustling them through the connecting corridors and tunnels that led to the officers' sector of the Refarian compound. She rarely visited the lodge, a large four-story cabin that served as housing for the king and queen and a small group of high-ranking officers. Their upper echelon took meals in the lodge, slept there, and obviously held top secret strategy meetings there, as well.

Upon entering the room, she saw Chris Harper already seated by Jared's side, and Colonel Peters from the USAF there on his other. None of this surprised Shelby, who had pretty much figured that their return would flush out all the big guns. Chris Harper gave her a slight nod, which she returned before glancing toward Tierny.

She couldn't help being intrigued by the relationship between Chris and Jake. Jake had years' worth of memories as the human's brother-in-law, memories that she couldn't begin to guess at. Had they mourned Hope together? Had they been tight-knit brothers or competitive adversaries? Chris and Hope were extremely close—maybe Jake had been threatened by that. She could have spent the next four hours speculating as to the memories hammering around inside

Jake's head, but looking at him she couldn't guess a dang thing.

No, whatever he might have felt, Jake betrayed nothing. He blinked back at the human for several long moments, and then it happened. Something cracked inside the guy, his entire body growing tense and edgy as if he might suddenly attack. Or as if being around Chris Harper tore open an old, festering wound, and he had to protect himself against further pain.

Harper shifted uneasily in his chair. "Tierny. Long time. Glad you're back on our team. That was some seriously good work over in Montana a few months ago."

"I'd do anything to protect Hope." Jake said the words like he more than meant them, dropping his gaze. "You would, too."

Shelby felt an unexpected pang of jealousy, that sense that she had no business getting involved with a man who still mourned his murdered wife.

Did Chris know the full truth about Jake? Shelby hadn't been debriefed on that point. From the thoughtful look in Chris's eyes, she guessed that he knew everything—and with the way Hope confided in her twin, it was impossible to imagine he didn't know exactly who Jake was to her. Besides, Chris was the one who'd conducted the deep background search on the "original" Jake Tierny and was the only reason she'd been able to give Jake that thick folder of intel back in Texas.

With a quick glance at Jared's expectant features, Shelby decided the formal route would make the best impression at the moment. Placing both hands on the shiny conference table, she lowered into a half bow. "My lord," she whispered reverently, hoping her king wouldn't upbraid her for having done such a piss-poor job of getting Tierny back to base.

"Please, Medic Tyler . . . rise."

She obeyed, placing both hands behind her back until Jared gestured toward one of the chairs. Next, his black gaze swung to Tierny, his eyes a pair of fathomless pools, glittering slightly with emotion. "My dear friend." Jared's voice was hushed, the feeling in the words undeniable.

Jake blew out a sigh, hunching slightly as he stared at the floor. "Hey, J."

"I realized you'd never come home if I didn't send a search party."

Jake shifted uncomfortably, still avoiding their king's gaze. "You know why."

Their commander nodded, then—as if suddenly aware that others were present—gestured for everyone to take a seat.

"The humans have formed a Joint Alien Task Force," Jared said, "spearheaded by the FBI. Hope and Scott are working with them over in Denver."

"So I've heard." Jake cocked back in his seat, folding both hands across his belly as if he were playing poker. "And what about Harper, here?" He nodded toward the human. "What's his role?"

Chris sat up straight. "I'm heading the task force."

Jake didn't seem the least bit surprised. "But this group of yours, it has both humans and Refarians in it?"

"We're working in cooperation," Jared replied, studying Jake curiously. Shelby could guess what their commander was wondering: Had it been different in the future, that alternate world that Jake had traveled from?

"That's good," was all Jake said, averting his eyes. "Much better that way."

Silence fell between them, a few awkward glances exchanged before Jared continued, "Jakob, one reason your return became such an urgent matter is that we have a line on the man you're seeking."

"Tierny? You know where he is?" Jake's eyes assumed a hungry, voracious gleam, and a chill ran through Shelby.

"Our source within the Antousian camp has spotted

him," Jared answered. "He's working with them now. Over in Idaho."

Jake ran his tongue across his upper lip, nodding wordlessly. Shelby couldn't help getting a strange, queasy feeling deep inside: Of course he'd been anticipating vengeance for years, but his downright breathless reaction unsettled her. This same man had made love to her only hours earlier, had made himself deeply vulnerable to her. Now all that intimacy had vanished, replaced by thoughts that were frighteningly transparent. There was murder in his bright green eyes.

Jared leaned back in his chair, folding his hands into a temple beneath his chin. "But there's more. The Antousians have been holding warehouse parties—raves?" Jared's voice turned up at the end, as if he wasn't entirely sure he was using the right word. "Raves where they let the alcohol and drugs flow pretty damned loose, and then seize the human hosts they want from the assembled partygoers. We know the location of their next event a week from now. We want you to infiltrate, impersonating Tierny."

Jake laughed low in the back of his throat, a dark, cold sound. "That shouldn't be hard."

"It will be dangerous," Jared cautioned, meeting Jake's thousand-yard stare. "You scent like an Antousian hybrid—"

"Which I am."

Jared barreled ahead. "And you're older than the real Jake Tierny is. . . . They could kill you without so much as blinking an eye. It's a significant risk."

Jake kicked back from the table, nearly knocking his chair over. "I'm all over it."

"Well, I'm not certain I'm so eager," was all Jared had to say.

The two friends stared at each other for a long moment, and slowly Jake slid back into his chair. "Tell me everything you know."

Chris Harper cleared his throat. "These raves move

all across the Southwest. Sometimes in Phoenix, other times in Albuquerque or Dallas. This one they're bringing much closer to their center of operations. We want to know why. It tells us something big is in the works or they wouldn't be changing the geography."

"I've been over that folder of yours," Jake told Harper. "Haven't really learned shit about what he's up to. Except electronics, he's big-time into technology."

"That makes sense, with what you took off of him," Shelby interjected. And just like that, the attention of every soldier in the room swiveled toward her.

And Jake was giving her the serious evil eye. *Uh-oh.* So he hadn't wanted that little bit of information about the Antousian chip to leak just yet.

"What's she talking about?" Harper asked. Jake rolled his eyes, digging into his jacket pocket, flinging his wallet onto the table. It skidded across the smooth surface, bouncing like a penny over open water, sliding to a halt right in front of Chris.

"Look inside," Jake instructed. "You should find this . . . enlightening. All of you will."

"I'll be damned," was all Chris could think to say. The alien squad had been thoroughly briefed by Jared and his lieutenants; they knew all about the neural implant chips that had started the war between the Antousians and Refarians. And for the past few months his crew had gotten a pretty good idea that the chips were being leaked here on Earth. An intercepted shipment down around Denver had revealed that much. But this? If Tierny had taken it off his nemesis—in the future? Well, this just might be the mother lode of all leads.

"The question I haven't been able to answer," Jake said, "not since taking this off of Tierny the night of the . . . uh, when he . . ." Jake coughed, struggling. "I've never figured out why a *human* was partnered up with the Antousians. Or why he was on the battlefield that day."

Chris flinched. The last thing he wanted was to picture Hope's murder. She'd told him everything over the past months, about what happened to her in the future, all the dark, sordid facts. He was as hell-bent as the man before him to stop that murder from taking place a second time.

Chris leaned closer across the table, spreading both hands flat. "We don't know why, not yet. But I promise you one thing, Tierny," he said. "We're going to capture that bastard and figure out what his role is in all of this."

"I'm your man. I'm ready to roll whenever you give me the green light."

"But as your commander says, it's a risk." Chris felt obligated—if for no other reason than because of Hope—to underscore that fact. But Tierny was a tough bastard, he'd hand him that.

"Hope told you the whole story?" he asked, kicking back in his chair like he might at a backyard barbeque. "You know what happened to her . . . and our baby?"

It was as if all the other advisers and lieutenants faded into the background. There was only the two of them, Tierny practically burrowing a hole in Chris with his brilliant, glowing eyes. "I know what happened," Chris answered flatly. "But it won't happen again. You can be damned sure of that much."

"Good. We're in agreement, then." Jake released his visual hold on him. "You just tell me where I need to go, and I'll do whatever it takes to stop my enemy."

Chris nodded, but an eerie shiver shot down his spine, as if he'd had this same conversation before, only he couldn't quite remember when. The sensation was so vivid, so totally intense, that he lost his train of thought for a few seconds.

Commander Bennett stepped in. "The warehouse party is in a week," he explained. "We've got a lot of prep work to do before then."

"I need to debrief you, Tierny," Chris said, sliding a folder marked CLASSIFIED across the table toward the other man. New information, more than he'd sent with Shelby Tyler in an effort to lure the alien back to base.

Jake nodded. "I'm all ears."

"And you need to debrief *me*, while we're at it," Chris added. "I want to know everything you've got on this man."

Jake retrieved the folder, flipping it open. For several moments he rifled through the papers, his eyes scanning the pages at hyperspeed.

Strange to think this was a future version of his sister's husband, Scott Dillon. He and Dillon had spent the past four months partnered up, gotten to know each other pretty damn well. It was hard to take the jaded, sad man in front of him and reconcile him with Dillon . . . to square them as two versions of the same man.

Hell, it was even spookier to realize that Tierny had scores of memories of being married to his sister—and of her murder. No wonder the soldier's eyes had that haunted, distant look in them, an expression Chris had seen before over at Warren on the faces of returning vets. Guys who'd experienced far too much of the War on Terror, that up-close kind of experience that left something hollow and dead in their souls.

"One week," Tierny murmured, his eyes riveted on the open folder. "We've got a lot of work to do, Harper. A whole lotta prep, but I'm ready."

"Good," Jared interjected. "Because we're all counting on you, Jakob. And I know you won't let us down."

LONG DISTANCE TELEPHONE CALLS

Date. . . . . Time. . . . . Charges. . . . .

CITY CALLED . . . .

Area Code. . . . . Tel. No. . . . . Order No.. . . . .

PARTY CALLED . . . .

PERSON PLACING CALL . . . .

REMARKS . . . .

. . . .

Collect ☐ Direct Dial ☐

Person to Person ☐

MED Form No. 20

Chapter Ten

"That must've been pretty strange."

Jake looked up from the open folder, surprised to find Shelby standing right beside his chair. As soon as the meeting had adjourned, he'd immediately gotten lost in the documents on Tierny and the Antousians, shocked to learn just how many humans had vanished in the past few months, all taken from the big warehouse parties Jared had described.

"What must have been strange?" He stared up into her beautiful blue eyes, startled by how clear they seemed beneath the meeting room lights. She brushed at a loose strand of blond hair, tucking it behind her ear with a sexy little gesture that hit him like a blast from a rocket launcher. Gods, the woman was as hot as hell, and after making love to her the night before, it took only the slightest movement of her tight, compact body to turn him on. *And what I wouldn't do to have that body right beneath mine*, he thought, with a glance at the long conference table. *Right here, right now.*

Instantly, thoughts of his enemies fled his mind, replaced by a quick rush of lust so jolting, it was all he could do not to draw her right down onto his lap.

"Jake?"

"Yeah?"

"Were you listening to me?"

He flushed. "Got a little distracted, sorry." He shifted uneasily in his chair, hoping she wouldn't glance down and see the serious tent that had just pitched inside his jeans.

She sidled up onto the table, facing him. "I was just saying it must be weird to be around Chris after . . . everything."

Bringing up his painful past hadn't exactly been on his mind. "Yeah," he agreed after a moment, "it hurts to be around him after so long."

"Was he still in your life? Right before you came back through time?"

He shook his head, swallowing hard.

"Was he dead, then?" she persisted, swinging her legs back and forth.

He planted one palm on the table beside her. "It's better not to talk about this stuff, Shelby. When Kelsey sent me back in time, she specifically instructed me to keep details of that other timeline under wraps."

"But you're here to stay now, and you have told all of us a whole lot of facts."

She kept swinging those shapely legs of hers back and forth, back and forth, and his fingers burned to reach out and stroke them. "It's bad territory for me, that's all."

Slipping one hand onto her knee, she bent closer toward him. "I'm good at listening. It's the ole bedside manner, always ready to kick in."

Another little swing of her leg, that miniskirt riding high about her thighs. Damn it all! His hand shot out, catching hold of the calf closest to him. He held his breath, slowly inching his fingers along the warm, smooth skin. With a glance toward the door, he was thrilled to confirm that it was shut. No one would barge in: They knew that he was studying the confidential file and would give him privacy to work. Shelby bent toward him, watching as he skimmed his fingertips higher up her leg, then higher still, until he was brushing his calloused hands up beneath the hem of that skirt.

"Talking isn't what I have in mind right now." He

growled low in his throat, tugging her closer to him. Scooting his chair back, he made room for her, sliding her right in front of him on the table. She sat facing him, her parted thighs an open mystery to him. He could see dark blond tufts of curling hair where her absent panties should have been. Unable to help himself, he released another throaty growl, rising up slightly in his seat.

"You like it dangerous," she murmured, reaching to touch his hair. Her fingertips lingered there; then she slowly stroked his cheek. "I've definitely got your number, boy, and you're an exhibitionist."

He pressed a soft kiss against her inner thigh. "I think that would be you, baby."

"Okay, maybe both of us," she admitted on a delicate little sigh, the muscles in her legs contracting.

"Nobody's watching. It's just you and me."

"And the whole lodge just outside that door." She gestured behind her.

"So lock it."

"Maybe I'm a little dangerous, too. Ever think of that one, Tierny?" She lowered her lashes coquettishly, parting her thighs a little wider. "If Commander Bennett walks in on us . . ." Her words trailed off, and she planted both hands on his shoulders, leaning into him. "Well, I guess he could kick me off base or could demote you. Wait! You're not a ranking officer. Forgot. So what's to worry about?"

Jake muttered a curse, then hiked her skirt up to her waist. "All right, sweet thing, if you want danger, you've got it." He bent his head low and forward, planting fiery kisses along her inner thighs, dragging his lips upward until he buried himself in those sweet folds of flesh. Oh gods, she tasted like nectar, and she was already so wet for him. Just gleaming and damp and perfect.

She dug one hand into his hair, scraping her fingers back and forth across his scalp. Her other hand tore into his shoulder, and he could feel her arch. She made soft moaning cries—quiet, but certainly intense—and he plunged his tongue within her, spreading her wider with his hand.

"Deeper," she murmured. "Please, Jake, . . . deeper." She began to rock her hips, thrusting them, teasing him harder.

A desperate moan escaped his lips, and a dim part of him hoped they wouldn't get barged in on; still, he couldn't keep quiet. His erection lengthened a little more, tightening to the point of painfulness. Almost as if she knew it, Shelby worked her little ass closer to the edge of the table, until she was as close to his own body as she could get. Then, with another delicate cry of pleasure, she slowly leaned back onto the table, opening herself wider to him that way.

He buried his face deeper, thrust his tongue faster and swirled it all about her mound, licking at every drop that she released for him. Just for him.

She began trembling, her thighs tightened about his head, and then quake after quake shot through her core. Arching on the table, she moaned—loudly—and Jake had to have more.

Fumbling with his fly, he rose to his feet, shoved his pants down about his legs, and mounted her right there on the table.

Shelby knew she was in seriously deep trouble. She'd known it from the moment Jake had begun eyeing her legs; now, well, she was just too far gone to care. Any moment and one of the officers was going to discover them having rock-hard, blazing sex on the meeting room table. Jake's heavy weight settled atop her, the wooden table groaning in complaint.

"Better not break this thing," she said, wrapping her legs about his waist.

"I'm not going to break you, baby." He pushed his tip against her opening, sliding in easily.

"The table." It gave another creaking groan. "You're a big, big boy." She settled him inside of her deeper. "A really big boy. God, Jake, you're *huge*."

He pulled back, giving her a lopsided grin.

"Couldn't get this deep on the hood of that truck last night."

Adjusting his hips, he worked his way in farther, and it was all she could do not to melt beneath him. He was beautiful, from his haunted green eyes to his dusky olive skin; his body was exquisite, with its roping muscle and surging power. And he made her feel things that she hadn't in such a long time. Oh, for such a very long time.

Sliding both her hands along his lower back, she outlined that big, gorgeous body atop hers. "You're . . . stunning," she murmured in his ear.

He dipped his head low, nibbling at her collarbone. "Even if I am a *vlksai*," he teased, and she stilled beneath him. "What?" He stared down into her eyes. "I was just joking, sweetheart."

She gave her head a little shake, staring up at him in shock.

"Shelby." He brushed her hair out of her eyes. "It doesn't matter what we are. . . . This is beautiful. Trust me."

That was the terrifying part—she did trust him. And she had no doubt she'd let this man do anything with her that he ever wanted. He leaned up on his forearms, watching her, his intense eyes growing brighter. She turned her head to the side. "Don't go gazing me, now. That's not fair."

He bent down, kissing her chastely on the forehead. "I didn't even know I was doing it. I can't always control my gift. Just call me on it if I do that again."

She nodded, keeping her face turned away from him. Finally, he released a quiet sigh. "We better try this again later." He moved off of her and into a push-up, bending to kiss her softly on the lips one more time.

She slid her hand behind his head, stroking his nape. "I—I don't want this to be over."

Jake opened his mouth to speak just as the meeting room door opened. He bolted backward, practically falling off the table. *"Meshdki fliishki!"*

Chris Harper appeared in the doorway, eyes bugging out of his head. "Holy shit, Tierny."

"You ever hear of knocking?" Jake shouted, grabbing at his clothes.

Shelby yanked her skirt down as low as it would go. How was it that she and Jake always seemed hell-bent on landing in compromising positions?

"You ever hear of the *bedroom*?" Harper fired back at Jake, shaking his head. "Fuck, Tierny, let me know when you're done so we can get back to work."

The door slammed shut, rattling in its frame. Shelby slid off the table, her face burning red-hot, and adjusted her skirt. Jake stared after Harper, a dazed, stricken expression in his eyes. She had a pretty good idea that it was far more than being busted by Hope's brother. For it to have been Chris of all people had to have triggered an avalanche of guilt within Jake's heart.

He stared at the closed door, his chest heaving. Shelby's throat tightened; some part of Jake would always be in love with Hope, she realized, and that meant some part of him would always be elusive, unattainable. Remote.

"I better get down to the medical complex," she said smoothly. "I have some patients to check in on after being away for the past ten days."

Jake caught her by the arm, spinning her up against his chest. "We're not done, Shelby. Not even close to done." His light green eyes blazed against his swarthy skin, electrified with unspent need and emotion.

"You've got a meeting, and I've got patients." She kept her tone flat and fixed her gaze just past his shoulder.

"What is it about me that you're so afraid of? Is it really because I'm a hybrid? Does the Antousian blood pumping through my veins turn you off that much?"

"I know how you must have hated that. Chris seeing you with me. How disloyal it must have made you feel." She pressed her eyes shut, tears appearing from nowhere. Jake must have seen, because his entire demeanor changed, and he cradled her head against his chest.

"Shh, sweetheart. I don't care what Chris Harper thinks." He stroked her hair.

"I'm not afraid of your hybrid nature, either," she told him in a thick voice. "I—I just feel so overwhelmed by you. Everything about you."

"I'm not trying to push you," he told her, running one hand down her back.

She tried to speak, but no words would come, and at last she sighed against him, feeling his fingers stroke her hair. Her tears wouldn't stop, and all the while just one thought echoed in her mind: *Gentle.* Jake Tierny, Antousian hybrid, deadly soldier, giant of a man, was so unbelievably . . . *gentle* with her.

Surely she would be safe with someone capable of this kind of tenderness—even if he was a *vlksai.*

Maybe that was true, but everything—all of it that was happening between them—was just too much, too fast. She pushed apart from him, wiping at her eyes. "I really do have to go," she said in a numb voice, staggering slightly as she made for the door.

"I'll see you later, though?"

"I have patients to visit."

"You already said that."

"Because it's true." She hesitated, her hand flat against the heavy wooden door. "But . . . I want to see you, too."

"Yeah?" Jake asked softly, stepping close behind her. His large hand settled on her shoulder, a heavy and comforting weight.

"Sure." She steadied her hand, trying to stop it from trembling against the door. "So I'll just, uh, see you around." She slid out of his grasp and was gone before he could catch her.

"Just tell me that Erica doesn't somehow know I'm ravishing her mother," Jared laughed, rolling onto his back and collapsing against the pillows. His body was covered in perspiration, his naturally dark face ruddy from their exertions.

"It puts her to sleep," Kelsey panted.

Jared's eyebrows lifted to his hairline. "You must be joking, love. How could anyone sleep through"—he slid an open palm over her breast, then down along her hip—"that. Sweet gods above, we'll be lucky if a battalion doesn't storm down our door after the noise we just made. They're probably afraid the compound is under attack."

Kelsey laughed, burrowing closer to Jared. "It's the rhythm of it. The back and forth is like we're rocking her."

Jared's eyes drifted halfway shut, and he flipped over onto his belly. "I know what she means. . . . I'm ready for a nap myself. You wore me out, sweet Kelse."

Kelsey began stroking her fingertips across his shoulders; he practically purred in response. He loved a good postcoital back scratching and always lapped it up, growling happily in reaction. So long as she avoided his scars; from the beginning, he'd always flinched or pulled away whenever she touched the rough striations on his back.

She wasn't sure why—maybe because of the growing closeness she felt with him now that Erica was almost here or maybe from some need to help him—but she took her fingers and deliberately touched the harshest scar that ran from his left shoulder all the way down to his hip. He flinched in reaction to her touch, but she didn't remove her hand.

"You never talk about how you got these." She skimmed her hand lower, moving across the firm musculature of his buttocks, stroking until she reached the banded scars on his upper thighs. "Or these."

If he hadn't been lying facedown on the pillow, she would have undoubtedly touched the faint scoring on his jaw and face as well.

He shifted his hips, propping his chin on both arms.

"Love, it's an ugly story. Not something you should have to hear."

Her voice was gentle. "But I *want* to know everything about you. I don't want there to be secrets. There's still so much you've never told me about your life here on Earth, about the war, your family. I love you, Jareshk. I want to know all the things you've experienced." She pressed her lips to the longest scar on his back, then pulled away and stared down into his eyes. "Please tell me how you got them."

He rotated onto his side so she wouldn't be able to see the ridged flesh on his back. Just the thought of her gazing on such ugliness shamed him, made him feel dirty inside, dark. He clenched and unclenched his fists around the covers, remembering his captivity at Veckus's hands. Only when she pressed her hand over his own did he realize that he'd begun to rip the sheet in half.

"I know it's hard to talk about," she prompted softly, reaching to stroke his temple. "Maybe I'm selfish because I want to know."

"No. No, you're not wrong. . . . I—I have never spoken of what was done to me. Only Scott knows . . . well, a bit of it, and it probably is time that I . . ." His mind flooded with twisted images, of his arms strung out overhead, the feel of the flaying whip against his back. If only the physical torture had been the worst of it.

"Time that you opened up about it?" she encouraged.

He swallowed, nodding as his head dropped heavily against the pillow. "When I was twenty-six, I was shot down over Idaho, the middle of nowhere. I had no choice but to eject from the craft. . . ." His voice trailed off. Gods, he hated the thought of Kelsey learning what they'd done to him. To his body . . . and his soul.

Of course she didn't relent. "And you were captured?"

He nodded. "Veckus didn't care about intel or what he could learn. He only had a taste for vengeance. He wanted me to suffer . . . and I did."

Kelsey nodded, calmly stroking his hair, but he could sense how her heartbeat quickened. "How long did they have you?"

"Three days." He gulped at the air between them, his throat tightening spasmodically.

"They beat you?"

Again he nodded. "But that's not what caused the scarring. Those wounds healed up . . . eventually."

Kelsey stroked her hand across her pregnant belly, studying him intently. Not pushing too hard, not forcing him to continue. The safety of her love and goodness nearly overwhelmed him. "At the end, they trapped me in my D'Aravnian form," he admitted thickly. "And beat me with pulsar whips . . . over and over. My energized body doesn't scar, but the torture left marks on my physical one." He lifted a hand to his cheek, outlining the long mark along his jaw.

He didn't dare look at her, his pain and shame at what had been done to him was that intense. Besides, it would be impossible for her—a human—to comprehend the thin line between his dual selves. Nor could she fully grasp the ambivalent feelings he had about his twin halves—and how Veckus had played those insecurities to the hilt. No, nothing had ever made him feel more perverse for simply being what he *was*—an entity of pure energy—than the feel of those spiny, cracking whips burning across his surging power.

And Veckus had laughed. Over and over the perverted bastard had mocked him, holding him in his natural form until he began to lose touch with his physical body. Putting that whip to his glowing D'Aravnian self until Jared thought he'd lose his mind from the shocking, torturous agony. Until the smell had sickened him to the core of his undulating, swirling being. During those three days, his primal golden body had been like a dying sun, flayed raw beneath the hands of its captors.

"I—I almost couldn't change back. They kept me in my D'Aravnian form for so long that the connection between my two forms was almost destroyed." He cracked his eyes open, daring to see if she was frightened of him, disgusted by how "other" he truly was to her human self. Still, after all these months together, he wrestled to grasp her pure acceptance of what he was.

"Oh, Jareshk." She bent toward him, struggling a little awkwardly to reach him because of her large belly. She pressed gentle kisses against his brow, over and over, just murmuring his name. "I'm so sorry you had to live through that."

"You've no idea how badly it hurts, the way my energy reacts to those Antousian whips. It's worse than anything I've ever experienced in this body." He thumped at his chest. "I wanted to die. I prayed the gods would take my life."

"But you didn't die," she whispered, stroking his hair.

He cringed. "What sort of king wishes to leave his people because he's not strong enough to endure torture? What sort of leader? I am still ashamed at the memory of it."

Kelsey had known the scars were linked to some deep pain, but nothing could have prepared her for the hidden suffering Jared still carried with him. And that he blamed himself for having wanted to die? That was probably what tore her up the most. "Jared, you were in pain. You didn't know if your people would find you. . . . You can't feel bad that you prayed for an escape."

She watched as Jared's whole body jerked and flinched, almost as if it were remembering the physical punishments it had endured. "That weakness is still inside of me. . . ." he finally whispered, thrusting an arm across his face. Like he was hiding from her. She fought the urge to peel away that freaking arm so she could just stare into his beautiful black eyes and make him understand that he was blameless.

But healing took time, and she knew that. This was just a first step, a beginning of his opening up to her about the full nature of what he was.

And that was when it hit her, a total insight into something they'd been wrestling with throughout their relationship. "Is that why you're so uncomfortable with your D'Aravnian form?" she asked. "Why you're always so afraid of being near me in your natural state?"

A fervent growl came from his chest, but he kept his eyes hidden behind his forearm.

"Is that a yes?"

Another growl. "Stop . . . pressing. . . ."

That was her answer. He worried that he'd hurt her, could destroy her—that much she understood. But there had always been a more complicated layer of discomfort that she'd never been able to find her way past. And here it was, at last brought out of darkness and into the pure light of their love for each other.

"Thank you, Jareshk," she whispered softly, bending low to kiss the top of his head. "I love you so much. Thank you for trusting me, for knowing I won't hurt you."

His arm dropped away, and he turned his black gaze on her. The fury and revulsion in his eyes shocked her. "I hate them for what they took from me, Kelse. I despise them for it. Don't you see? That's the ugliest part of it all. A part of my soul was stolen during that captivity. . . . They made me hate, made me less than what I was. They made me," he whispered meaningfully, "at least a little bit, like them."

"You're nothing like they are!" she cried, struggling to sit up in bed, but Jared had already launched himself onto the floor. He paced back and forth like he'd been caged; maybe because he was remembering his captivity. His naked body gleamed with sweat, and he rolled his shoulders, the muscles bunching tensely.

And then he stopped. Right in front of her, he pulled to a halt, his midnight eyes blazing ferociously.

"I cannot forgive them for what they did to me during those three days."

"Nobody expects you to."

"*I* expect it!" he roared, the words bouncing off the overhead beams like a pinball. "I expect myself to be better than they are, to not become less than . . . what I'm called to be, Kelse." Jared thrust a hand through his hair, trembling slightly. "I am a leader, and as much as it makes me uncomfortable, I am also a king. A king does not let bitterness take root in his soul. He has greater character and strength than that."

Kelsey wobbled up onto her feet, wrapping her arms about Jared from behind. She pressed her lips against his longest and most brutal scar, trailing her mouth down it in a healing gesture, lapping at it with the tip of her tongue. "They tortured you, sweetheart," she whispered at last. "You had a normal human . . . well, normal *Refarian* reaction. You're a good, kind man."

"I prayed to All every day after that, prayed that Veckus would be killed." The words were dark, threatening. "And he did die. But perhaps there's a cost; perhaps I'm going to be punished for those prayers."

Kelsey dropped her arms from about his waist, then stepped around him so she could stare him straight in the eye. "Veckus was a cruel killer who has taken more lives than we even know about. Of course you were right to pray that."

Jared's jaw tightened, ticking slightly. "I do *not* want to be like *they* are."

Kelsey realized that this battle had been waging itself inside Jared for a lot longer than she might have guessed—ever since his captivity. She could also understand why he'd never spoken about it, or his trauma or the scars. He'd been at war for years now, more years than she could even begin to fathom, and this was the area where his foundation had crumbled a bit.

"When Scott found me and freed me, I torched the entire camp."

"What do you mean? You dropped a bomb?"

Jared shook his head. "No, I torched it. In my D'Aravnian form, after Scott released me from the containment cell. I moved over the whole place, whirling like a hurricane, and killed every last Antousian in the place. I wanted to murder. I wanted to destroy . . . and I wanted Veckus obliterated from the universe."

"How did he get away?" Kelsey sat back on the edge of the bed, watching Jared's intense expression. For long moments, he seemed somewhere else, kept stroking his hands down the length of his long black hair.

"Jared?"

He jumped slightly as if he'd forgotten she was with him. "I never knew how he escaped. But I thank All every day that he finally died, that Jake killed him in the warehouse. But my hatred didn't die with him. Now I want Raedus. I want him with a vengeance I can taste. And I want the human Jake Tierny, want his life because of what he did to Hope and Scott. . . ." Jared bowed his head, his eyes sliding shut. "Now you see why I do not discuss my scars. I'm ashamed for you to know the bitterness that rages inside my heart."

"They killed people you love, Jared." She gripped him by the forearms, wanting to physically shake some sense into him. "They are the enemies of your people. You talk about being a king—of course you hate what they've done. I know you—really know you—and you don't hate them. You hate that they subjugated your people."

He blew out an exhausted sigh. "Once again, you understand my heart completely."

"Well, *yeah.* Always." She laughed softly.

A slow, sideways smile slipped onto his face. "You never fail to link me back to myself, sweet love." The desperate, haunted look in his eyes faded a little. "And I suppose if All had been judging me, he never would have brought you back into my life."

"Our mating is the only proof you ever need that

God loves you." Kelsey stood and cupped his face within her palms.

"Across this fathomless universe, He did draw us together."

"We could have wandered forever, you know. Never found each other. It's scary how easy that would have been." She leaned upward, kissing his cheek. Her belly, so large and ungainly, bumped right into his hips. Jared slid fingertips between them, touching her stomach.

"This babe, too, is perfect proof of All's existence," he whispered, his eyes gleaming with emotion. "She's our gift from him. When I was nearly past my fertility, we conceived this beautiful child . . . against such odds. A hybrid child that could so easily have never been. Oh, yes. *That* was a miracle. Almost as great as All himself drawing us together."

"Yes, it was." She leaned into him, wrapping her arms around his body, just wanting him to feel her love. Needing him to feel the healing in that love. "Remember that when you doubt."

"I never doubt your love, Kelsey. Or the love that brought us Erica."

She nestled up against him, focusing on the primal heat and energy that thrummed within his body. She willed everything else to the sidelines, every doubt and fear about their future, of what was yet to come with his enemies. And silently—so very silently within her mind—she prayed that he would never be captured, not ever again.

But none of her prayers could stop her from shivering.

Chapter Eleven

Shelby trotted through the medical complex toward her room, thankful that she was finally heading for a shower. She hadn't gotten a chance to freshen up before the meeting with Jared—a little disgraceful, really, considering she had a serious case of bed head and her clothes were rumpled from sleeping in the truck. Plus, Jake's sex had to be all over her, just had to be, but maybe the folks in the conference room had been too focused to notice their shared mating scent.

Spotting several other medics at the main station desk, she ducked covertly down the side hallway that led to her room. Making quick work of the door's lock, she shoved herself inside, collapsing on the other side of the frame. Good lord, that Jake Tierny was dangerous. Danger Incarnate with a capital *D* and *I*.

Leaning her shoulder against the door, she struggled to find her breath, and it had nothing to do with the long hike down from the main lodge. Nope, it was all about her body and how Jake had teased her out to a very dangerous precipice. Her eyes slid shut as she remembered the feel of his warm mouth between her thighs. A strange, low sound shocked her, and only then did she realize she'd moaned aloud, releasing her pleasure at the memory of his tongue and what it had done to her.

This just ain't gonna do, she thought, crossing the room and dropping her bag on the bottom bunk. The other female medic who shared her quarters had recently been transferred to another facility, so Shelby had all the alone time she wanted. She could be quiet and sort through her thoughts without interruption.

She sank onto the mattress and buried her head in both hands. *What have I gotten myself into?* she wondered, thinking about Jake's physical needs, his loneliness . . . and his very alien nature. She'd followed him to Texas because Jared had asked it; more than that, she'd yearned to go because she hadn't been able to shake Jake from her mind. So what was the big deal, now that they'd gotten together—and were clearly going to keep on getting together if he had his way about things?

It was Texas, a quiet voice prompted. *All because you went back.*

And didn't she know it? Going down south had unearthed a mountain of memories and pain. That, coupled with, well, *coupling* with Jake, had pretty much sealed the deal. The trip had launched her into an emotional tailspin the likes of which she hadn't felt in years, not since the fire had taken the lives of so many of her friends . . . and of her lover. Nate. *Gods, Nate.*

Barely lifting her head, her gaze fell on a small dark suede box on the desk across the room. *Oh, no you don't, girl. Don't you dare.*

The box was as dangerous as the sex with Jake had been. *Or had it been just sex?* another quiet voice whispered. Wasn't it more like lovemaking, what they'd shared both times he'd been deep inside of her? As rough as it had been, it had still been filled with such passion and need and intensity, surely it wasn't just sex.

She gave her head a clearing shake. It was all because she'd gone back to Texas; that was it, really. It definitely didn't have a thing to do with the sad-eyed, gentle Antousian who had already begun to steal her heart. Not a thing at all.

With a shudder, she crossed the room and reached for the suede box . . . and unlocked that powder keg for the first time in at least two years.

Jake strode through the connecting corridors that led down to Shelby's quarters in the med area. He'd located her room on the confidential map, thankful for his very high clearance level. At least one thing could be said for the way everyone on base treated him like he was still Scott Dillon: He had the highest level of authority, whether he cared to accept it or not. Good thing, because as he'd told Shelby, they weren't finished, not by a long shot. Now that he'd done his duty by meeting with Chris, he couldn't get to her fast enough.

"I heard you were back," a warm, familiar voice called out, startling him from behind. He might not have seen her for months, but he'd recognize Anna Draeus's voice anywhere, and he drew to a dead stop.

Slowly he pivoted to face her—and got his first real shock of the day, which was truly saying something. Anna was wearing a thin black turtleneck with neat black pants, dressed totally as a civilian. More than that, her belly protruded like she was three or maybe even four months pregnant. She'd been unmated when last he'd seen her during their battle over in Montana.

He pointed with his forefinger, wordless. She just laughed, touching a light hand to her stomach. "Yeah, go figure, huh?" Then she lifted both arms, pulling him into a strong embrace. "You made it back," she said, beaming up at him.

They had always been close, and years ago he'd been into her—had even tried kissing her on a mission one night. But the events of a few months back, the way she'd ministered to his wounded soul, had left him with a true soft spot for the soldier—enough so that he quickly grew uncomfortable with her closeness and ducked out of her grasp.

"Man, I missed you. Glad you're home."

"So who's the lucky soldier?" He couldn't help glancing down at her belly again. "You are *really* pregnant, friend."

She tugged on her ponytail, blushing slightly. "You didn't hear? Nothing at all?"

He felt like a big, dumb lug but just shook his head. "Shelby didn't tell me a thing."

"I'm with Nevin Daniels."

She might as well have popped him upside the jaw. "What?"

"Lieutenant Daniels—"

"Yeah, Anna," he cut her off, "I know who he is. Holy shit! He's . . ." *In his maturity*, he wanted to say, remembering the security adviser's full head of silver hair, the first outer sign that a Refarian male could no longer sire children.

She shook her head, beaming. "We're expecting twins."

And now his eyes truly bugged right out of his head—to the point that he just wasn't sure he could think of a damned thing to say.

Her face assumed a giddy blush. "A very, very long story, trust me."

"But the guy's such a tight-ass."

She giggled, touching her face shyly. "You just don't know him like I do." From the dreamy, half-sexed expression on Anna's face, Jake got a very clear picture that the Daniels he knew in the *meeting room* was obviously a lot less inhibited in the *bedroom*. Still, he could only picture the lieutenant's silver head of matured hair.

"But he's infertile." What he remembered from only a few months earlier just wasn't adding up at all. "Totally mature."

"Uh, I don't think so, Tierny. He's going to be a daddy pretty soon. I'm only one month in, and look." She patted her belly. "The doctor said it happens sometimes, a male in his maturity just kind of . . . gets really, really fertile again."

"Really fertile," he repeated, and this time he was the one blushing like crazy.

"Your kind doesn't go through that, do they?" she asked, tilting her face up toward him with genuine curiosity. "I mean, Antousians don't . . ."

He swallowed, shaking his head. "Nope. Works like it does for the humans with me and my kind. I'll still be fertile when I'm an old dude."

Then, all of a sudden, the *look* came into her eyes. That embarrassed, almost pitying gaze that told him she was remembering how he'd lost Hope and baby Leisa. He backed a step away from her, his chest tightening painfully. "Look, we'll catch up," he blurted in a strangled voice. "Soon. I want to hear how you and the, uh, babies are doing. And Nevin." He jogged backward a few more paces. "I'll come find you later."

"Jake, don't leave yet." Her voice was soft as she extended her hand.

"Gotta go. Have something to handle," he replied gruffly, then turned and walked as fast as he could toward Shelby's quarters.

Shelby stared at the holographic chip in her palm. It had been years since she'd dared to activate it and once more view the digital images it contained. She closed her fist about the disk, then dug deeper into the box, finding a silver chain coiled against some papers at the bottom.

Slowly she withdrew the necklace, allowing it to dangle from her fingertips. A gleaming silver stone caught the light, a primexia, one of the most prized jewels back home. It was a mating stone, given for only one purpose ever—as a promise of deep bonding between two Refarians.

Her vision blurred, and time folded back. Beginning to sway, she felt the gauzy window of the last five years open wide. Nate stood behind her, brushing the hair away from her neck. "Keep your eyes closed," he whispered against her ear. "It's a surprise."

She giggled, feeling breathless. He'd told her that something big would happen tonight; she'd thought he might sneak her off base to the local movie theater. But then the dull thud of something heavy came to rest just above her breasts, the tinkling of a chain folding about her neck.

"What is it?" she asked, reaching for it, but Nate caught her hand.

"Not yet," he told her in that gruff, gravelly voice of his. He made an adjustment to the necklace, heavy and cool as it joggled against her breastbone, his hands touching her skin ever so slightly as he did so. At last he pressed his lips to her bare neck. "Now you can look, *nanlia*." *Nanlia.* Refarian for "dear one." "Now you can look."

With a downward glance, she gasped. A bonding stone. The promise of a mating. In a tangle of hugs and tears and kisses, they pledged their love for each other that day, confessed their desire to bond—to mate totally, as signified by a formal ceremony. They would be one, he promised, for all eternity.

She rocked, watching the scene . . . no, not watching it. *Living it.* She had transported through time, had walked her way back into the painful memories, allowing herself to experience that last perfect day with Nate. How desperately she loved him, and how willing she was to give herself to him, totally and freely. Ah, yes, the emotion jetting through her veins was nothing less than true love.

Their friends clapped them both on the back, and Brian, their card-shark buddy, even made a big joke of kissing Nate right on the mouth and pouring champagne over his head. It had been the happiest of days. The very, very happiest of all her days, more joy than she'd experienced in years . . .

Something distracted her, though, and this part wasn't right. There hadn't been a loud banging noise that day—that had come later, as the grenades started going off and the Antousians began storming the hangar. She scowled, rocking harder, walking the thread of time to its farthest possible extension, a shaky boardwalk out over the depths of space.

"Bond with me?" Nate whispered against her cheek. "Wear my promise chain until we are sealed?"

More banging, harsh and urgent.

But she wasn't ready to leave the time walk, still needed to nurse on the bittersweet memories.

"What the hell are you doing?" A deep, masculine voice demanded, wiping past her visions.

She gave her head a shake, lying back on the floor, focused on Nate's soft brown eyes, memorizing the way the champagne poured down his throat.

"Shelby! What's wrong?"

With a spasmodic jerk, she blinked upward, blinded by the lights of the hangar. Gods, they were so unbelievably bright, and something had tackled her. She swatted at it, but it was too dang heavy, just pushing her down, down into the floor.

"Shelby!"

The seizures kept on ripping through Shelby's slight body, even though Jake had her pinned down by both arms. "Shelby!"

More jerking, her thin arms whipping at her sides. Her lovely blue eyes were rolled back into her head, her legs and torso gyrating like mad. He glanced at the door, his heart hammering as he calculated how long it would take to run for one of the other medics.

This felt too familiar, too much like all the times he'd been with Hope during a diabetic seizure. Shelby was in such desperate shape, and he had nothing—not even a prayer—to offer her. She just kept on flailing and groaning, writhing beneath his big body. He tried to pin her down harder, did anything he could to calm her spasms. Hope's diabetic seizures had never been so traumatic; this was a whole new territory for him.

In All's name, not again, he half prayed, memories of losing Hope tearing at his consciousness. *No time for regrets, not now.* Bending his face low, he got right up against her, nose to nose. "Shelby, listen to me. It's Jake. Jakob!"

No answer.

"Shelby!" he tried, louder this time. "It's me, Jake. . . ." He paused, and then said, "It's *Scott*! I'm here with you—gods, I'm right here." Her body shook, then stilled, as if his voice—his very self—had settled her. She was covered in sweat, totally soaked. "It's Scott," he whispered again, drawing her damp head into his lap. "I'm right here, sweetheart," he said quietly. "It's me . . . Scott."

Just to call himself by that name was enough to rend his very soul, and the only reason he kept repeating the godsforsaken thing was because, more than Jake's name, it had seemed to soothe her. She twisted against him, rolling her head to the side within the cradle of his crossed legs, moaning. He kept petting her hair, his heart rate slowly settling down; with one last glance at the door, he wondered whether he should go for help, but the idea of leaving her—hell, any woman in bad shape—just didn't sit well with his memories.

He started to pick her up and carry her, but she released another small moan and kept murmuring a word he couldn't make out. Leaning over her, he bent his head low, just stroking her hair in a soothing gesture. "What is it, Shell? I'm right here. . . . Tell me."

"Time." She groaned, pulling her knees up tight against her body, cradling herself like a baby. "Oh, *time*."

Jake jolted, sitting upright, his hand frozen against the top of her head. She'd been time walking—that had to be it. A flash of guilt hit him. *This* was what he'd tried to bribe her into doing for him? When the cost was clearly such spearing pain? What a bastard he was. If he'd known, he never would have asked, not when this was the price she had to pay. Maybe she'd even been trying to time walk for *him*, he thought darkly, but that was when he noticed the bonding stone clasped loosely within her right hand.

It dangled, the chain dripping from her flaccid fingers like a dead weight.

Very delicately he worked the necklace out of her grip, lifting it to eye level. The primexia gleamed beautifully beneath the dim lights of her room, definitely not a cheap bonding stone by any stretch of the imagination. *Nate*, he wanted to curse, that stupid bastard of an Antousian spy who'd taken her heart and broken it. An unexpected rush of protectiveness shot out of his core—something so male and ancient, it had to be truly murderous in its intent. With a final glance at the dangling bonding stone, he slipped it back into the suede box; at least she wouldn't have to see it again that way.

She stirred slightly, her head shifting in his lap as she rolled onto her side, and that's when he saw the other piece of evidence, the telltale sign that she'd been walking back into her broken past. Gleaming within her other palm was a small holographic disk. He frowned, stroking her hair slowly, wondering what harsh memories might be frozen within the disk. A check of the chip's monitor revealed that it hadn't been engaged in more than two years. So that wasn't what had sent her into the seizures—those had definitely been the result of her time walking.

Stroking her damp hair, he studied the chip within his hand. It had to be his fault that she was in such raw pain, all because he was a *vlksai*, just like Nate. There could be no other explanation for her digging into the past like this, not with what had just transpired between them up in the meeting room. Clearly just being with him unlocked too many painful memories, all because he was Antousian.

Rotating the silvered chip, he deliberated.

She was out cold; he could look—couldn't he? Just take a small, guilty glance into her past. Cursing himself as no better than Nate, knowing that some part of his soul was cold and wrong, he flipped the small disk into the air and engaged its images.

The 3-D replay opened wide within her room, right

in the center. Whoever had recorded the fucking thing had done a great job of capturing Shelby's joy that day. She kept fingering the stone about her neck, her face flushed with emotion. Friends gathered around her, kissing her, and then someone dumped the last of a champagne bottle over her long, flowing hair. Gods, the thick golden waves had been down practically to her waist, and she'd been wearing them loose that day.

Weird for a soldier, he thought, placing a protective hand against her forehead. She didn't stir at all, and he felt totally guilty. In fact, he almost snapped the holographic disk shut, but something compelled him onward.

Something? *Someone.* It had to be Nate. The Antousian, the man she loved, was definitely somewhere on this strip of memories. He growled at the thought, the hoarse, possessive sound escaping from deep within his chest before he could stop it.

The scene continued; then a tall, dark-haired man, his hair soaked from champagne, stepped into the action. With a dramatic sweep of his arm, he dipped Shelby into a swooning dive of a kiss, dropping her halfway to the floor. Her hands slid about his neck, holding him close, and Jake nearly exploded right out of his skin with jealousy.

And hatred. And bitterness. How could that fucking *vlksai* have treated her so callously? He'd been using her, and that should have been enough right there. Why the pathetic ruse, the heartbreaking effort to pretend he loved her?

Abruptly the images ended, retracting back inside the disk until the only sound within the room was Shelby's uneven, startled breathing. Jake glanced down at her and realized that he had her in a thoroughly protective posture, one arm thrust across her torso, the other cradling her head. With a gentle gesture, he rubbed his thumb back and forth across her cheek.

"It's going to be okay, Shell." She suddenly seemed

as fragile as a baby bird, its frail heart thrumming nervously. He stroked his fingertips down to her chest and began massaging his thumb over her pounding heart, willing it to slow its tempo.

"I won't let you get hurt again," he promised softly. He'd seen enough of good women dying in this war. The love of his life had died right on his watch, and although Shelby's life wasn't in danger, her heart most definitely was. Hell, he had the power to back off right now and prevent the possibility of causing her any more pain.

Right then and there, a vow bubbled up from deep inside of himself, uttered before he could hold it back. "I will protect you, sweetheart. I promise."

And at that same moment he knew one thing for certain; he could *never* stay away from her. So he would protect her—if need be, from himself.

Chapter Twelve

It was nightfall. Shelby stirred on the floor, disoriented at first, surprised by the darkness of her room.

Oh, crap. She'd skipped time again.

She drew her knees tight against her chest, pressing her forehead against them with a banging thud. *Way to go, girl. Like you really needed that lovely stroll down memory flippin' lane.*

It had been months since she'd "gone under." Then again, she hadn't exactly time walked in months, either. And Jake wondered why the commander didn't expect her to operate in her gift? Well, this latest seizure would be the answer to that one with a big fat *bingo.* The blackout stunts kept her on a medical exemption.

She stretched her arms overhead, groaning at how sore her muscles felt. Yep, she'd obviously done a great job of seizing all over the place.

"I was afraid to move you," came Jake's voice from out of the darkness. "I'm sorry you had to rest on the floor."

The deep, raspy sound of it, totally unexpected, startled her. She blinked her eyes and saw him propped up on her bed, arms behind his head. He wore a haggard expression, and a late-day growth of beard covered his jaw as if he'd been watching over her for many hours.

She rubbed her eyes. "When did I black out?"

"A couple of hours ago. I stuck around to make sure that you were all right."

"You saw . . . it? What happens to me?"

"Yeah."

She groaned, feeling her face burn shamefully at the thought of Jake watching as her arms and limbs jerked . . . her whole body rebelling in spasms. "Sorry."

"Nothing to apologize for. I have some experience with seizures, you know. Hope was . . . is . . . well, *was* a diabetic." He had to keep reminding himself that in this timeline, her diabetes had been totally cured by genetic therapy.

He didn't say anything else, and she was thankful. She cringed at the thought of what he'd witnessed. There was a rustling on the bed as he shifted, then the full, quiet sound of him sighing. She worked her way into a kneeling position, feeling in the semi-darkness for her bonding stone and the disk, but there was only smooth wood beneath her fingertips.

"I put it all away on your desk."

"That isn't none of your business, that stuff," she snapped, wondering what in the world had possessed him to pull a little cleanup job while she was out cold.

He swung his legs off the side of the bed. "It looked to me like you were . . . upset. So I figured I'd put it away before you woke up. So you wouldn't, you know, have to deal."

"Why, Jakob Tierny! You're the protective sort. Who'd have guessed it?" Her anger totally dissolved at the image of Jake bustling around her room, trying to take care of her. Something warm burned inside her chest, too, at the very thought of his kindness.

"A regular godsdamned knight in shining armor, that's me." He laughed, the sound causing a warm flood of desire to shoot through her whole body. "You got my number, baby."

Baby. It was the way he said it, how his voice got huskier, throatier. *Hotter*.

Abruptly, he stood. "You're okay now, right?"

She bobbed her head, struggling to tamp down the instantaneous lust that he'd just unlocked within her. "Fine and dandy."

He strode slowly across the room, his gait slightly uneven as if maybe his leg was bothering him. As he moved past her, he brushed his hand gently atop her head, letting his fingers trail tenderly over her hair.

"Are you limping?" she asked, watching him move haltingly toward the door.

He stopped, turned back to her. "Old war injury, that's all."

"What happened to you?"

He thrust a hand through his hair, his whole body trembling visibly at her question. "Bad shit, Shell. Let's not talk about it."

She struggled onto her own feet. "If your knee is bothering you, let's go over to the med center. I can wrap it, ice it—"

"It's *fine.*"

O-kay, so she'd stepped into something here, obviously, but then he chuckled quietly, his demeanor softening.

"My legs were shot out from under me during a big battle down in Denver a couple of years ago."

This time it was Shelby who trembled. "That's . . . that's what happened to Scott back in December. That's how I met him. Only he was wounded at Warren."

"Yeah, I know." He laughed again, a darker sound. "That's why I figured it was better to keep quiet about it with you. It's spooky even to me, the way my path and Dillon's have crossed . . . and separated. Too bad I was wounded in this body, Jake's body, so I'm stuck with the ongoing pain."

"Was . . . anyone there, to help get you to safety?" Shelby asked him softly, and he followed her line of thought. She could see the flash of pain in his green eyes.

"Hope was already long dead by then," he said, then hesitated, clearing his throat before he continued.

"I was left by my enemies, bleeding out on the back alley where we'd had the street fight. I come from another world entirely, Shell. Everything there is in ruin, and society has slipped into chaos. It all went straight to hell after our own version of events at Warren."

As if reading his thoughts, Shelby whispered, "What happened at Warren in your time?"

He sighed, closing the distance between them, and squatted down right beside her. Without speaking, he reached for a lock of her hair, rubbing it between his fingertips thoughtfully.

"It played out very differently, that's what. Our whole war changed because of what the Antousians did with those missiles. In this time . . . everything's new. Strange to me."

She turned her cheek against his hand, resting it in his warm, rough palm. "So maybe things are gonna go differently for you, too, then," she suggested gently. "Maybe?"

Maybe you can have a future, a good one, where your wife doesn't die and your baby daughter isn't lost to you.

"I'd like to think that."

"I—I wish you weren't going to be part of that warehouse operation," she admitted in a rush. "It scares me."

"Did you time walk that, too?" he asked, dropping his hand. She heard panic edge his words.

"No, not even close," she reassured him. "It's just a really big risk, going into that nest of vipers."

"You know I have to take Tierny down, Shelby. And you know why."

She reached for his big hand, drawing it close against her knee. "But if this time is different, and everything is happening differently, why do you have to go after him? Let us send a team in; don't walk in there with a flipping bull's-eye on your back."

He took a long time to speak, then finally said,

"You care about me. That's what this is about." He sounded . . . pleased. A little excited. Optimistic. As if, despite her ditch-and-run job up in the conference room earlier, they might still have a chance.

Which was totally the truth.

"Of course I worry about you."

"*Care* for me. You care for me—don't you? Even knowing what I am, my twisted genetic map . . . you still have feelings for me."

She swallowed hard, gripping his hand tighter, refusing to meet his gaze. "Yes."

Before she knew what was happening, his mouth was against hers and he was drawing her close up against his hard chest. Gods, his hands were traveling all over her body—down her back, around her waist. She looped her arms about his neck, plunging her tongue deep within the warm cavern of his mouth. He tilted her head back, one palm coming to rest against her cheek, and thrust his tongue deep inside her mouth, swirling it back and forth.

Her breathing became ragged, and she ached for all of him—to be swept within his arms to the bed across the room, and taken soundly beneath him. Breaking the kiss, he pressed his face against hers, dragging in long, slow scents. She dared to do the same, her body quaking with tremors in reaction. He smelled like fresh snow, mountain rain, the scent of him so gorgeous she could have drunk from it for hours.

He pressed his forehead against hers, gripping both of her arms tightly in his. "I better go."

"Why?"

"Because you need your rest." With a slight whoop, he bounded to his feet, his leg suddenly much better. Planting hands on both hips, he began to laugh, a strangely innocent, almost boyish kind of giggle.

"What's so funny?" She quirked an eyebrow, not sure how kissing her had elicited this particular reaction. "It ain't exactly complimentary to laugh at my kissing technique, you know."

He glanced down with a lopsided grin on his face. "I'm laughing because, sweet Shelby Tyler, you just gave me the best damned news I've had in months."

She gave her head a little shake in confusion. "News?"

"That you care about me."

Before she could react or respond, he swooped down, planting another wet kiss right on her lips, and murmured, "So I'll see you tomorrow."

"See you tomorrow," she repeated, too stunned to even argue.

As the door closed behind him, she pressed the back of her hand to her lips, still feeling the taste of him on her mouth. He'd just declared his intention to pursue her, hadn't he? Wasn't that what he meant?

Lord, how could she have ever thought she could stop a warrior like Jake? Not when he'd chosen pursuit. Not a chance in hell, not for her: She'd been a goner to the man ever since that beer brawl down in Texas. No, nix that. She'd been a goner since Scott Dillon had come into her medical area five months earlier.

See you tomorrow. . . .

Which would leave exactly six days until he put himself right in the line of fire with their enemies, the same enemies who had destroyed so many of her friends five years earlier.

Chapter Thirteen

"I don't need a partner complicating things, and I sure as hell don't want a human going in with me." Jake eyeballed his former brother-in-law across the table, unable to believe what the human had just suggested.

For the past three days they'd been going over details, strategizing together, but this suggestion that Chris go in with him was a brand-new one. Besides, he'd already heard the same thing from Shelby—at least on those few occasions when he'd actually had time to swing by the medical complex and see her. He didn't like the idea any better coming from Chris than he did from Shelby, the notion that he needed a partner of some kind on the op.

"You need someone to watch your back," Chris argued, kicking back in his seat. "It's not enough that we'll have the team in place nearby."

"Then we bring along a Refarian, a group of them—no way a human goes in."

Chris coughed awkwardly. "I figured you'd have more respect for my species, seeing as how you were married to Hope for all those years."

Heat rushed into Jake's face, and he had to dig both fists into his thighs to stop the sudden onslaught of memories Chris had just unearthed. Being around Chris was downright hellish; not the man's fault, but still an absolute fact. Too many memories ran between them, the pull of the emotions almost enough to yank Jake under.

"Got no problem with humans," was all he grunted.

"But you're saying that I wouldn't be strong enough to hold my own."

Damn you, Christopher, he wanted to shout, *you're a first-class hard-ass, and don't I know it.* But he kept the past out of it. "A human's got no business stepping into that place willingly," was all he said. "Far too dangerous."

"I'm not just a human, Tierny—I'm a special agent with the FBI. I'm trained to deal with scenarios just like this one."

"No, you're *not* trained for what I'm facing. You don't truly understand what our enemies are capable of, or of what they love to do to your kind."

"And to yours," Chris added softly. "So it's a risk for both of us. Probably more of one for you, considering who you're going to be impersonating. You need some serious backup when you go in."

"You do realize those *vlksai* freaks could easily snatch you? That if they sniff out who you really are, they'd take special pleasure in torturing you, then serving you up on a platter to Raedus . . . or maybe they'd just do the body-jump routine, snuffing you out in one second flat." He shook his head. "Hope would never forgive me if you got killed on my watch. So you don't go in. Period."

Chris's fair face reddened, a flash of hot anger filling his eyes. "I'm the one running this squad."

Jake slammed a fist down on the meeting table, the wood frame jarring loudly. "But it's *our* war, a war you humans are just beginning to figure out," he said, his voice rising. "You may be heading the squad, but we work together, man."

"Exactly. So you don't call the shots, and you sure as *hell* don't tell me I won't go in on my own goddamned assignment!"

Jake threw his hands in the air. "Then it's your death warrant, buddy, not mine. And you won't take me down with you. You insist on this, and I don't go on the op at all."

Harper cocked back in his seat, a crooked grin forming on his lips.

"*What?*" Jake demanded hotly.

"Nothing." Chris laughed. "Just that Hope told me that's what you'd say."

Jake glanced away. "Yeah, your twin knows me pretty damned well. Kind of fucked up, isn't it?"

"She still cares about you." The words were quiet, a sudden point of stillness between them.

Jake pressed his eyes shut. "Don't go there. Please? Just don't . . ."

"She wanted me to tell you that."

Turning away, Jake tried to stop Chris from going on. "Let's talk about the op. We've got too much to plan to talk about the past."

"She wanted to know about Shelby because she thinks that medic has the hots for you." Harper coughed significantly. "And, uh, yeah . . . enough on that one, I guess."

"Harper, you are one stubborn son-of-a-*bitch*! Let it go, man. Let. It. Go."

Chris didn't say another word, and the room fell completely silent—not even the rustling of papers or a cough punctuated the deafening stillness. Jake slowly turned in his seat and discovered that Chris's gray eyes, so like his twin's, were fixed coolly on him.

"Tierny, you got a problem with me?" Chris asked in a quiet voice.

"No problem at all." Jake really did not want to have this conversation; in fact, he desperately hoped to avoid it. He dropped his head, staring at the open file in front of him. "I'm on edge, I guess, ready for Friday night . . . ready to get in the game."

"I'm pretty damn sure that's not it." Harper's voice was tense, angry. His brother-in-law always had been a hothead.

Jake sighed, shoving the papers aside. "So tell me, then. Tell me what you think is wrong with me. Because I know you're going to do it whether I want you to or not." Jake gestured at his chest, like he was urging Harper to take the first punch. "So just go on. Have at me."

It was spooky how easy it was to fall into a sparring match with Chris, how familiar it was dropping into old patterns. The last time he'd seen him had been five years ago, a few days after Hope's death.

Chris eyed him hard. "I think you hated my sorry ass in that future of yours, that's what. And so you still hate me now."

"Chris . . ."

Harper folded both arms across his chest. "I'm right, aren't I? Were we enemies? Or did you just dislike me on principle?"

Jake shoved back from the table, making for the door. "You don't know jack about the world I came from."

Chris bolted to his feet, instantly between Jake and the exit. "Every time you're around me, you act like I've got the goddamned plague," he said in a low voice. "I know that much."

Jake held up his hands. "No problems between us, man. Nothing wrong at all. Totally copacetic."

"Maybe it isn't about the future, then."

"It's not."

"Maybe you just resent that a human's running this squad?" Chris raked his gaze over Jake, his eyes searching for something.

A part of him knows everything. Senses what happened between us, even if he didn't live it . . . "Already told you that joint cooperation was a good idea—I said that in our very first meeting about all of this. Trust me, it took way too long for our species to work together in that other timeline. Interspecies teamwork is our best bet for the future, and you're the man for the job, Harper. I'm not complaining at all."

Chris nodded. "Thank you."

"No problem." Jake made to step around the other man, but Chris blocked him. The human's brown eyebrows lowered intensely, and Jake had a serious feeling he wasn't going to like what came next. "What?" Jake demanded.

"You do realize I interrogate people for a living. That reading body language and tells and all that shit is what I'm trained to do."

"Your point?" Jake's chest began to ache, a gnawing depth of pain from his past choking upward, threatening to steal his breath. *Gods, Chris, leave it alone, man. Just leave it be. . . .*

"You're lying about what happened between us in your world. And you're not even doing a good job of it." Chris released a loud, bitter laugh. "So, Tierny, I'm gonna ask it again—what's your problem with me?"

Jake turned and walked to the far side of the room, bracing his hands on the fireplace mantel. "I don't want to do this right now. I really just don't, so if you're smart, human, you'll back off." Jake's eyes slid shut, and he heard voices from a past he'd done his level best to forget.

"You know, it'd be a whole lot easier to work together if you'd let me know the score."

Jake spun back around. "The score? The gods-damned fucking score? I married your sister. I spent the five happiest years of my life married to her, and she died on my watch. That's the score, Harper. Does it make more sense to you now?"

"I already knew all of that."

"But you don't remember any of it—I do. And I remember how you shut me down after that. We'd been close, you get it? You and me." He waved between them significantly. "You were my brother in every sense of the word, and then—"

"And then?"

"It was my fault. All my fault that she was murdered. And things got ugly after that. Way, way ugly, and I still carry all those memories, all that shit around inside this big, dumb skull of mine."

"All right, all right." Harper planted both hands on

his hips, staring at the floor between them. "You're angry at me for things I did . . . I do . . . in the future."

Jake's fists tightened at his sides as he remembered how Chris had jumped him the day after Hope's death. Chris had been irrational, over the edge—and he'd probably said things he'd always wished he hadn't. "You were the angry one, my friend."

"What did I do?"

"You blamed me for Hope dying. For Leisa never being born. You told me our friendship was over, done, and that you'd never forgive me . . . and then you just left. You never even resigned from your post, never told Jared you were done. You just"—Jake made a waving motion with his hand—"vanished, disappeared . . . and you never came back."

Chris stared at the floor. "That explains it, then."

"Pardon?"

"It explains why you're so pissed off at me all the time. And sounds like I deserve it."

Jake groaned. "Would you just let this one go? Please, could you just leave it alone?"

Chris didn't say anything at first, and when Jake glanced up he discovered that Chris had extended his hand.

"What are we shaking on?" Jake stared down in confusion.

"On a fresh start." Chris kept his hand extended. "I mean, it's kinda strange to apologize for something I didn't exactly do, but I want to work with you, Tierny. And I respect you. If I blamed you for Hope's murder . . ." His voice trailed off; he coughed, then finally continued. "You know how close she and I are," was all he said, then shrugged. "I'm really sorry, man. Sorry for everything that happened to you."

Jake reached slowly for Chris's hand, almost afraid to take it. The whole moment between them was just too messed up to begin with—but this? Chris trying to make up for his future self's grief-induced madness? It was almost more than Jake could handle.

They shook hands briefly, Jake pulling away first. "Thanks, man."

Chris walked toward the table. "Good. Now let's get down to brass tacks on how Friday night's going to unfold."

Jared lengthened his stride, determined to get in a few more laps around the track that circled the top of the hangar deck before his upcoming linkup with the elders. He was dripping with sweat, his body pushed to its limits, but still he had to force himself to go harder. Faster. Longer.

His heart slammed within his chest, but the chilling images from his dreams drove him onward. Something dark was coming, something so dreadful that it was critical for him to be prepared, to have his body honed into a fighting weapon in its own right.

At least Jakob was back, he thought with a quick prayer of relief, which meant one particularly disturbing vision had been averted—although the upcoming undercover operation over in Idaho concerned him greatly. Still, they had no better choice than to use Jakob in the op. Besides, if he could take down the man who'd murdered Hope, it just might help him embrace life here in this time.

Jared had a strong instinct about Shelby, too, and hadn't missed the way she'd kept her eyes on Jake all through the meeting the other day. He'd seen her in his visions of his friend, seen that she was a critical part of what Jake needed to move on.

His comm vibrated against his wrist, and he punched the button, not breaking stride. "Bennett."

It was Lieutenant Daniels. "Sir, there's a relay call for you down here in the hangar. It's Kelsey's father on the line."

Jared came to an abrupt halt, bending over and planting his hands on both knees. Gasping for air, he answered, "Hold . . . the . . . call, Lieutenant. I'll be right down."

He hit the stairs, taking them two at a time, snagging a water bottle from the refreshment table as he trotted past. Gulping it down, he used his T-shirt to mop the sweat from his face. By the time he reached the far side of the hangar, his breathing was at least close to normal. Lieutenant Daniels stood waiting, holding the phone out to him.

"Thanks," he said, pressing the phone to his ear. "Hello, sir."

There was a moment of hesitation on the other end. "This is Jared Bennett?"

"Yes, sir—thanks for calling me. Do you have news about our . . . matter?"

Again, more hesitation, then, "I think I need to come back out there, Jared. You're right . . . the situation with the vice president is very disturbing. I have no idea how to proceed."

Jared nodded, not that his father-in-law could see him. "How long would it take you to get to Warren?"

"I'd have to book the ticket, find the flight . . . might be really late tonight."

"That's too long." Jared thought, flipping through possibilities. "Where is there an open area near you? Some place discreet."

"Roosevelt Island, but what do you have in mind?"

"I'm going to send one of our stealth crafts for you."

"Whoa, Bennett, there are all sorts of no-fly zones and restrictions around D.C."

Jared laughed softly, realizing how very little Kelsey's father knew about their clandestine war. "Sir, trust me on this: We fly *way* under the radar. They'll never know we were there."

There was silence on the other end for a beat, and when his father-in-law did speak, his voice was hoarse and pained. "Bennett, I've known the vice president for a long, long time. *Years.* We've been friends for years. And that friend was not the man who ate lunch with me yesterday."

* * *

Well, Chris had to hand it to Jared Bennett: He was as elusive as all get out, seemingly everywhere on base and nowhere at the exact same time. Chris had spent the past hour chasing him from the lodge to the med sector, back over to the athletic complex, and now finally in the hangar. All in hopes of buttonholing the commander for a quick conference.

At the moment, Bennett was supposedly finishing up with his elders in the council room. This fact had been confirmed by the closed chamber door. So Chris marked time outside in the hallway, going over his action plan. Hope had said that if anyone could get through to Tierny, it would be his lifelong best friend. And since arguing with the Antousian soldier had gotten Chris exactly nowhere, it was time to bring in the big guns. Hope had nearly freaked when he'd shared Jake's intention to go the mission alone, her normally soft voice shrill across the cell phone. He was in total agreement with her, and since Tierny wasn't listening to reason or persuasion, Chris had decided to lay the issue at Jared's royal feet.

Chris propped back against the wall, reading over his latest notes on the upcoming rave. They had three more days until Friday night. His most recent debriefing from headquarters revealed that not only were the Antousians trafficking in human bodies so they could use them as hosts—but apparently some kind of sex slavery ring was going on, as well. This was new and totally disturbing information. Just thinking about what those aliens might be doing to the women they kidnapped left him feeling queasy. It also meant it was more critical than ever that their team be configured in exactly the right way.

The door across the hall burst open. Bennett appeared in its frame, a glowering expression on his face. Whatever his elders had just said, he wasn't a happy camper about it. Jared muttered in Refarian, never even noticing Chris as he stormed down the hall.

"Bennett!" he called, trotting to catch up. "Hold up!"

As if seeing him for the first time, the commander halted. "Harper."

Chris cleared his throat. "Look, we need to chat. I need a little help with your boy Tierny."

The dark expression on Jared's face grew even darker. "What's the problem?"

"He's insisting on going in alone on Friday night, and that's just not gonna cut it."

"I agree." Bennett glanced past him, farther down the hall, seeming very distracted.

Gee, could the guy be any terser? Or maybe he just had bigger interplanetary fish to fry. It was tough to gauge. "Is this not a good time?" Chris finally asked after a drawn-out moment of silence.

Bennett swung his gaze back on him. "We do need to talk, Agent Harper, because I received some very disturbing news just a short time ago." Bennett seemed to think a moment, then said, "Let's go up to my quarters. It'll be more private that way. And Kelsey should be part of this meeting, too."

Chapter Fourteen

Kelsey knew trouble was brewing the minute Jared crossed the threshold of their chambers, Chris Harper in tow. Both men wore identical expressions, a mixture of apprehension and fury. Jared's black eyes were narrowed practically to slits, and Chris's mouth was drawn in harsh lines.

"Kelse, we need to talk," Jared announced, dropping his uniform jacket onto the foot of their bed.

Chris stood in the center of the room, glancing subtly about him. The agent had never entered their chambers, and his curiosity was palpable. "Hello . . . my lady," he greeted her awkwardly, then shoved both hands in his pockets and stared at the floor.

It always surprised her that such a blustering alpha male could occasionally possess such a shy streak.

She smiled. "Like I've told you before, Agent Harper, Kelsey's just fine."

"Chris is, too." He flashed her a grin, the tension in his features easing up just a little. And then just stared at the floor some more.

She could only imagine that the guy found it more than slightly strange that she, a fellow human, was queen of the Refarian people. No wonder he always seemed so totally at a loss around her. She felt the same way sometimes about her newfound role.

"Harper, follow me." Jared indicated the sitting area that adjoined their bedroom, then opened his arms wide to Kelsey. "Come here, sweet love," he murmured against her cheek as he folded her into a strong embrace. Keeping his arm around her, he walked with her into the next room.

"What's going on?" she asked under her breath.

"Heard from your father." He kept his voice low, following Chris toward their study, a small room dominated by a pair of plush leather sofas and a too-small desk.

After waiting for them to be seated, Jared reached for the desk chair, flipped it backwards, and settled his body onto the flimsy frame. His heavy arms draping across the back of it, he focused squarely on Chris. "Tell me about Jake."

Chris began, "To use human vernacular, Commander, he's acting a fool."

For the first time since entering their quarters, Jared cracked a smile. "Oh, now, this I find impossible to believe."

Chris leaned forward, not an easy task on the deep sofa; Kelsey had sunk into the cavernous thing and wasn't going to be wobbling her pregnant way back up without assistance. No wonder Jared had chosen the straight-back chair.

"Seriously, sir—"

Jared cut Chris off. "I was being sarcastic." He laughed, brushing a hand through his long hair. "I've known the man for my whole life, and he's a hothead, a loner, and . . . the best damned soldier I've ever fought beside. So tell me what Jakob's trying to pull this time."

"He's not agreeable to support on Friday night. Doesn't want to risk the lives of anyone else—or his own deep cover. He believes that having others involved will compromise the integrity of the mission, especially concerning his ability to impersonate the human Jake Tierny."

Jared nodded thoughtfully. "He might well be right."

"From one hothead to another, sir," Chris replied, "I think he's going about this all wrong. And he's not going to listen to me; that's been made perfectly clear."

A frisson of fear shot down Kelsey's spine as she imagined Jake completely alone, facing their enemies. "But he will listen to *you*, Jared," she said, following Chris's train of thought.

"My point exactly." Chris nodded vigorously. "This might be our one real chance to figure out exactly what they're doing at these raves. I can't risk fu—*screwing* it up," he said, catching himself with an apologetic glance toward Kelsey, "because of his vendetta."

Kelsey kept her gaze on Jared, curious as to how he'd respond. He nodded thoughtfully. "Well, with what I just heard from Kelsey's father, I agree completely on this one."

"What did you hear?" Chris blurted before Kelsey could even get her own question out.

Jared filled them in on the details of his phone call from Patrick Wells, about his meeting with the vice president, that he was certain that the leader had been "replaced."

"Oh, damn," was all Chris could say, sinking back into the sofa. The words that came to Kelsey's mind were far more *choice* than that.

"So Dad's on his way here? Today?"

"He'll arrive in approximately four hours," Jared answered in a grim tone. "He will give us a full debriefing at that time. But he made one thing patently clear—that the man he met with yesterday is not the one he's known for many years."

"And what about Jake?" she asked, thinking about the danger their friend seemed determined to step into.

"He won't go on that operation, not without a full team. I concur with Harper completely."

Jared punched the comm on his forearm, hailing Jake, whose hoarse voice answered within seconds.

"Jakob, come to my quarters, please," he replied crisply. "Right away."

* * *

"And who else do you propose should go in on this thing?" Jake stormed, pacing the small sitting room in agitation. "Huh, J? Whose lives are you willing to lay on the line?"

The three of them—Kelsey, Jared, Chris—all stared at him with sickeningly patient expressions—and he felt totally jumped, physically and emotionally cramped in the oppressively small room. "Seriously," he barreled ahead, "tell me who you're willing to nominate for this ugly job. Who you're willing to lose."

Jared stood, facing him, and planted a heavy hand on his shoulder. "Certainly not you, Jakob."

"That's my call, not yours."

"I beg to differ, friend," Jared answered with a calm that only served to irritate Jake even more. "You go with support, or you stay back here on base."

"*Meshdki*, J, you're not being fair."

"It's not my job to be fair—it's my job to watch over my people, including you. Especially you."

Jake glared at his king, muttering low Refarian curses. "So who else do you propose? Tell me that."

On the sofa, Chris cleared his throat, unfolding a piece of paper. "Here's the lineup . . . you, obviously. Me—"

Jake growled despite himself. "Already covered that idea, Harper, a few hours ago."

"What's your problem with me going in?" Chris asked angrily.

Jake sighed, planting both hands on his hips. "Because if something happened to you on my watch, Hope would never forgive me."

"Funny, but that's exactly what she said to me about you going in alone."

"Whatever."

Jared interrupted. "You're not getting your way on this one, Jakob. Who else, Agent Harper?"

"Shelby Tyler, because she's already briefed in, and if there are any medical needs, she can cover them."

Jake hit the proverbial roof. "No way in fucking, godsdamned hell is Shelby coming!" he roared.

The entire room fell silent, the other three staring at him in shock. "Really," he added in a much calmer voice. "She's been through enough."

Nobody said a word; understanding glances were exchanged until Kelsey finally broke the tension. "So tell us how you really feel about her, why don't you, Jake?"

Tossing his hands into the air, he stormed out of the room, just needing some space. A moment later and Kelsey was right on top of him.

"Talk to me, Jake." She stared up at him patiently, such kindness and sympathy in her eyes that he felt like a total jerk for just wishing she'd leave him be.

"She has been through enough," he answered slowly. "You get me? That woman lost everything in the Texas fire, and that's enough in my book."

Kelsey reached for his arm. "Kind of like you?"

"Nothing like me."

"Look," Kelsey said, walking to the door that separated the two rooms and closing it. "You can talk to me. What's going on between the two of you?"

Jake dropped onto the end of the bed, raking a hand over his short-cropped hair. "I don't want her at risk like that. Okay?"

"Are you two involved?"

He muttered several curses. "You could say that."

"Then maybe she shouldn't go. I can get them to pull her off the roster if that's what you want. Jared would understand."

Jake lifted his eyes to hers, thinking how very much he loved the woman standing before him, his queen—yet she had none of the same memories that he did. "I'll do whatever you ask of me, Kelsey. *You.* I trust your wisdom."

She nodded, slipping both palms over her pregnant belly protectively. "I know all about Shelby's story, and so does Jared. I know the people she lost, what happened in that fire. My guess is that she'd want in on your fight . . . all the more so because she cares about you."

He waved her off. "She doesn't care about me. That's not it." He was lying right through his teeth, but he was willing to attempt subterfuge if it meant protecting Shelby.

"Oh, really? Then why did she jump at the chance to go fetch you from Texas? With all the heartache that just going back there had to have meant to her? Tell me, Jake, why would she have gone?"

He dropped his head heavily. "I hate the idea of a woman—especially her—being at risk."

"But she knows the Antousians, just like you do. She could offer strong support."

"Because she knows them, she shouldn't have to go through that."

"Maybe. But I have a suggestion."

"Yeah?"

"Let's ask her what she wants to do." Kelsey's innate wisdom shone forth from her eyes. "It should be her choice, not yours, Jake. She's strong, and it should be her call."

"But—"

"No arguing," she said, cutting him off. "As your queen, I have made my decision. Shelby calls her own shots on this one."

Chapter Fifteen

"Damn you, woman," Jake cursed, pulling Shelby up onto his lap. They were in his new quarters, a set of rooms on the fourth floor of the lodge that were more lavish than anyplace he'd lived in years. "You got a death wish or something?"

She snorted, nuzzling up against his neck. Of course she'd jumped all over the chance to go on the op, leaving him little room to argue. "Oh, now, look who's talking."

"I honestly thought you were smarter than this." He pulled away from her, leaning into the back of the sofa so he could stare her right in the eyes.

She gazed up at him through lowered lashes, her voice husky rich. "I am smart, but that doesn't have anything to do with this situation," she murmured without one trace of a southern accent. "It's knowing where I need to be. And that's fighting beside you, Jakob."

He growled, cupping a hand around the nape of her neck, yanking her close for a ferocious kiss. He was pissed, and yet he wanted her so damned badly that his body burned with it. Ached with it. Her sweet little mouth just opened right to him, zero resistance, and her hands plunged through his hair.

Tilting her head, she sidled closer, her legs curling across his knees. With another shimmy of her hips, she brushed her thigh against his lengthening erection.

She broke their kiss with a sighing "yes" at the contact, and his cock pushed up inside his pants.

The traitor—the thing had a mind of its own, and clearly it didn't give a crap about how angry he was supposed to be. He took hold of her shoulders, prying her off of him. "We need to talk, Shell, and not like this."

"I'm listening." But then she reached up and unfastened her hair, shaking it out across her shoulders. It fell loose and long, a golden shimmer of femininity that she *knew* would tangle any of his lame arguments into knots.

He cranked down his eyebrows, scowling at her ferociously, but her only reaction was to laugh right in his face.

"You are so adorable when you get all cranky like that." She smiled, her gaze drifting down and to the left, and he knew she was thinking of someone else. That look on her face was no less than a rifle shot, fired right over the bow between them. The jealousy that answered inside his heart was instantaneous. He wasn't into sharing, and he swore that if she was having some memory of Nate, or any other man for that matter, he'd go flipping ballistic on her.

What is happening to you, man? he wondered dimly. *You need to calm the hell down.* But his self-lecture didn't prevent him from gripping her shoulders tight and getting right in her face. "Who?" he demanded, a low rumbling growl beginning in the back of his throat.

"Who?" She repeated with a mild expression, more confused than anything else. "Who are you talking—"

"You were thinking of someone else just then—another man. Now, tell me who." His growl grew deeper, richer, and certainly more impatient.

Her eyes widened in surprise, and with a terrible blush, he realized that he was behaving . . . Antousian. This kind of mating ownership went far beyond the Refarians' natural ways. Something about Shelby, though, just brought out the beast inside him.

She reared back. "I was thinking about you . . . Scott, I mean. *You.* Not another man."

"He is another man," he bit off, the thunder in his chest growing rabid. But as his growl reached an almost uncontrollable pitch, she planted one small hand against his chest, and he was instantly soothed.

"Hey, now. No need for all that. I'm right here." She rubbed her palm gently across his pecs, back and forth, and then finally centered it right over his heart. The woman truly had the gift of healing within her fingertips. Maybe not as a spiritual ability, but certainly in her very being.

He released a peaceful sigh, tugging her back against his chest. "Sorry."

"Are you kidding? A jealous man is a hot man, at least in my book." She wrapped both arms about him, pressing her face against his neck.

"No excuse; not for . . . that."

"It's in your blood, Jake."

The burn in his face intensified. "You bring it out in me. Not sure what that means, either."

"Means you adore me, baby doll." She gave him a self-satisfied, feminine smile that sent fire jolting through his veins. "And a girl can only love that. And I mean really love it."

"You're a confident little thing." He slid a hand along her thigh, outlining the muscled shape of it. She was still sitting sideways on his lap, and she swung her legs girlishly. No more miniskirt, much to his massive disappointment; she'd been back in uniform for days, the sleek dark pants not nearly as revealing as the postage stamp–sized mini had been.

"But I miss your miniskirt."

"I'll play dress-up for you anytime." She trailed a hand significantly down her chest, lingering dangerously close to her right breast.

Gods in heaven, he had to get a grip. They had business to discuss, and this mutual seduction scene was one unnecessary distraction. "Get off," he said gruffly, taking her by the hips.

"Gladly." She giggled, leaning right up against his chest.

He rolled his eyes. "Off my lap, Shelby. We've got to talk about this warehouse raid."

She slid onto her feet, beginning to prowl his room. She'd been up here at least five times in the past three days, but she wandered the length of it like it was the very first time she'd seen it. He knew better; the woman's mind was flying fast and loose, preparing arguments.

Clearing his throat, he told her forcefully, "I don't want you to go." Then he waited, gauging her reaction as she kept her face utterly unreadable. Her only visible response was the slight lifting of one of her feathery eyebrows.

"I don't want you to go at all," he repeated. "Period. I want you staying here on base."

She made a swooning gesture. "Oh, waiting for my soldier back at home, pining away like the little woman that I am?" She fanned herself, exaggerating her southern accent. "After all, I'm just a frail, delicate, *helpless* woman. I shouldn't go playing soldier with the big ole men."

He stared at the ceiling. "Fuck that. You know that's not what I'm saying."

She spun on him, the fire in her eyes jolting him backward. "Now, hear this, Jakob Tierny." Her voice was like a steel vise as she pointed a trembling finger at him. "I'm in this fight, just like you. Those bastards took my friends, my family—you've never asked me about my family back home. But I had two younger sisters who I lost in this war. I'm alone because of what the *vlksai* have done, and I'll be damned to hell and back if you treat me like I'm fragile."

He could only blink at her wordlessly.

"You don't have nothing more to say? Huh, now, boy?" She planted a hand on her hip, the uniform shirt tugging tight across her breasts, outlining their round, gorgeous shape. "You ain't gonna deliver more lectures about how I don't have the strength to fight, are you? You know, I trained with a K-12 and a whole arsenal of luminators before I ever left Refaria. I'm a good shot, too—not to mention being pretty damned handy with a grenade."

His chest tightened spasmodically. Not again. Not another time. Never again could he hold in his arms the lifeless body of a woman he cared for. He gave his head a clearing shake, hating the way his eyes burned.

"Yeah, so you got nothing else, Tierny." She harrumphed in self-satisfaction.

He stared at the floor, at his boots, at his worn laces—anything to keep from having to lift his gaze and simply look her in the eye. "I don't want to lose you," he admitted quietly. "Okay?" Slowly, he looked up, afraid of what he'd see. More anger, judgment, pity?

But she just cocked her head sideways and studied him, a tender expression on her face—all the fierceness totally gone. Then, after a considering moment, she bit her lip and walked toward him.

She crossed the distance that separated them and, crooking her finger, motioned him onto his feet. He unfolded his large body, rising slowly. The knee was hurting again, so he took an awkward step until he gained his footing. Facing her, he stared down into her eyes; she wasn't as small as Hope, but she wasn't that much bigger, either. Probably five foot three or four at the most, which put him more than a foot taller than she was.

She tilted her head back, craning to meet his gaze. Sliding both her arms about his torso, she dragged him flush against her, still not speaking. His heartbeat quickened; he felt vulnerable, totally skidding out of control. Wished like hell she'd just say something in response to his declaration.

Still, when at last she did speak, nothing could have prepared him for the words that came out of her mouth.

"Jake." She nuzzled closer, holding tight to his back. "Just cause you care about me doesn't mean you'll lose me. Those two ideas don't necessarily go hand in hand." She braced herself, ready for a blustering outburst, but none came. "Look, we've got a few days; why don't we just have fun together?"

"What do you have in mind?" His voice was pure gravel, rough with need and heat.

"I think you know."

"I might have an idea—but tell me what you want."

The big lug was in dire need of some serious seduction, something to just lighten him up and remind him that he was still among the living. She took several steps back, looked him hard in the eye, and said, "Go sit down." She waved him toward the sofa. "Over there."

"You're going to strip for me again?" His blazing eyes narrowed, and the front of his jeans bulged instantaneously with a massive erection. She smiled in pleasure, feeling the place between her own legs grow damp.

"Nope. Something different."

With an uncertain look, he settled back on the sofa, and she approached him, unfastening her shirt so that it fell open. "It's a little . . . game. The question game."

He traced his tongue over his upper lip, the pink tip of it making her want to forget her action plan and just jump him completely. "All right," he said at last, his gaze glued to the front of her chest and the lacy bra she was wearing.

"Question one," she began, reaching for the button of her uniform pants and unfastening it. "If you could have any part of my body . . . what would it be?"

"*Meshdki,* Shell . . ." He muttered more curses, a thin band of perspiration appearing on his forehead.

"Answer the question," she chided playfully, thrusting her chest out so the hardened tips of her nipples were visible through the thin fabric of her bra.

"I have to choose?" He gulped, his Adam's apple bobbing visibly.

"It's the game."

He leaned forward, practically bounding off the sofa. "That sweet spot between your legs."

She giggled, letting her pants slide to the floor. His gaze fastened on the dark blond tufts of hair between her legs and the rest of her folding warmth.

"Question two," she continued, stepping out of her boots and kicking off the pants. "If you could do anything with me—right now—what would it be?"

"Fuck you blind," he blurted without hesitation, his startling green eyes growing brighter.

"So do it."

"First I have my own question for you."

"Fire away, boy."

"Where? I'll take you anywhere you want, any way that you want. Name your pleasure."

Heat rushed to her face, her sense of control slipping right out of her hands. But he was letting her set the stage, letting her have that physical power over him that he knew she craved.

"Your bedroom—from behind."

He stood, glanced at her only briefly, and led the way.

"Take hold of the headboard," he instructed hoarsely, grasping her hips and easing her forward in front of him. She could feel the silky hairs that dusted his inner thighs as his legs cradled her hips, urging her into a prone position beneath him. "And grip it tight because this isn't gonna be gentle and it isn't gonna be sweet."

It was exactly . . . dang, absolutely *everything* that she craved from him. A little roughness, the feeling of being in control yet being lost. She complied, grasping both hands about the wooden sleigh bed, curling her fingers against its polished surface. She was bowed forward in a posture that was halfway between kneeling and lying down, perfectly naked. Astoundingly needy.

One of his large arms looped about her waist and he pushed himself up behind her. "Hold on for me."

She felt his thick length push up against her slick opening, and he almost entered her, but then seemed to stall out, unable to penetrate at the right angle. She smiled, pressing her eyes shut, and reached right between her thighs to guide him in. "I can help," she murmured softly.

This time he slid inside her like a greased-up piston, plunging all the way into her core. She groaned at the impact, but Jake didn't back down. He gave her hips a little jerk, securing her against himself with one large hand. And then he pumped and teased her . . . and pumped some more. Until she could only throw her head back against his chest, moaning over and over. She was so close to coming, already, and it was abundantly clear the guy was only just warming up.

She jerked when, winding a hand between his own legs, he caressed the forbidden place between her buttocks, stroking that erogenous zone while he pumped into her, over and over. Clutching at the headboard, she could barely stifle a rough shout of pleasure. And then, very slowly, he slid a finger up inside of her, and that one little stroke up her ass sent her into waves of orgasm. Her body gripped at his, quaking, releasing.

And in a very dangerous voice, he bent over her and whispered, "We're just getting started, sweet thing."

Jake woke with a dreamy yawn. Opening his eyes, he slowly realized that like some sated wildcat, he had fallen asleep with his head resting on Shelby's back. She was flattened beneath him, her cheek tucked sideways against the pillow, somehow bearing his massive weight. And sleeping through it, he thought with a grin, sliding down her length with a naughty growl. Hell, he knew how to wake her up.

He worked his way low, inching softly so as not to rouse her—at least not yet, and with a deft move, parted her thighs and plunged his face deep inside her warm, damp depth. She tasted like him, all salty and thick with his seed. He lapped at her folds until she jerked awake.

"Jakob!"

"Hmm . . ." He licked some more, swirling his tongue, loving the taste of their mingled sex.

"I thought I was dreaming," she purred, moving beneath him, grinding her hips into the mattress.

"Maybe we both are."

He kissed her between the legs sweetly, then rising up on his haunches gave her a playful slap on the bottom. "Much as I hate it, I've got to get back on duty."

"Buzz kill."

"Pardon?"

"More pop culture, dude. All the more reason—like I said about Texas—you need a guide on Friday night; you're just a teensy bit clueless about human culture."

"I take offense at that." He snorted. "I spent years roaming the bars around this town."

She mumbled something he couldn't make out.

"What was that?"

"I was just saying that you obviously had only one thing on your mind while prowling around those bars—and it wasn't music or television or sports."

He chuckled. "How's this for pop culture, then? Bite me."

"Wow, I'm impressed."

"Thought you'd like that one."

"You're the regular courting type."

"Oh, I wasn't aware you needed wooing. Let me get back down to it, then." He bent low, kissing the base of her spine, slowly licking and nibbling his way along the notches of her backbone. She squirmed in pleasure beneath him, and when he reached her neck, he brushed her hair to the side.

Pressing his lips to her nape, he murmured, "You're on my team for the operation, baby, on one condition. No matter what happens, we both come back, and we do a helluva lot more than just this."

She started to reply, but he bent down, silencing her with a kiss. *Three more days of heaven*, he thought, and promised himself that she wouldn't get hurt on his watch.

Chapter Sixteen

Sitting at the dining room table of the main lodge, Kelsey watched as Jared poured her father a drink. Whiskey, single malt, aged to perfection—Jared's favorite, and as it happened, her dad's, too. The only difference was that Patrick took his on the rocks.

Her father was visibly upset, his naturally freckled face paler than usual, his hands trembling as he took the drink and settled across from her at the table.

"Here," Jared said, sliding the bottle toward him. "Reinforcements as necessary."

Patrick smiled at him, and the expression of camaraderie that flashed in his blue eyes warmed her heart. This was what she'd dreamed of, that the two men would find an affinity for each other despite their differences; she only wished it weren't happening under such threatening circumstances.

"I'll admit that I wouldn't have pegged you for the whiskey type, Bennett," her father laughed, tossing back his drink.

"Hit you again?" Jared asked, and Patrick nodded, offering his glass. Jared filled it and said, "I'm a great fan of Earth's many fine inventions, whiskey at the top of the list, Glenlivet in particular."

Both men laughed softly, but then her father's expression grew grim. "I can't believe what I've wandered into the middle of." He lifted his gaze, looking at Kelsey where she sat across the table poking at a salad that Cook had made her. "How are you feeling, sweetheart? You look a little pale to me."

She dragged her fork through the greens on her plate, giving him a halfhearted smile. "I'm ready to have the baby, Dad. That's all."

"You're not eating. You have to keep your strength up, for you and the baby."

"I have told her as much before," Jared said, and the men exchanged a worried look.

She laughed. "Geez, isn't one conspiracy enough right now? I don't need you two ganging up on me."

The truth was that nothing appealed to her stomach anymore, but the medics all insisted that she had to keep forcing sustenance down. They also said that unlike with human pregnancies, the worst nausea came at the end. *Yeah, no kidding*, she thought, setting her fork aside.

Jared scooted his chair closer to hers, slipping an arm around her shoulders. "We both love you, that's all."

"And it's an alien pregnancy," her father reminded her. As if she could ever forget.

"Daddy. Jared." She glanced from one to the other with a pointed expression. "I am fine. If you can call throwing up two to three times a day fine. Want more details?" When both men demurred, she laughed. "Yeah, didn't think so. So stop talking about me and this pregnancy, and let's get down to the real order of business."

Jared smiled at her admiringly. "Spoken like a true queen."

Patrick blotted at his forehead, then began, "I had lunch with Bob yesterday—Vice President Clarke—as I mentioned on the phone. Overall, everything seemed status quo. He asked about you, Kelsey. Talked about campaign strategies, the like, and he seemed very much like my old friend." He glanced at Jared. "All very normal, and I nearly finished the meal, Bennett, thinking this whole theory of yours was half-cocked and insane."

"So what happened to change your mind?" Jared's black eyes narrowed shrewdly.

Patrick hesitated, raked a hand through his hair. He said nothing but reached for the whiskey bottle again.

"Go on," Jared urged, pouring the drink for her father, whose hands had suddenly started trembling much more violently.

After a very long moment, Patrick lifted his gaze and stared into Jared's eyes significantly. "Kelsey. Bob started asking me about Kelsey . . . in detail. In very significant detail, almost as though he were grilling me."

Kelsey's blood ran cold, and she jolted back in the chair. "Oh, my God," was all she could think to say.

"There's only one reason he'd be asking so many questions about you, sweetheart," her father said, swinging his gaze on her. "And that's because of your enemies' interest in you as the . . . queen." He said the last word as if it pained him, as if it were an uncomfortable weight that he didn't quite know how to shoulder.

"I know, I know," she murmured, feeling her stomach drop like a ten-ton freight elevator. "Oh, man."

"Do they know you've married Jared? I mean, surely they must."

"They know all about me, according to our intel, Dad."

Jared cursed, sliding back from the table with such a violent gesture that he knocked the chair over. "Godsdamnit! Anyone but my family. Anyone but you, Kelsey," he raged, hands balled at his sides. "If they're targeting you in some way . . ." His voice trailed off as he paced the dining area.

"I stuck with your original story about the research trip."

Kelsey wrestled to stay calm, training her full attention on her dad—and trying her best to ignore the fact that Jared was working himself up into a furious lather. "And what was his reaction, Daddy?"

"Questions . . . and more questions." He buried

his head in both hands. "I was so frightened for you, sweetheart. So stunned, I didn't think fast enough. I should have put him on the defensive, but . . ." His voice trailed off for a moment; then he dropped his hands. "You're my baby. Just like you already love Erica, that's how I feel about you. Imagine how much this terrified me. I think it's far more than them wanting to know about where you are. I think they mean you serious harm."

She rose unsteadily to her feet, easing around the table. "It's okay. This is good information, really good intel for us." She stood behind him, squeezing his shoulders. "And don't worry about me. It's like being locked in NORAD up here. The levels of security surpass anything from the human realm. They've never penetrated the base, not once since Jared and his people arrived almost a decade ago."

He glanced over his shoulder at her. "But what do we do with this information? How can the FBI proceed? Who do I even take this to? What must our enemies be planning if they've replaced someone at the very highest level of our government?"

Jared wheeled around, and when Kelsey saw his eyes, they held a vicious expression that she'd never once seen on his face before. She met his black-eyed stare, whispering across their bond. *Calm down, Jared. I'm okay. I'm right here and I'm safe.*

He gave his head a slight shake. "If they mean to harm you, I will strike at them with such vengeance, it will make every battle they've ever fought against us look like a holiday. Like a pleasure banquet." Then he reached for the whiskey bottle, sloshed a long shot into a glass, and tossed it back. "If they make a further attempt to harm all of humanity? These people that I love so dearly?" He slammed the empty glass on the table. "I will chase them across the universe to extract payment. So, Patrick Wells, don't worry about your next move. You've done fine. It's the *vlksai* who need to worry now."

"Jared, what do you have in mind?" she asked, feeling a roiling wave of nausea overtake her. And it wasn't from the baby; it was that look on Jared's face, the wild menace that had come roaring to life in his eyes. She knew that mated Refarians were insanely protective—she'd seen that much repeatedly in her relationship with Jared thus far. But she'd never heard how one might respond if his mate—especially a pregnant mate—were physically threatened. She had a feeling that this rabid display of fury went beyond a husband's love and protection of his wife; it seemed very much a part of Jared's alien nature. His face and hands had even begun to glow slightly, as if, quite against his will, he was on the verge of Changing.

Yeah, her dad would totally know what to make of that. An alien husband was one thing, a glowing ball of fire as her mate was quite another. She had to do something, and fast.

"I am fine, Jared," she told him, crossing the distance that separated them. "Look at me. Right here." She patted her chest, then her belly. "Both of us. We are safe, secure within the compound. They probably just hoped to get a line on where your base is located."

A low rumbling began at the back of Jared's throat, and she grabbed his hand. Her dad wouldn't know what to make of his Refarian growls either, especially since they were deeply tied to the mating instinct. Jared's eyes drifted shut, and he gave a slight nod, cutting off his growl right as it began.

"Let's all stay calm, here," she told him slowly, squeezing his hand. "Meet with our advisers, then let Daddy head back home. The best thing will be if he doesn't tip his hand with the vice president. That means he needs to be back at his desk tomorrow morning."

Jared murmured his agreement, but when he opened his eyes, it was as if he were staring right through her. The murderous look on his face sent a chill right down her spine.

* * *

Chris Harper had just put a pillow over his head, hoping for a few hours of shuteye, when a loud, aggressive knock sounded at his door. Leaping to his feet, he hurried to find out what was going on. As an FBI agent, he was more than used to being woken up at all times of the night, and in this case, it wasn't all that late. He was just bone tired.

He opened the door, and Jared Bennett loomed over him. The alien was a force of nature to begin with, but the glowering expression on his face was enough to have Chris automatically reaching for his sidearm in order to protect himself.

"I'm going in with you. At the warehouse," Jared announced, his lips drawn into a tight line.

Something had obviously tripped the guy's wires in a serious way; it didn't take a genius to realize that the king had absolutely no business going on a dangerous op like the one they had planned. And given how adamantly he'd wanted to protect Jake Tierny, something wasn't adding up right.

"I don't think that's advisable," he said slowly, opening the door. "You're far too visible a target."

"I'm a shape-shifter, Harper. I can take whatever form I want. And I'm going. Oh, trust me, I am there on Friday night."

"Don't you think you should come in? So we can discuss this more privately?"

Jared waved him off. "This whole lodge has top clearance, and I'm not staying to make small talk. I'm on the team, period."

Chris planted his hands on both hips, staring at the floor as he gathered his thoughts. He sure as hell didn't know the right protocol for standing up to the king of Refaria. *Here goes nothing,* he thought, clearing his throat.

"With all due respect, Commander, it's too grave a risk to your safety. You're needed, not just by your own people, but mine as well."

Jared shoved past him, seething with aggression.

Slowly, he pivoted to face Chris once the door to the room was closed.

"So you're going to tell me what's really going on now?" Chris asked, then for the sake of peace making tacked on, "Sir."

"The vice president has definitely been replaced. Confirmed by Kelsey's father."

"We already suspected as much."

"They're asking questions about Kelsey. My wife. All kinds of questions."

"That doesn't mean they're after her—it's you they want. We've always known that."

"The questions . . . are not acceptable to me. This must be stopped. A message must be sent."

"So why are you the one to do it?"

"Do you have any idea what I'm capable of? The battles I've fought, the enemies I've scorched just by my very presence?"

Hope had told him in detail about Jared's D'Aravnian side, although few ever saw it. "I have heard, sir."

Suddenly, the air around them seemed to separate in half, a scorching blast of heat waving around Bennett's body, and then the alien was no longer there. In his place was what could only be described as a compact sun; the waves of energy were so intense that Chris was knocked back against the door, forced to shield his eyes.

"I get it, Commander. I concede the point." He gasped.

The room cooled by quick degrees, but not before the air-conditioning unit clicked into gear. When he dared to drop his forearm away from his eyes, the commander stood before him, his face lined in perspiration.

"I can take them all," Bennett said coldly. "We just have to find them. That part's your job—now, let me do mine come Friday night."

Because he really wondered how Bennett would

handle breaking this news to the queen, he couldn't resist asking. "You'll tell Kelsey? And she'll support you?"

The commander headed for the door. "That, Agent Harper, is most decidedly not your problem. I'll take care of things at home. You just work me into your plans."

Chapter Seventeen

The music inside the warehouse was little more than a droning, hypnotic beat. Unfortunately, Shelby's tastes ran in an entirely different direction. She kept trying to fall into the techno rhythm, searching for some sort of danceable groove while the throbbing, sweaty crowd pushed her along. So far, no dice—and, so far, no Christina, no Fergie, and sure as heck no Tim McGraw.

She'd dressed for the rave like she would any scorching-hot date: wraparound black dress and knee-high black boots with stiletto heels, her hair loose and curly, falling below her shoulders. When Jake had first seen her boarding the craft to fly them here to Idaho, his eyes had nearly bugged right out of his head.

She'd smiled in pleasure, slipping into the seat beside him. He'd rushed to harness himself in, clearly trying to hide something with the large buckle. "You look too damned hot for this mission," he'd complained under his breath. "You're going to jeopardize things for me."

The poor guy—he'd actually sounded like he halfway meant it. In reply, all she'd done was to snuggle closer, giving him a wicked, tempting smile. "Careful with that harness, soldier," she'd teased. "Wouldn't want you to injure yourself. You know, like getting something caught in that buckle?"

"Don't worry, got it covered."

"As it were," she added, eyeing his harness pointedly while he fastened it.

He cursed at her, folding his hands in his lap. Still, she could see the way the buckle of the harness jutted straight up because of the "package" hidden underneath it.

She leaned close, whispering in his ear. "Thought you'd like this dress."

"It's the boots," he barely choked out. "Well, and the dress. Both. Damn you, woman. I knew this idea was shit."

She flashed him a grin. "I have a dagger in my right boot, a mini-luminator in my bra, and am wired totally for sound. I'll be safe."

He muttered something under his breath that sounded a lot like, "Now I really have a stiffy."

Besides, he had plenty of nerve, complaining about how sexy she looked. With his black jeans and cowboy boots and loosely buttoned black shirt, he was smolderingly sexy. In fact, from the moment they'd entered the warehouse, girls all over the joint had been checking him out, and she wasn't sure whether she should feel proud or possessive.

Stepping out of the way of a drunk girl who lurched toward her on the dance floor, she searched the crowd for him. Although they wore concealed earpieces, it was impossible to hear transmissions over the music. Their entire team—Chris, Jake, Jared, and herself—would be meeting in one hour. That didn't give her long to try to scout out her own take on the situation.

Chris had told them that they had two major objectives. First they had to figure out the Antousians' strategy in infiltrating these warehouse parties, from which they had been kidnapping humans and others—in some cases, their intel showed, for the purpose of sex slavery. The task force had speculated that they were drugging their selected targets, but witnesses interviewed by the FBI all claimed that their friends seemed lucid and coherent right up until the time they suddenly vanished. It was as if they were disappearing from the dance floor itself, was how several statements had described the kidnappings.

And second, they needed to find the real Jake Tierny—the human Jake, as Shelby had come to think of him.

Moving along the dance floor, she kept her eyes wide open, all the while doing a damned good imitation of a girl out for a good time. She was just hitting a pretty smooth groove with the techno when the light display suddenly became very erratic. The volume of the music increased sharply, and she felt dizzy and disoriented. Working to block out all the stimulation, she focused on the people around her—what little she could see of them. It seemed to be mostly women bobbing beside her in the sweaty darkness, some of them barely twenty years old.

She thought of her little sisters, how they'd needed someone to protect them during the war, and determined that she'd learn whatever she could tonight on the sex-slavery ring. Reaching about her waist, she loosened her dress slightly, so that the tops of her breasts were more exposed. She also began to move her hips much more suggestively. After all, what better way to get intel than to use herself as a moving target?

Again the music intensified, became confusing; darkness folded in on her, the light show becoming trippier and trippier. Shelby stopped cold on the floor, extending her hands about her in a steadying motion. If she wasn't careful, this sensory overload was going to make her faint. Or worse still, it could trigger an involuntary time-walking episode, leaving her completely vulnerable.

Someone jostled her from behind, nearly knocking her to the floor. "Hey, watch it!" she called out over the noise, turning to see who had just rammed into her.

When she saw his face, it was as if time itself ground to a painful, precarious halt. As if it grew compact, hard and small, then unraveled from the inside out.

She gaped at the person in front of her, wide-eyed, trying to move her mouth, and then her entire world went black.

Kelsey entered the dining hall, her eyes searching the room. She'd spent the past fifteen minutes trying without success to reach Thea on her comm. It was utterly unlike her friend to ignore her—or anyone else for that matter—and a nagging, bottomless feeling had begun in Kelsey's chest. Jared had told her he'd be staying on the battle cruiser during tonight's operation. She hadn't liked his leaving base, not at all, but she'd understood that such risks were part of the cost in leading his people.

But only a few minutes after he'd left her in the hangar, something had begun to nag at her consciousness. It was the way he'd crushed her against himself, not wanting to release her—and it was the look in his black eyes when he'd finally stepped away. It was the same ruthless, dark expression he'd gotten the other night when her father had relayed the information about the vice president—and with the same terrible air of desperation.

"Jared?" she'd called out, but he'd just given her a little wave as Lieutenant Daniels accosted him. The two men had walked together toward the main craft, boarding it as they continued speaking. Her last image had been of Jared ducking through the hatch, his broad shoulders barely clearing the space.

After watching the craft catapult out of the mountainside and seeing the hangar door snap shut, she'd continued sitting off to the side, listening to the hum of machinery and the shouted commands and responses of troops on the deck. A few of the engineers had glanced her way uncomfortably while she sat on the bench, both hands perched on her knees.

Something just didn't feel right about this mission. But it was more than that: For the first time in her relationship with Jared, she had the feeling he'd lied to her. That he was far more deeply involved in this op than he'd let on. So after hailing Thea without a response, she'd come to a very disturbing conclusion: Jared had put himself directly in the line of fire.

Around the dining hall, the loud din of voices fell quieter as she moved down the aisle, navigating the rows of tables. It was Friday night, so that meant those who were off duty got served alcohol and were allowed to let it all hang out for a while. For ten p.m. things seemed fairly tame so far, but it was obvious that her unexpected presence had the gathered soldiers at a loss. Some bowed over their tables and some rose and bowed, even though she tried to wave them off. Suddenly, she found herself standing in the center of the mess hall, surrounded by at least a hundred bowing and genuflecting Refarians.

She lowered her head and muttered under her breath. Even the music had stopped, leaving her stranded like a tall pregnant island amidst a sea of her people.

"Please . . . please, just go on with what you were doing. No bowing. I—I . . . am just looking for Lieutenant Haven. . . ." She had the sense that she'd wandered into some sort of demilitarized zone, a no-man's-land for queen-types, and it was all she could do not to back out of the hall as quietly as she could.

"Kelsey!" Thea trotted across the room, darting between tables.

She wanted to weep with relief at the sight of her friend. Thea reached her, slipping an arm through the crook of her elbow. Under her breath she whispered, "You're not supposed to come in here, my lady."

"Don't 'my lady' me, Thea," Kelsey shot back. "You're in on it."

Thea tugged her by the arm. "Look, they don't know how to respond. Jared never comes here, and it's not a good idea for you to visit this place, either."

"*You're* here."

Thea shook her head. "That's different."

"Because you're Refarian?"

"Because I'm not their queen," she explained, practically dragging her toward the door while more of her people bowed around her.

Kelsey tried to disengage her arm without letting the gathered soldiers see how upset she was. "I'm still pissed at you because I know you're in on it," she told Thea under her breath, "and you're also changing the subject."

"Wait until we get outside."

At last they reached the exit door, and as it closed behind them, Kelsey practically collapsed against it. "Don't worry," she told Thea, "I won't be repeating that maneuver again anytime soon. And if I'd been able to reach you on the comm, it wouldn't have happened at all."

Thea looked at her with a composed expression. "I never heard you."

Kelsey gave her friend a light shove on the shoulder. "Please. Don't you lie to me, too. I know he's going in on that op."

"I'm not sure I know what you mean," Thea answered blandly.

"Oh, really? You don't realize that Jared plans to go into that warehouse with the team? You mean, you never heard that stupid, idiotic, asinine plan pass my husband's lips?"

Thea sighed, staring at the ceiling. "I can't lie to you. Not you, Kelsey. It wasn't fair of him to ask me to do it."

Kelsey felt the world grow unsteady all around her, the lights of the hallway swimming before her eyes. "So I'm right."

"He didn't want to upset you, not with the baby due so soon. He didn't want to worry you."

"But he was willing to put himself right in the line of fire!" she shouted, throwing her hands in the air.

Thea tried to put an arm around her, but Kelsey shook her off, storming ahead of her down the corridor. She didn't even want to hear Jared's lame excuses, and she sure as hell didn't want to argue with

Thea about why she'd allowed him to endanger his life.

"Kelsey, please don't leave. Let me talk you through this." She could hear Thea's booted footsteps echoing behind her.

That was it. Finally, after all the past weeks of tension, the endless churning and discomfort in her belly, and now this knowledge that Jared might get himself killed—the dam inside of her broke. Something simply crumpled right in her center, gave way until she was free-falling, sobbing uncontrollably in the middle of the hallway. Wrapping her arms about her round belly, she hugged herself, hugged Erica. Wished she could hold Jared tight in her arms, and kept on sobbing.

Next thing she knew, Thea was tugging on her arm; Kelsey just dropped her head and wept some more. "Kelsey, please," her friend whispered, but Kelsey gave her head a little shake, feeling a current of nausea overtake her.

Thea placed a hand against her back, whispering something she didn't understand. Refarian words that were useless to her right now, only . . . they soothed her somehow.

"Wh-what are you saying?" She sniffled, turning slowly to look at Thea.

"I'm praying for you. Sending words of comfort from All to you."

Dimly aware of a few soldiers walking past them and keeping a wide berth, Kelsey wiped at the hot tears that kept streaming down her cheeks. "And now our people are going to think I'm crazy. I just . . . I made a fool of myself in front of at least a hundred Refarians in the mess hall, and Jared's in such danger. . . ."

Thea stepped forward, wrapped both her small arms about Kelsey—quite the feat with her large belly—and held her tightly. "Shh, now. The people love you. All our people love you. . . . Shh, you're the Beloved of Refaria."

"But Jared—"

"Is a fantastic soldier. All these years he's been fighting, and he's only been captured one time."

Kelsey winced, stepping out of Thea's embrace. "That's what I'm thinking about—the things that Veckus did to him over in Idaho."

Thea's expression grew grim; she opened her mouth to speak, then closed it, and finally opened it again. "You're married to a military commander, Kelsey," Thea told her slowly. "It's not an easy road for you . . . or him. But you did sign on for this. You knew what his life was like when you mated with him."

Kelsey wiped her eyes angrily. "I don't need a lecture, Thea. In fact, it's the last freaking thing I need right now."

Thea took hold of her shoulder, looking up into her eyes with an intense expression. "It's not a lecture. I'm reminding you of who you are. You are our queen. Your people need your strength right now; so does Jared. And most of all, so does Erica."

"I keep wanting to use our bond. To tell him I love him, in case it's the last time, but . . . I don't want him to hear how upset I am. I don't want to distract him or put him in danger, but this need to have some sort of link with him is almost more than I can stand."

"He will come home, Kelsey. I feel it with my intuition."

"Is your gift ever wrong?" Kelsey asked, rubbing her palm across her stomach, needing to be closer to Erica.

"Not very often."

"Then I'm going to hang on to what you've told me. I'm going to believe he will return."

Shelby blinked groggily, the ceiling above her head spinning like a whirlwind. Only, what ceiling? Last thing she remembered, she'd been on the dance floor, trying to move to that numbing, mesmerizing rhythm. The lights had sped up weirdly; then she'd blacked out—almost as if the light show had triggered one of her seizures.

"Ohhh," she groaned. She was lying on a soft surface, something like a bed or a sofa, although she couldn't manage to look at anything other than the rafters overhead. Even they were more a gyrating kaleidoscope than anything solid. She moaned softly, trying to turn her head to the side.

"So you're coming around," a deep, familiar voice said. Only it was devoid of all warmth, lacking any kind of compassion at all. With a woozy effort, she managed to rotate her head, feeling something heavy clamped against her throat. Her gaze locked on a pair of legs, thighs that were thick like tree trunks.

"Jake?" she murmured, the words gauzy as they passed over her tongue. "Oh, gods, I'm going to be sick."

"Don't do that, not in here." Again, coldness, a hollow sound to his voice.

She winced, and managed to follow the pair of legs upward, realizing dimly that Jake wasn't wearing what he'd had on earlier, the black jeans and shirt. He now sported a biker jacket with metal studs across the front.

"What's going . . ." The words died right on her tongue. The man staring down at her had a smirking, lecherous grin on his face. His eyes lacked any sort of vibrancy or life. They were like hard green marbles, lifeless and cold, a chilling contrast to his swarthy face.

The sick feeling in Shelby's stomach spread to her heart. This couldn't be good. No way, no how. There wasn't any positive spin she could put on the situation, not when confronted with this vile expression on the face that she'd come to know and care for so deeply. She tried to move her hands and feet, but something heavy held them, pinning her down.

Stupidly, she mumbled, "You're not Jake."

"Oh, yeah, I am," he replied, sneering at her. He reached for a lock of her hair, stroking it suggestively, but before she could even pull away from him, he tossed it against her cheek. "But you're right. I'm not the Jake you're looking for. Don't worry; he'll be along soon enough."

Alarmed, she struggled to sit up, but the Jake before her—the human, murdering one, she was now certain—shoved her back onto the mattress. Only then did she glance sideways and realize what the heavy weights on her hands and neck were. She'd been manacled with hard, metallic bands.

"Let me go!"

"That won't be happening, sweetheart. Not anytime soon."

She tried to move her hands, but the grip about her wrists tightened, almost as if in response. *Oh, All, help me.* They'd fastened her in reflexive metal, a psychic alloy that originated on Antousia. If you resisted, it understood and tightened; if you complied, it rewarded you by loosening slightly. She'd heard of soldiers driven insane by captivity within their harsh confines. Hope and Scott had been held with similar restraints back in December and had managed to undo them because of their lovemaking and deep feelings for each other. Here, in the presence of such a threatening man, she had no such promise for liberation.

Jake trailed his fingers down the length of her arm, and dipping inward, he grazed her breast lightly. Shelby jolted, but he continued touching her body.

"Where am I?" she asked, ignoring the maneuver. Intimidation tactic, plain and simple.

"In my world now. You can kiss your old life good-bye."

She blinked up at him. "What do you mean?"

"I have plans for you, girl. Very lucrative plans. Well, lucrative for me, of course. For you, I'm afraid they won't be so good." Jake stroked a hand along her cheek. "Or, to be more specific, I have plans for your body."

And with that, Shelby knew that she'd stumbled right into the heart of the sex-slavery ring.

"Where is *my* Jake?" she demanded. "You tell me right now!"

As she tried to move her legs, the bands around her ankles tightened; he had her pinned flat on her back. With a lift of her chin, she glanced down her body and finally understood exactly what this Jake had done to her: She was splayed out on a padded table, hands and feet bound against the surface. It was clear he made a regular business of this routine, too, because the fastenings were tarnished and grimy. The black table had worn places in its leather, a rip running beside her thigh.

"I'm sure you know how these bands work," he told her softly. "The harder you fight, the worse it'll be for you."

He put his back to her then, walking across the room, and Shelby worked to focus her blurry vision and see what he was doing. The room was mostly dark, and she became conscious of a thrumming beat, heavy bass notes pounding above them. Obviously, she was still somewhere inside the warehouse, and that meant she had a prayer of survival. No, she was *under* the warehouse, she corrected herself, feeling a chill and deciding she'd just concentrate on the survival part.

Jake fiddled with something on the far wall, a clanking noise sounding as if two chains were dragging together. After a long moment, he pivoted slowly back toward her. "How many different ways do you take it?" he asked, approaching her with something in his hand. "The more the better, as far as my money goes." He looked her up and down with those empty eyes. "But I figure you can be made to do whatever needs doing. And the first thing is to tell me your name."

As he stopped beside her, she strained her head upward and spat, missing him by a *ketro*. He just laughed right in her face, rubbing a sinister, dark object in his hands that she couldn't get a good look at.

"Here," he told her coolly, "let's get down to business." He fastened whatever it was against her neckband; then at once the manacles around her ankles and hands sprang free. With a deft movement, she rolled to the side, throwing a kick at Jake's solar plexus as she did. She might as well have tried to drop-kick a mountain; her whole body was jerked back with such force that at first she swore he'd broken her neck.

Feeling with her hands, gasping for air, she realized what he'd attached to her collar: a thick, velvet leash clamped to the circular band.

And now he had the controlling end grasped right in both of his beefy hands.

Chapter Eighteen

The first thing Jake thought, as soon as they grabbed him, was that he and the others had come into this place completely unprepared. As battle hardened as his team was, as many times as they'd gone up against these same enemies, they damned sure should have known better. But it had all happened so quickly, he tried to tell himself; still, that was no excuse. All the planning and preparation they'd done amounted to *meshdki* now that they were in the thick of things.

He and Jared had been walking along, trying to blend into the crowd while they searched for Shelby, when for the first time he noticed a barricaded back stairwell shrouded in darkness. He turned to look back at Jared, who just then was being approached by a tall, curvy brunette. Only this wasn't the Jared that the *vlksai* would know, at least by sight, because for this mission he'd adopted the form of a rugged blond ski bum. *I'll leave him to deal with that situation,* Jake thought to himself as the woman leaned toward Jared's ear, shouting to be heard over the loud music.

Jake slipped across the dance floor to the back stairwell that had caught his eye. The steps led upward to a balcony where partygoers stood surveying the scene below, but what interested him more was the flight that led downward, a dark, cavernous space filtered with shadowed light.

After climbing over the barrier, he crept carefully down the steps and through a door that opened onto a hallway made of jagged stones. Their surface was illuminated by a dim light that seemed to be coming from farther along, around another corner. He inched forward, the noise from the dance floor pounding above and behind him, but when he stopped to peer down that next hallway, his breath caught in his lungs.

It wasn't just the fact that the man ten *ketro*s away looked just like him, only younger—or that he'd finally found the prey he'd been hunting for five years now—it was the dungeonlike room he was coming out of. The walls were bordello red, and an array of barbed whips and chains dangled from above like some grotesque type of curtain.

With a sick, helpless feeling, Jake realized that he hadn't seen Shelby in more than thirty minutes.

It was all he could do not to lunge at the human and choke the very life from his lungs—for a second time—but he forced himself to remain hidden, knowing that Shelby's life depended on it.

Down the hall, the human looked first one way, then the other, before entering another room. Jake stole along the passageway to the dungeon and gently pushed the door open. Past the torture implements hanging from the ceiling, he could see a large padded table on which a woman struggled, the shiny blond of her hair painfully familiar.

Catching sight of him, Shelby struggled against her restraints, a mixture of relief and despair in her vulnerable eyes. "Watch out!" she whispered hoarsely, just loud enough to be heard over the throbbing bass notes from above. "He'll be back any second."

"I know," Jake answered, stepping toward her. "I just wanted to make sure you're okay—now I'm gonna go get help."

"Jakob," she told him with a faint moan, "be careful. Please. Look after yourself."

"I'm going to look after you, Shell. I'm getting you out of this hellhole."

When he turned around, all his plans faded to nothing as he found himself staring at half a dozen burly guys in security T-shirts. Not human, not by a long shot, even though they occupied that form. The Antousian scent wafting off the gathered men was downright sickening. *Well, well, well,* he thought. *So the stakes just got a hell of a lot higher.* His finger twitching against his hip, he felt the hard outline of his luminator.

"So," the tallest one of the group said as he stepped forward, chest thrust out for maximum intimidation, "mind telling us how you got in here, Mr. . . . ?"

Jake tried to force a laugh. "Hey, it's me—Tierny."

"Oh, yeah . . . Jake," the tall one replied, looking around at his men with a sneer—clearly he was their leader. "Funny how you not only managed to change clothes, but you even aged at least five or ten years since we saw you a few minutes ago." Now he stared at Jake with a menacing expression. "But that's not the main reason we know you're lying."

Jake said nothing. The *vlksai* stepped in close about him.

"You don't want to know how?" the leader asked. "Well, I'm gonna tell you anyway. It's because the stench"—to emphasize that word, one of the Antousians landed a punch against Jake's stomach—"on you isn't"—and now another one, who'd somehow managed to get behind him, hit him over the head with a hard object—"strong enough."

It took four of them to pin him down in the hallway, but eventually they did. The leader stood by, looking almost amused, as Jake struggled with them. "Come on, now; don't fight it," he said in a soothing voice. "Ease up, man. Just let yourself go."

"Okay," Jake responded, gasping for air. But a second later, he shoved his elbow into the ribs of the nearest one, dropped low, and punched another in the gut. He was just about to turn his attention to the rest of the *vlksai* when several of them jumped on him at once and grappled him face-first to the floor. Jake cried out, a muffled sound against the slick concrete beneath him, and found himself pinned by something heavy. Must have been one of the freaks who'd jumped him, he thought.

"What the fuck?" he tried to protest, but with another jerking movement, they had him on his side.

Someone shoved his shirtsleeve up his arm, and from the side of his eye he caught the metallic glint of a hypodermic. *Shit, they're gonna inject me,* but he hardly had time to process the thought before a sharp prickle of pain shot down his forearm and his mind suddenly grew numb and hazy.

"What in hell," he tried, but the words felt gauzy—sounded gauzy. A rending pain shot through the whole of his body, accompanied by severe muscle spasms up and down his backbone.

"No!" He slapped both palms against the floor, arching in protest. "In All's name . . . no!"

But there would be no stopping it. A deeply primitive sensation rang through his core as bone and sinew stretched, as skin yielded to hide. His clothing, suddenly far too small, pulled and tore to shreds. Ropes of muscle tugged against enlarged bones, his jaw lengthened, and all the while he screamed. Screamed and screamed, making his agony known. Not just because of the physical onslaught, the horrific transformation—but out of sheer terror at what they were forcing him to become. Screaming and screaming, the pain almost too much, at last he fell still against the warehouse floor, monstrously big and large eyed.

He lay naked, surrounded by his own kind, who cackled and mocked him. "So you're a human, are you?" one of them taunted with a kick at his side. "We can smell our own kind from a mile away. There's no use impersonating what you most clearly are not."

"I have nothing in common with you. The only thing that we share," he gasped, struggling to get the words out, "is DNA. That's it."

"Welcome to our world, brother," another one

chanted from the veiled darkness. "Welcome. Welcome."

His mind was fogged over, his body at war with itself as he struggled to his knees, tatters of his clothing falling to the floor around his utterly naked body. "Why?' he tried asking, horrified by the garbled, mangled sound of the human words passing over his Antousian vocal cords. Vaguely he wondered if Shelby could hear him from the room where she lay captive, and he shuddered at the thought. "Why did . . . you . . . do this?"

"Why?" another faceless enemy taunted from above him. "Pretty simple, Antousian brother. Because you can't leave this warehouse if you can't show your face." Jake managed to rise and turn sideways enough to see the gathered men through first one eye, then the other.

He shook his head, trying to clear it. "What do you . . . mean?" They'd injected him with a form inhibitor, quite obviously. A drug that forced him into his most base and natural body. But how long would the effects of the drug last?

As though reading his mind, the leader said, "You won't be able to change back." For emphasis, he kicked Jake's ribs, driving him face-first to the floor once again. "You can't so much as take one step into the human world without being seen for what you are—what you clearly refuse to believe you are—an Antousian, just like us. You have 'alien' stamped all over your body and your face."

"You don't know anything about me," Jake said with a groan.

The leader dropped to his haunches beside him, his menacing black eyes like pinpricks of malevolence. "We know you're aligned with our enemies. That's enough right now."

"Can't . . . keep me this way." Jake grasped at the floor, sucking burning breaths into his four lungs. "Not . . . possible."

"We can hold you in this form for the rest of your life if we see fit," the leader taunted. "You're ours now, *brother.*"

Though Jake didn't know it, Jared had disengaged himself from the lovely brunette, found his way down the stairs, and located the dungeon. Not that any of that did much good, Jared thought to himself as he watched in horror while his friend, now held captive in his Antousian form, struggled against a bunch of *vlksai* gathered around him.

There wasn't time to go for reinforcements; he had to act now—and fast. Crouching low against the turn in the hallway where he'd been concealing himself, he reached inward and allowed his internal energy to overtake him with an aggressive sweep. He became the powerful, surging being that he always held at arm's length, and in an instant swirled into a blaze of murderous energy.

They would not take his friend and comrade; nor would they capture Shelby Tyler, not if he had anything to say about the matter. Shooting down the hallway, he spun and gyrated, taking out at least two of the Antousians who stood in his way. *Can . . . eliminate . . . them.*

But as a sickening crack resounded against his glowing core, he knew these Antousians had arrived prepared. From seemingly nowhere, they struck him, again and again. Their power tethers spun through the air, pursuing him like horrible, flaming blue lassos. With a roar, he flung his energized self down the corridor, ricocheting off the far wall, and in the process grazed two Antousian soldiers, both of whom collapsed to the floor in agony.

He thought of Kelsey and Erica, remembered all the reasons he had to escape—his enemies couldn't capture him, not this time. And he thought of his lifelong best friend, collapsed against the concrete floor, a man who had already lived enough torment to last too many lifetimes.

Still the blue lassoing lights kept circling him, slapping off of his surging power. With a terrible wave of despair, he felt his own energy dim, grow weaker. All the intensity of his energized body wasn't going to be nearly enough to withstand the relentless onslaught. The bands encircled him, spinning faster and faster, and with stinging welts, the Antousians' energy whips made contact with him. Lethal talons seared his natural D'Aravnian form, punishing him, whipping him to shreds.

Kelsey . . . Erica, he thought, taking a driving lunge at the soldier who held the largest whip. *Home . . . them.*

The Antousians pressed inward, cornering him, beating him, over and over again, with their powerful, flaming whips. He struggled, expanded, but felt his energy growing dimmer. He would never make it out of this battle, he realized with a hopeless, grief-stricken spasm. Right then, an electric blue power grid began rotating in the middle of the air, and he could no longer move. He was trapped on all sides, frozen, left undulating midair in soundless captivity. He sensed more than saw what happened next.

From the ceiling, six clear sheets of material—like giant Plexiglas shields—descended, rotating mechanically until they centered in upon the power grid where he was held churning in midair. First one transparent wall came toward him, then another, then the final four until they joined and he hung captured and suspended within the narrow glass prison like a butterfly in a jar.

In that moment, J'Areshkadau B'nt D'Aravni, king of Refaria, knew he was at the mercy of his enemies.

A creeping, itching heat smoked across Jared's belly; when he woke, he smelled it, like singed wool pulled over his eyes. At first, he had no memory of what had brought him here, just the thin awareness that he wasn't in his Refarian form—he was natural. *All natural.* He moved to stretch but met opposition.

Feeling drugged, he tried again, opening himself so that he might see where he was. *Something off . . . natural form wrong.* Again he met the opposition of a hard, flat surface. Panicked, he came fully alert, opening his mind and senses full throttle.

Pressing up against a barrier of sorts, he realized once again that he had been closed in, glass all around him. His entire being was under their control, held prisoner by the familiar swirling helix of an Antousian power grid. Pressing hard against the flat surface, he tried to make out his surroundings.

Kelsha! he cried out across their bond, knowing that it would be nearly impossible to make a connection from so many miles away. Thinking hard, he grappled for words. Even his native tongue seemed lost at the bottom of a thick bog. He'd been in this form too long—by now, it had to have been hours since his Change—and clearly he'd become pure energy. In the process, he'd lost everything that came with having a material form—even the capacity for language.

Kelshaaaaaaa! he cried again, slingshotting the word toward his wife. As if in reaction, the boundaries of his confinement tightened about him—he sensed them contracting, their tension painful to him. He spun within his glass prison, rotating so he could gaze upward, then around.

His energy escalated; in Kelsey's fragile condition, she could not tolerate his capture. There would be no one to save her, no one to protect her. She'd have to lead their people alone . . . raise Erica alone.

Fear began to choke him, and he pressed harder to reach her through their bond, trying to find words—in *any* language—that she might recognize. But all he could speak was her name.

Trying to calm himself, he focused in, stilled. Forced himself to seek her with his energy and his heart. Finally, he found her, and she was sleeping lightly. He felt her heartbeat thudding out a very slow rhythm. Her belly—what did he sense there? *Erica, was Erica okay?* Panic tried to close in, but he shoved it aside, honing his sensory experience.

There, he had it! She glowed. Her abdomen, full with their baby, radiated pure energy. *His* energy—Arganate. *This could not be!* Kelsey could not survive the baby's changed state! The little one, what was she doing to her human mother?

They had him right where they wanted him; his enemies knew what they were doing. They'd left him vulnerable in the worst possible way: tethered, trapped, and unable to communicate with his human mate when she was at her most delicate stage.

"J'Areshkadau, wake," came the dull voice of his captor. "Time to work, J'Areshkadau."

He stirred, feeling the drugs seep through his energized system. They spoke in some universal language, one he could understand. Not Refarian, not English . . .

"Do you understand, J'Areshkadau?"

Mind Talk. That's what the voice used. Preverbal, it was the only thing he could possibly grasp after so many hours in Form.

He spoke back to the voice: "Yes."

"You miss your physical body?"

He refused to answer, sliding toward the bottom of his prison.

"We're told the D'Aravni relishes his natural form. Yet you seem quite vexed," the voice said.

So much power, banking all through his synapses, his cordoned stretches of energy—yet to be incapable of flexing it, it was maddening.

"Maddening, yes."

The Voice had heard. He had not mind-spoken, yet the Voice knew. He vowed to silence himself.

"Wife?" he managed, unable to hold back the question.

"She lives, D'Aravni."

He stifled a cry of relief.

"She still carries your child as well. For now."

Gods, they know about Erica!

From seemingly nowhere, an Antousian soldier appeared. Dressed in full battle gear, he bore the unmistakable air of authority that identified him as a high officer. Circling the glass containment unit, he studied Jared as he would an animal. "We will be transporting you back to Refaria, rebel," the man said coldly.

The words came through to Jared, but the other man was speaking in ordinary language; clearly someone was translating the officer's thoughts into Mind Talk. Jared felt around the room and sensed a faceless Antousian intuitive in the corner.

"Raedus wishes to study you," the officer continued, "like the shameful creature that you are, alien."

Were they on a transport now? Or in a bunker somewhere on Earth?

"The child will be studied also," his captor continued.

Jared held on to the hope that they were lying, but his fury had to have some release, and he slammed against the glass in protest.

"And why would you think you could take a human as mate?" the officer laughed, tapping the power grid with his fingertips and sending a shock wave through Jared's whole body. "That kind of interspecies lust is shameful. Utterly disgraceful. When we are finished, your bedmate will be given to one of our own officers as a reward."

Jared reached desperately for Kelsey.

"Don't feel for her," the man instructed, staring in at him like he was a wild *gnantsa* on public display. "She doesn't belong to you now."

Bond! Bond! There, he'd managed to lay hold of one very important word. But, he thought dimly, if he had it in his mind, then . . .

"The bond is broken," the Antousian said, his eyes growing large. "Do you understand, J'Areshkadau? Broken? You understand this word?"

Jared swelled, his energy roiling high, wide, deep. In answer, the containment system closed in on him, smothering all his power with a single, excruciating blast. *No,* he moaned. *No! No . . .* But then all his facility with communication—in Refarian, in English, even Mind Talk—all of it fizzled to nothing as he pictured his wife and baby ripped right out of his arms and handed over to his enemies.

In the background noise of his brain, he heard more Mind Talk but found he could no longer focus on it. Not with the Image there. Over and over he saw the murderous Antousians raping Kelsey and taking his baby, gods knew where. They must have implanted this image in his mind, because it came through so clearly. And it was having the effect they wanted: panting, he rolled onto his side, weeping inside his soul.

Harsh words that he couldn't understand flew past him—these Antousians were angry at him. They wanted something, a performance of sorts, but knew they could not get it out of him today. Jared slid to the bottom of the glass cage, feeling his energy grow dangerously cool.

Shelby lay strapped on the table, straining to listen for any hint of sound out in the hallway. Where was Jake? She didn't even want to ask the question for fear of what she knew might be the answer.

From what she could hear, it sounded like someone had gotten into a horrific struggle out in the hallway. After that, there was a long period of agonizing silence, broken finally—she'd already begun to lose track of time here in Tierny's dungeon—by a massive blast. A blast so powerful she could feel the heat from it in here as if a giant searchlight was trained on her face from three feet away.

That was when she knew it for sure: Not only was Jared there, but he'd Changed into his natural form.

And then, just like before, a long silence. *Wait,* she thought. Something was wrong—something else. And then it hit her: the silence. The music had stopped, and that meant . . . well, that probably meant that the dance club had closed up. Hours had passed since they'd taken her, but that wasn't her first thought upon processing this information. *If everyone else is gone,* she thought to herself with a shudder . . .

She couldn't bear to think of what they might be doing to Jake—from what she'd been able to hear in the hallway, they'd captured him in a vicious manner. And her king . . . she kept offering prayers for his safety, blabbering aloud in her native Refarian, begging that All would watch over both men.

In the painful, endless stretch of time that she'd been captive, one thing had become vividly clear to her heart: She had fallen in love with Jake Tierny. *Her* Jake, not the horrible, murderous one who had awful plans for her body. Shuddering, her eyes drifted shut. At least Chris Harper was still out there somewhere—she only hoped he hadn't been taken prisoner. It had been freakishly easy for the Antousians to overrun them, almost as if the raid had been a trap—which made no sense because Thea's spy had been totally reliable, rock solid. Whoever the Antousian woman was, she'd already helped free Scott and Hope back in December, so why would she have now been setting them up?

A cranking steel sound jarred her, and with a struggling glance over her shoulder she saw the human Jake returning, still clutching that velvet leash of his with a greedy look of expectation. Like hell was she letting him get a piece of her, she thought, bracing for combat as soon as he sprang her free from the restraints once again.

"So did I miss anything?" Jake drawled, slapping the leash in the palm of his hand.

Twisting her right hand, the one closest to him, she managed to give him the finger—and didn't give a crap when the reflexive binding reacted by crushing against her bones.

Tierny laughed. "Well, well, well. You've got more spirit than most of the girls I bring down here. Then again, you are alien, so that would explain it, I guess."

"How did you wind up with the Antousians?" she demanded.

He held up a palm, silencing her. "The questions are for me to ask. But first, we're going to take a little trip, you and me." He fastened the leash against her collar once again, and her hands and feet were instantly freed. She tried lifting her leg to kick him as she'd done earlier, but after being bound for so long, her whole body had gone prickly and numb. She was just too weak.

"Get up," he told her, yanking on the leash hard, driving her up against his chest.

"Give me a damned minute," she spat back at him, trying to settle her hands against the table. "You've kept me pinned down so long, I can't sit up right."

With a rough gesture—with hands so painfully familiar, yet all wrong—he lifted her to the floor. "Here. Walk with me," he told her, wrapping the velvet cord about his hand in a loop, giving him more control over her.

It was all she could do to follow him, her stiletto boots stumbling and dragging in the wake of his long strides.

I'm glad Scott killed you in the future, she thought. *And if I have my way about it, we'll* both *kill you this time around.*

He nearly dragged her toward the far end of the stone corridor, then around a bend, and at that point she glimpsed a large steel door. It reminded her of a submarine hatch or some sort of bunker. Maybe the whole place down here was far more than the basement of a warehouse, she suddenly thought. What if the seemingly innocent structure up above actually perched atop one of the Antousians' own bases, much like Jared's lodge capped off all of Base Ten?

Jake halted, yanking her flush against his side. She trembled, desperately wanting to shove out of his grasp—he had the same bulk, the same build and height as the man she loved, and yet everything about him revolted her completely.

He punched a code into a panel on the wall, shoving her head down cruelly before he did so. He kept her held by the nape of her neck, pinned against his hip, until a beeping noise sounded, and the armored door before them swung open.

With a pinching gesture, he dragged her back upright. "Come on," he told her with a gruff shove. "Get in there."

Shelby blinked at the bright lights on the other side of the door, a contrast to the darkly lit hallway. As grimy and dank as her cell had been, this room nearly sparkled. At the far side was a chrome desk, an array of computers—a whole bank of electronics, in fact—and other monitoring devices. A man with dark hair sat on the other side of the desk, his back to them as he studied some sort of screen.

"I've got her, boss," Jake told the man. "Take a look. Think you'll be impressed."

With a quick sniff, Shelby tried to scent the leader, to determine whether he was alien or human, but came up blank. Odd, usually she could get a reading right away.

But then he slowly rotated in his shiny metal chair, still keeping his gaze on the monitor. "So, looks like my boy's brought us another fine young woman," the man said, at last fixing her with his brown-eyed gaze. When he did, Shelby actually swayed on her feet so badly that Tierny gave the leash a jerk to punish her.

"Stop that!" the alien on the other side of the desk roared. "Release her right now, Tierny."

"But—"

He rose to his feet, sweeping past the desk. "I said release her," he repeated much more softly, his shocked gaze riveted on her face.

Dully she was aware of being unfastened, of Tierny's leash falling with a thud to the floor. Of time itself grinding down, then speeding up.

"You must have drugged me," was all she could think to say, giving her head a little clearing shake.

"No," he half whispered, then addressed Tierny: "Get the hell out of here. I need to talk to Shelby."

"You know this *nank*?" Tierny stepped backward in surprise.

The man looked him up and down. "Just get out."

With a shuffling movement, the human was gone, leaving her to stare up into a pair of eyes that she'd never thought to see again. It wasn't possible; he couldn't be here. She'd watched him die; he'd been inside the Texas facility when it exploded. . . .

"Nate?" she whispered uncertainly, feeling the floor grow unstable beneath her feet.

Chapter Nineteen

The emotion in his eyes was undeniable as he lifted a hand to her cheek. "Shelby," he said softly.

"Don't touch me."

He stepped closer. "Listen to me—"

"Nate is dead." She wheeled to face him, thrusting a finger at him. "You ain't Nate, no way in freaking hell! You're some sort of shape-shifter, trying to manipulate me."

"No," he told her slowly, guiding her with him toward a sofa, "I did not die."

"I saw it happen!" she shrieked, ducking out of his grasp. "I watched as Nate changed into . . . into . . . a *vlksai.* And then he had me dragged out of that warehouse before it exploded. He was still inside. *You* were still inside. So you're not here, and you're not alive. Whoever you are, you're just another *vlksai* trying to mind-fuck me."

The alien stared down at her, dark emotion in his eyes. "I survived," was all he said, his gaze never wavering.

"You survived," she repeated bitterly. "Made a miraculous escape, huh? Wow, you're a regular freaking Houdini. Imagine that."

"Do you still have the primexia stone I gave you? Did you keep wearing it?" he whispered, his eyes glinting with emotion. And that was when her tremors truly overtook her, and she had the dull thought that she was heading straight into shock.

"You could have lifted that from my memories, too," she argued weakly, even though her mind was beginning to draw terrible, horrifying conclusions about the Antousian in front of her.

As if sensing her panic, he reached for a bottle of water on his desk. While he was turned away, she took advantage of the moment to study the alien's profile. It was amazing how much like Nate he really did look—but any shape-shifter could easily have accomplished that. "When they drugged me," she said, "they pulled Nate's image from my memories. That's got to be how you're doing this."

"Here," he told her, pushing the cup of water into her hands. But she flung it at him furiously, drenching the front of his tight black T-shirt.

He brushed at the wet fabric. "Shelby, I realize this is all a great shock."

"Don't!" she screamed in a blistering voice. "Don't try and soothe me, not about this!"

She backed away from him, folding her arms protectively across her chest, but stumbled over a small chair right behind her and went sprawling. Nate advanced upon her, brown eyes suddenly blazing bright gold; she scooted backward, closing her eyes.

"I got out of there before the explosion," he explained.

"Lies and more lies." She waved a hand between them. "That's what you trade in. Just like all of your people." She couldn't stop shaking, her whole body wracked with jarring tremors.

The man sighed, squatting down in front of her. "Shelby, whether you want to believe it or not, I'm your Nate."

She began laughing hysterically. "My Nate? *My* Nate? Oh, puh-lease. Even if you did survive, you sure as hell weren't ever *my* Nate." She looked him in the eye. "Don't even try going that route. Nate betrayed me. Betrayed me and our friends—and so many people who I loved died because of what he did." He couldn't seem to meet her gaze. "Nate broke me, my spirit, my heart. . . . He took everything good inside of me and . . . and . . ." She couldn't finish.

The man before her winced visibly. "Too many people died that day," was all he said, and a sick feeling began to crawl across her skin. "I've always regretted that fact—and, whether you believe it or not, I've always regretted hurting you."

"Hurting me?" she scoffed. "Hurting me? You used me, boy, plain and simple. If you *are* Nate, that is."

His expression hardened. "I did what I had to do . . . for my people."

"Nate." She blinked, pressed her eyes shut, then opened them again. "Tell me how it was I watched you die, then. Huh? I mourned you and grieved you for years. For *years.* Why would you let me hurt like that?" She dropped her head heavily into her hands.

"You saw what I wanted you to see, Shelby." She felt fingertips skim across her forehead, a brush of energy touching her consciousness. "It was safer if you thought I was dead. I wanted to protect you. It was the least I could do after . . . well, everything. I never intended for us to fall so deeply for each other. It wasn't supposed to happen that way."

If I just stay like this, tight as a ball, the nightmare will end. She drew deep inside of herself, pulled at her energy until it grew intense and centered right in her core. She struggled to focus on memories, sensations, anything to protect herself from actually feeling the moment.

"What are you going to do to me?" she mumbled, burying her face in her arms. "What are your people going to do?"

"I'll take care of you."

She would have believed that lie, too, once upon a time. And maybe that was why that sick realization became more certain inside of her: Nate had always promised he'd protect her, and even now . . .

She dropped her arms away from her face. "You didn't have to ask me to bond with you or give me that stupid mating stone. . . ."

"Like I said, Shelby, I never intended"—he coughed, cleared his throat, then continued—"I didn't mean for it to go so far. It wasn't the plan."

"Why play me at all?" she shrieked, throwing her hands up. "I was just a flipping medic. I didn't know anything of value. I couldn't have been worth anything to you."

"Having relationships made me look believable. You were part of my cover."

"Fuck you!" she spat.

"This is war, Shelby. You know it, and I know it." He shook his head. "Your people are insurgents, and I did what had to be done in order to stop them."

Without thinking, she drew back her hand and slapped him so hard that her handprint glared harsh red against his fair cheek. He kept his head to the side for a moment, then slowly turned to look at her again. "I'll let you get away with that. Once. I owe you that much. But don't strike me again, Shelby. I don't care who you are or what you once were to me. I won't put up with that kind of thing."

"That was for asking me to marry you when you had no intention of following through."

"I did care for you."

"Yeah? Well, I *loved* you! I loved you, and you took that and just . . . just . . ." She drew her hand back again, unable to stop herself, but this time he caught it in his firm grasp.

"Don't hit me again, Shelby. We may have a past, but you're my captive now."

Only then did she realize she'd begun to sob uncontrollably, her shoulders and body shaking with it. "You used me."

"I'm sorry," he said, pulling her against his body with shocking gentleness, "but I'm going to have to put you under."

Then, once again, her entire world went black.

Kelsey heard Jared whispering in her ear, his voice tickling at the fringes of her consciousness. She groaned, shifting on the bed, and reached for him. She'd been so incredibly exhausted, she couldn't stay awake.

"You're back?" she mumbled, her eyes fluttering open. Relief washed over her as she rolled toward the sound of his voice.

Kelsha!

She jerked awake in alarm. The sound of his voice was panicked, edged with terror. Struggling to sit up, she glanced all around their bedroom. "Jared? Are you here?" she called out.

No answer. With a frantic look at the bedside alarm clock, she realized it was well after two a.m. Without meaning to, she'd slept hours when she'd intended to take just a quick nap. But that wasn't the only thing that frightened her. The semidarkness was being illuminated by Erica: Her entire belly was glowing brighter than it had at any other time during her pregnancy.

What could have sent Erica into her Change like this, and so dramatically? She thought of hearing Jared cry out to her just before she'd woken up. What if Erica sensed something, somehow knew that her daddy was in danger?

Jared is fine. Jared is safe, she tried telling herself. *You're imagining things. Any minute and you're going to hear from Thea that the mission was a success and that he's back on the hangar deck.*

Then she swore she heard Jared once again, his voice so vividly strong, he might as well have been in the room with her . . . and he sounded agonized. Hands fluttering against her belly, she squeezed her eyes shut and tried her best to tap into the bond, but she couldn't feel him at all.

Kelsey's heartbeat went crazy inside her chest, and she struggled to calm herself so she could soothe Erica. "Baby," she murmured, rubbing her blazing-hot belly, "baby girl, you need to settle down. You're okay, just shh . . . calm down." In response, her stomach seemed to glow even brighter, and a sharp dagger of pain nailed her in the side.

Not now. I can't go into labor now, not like this.

Between her legs, she felt a faint trickle of dampness, and that was when the full-bore panic descended, robbing the very breath from her lungs. *I have to get help.*

With a careful shove, she moved sideways, and the trickling between her legs got warmer and wetter. Sliding across the bed, moving slowly and cautiously, Kelsey finally reached her comm. Taking a deep breath, she signaled the med complex and tried to convince herself that both Jared and Erica were safe.

Thea tore down the back stairs that led to Jared and Kelsey's quarters. The horrible news seemed to only be getting worse, with the comm transmission from the med sector indicating that Kelsey was in the midst of a medical emergency and that Erica was in crisis. She practically tumbled down the final two steps, and the image that greeted her, of the medics working on Kelsey, who lay flat on her back in bed, brought tears to Thea's eyes.

Jared's capture—as well as Jake's and Shelby's—had been terrible enough, the news so horrible that Thea had spent the past hour deliberating how to break it to Kelsey. But this? Seeing their queen laid out, an oxygen mask over her mouth, and Erica glowing so brightly inside her belly that it was a wonder Kelsey hadn't been scorched alive from the inside out . . . well, it was almost more than Thea could bear.

She took slow steps inside the room, and the chief medical adviser glanced up at her, his expression intent. "I don't want to move her, not yet," he explained.

Kelsey's eyes widened when she caught sight of Thea, and she gestured wildly. "Keep still, my lady," the doctor told her, trying to settle her hands, but Kelsey grew only more agitated, waving at Thea.

The doctor turned to Thea, his expression severe. She wondered if he'd already heard the news of Jared's capture because he gave his head a slight shake—as if to say, "Don't tell her, not now."

Thea swallowed and slowly approached the bedside. Kelsey writhed, yanking at her oxygen mask, and even though the medics tried to stop her, she managed to pop it off. "Tell . . . me . . . he's safe," she gasped.

Thea gave her head a slight bob, praying Kelsey would forgive her this lie. "He'll be here . . . soon. Soon he'll be back," she whispered in a wooden tone, knowing all the color had to be drained out of her face.

Kelsey's eyes welled with tears, and then slid shut, and then the medics positioned the mask back over her face. Thea knew then and there that Kelsey had already guessed the truth: It was the reason that she and Erica were in such crisis. Thea walked to the far side of the bed, the one where Jared normally slept, and climbed onto the mattress. The medics were at Kelsey's other side; Thea kept herself out of the way, sliding cautiously across the covers until she was right beside her friend, who was covered in wires and surrounded by beeping monitors. Thea reached for her hand, and Kelsey stared up at her, blinking helplessly, tears still streaming down her cheeks.

"It's going to be okay," Thea promised. And she meant it: She would not let Jared's enemies win this battle; she would do everything within her power to bring him home safely. "You just be strong for Erica. That's your only concern right now, all right?"

Through the mask, Kelsey spoke in a muffled voice, and even though the words were slightly garbled, Thea understood them nonetheless: "They have him."

She squeezed her queen's hand. "For now," she admitted quietly. "But not for long, my lady. I promise you, not for long."

"You tell me where Shelby is—right now." Jake tried desperately to ignore the hideous garbled sound of his words as they passed over his Antousian vocal cords. Like water breaking over rocks, only with more vibrato and distortion. He'd been transported, blindfolded, through a long series of winding corridors and shafts, held naked and at gunpoint by a female Antousian who had introduced herself as Kryn Zoltners. It was the same curvy brunette he'd seen Jared talking with right before all hell had broken loose.

After some waiting, he'd been taken in a vehicle over bumpy terrain, nighttime air cold against his bare skin. Then, with a graceless shove, he'd been hiked up a small flight of stairs and brought inside what he'd come to realize was a small cabin of sorts. Kryn had explained coolly that Shelby was being held elsewhere—and Jared, well, that wasn't information she was prepared to dispense.

"Where is Jared Bennett? Shelby Tyler?" Jake demanded. "You tell me where they are. Now!"

"In good time, Jakob." Kryn spun to face him, a long velvet-covered belt in her hand, and she tapped it against her open palm like a whip. "First you'll tell me who you are, imposter. We know you aren't the Jake Tierny who's been supplying us with humans. He's a human, and you"—she raked her gaze up and down his naked form—"you are quite *clearly* not. So why don't you tell me how it is you chose to replicate Tierny's body? Shape-shifter? Or something else?"

Jake slid on the modular settee, backing himself—quite literally—into a corner. With one palm, he worked to hide his permanent erection, cupping it protectively; with the other arm he covered both of his nipples. He didn't want this Antousian bitch to see any more of his naked body than she had to.

"My, you are a shy one," she hissed, clucking her tongue. She dragged her gaze up and down his nude body once again. "Surprising, too, since from what I can tell, you are quite the *physical* creature."

Jake was aware that his breathing increased slightly, and his fingers twitched protectively against his cock. "What do you know about my physicality?"

She leaned close, whispering in his ear. "Just look at you. You're magnificent."

In a flash, he had hold of her ponytail and used it to drag her down atop the settee; she practically landed in his lap. Drawing his face up against hers, he snapped his distended jaws menacingly: He might not be Antousian in his heart, but the blood still flowed in his veins. "Bring Shelby to me. Bring her, or you die." The words mingled with his quick panting, modulating over his rough vocal cords.

With a second jerk of her ponytail, he had her neck exposed. "I could end your life right now." Another snarling snap of his powerful jaws just over her jugular. "I could choke the life out of you, little girl. But then you would be of no use to me—so you're going to get Shelby and bring her to me. *Now*."

Jake grabbed hold of her velvet whip, wrapping it tightly about both of her hands until he had Kryn straddled. As if he were roping a calf, he used it to bind her. Once he had her hands tied together, he backed away from her, not bothering with modesty. Hell, he had a nine-inch hard-on jutting right at the woman's face, but it wasn't a moment for shame.

"And I need clothes," he said.

"You aren't going to get any," Kryn announced, staring down at her hands.

"I won't spend another moment naked like this—not in front of you, not in front of your people. Call for someone, and get me some fucking clothes."

She gestured with her bound hands. "I can break out of these bindings easily."

"I'm aware of that." He gave the tie a securing tug. "And yet you were going to bind me with the same cord?"

She lifted her eyes meaningfully, and the dark irises flared. "Perhaps I wanted you to have freedom of movement." With a flick of her tongue, she licked her lips seductively.

Jake only scowled back at her. "Not interested, Kryn."

"That's right." She tossed her head back, giving her mane a shake. "You've only got eyes for your Shelby Tyler. I wonder what she'll say about you in your . . . natural form." Kryn scraped her gaze across his hide-covered chest, then lower over the hard plates that covered the center of his abdomen and stretched toward his naturally elongated cock. When he was in his Antousian form, it was fully erect and one hundred percent ready to go—any day of the year. A perverse fact of their evolution, it ensured that their bodies were capable of procreation, no matter how harsh the conditions back on their home world.

He bellowed angrily, throwing back his head and releasing a trumpeting sound of frustration. "Shelby knows who and what I am."

"Interesting. So it's only *you* who can't accept it?"

He clamped his long jaw, tilting his head slightly sideways so he could meet her stare full on. His nostrils flared with huffing, furious breaths, and it occurred to him that he sounded—and looked—every bit the monster he had long known himself to be. This was what flowed in his veins; this was what he truly was.

He rubbed the rough ridge that ran from his nose upward onto the crown of his head. "Why don't you assume *your* natural form, Kryn? If you're so proud?"

She gave him a coy, wicked smile. "I like being human."

"And so do I!" he roared. "So you're going to help me, or you'll die at my Antousian hands."

"I can't help with the shape-shifting." She gave a halfhearted shrug. "You're stuck until the drugs wear off."

"How long?" he gritted.

"A day, maybe two or three."

"Days? I'll be this way for days?" He rubbed the ridge atop his head again. "I can't go anywhere like this. I'm fucked."

"Their plan exactly." Odd, but her use of "their plan" struck Jake as meaningful—as did her tone. She wasn't gloating at all. "They can keep you here indefinitely so long as they keep injecting you—obviously you can't set foot outside in your Antousian form."

With a shudder, he imagined Shelby's reaction to seeing him this way. A terrible wave of shame crested over him as he thought of her reaction to him—so monstrously huge, so rough and alien.

Then he stopped and looked at Kryn. Something told him that she wasn't entirely his enemy, that there was the possibility of finding common ground. Instinctively, he began to soul-gaze her.

What he glimpsed inside of her caused him to stagger backward a step. At first she didn't notice—she'd been tugging at the velvet binding—but then she looked up. "You're gazing me, you bastard." She struggled to avert her gaze, but he reached for her face, roughly turning it upward so he could get a better look into her.

He intensified his soul-searching, delving deeper, and took yet another step backward from her, shaking his head in disbelief. A vulnerable, skittish look filled Kryn's eyes: She knew everything that he'd just intuited.

She lifted a shushing finger to her lips, a barely perceptible motion that said, "Silence."

In All's name, please help me! he wanted to cry, but instead he heeded her warning and pretended that he hadn't just seen everything about who Kryn Zoltners truly was.

"I need Shelby," he whispered in a hoarse, fractured voice. Working at his jaws and lips, he tried to gain better control of his speech. "I need to see Shelby Tyler—sooner, not later."

"I don't know what I can do about that."

"And please, I'm begging you"—he blinked his overly large eyes at her—"get me some kind of clothes."

The clothes that Kryn managed to find were an odd assortment of leather and denim: a worn pair of blue jeans that were perfectly sized to his extraordinarily long legs. He was, after all, six foot seven in his natural Antousian form. The only other clothing item was a black leather vest that barely managed to close over his rough chest, and unfortunately still revealed a bit of the thick hide that formed plates across his pectorals.

"A T-shirt? Nothing?" He tugged at the tight-fitting vest, struggling to fasten it across his bulky sternum.

"I couldn't come up with one. You look fine."

His face flushed. "She can't see this. I need"—he shook his head, swallowing the words at first—"well, more coverage." He tapped at his chest meaningfully.

"Open it," Kryn said, surprising him, but he shook his head. "Seriously, just wear it open."

He toyed with the top snap, loosening the vest. "My hide. I don't want her to see the thickness of it. . . ."

"She's seen plenty of Antousians before. She's a nurse."

He felt suddenly vulnerable—horribly vulnerable in a way that he hadn't since he'd first fallen in love with Hope, so many years before. Naked, exposed. It had taken years for him to allow Hope to see his natural form; he'd known Shelby for only about five months.

"But . . ." *We're lovers*, he wanted to say.

Kryn made a little cry of frustration and with a jerking motion unfastened his vest until it fell loose across his abdomen, revealing him for exactly what he was. With a nervous look down, he noticed the one plain fact that couldn't be avoided: the thick bulge in the front of his pants. He shifted, trying to adjust himself, but nothing helped.

Kryn seemed to read his mind. "You need a sling, but I couldn't find any."

He tilted his head sideways, studying her with his left eye. "What kind of sling?"

She scowled at him. "I'm amazed at how little you know about your own people."

"I'm Refarian!" he bellowed angrily, thumping at his chest.

"I can see that." She rolled her eyes. "A sling, Jake—a *sling*? It's how our males hide their, uh, state. It's like Antousian underwear—for men."

He gaped downward, studying the immense bulge

in the center of his jeans, and tried to imagine what sort of device a "sling" might be—how it could possibly control or conceal his permanent erection.

"Get me one, damn it. Fast."

"I'll keep looking."

She started to leave the room, but he caught her by the arm. "We need to talk," he murmured under his breath.

With an alarmed expression, she shook her head, silencing him. "I'm going to see what I can do about having Shelby transported here, *nank*," she said loudly, then leaning into his body space, she whispered, "Keep quiet."

"We need to talk," he repeated urgently. "Where is my commander?"

She took two steps back, lifting both hands. "The fate of the Refarian king has already been decided." His heart plummeted. "He is being prepared for airlift to Refaria, where he will be tried for war crimes and where his D'Aravnian body will be studied as a potential chemical weapon. There is nothing you or anyone else can do to help him now."

Jake shook his head. "Godsdamn you all."

Using only her eyes, Kryn seemed to plead with him. "I'll do what I can about more clothing and getting Shelby moved."

And with that, the woman who certainly had to be Thea's well-placed spy left him alone, bolting the door behind her as she departed.

Chapter Twenty

When Shelby finally came to once again, it was still nighttime, and she'd been transported somewhere far—or maybe not—from the warehouse in Idaho. Rising unsteadily onto her bare feet—someone had removed her black boots and left them beside the bed—she walked to a window and stared out. All around, as far as she could see, were empty fields, with a large stream bisecting the one closest to her. Pushing her face up against the window, she could see that hers was just one cabin in a long line of others, with perhaps fifteen in total stretching along the stream bank.

It had to be an abandoned fishing camp of some sort. Or they were on a ranch, maybe. She couldn't tell for sure, although one fact was abundantly clear: She wasn't going anywhere. Two armed guards kept watch in front of her door, and although they appeared human, she had no doubt that they were Antousian-human hybrids. She shivered.

That was when she remembered Nate, and she pressed the heel of her palm against her temple, groaning. *I can't go there, not right now,* she thought. Seeing him again had nearly torn her heart out. All the betrayal, all the grieving . . . and to know he'd lied to her from the beginning? And supposedly for her protection? Yeah, right.

"Alien bastard," she grunted out loud.

Almost as if in answer, a door opened behind her;

she hadn't noticed it before, and she lurched against the wall, falling into a protective stance. "Who's there?" she demanded, spreading her feet slightly apart. She'd rush any *vlksai* who tried to harm her—and she sure as heck wasn't going to let the human Jake drag her around by a leash anymore. Hopefully Nate had at least put the kibosh on that nasty maneuver.

A hulking *vlksai* entered from an adjoining door, and just beyond him she could glimpse a bed and a simply furnished room. "Who are you?" she demanded, wishing like hell that she hadn't been stripped of her weapons.

"Shelby," the alien whispered, his black eyes growing wide with what appeared to be relief, of all things.

"Just stay back," she insisted as he took several loping steps toward her. "Keep the hell away from me."

"Shelby, it's . . . me. Jake."

After all the strange, twisted events of the night, she wasn't about to fall for this flimsy trap. She rolled her eyes, relaxing a little. "Oh, just shut up already. I ain't that dumb."

Jake cried out in frustration. Of course she didn't believe him—she'd never once seen him in his Antousian form. Working at his distended jaw, he struggled to form English words. Strange, but the language felt foreign to him now. Hours he'd been like this . . . maybe even several days for all the confusion garbling his mind, but the sum total was that he was becoming more feral with every passing minute. Less tied to the Refarians and humans that had defined his world. Snapping his jaws, he managed to find his voice, though it required a good deal of labor. "Shelby, it's me," he repeated hoarsely.

She pushed up against the door to the cabin, flattening herself. "Don't say another word, *vlksai*!"

"Shelby!" he managed to bellow gracelessly, swinging his gaze first one direction, then another, to try to get a good, clear look at her. "It is really me. Jakob." He thumped his chest significantly. "*Me*, sweetheart."

She began to tremble visibly, sucking at the air around them. The terror in her eyes nearly broke his heart; to think what she must be feeling, seeing him this way. To imagine how little she trusted the image before her eyes.

Sliding along the door, she crumpled in a heap against the floor. "How can I know for sure?"

Gingerly, he approached her, doing his best to control his ungainly steps. Squatting down beside her, he reached for a lock of her hair. "You're . . . my little Texas tamale," he said, the words vibrating. "The hood . . . of that truck. Boardroom. My . . . quarters." Every word he called forth was a labor, but her entire demeanor transformed, relief and faith returning to her clear blue eyes, even as she began to sob. "It's me," he repeated, opening his arms to her, and she flung herself at him so hard that he almost toppled backward.

He didn't even care that she burrowed her face against his rough chest, or that the hands he stroked her with were large and brutal. All that mattered—the only thing in his heart for that one moment—was how precious she was to him. And that for the moment, he had her back in his arms. Where she belonged.

She clung to him, wrapped her much smaller arms about his barrel of a chest, and murmured his name over and over, weeping. "You're safe," he told her, wondering how in hell he'd ever spring her from this fortified compound.

"Why're you like this?" She drew back, staring up into his eyes. "What did they do to you?"

"They injected me," he told her, wincing at the memory of his painful transformation. "They forced me to shift, and I can't change back."

Her eyes grew horrified and wide. "Ever?"

He hung his head. "Not until the effects of the drug wear off. Sorry. I know this body must be . . . Well, it's distasteful to me, too."

She shook her head. "No, that's not it."

"They've trapped me. Limited my ability to escape because I can't show my face among humans. Pretty nifty little trick, huh?"

"Fuck that," she said, reaching a hand to his cheek. "Did they hurt you?"

"The transformation was a bitch." He gazed down his body, hoping she didn't notice the massive bulge in the front of his pants. Kryn still hadn't brought him one of those slings she'd mentioned. "But that's nothing in the greater scheme of things: They also captured Jared."

"Oh, gods, don't tell me that. Please."

He said nothing for a long moment. "They have him in his natural state, totally locked down, and prepping him for transport back to Refaria."

"We have to do something. But what?"

Jake shook his head, staring up at the ceiling. "I have no idea. I've never felt so powerless. We're under way too many armed guards here to do anything." He wasn't about to explain that he'd placed whatever flimsy hopes he did have for Jared's survival in the hands of Kryn Zoltners, an Antousian.

"Listen, Jake, I have something else to tell you." She leaned back against the door. "About who's running this whole show." He nodded his encouragement, and she blotted at her forehead, her hand trembling. "I saw Nate."

"But you told me he died."

"He did die . . . or so he let me believe, but he's alive and he's the one in charge, from what I gather."

Jake couldn't help it; as irrational as the reaction was, he felt a horrible stab of jealousy. "You saw him?"

She nodded, averting her eyes.

"How did that go?" he practically barked at her. "Seeing him must have been interesting."

She fiddled with her hands, staring into her lap. "It

doesn't matter what he said. But I do think that my connection with him might be our only prayer of getting out of this place."

"Or for you to get out." Jake shook his head. "Once they figure out who I am, they won't ever let me go."

Her gaze snapped upward. "Don't say that." With a nervous glance about them, she added, "You have no idea who might be listening in."

He reached for her hand, holding it tight. "If you can get out of this place, do it, Shell. Don't worry about me. You look after yourself."

"I won't walk out of here without you," she disagreed fiercely. "If it comes to that, I'm staying with you."

"No, you'll take care of yourself, Shell," he insisted. "It's all I ask of you. Please do that for me."

Thea paced the meeting chambers, wishing desperately that Kryn would contact her. Had the woman set them all up? Or had she somehow been betrayed herself? That would certainly explain how their team had been taken out so thoroughly and surgically. Behind her at the table, Chris Harper called her back to the moment.

"No contact from the spy yet at all?" he asked.

She shook her head. She had her data portal open and would know as soon as any message arrived: so far, total silence. "I have to believe that she's working to help them, even now."

Nevin Daniels sighed. "We have little left to us at the moment, not knowing where they are, where they've been transported."

"At least Kelsey and Erica have stabilized," she told them grimly, and Marco gave her a small smile of support from across the table.

"I hate this wait-and-see bullshit," Chris muttered.

"Well, what's the status on the situation with the vice president?" Thea asked. "That's something else we can focus on."

"And at least it's good news," Chris told them. "He's been taken to Warren for questioning."

"But how will they prove his real identity?" Thea asked.

"It may not be possible, but at least based on Patrick Wells's statements, we had enough to go on to bring him in. Not an easy feat when you're talking about the VP. But thankfully headquarters got the president to listen."

Thea was about to suggest DNA testing as one route but remembered that whenever Antousians seized human hosts, the genetic match remained identical. Retinal scans, DNA swabs, none of it would help. "Surely he didn't have access to the right security codes and so forth, the kinds of things that the vice president would have memorized."

Chris shot her a dark look. "Haven, we have no idea how deeply the White House has been infiltrated or compromised."

"Thanks for the pep talk, Agent Harper," she complained, and then her data portal beeped, signaling a new message. Every set of eyes in the room riveted right on her.

Staring down at it with trembling hands, she said, "It's from Kryn."

Quickly she scanned the coded message, breathing a quiet and heartfelt, "Thank All," as she did so. When she was finished, she turned to face the other gathered advisers. "All three of them are alive. Jake and Shelby are being held together in a cabin roughly twenty clicks away from the warehouse itself. They're in an abandoned fishing camp."

"And Jared?" Marco asked, the deep emotion in his voice undeniable.

Thea swallowed. "They have Jared in a containment cell, trapped in his D'Aravnian form."

Marco and Nevin cursed in unison.

Thea leaned over the table, planting both hands heavily on its polished surface. "Gentlemen, I think we all understand the gravity of this situation. The longer Jared is held in his natural form, the riskier and more jeopardized his return grows. But it's more than that. Kryn says that they're moving quickly to get him off-world, back to Refaria."

Nevin stared at her, his black eyes shockingly wild with emotion. "They will not take my king back to face his enemies."

"Agreed," Marco muttered with a sharp growl.

"We take in a full team," Chris added. "We go back in, based on her coordinates, and we bring in the USAF, the FBI, and your people . . . and we spring all three of them."

"How long for us to put together that kind of coordinated attack?" Nevin asked, tapping the table with his fingers thoughtfully.

"I'd say by early tomorrow morning," Harper replied.

Thea shook her head. "That's too long. Way too long."

"If we go in too soon and too sloppy, they might kill Jared. This plan has to be executed carefully."

"Chris," she said, "execution is exactly what they have on their minds. If they load him on a transport to Refaria, he's as good as dead already."

Kryn jogged through the assembly plant, past the rows and rows of mechanized systems that were responsible for creating their chip-based technology, the minute electron processors that Raedus planned to spread among the human population. The chips represented his latest plan for subjugating the human population, a way to mass-control them. Yes, it was quite the deal her so-called leader had struck with Tierny down here on Earth, getting the heartless bastard to supply human hosts for experimentation in exchange for cold, hard cash. And loads of it.

Living through the virus back home had been all she ever needed to see of the potential implications of a plan like Raedus's, and she'd decided to do whatever she could to stop the Antousian leader's strategy to vanquish mankind. But it appeared that her number was almost up: The intel that she'd been fed about the rave had been entirely bogus. All those in attendance had been either their own soldiers or humans who had already been successfully implanted—and controlled. It had made picking out Jared Bennett and most of his team from within the gathered crowd painfully easy, like shooting fish in a barrel, as the humans were fond of saying.

That was why she planned to meet with Nate now and learn whatever she could about the scheduled lift-off in the morning—then feed that ETD back to Thea so hopefully she and her people could abort the mission. And strike at the heart of this mechanized warehouse, she thought, hating the image of the chips and technology all around her. Back on Refaria these same chips had led to the deaths of millions of her people. She wouldn't stand by idly and let it happen to another race, not again.

Exiting the plant on its far wall, she entered the circuitous series of corridors that led to Nate's office. Arriving at his door, she entered the latest security code, and after a moment, the steel door swung open. Nate was expecting her.

"Come in," he called, never looking up from his desk.

Nate was a complex leader—years ago, she'd admired him; in fact, he'd been the reason she'd been caught up in the war. A famous figure within their military operation, he'd been charismatic and convincing, a brutal warrior who'd also seemed to contain an instinctive level of compassion.

But that had been what she'd believed before—before all the heinous acts on his part that she'd witnessed while serving under his command. Now she'd much rather take a luminator to his head and execute him than follow him another single day.

She stood, waiting for his attention, and he let her stand. A power move, the sort she'd long ago learned to ignore. When at last he glanced up at her, his normally brown eyes had turned gold and icy.

"Tell me, Kryn, what is the status of our prisoners?" He leaned back in his chair, studying her shrewdly.

He suspects I'm the spy, she thought, choking back a wave of panic. Nate's eyes changed color only when he was furious or deeply emotional.

"The one named Shelby Tyler is now being held with the Antousian." The less she said, she figured the better it would be for her. "At the fishing camp."

"Have you learned the nature of their connection yet? How it is an Antousian has come to be fighting alongside the Refarians?"

"I'm not sure, sir," she hedged, "but they seem to be involved in a relationship together."

His eyes flared oddly. "What has been their reaction to being brought back together?"

She shook her head. "Shelby was still sleeping off the injection when I was there. They haven't had the chance to speak or interact yet."

"There has only been one Antousian working alongside Jared Bennett—ever—and that's Lieutenant Scott Dillon."

"Our latest intel shows Dillon as well as his human mate both at Warren Air Force Base working with the Joint Alien Task Force."

"I realize that," Nate told her with a hint of impatience. "I read the daily reports just like you, Lieutenant. But I'm remembering something. Back in December, Veckus was convinced that a time traveler had used the mitres; he sensed it when an Antousian penetrated interdimensional space. It was *that* man we were chasing when you captured Dillon and Hope Harper in Yellowstone. You remember this?"

"Of course." She wasn't an idiot, after all.

"So I have a theory . . . I'm thinking that perhaps our mystery Antousian over at the fishing camp is none other than our time traveler. The one Veckus intuited back in December. Again, only one Antousian has ever worked with Jared Bennett—and that's Dillon. And the man in Yellowstone had a personal interest in Hope—just like Scott Dillon does. Conclusion? That Scott Dillon is our missing time traveler, and that he killed Tierny at some future point, taking his body. In fact, that's exactly what I'm thinking."

"An interesting idea." She thought of the man she'd left back in the cabin, his honesty and frankness—and his desperation. She couldn't bear the thought of what Nate might have in mind for the soldier.

"Stay with me on this one," Nate continued. "What if I'm right about his identity, that he seized the human Jake Tierny's body in the future? It would explain how the version we captured appeared so much older. And our boy Tierny certainly has a significant score to settle with Dillon. I've never known him to hate anyone like he does that bastard. Perhaps they got into a scuffle in the future, and Dillon came out the winner, and thereby took his body."

Kryn's mind whirled. Nate was making crazy leaps of logic, and yet—he was also making a terrible kind of sense. "Are you saying that our prisoner might be Scott Dillon . . . from the future? Is that your suggestion, sir?"

He gave her a half smile. "Perhaps. Or perhaps he's just another Antousian who's aligned with the rebels. But if he is Dillon . . . I don't have to tell you what a powerful moment this truly is. To have captured Jared Bennett and his lieutenant? All in one night's work? Well, I'd have to"—he rose to his feet, stepped around the desk, and cupped her face in both hands—"reward a woman who helped me bring that about."

She feigned a blush, dropping her head. "Oh, I can't take credit for that, sir. I didn't have anything to do with it."

"Someone did," he said icily. "Some traitor in our midst fell for our bait and passed the intel to the rebels."

Forcing her head back, he kissed her on the mouth,

then whispered, "I'd hate to think that traitor might be you, Kryn."

She tried to return the kiss, struggled against the revulsion he elicited in her body. She was accustomed to his occasional physical "outbursts," the way he tried to intimidate her sexually. "Sir, I am . . . loyal. You know it."

"That remains to be seen, but I'm watching you, soldier. So is everyone else." And with that, he released her, sending her stumbling slightly backward.

"What is our next move, sir?" She tried to compose herself, trying to believe that he'd not read the fear in her mind and body.

"Take Tierny to the captives—see what the result of such an encounter might be. Because if our Antousian is Dillon after all? Then that meeting should reveal the truth."

She swallowed. "Certainly, sir. But when?"

"Give them until the morning. I want to catch them off guard, let them fall under the spell of safety for a bit," he said, returning to his desk. "But one mandate is imperative: Shelby Tyler is not to be harmed. Not under any circumstances."

Now, this little directive was more than slightly interesting. She just couldn't help herself: "I'm curious sir. Why not?"

He shot her a withering look. "Because I said so, Lieutenant. Dismissed."

Chapter Twenty-one

Inch by inch, Jake carefully worked his way inside Shelby, as cautious as if he were holstering an unpredictable weapon. He knew his strength and massive size could hurt her; hell, his nine-inch cock wasn't ever intended for a woman of her much smaller dimensions. But by the gods, after everything they'd been through tonight, he had to get into her—deep into her—as far as he could possibly sheath himself. He needed to feel her close about him, needed the intimacy as desperately as he did his very next breath. Damn their captors or anyone else who would try to stop the two of them from joining.

Bracing upward onto his elbows, he turned his head to the side and stared down into her clear blue eyes. He had to be sure she was all right making love to him in this form; hell, the scent of her alone had driven him into a frenzy, but he had no illusions that she felt the same. In this state, he was grotesque and huge, the skin of his chest and thighs as rough as sandpaper against her much softer, satiny flesh. "Shelby?" he asked, swallowing to adjust his voice. "Are you . . . sure?"

She blinked back at him as he worked his way another inch inside of her. More than half of his hard length was in her now, but man, he needed more. To be deeper, to feel this woman all about him. She lifted a hand to his chest, placing her palm over his heart, and he stilled his hips against hers.

"Too much?"

She shook her head. "I just wanted to feel you here," she said, fixing him with her gaze. "I remember how you reacted the last time I stroked your chest."

He felt his face flush. The thick hide across his muscular chest was actually pliable and very sensitive to stroking. He arched his back, purring in pleasure, his eyes drifting shut. Shelby worked her hands over his nipples, budding them beneath her fingertips, then caressed outward in spirals. In reaction, he began to move within her, working his cock back and forth inside her slick heat.

He slid a hand to the place where their bodies were joined, trying to angle a bit better. "I'm sorry I'm so big," he whispered. "That there's so much of me."

"You're beautiful," she murmured, staring up at him.

Deeper he went, and a little deeper still, his lips parting with a sweet cry of pleasure. He didn't even mind that he sounded Antousian; didn't even bother stopping the humming vibration that had begun in the back of his throat—his species' truest expression of sublime and total pleasure.

Shelby let her eyes drift shut, wrapping both arms around Jake's tough, muscular back. His was the body of a warrior, or some sort of mythical creature; hewn of leather and softness. The whole of her being was quaking at his touch, reacting with tremors that shot through her core, over and over again. Already, she'd come at his touch, her body tightening about his, reacting and thrusting, and they'd only been at this for such a short time.

Oh, yes, she thought, arching at his strokes and touches, lapping up every single one of his caresses. This was the sweetest place, the most heavenly one that he'd ever taken her so far—in any form.

In any form, she thought, a dark pall coming over her.

If she just kept her eyes shut, she wouldn't have to remember that he was Antousian—that he looked

Antousian. She wouldn't recall that he shared blood with Nate and with her enemies. The man was a rutting stallion, with his mighty, long cock that couldn't quite fit all the way inside of her, and his heaving chest that kept sucking at air helplessly. She tried to focus on the thrilling sensations he was arousing in her, and blocked out everything else.

But even with her eyes shut, she heard the vibrating purr emanating from the back of Jake's throat, totally alien—and growing louder by the moment. She'd never been around a happy Antousian, only bloodthirsty ones, but as he nuzzled her and hitched her legs tighter about him, the rumbling grew even louder. Alien. *Good lord, after everything I've been through, how is it I'm letting myself be screwed senseless by an Antousian?*

She shivered, involuntarily clasping his hips and stilling him.

His eyes flew open and he fixed his stare on her. "What's wrong?" The vibrato stopped.

She shook her head, leaning back into the pillow. "Nothing, Jake. I'm just fine." She stroked fingertips down the length of his ridged nose. Jake stared at her, his black eyes growing bright. "Don't gaze me," she said, "just don't do that."

He blinked, roughly stroking her hair. "Sorry." He made a rumbling sound. "I thought you were enjoying this."

"I am enjoying it!" She drew him much closer, pulling his face into the crook of her neck. "I'm also scared shitless, baby, but you're doing amazing things to me. Incredible, beautiful things."

Lifting his head, he made eye contact again, his brow creasing. "You're frightened of me? Because I'm like this?" His voice cracked over the last word, and he cleared his throat self-consciously. "I'm Antousian. You've always known it."

She cupped his face, taking hold of his distended jaws. "But I've never made love to an Antousian before—at least, not in his natural form. You're a first for me, that's all," she said, working desperately to silence the quiet voice of dismay that sounded inside her heart.

Shaking his head, he raised his hips and unsheathed himself.

"Hey, don't do that." She took hold of his shoulders, pulling at him, but Jake could only retreat.

This had been the ultimate vulnerability for him, sharing his Antousian form with her on such an intimate basis. Lifting off of her, he strode toward the far side of the room, where his clothes lay in a heap, aware that his ungainly steps were more stalking than actually walking.

Reaching for the jeans, he stepped into them, and tossed the leather vest on next. With a glance in the mirror he saw himself—truly saw himself—as Shelby probably had. A man who was gigantic in proportion, with a chest like a tree trunk and with large, doleful black eyes that were set slightly to the sides of his harsh-planed face.

He lifted a hand to his jaw, long like a wolf's, and ran his fingertips over the ridges. "I don't blame you," he said softly, not turning to face Shelby. He caught sight of her in the mirror, the blanket gathered about her naked body, shimmering tears in her beautiful blue eyes.

"You don't understand, Jakob."

"Oh, but I do. I am everything the Refarians hate." He scraped his palm over the top of his bare head, feeling the plated ridge that ran from his nose all the way to the top of his spine. "And I'm everything I have always despised, so I can hardly blame you, Shell." With a parting glance at her he said, "Don't worry—it won't happen again."

She tried to call after him, but before she could get a word out, he'd already closed the door that joined their two rooms, leaving her speechless—and wet and desperate, without any real release. *Damn you, girl,* she cursed herself. There she'd gone again, putting her foot right in it.

Collapsing back onto the bed, the sheets still warm from their bodies—especially Jake's hotter-blooded one—she drew herself into a ball and began to cry for real. It had been so many years since she'd loved a man like this; hell, who was she kidding? She'd never loved any man like she did Jakob Tierny. And after all that time, to fall in love with someone who was so ill equipped to feel and receive her love, who was haunted by the demons of his past and of what he truly was. Just as she was haunted by her own history.

Burying her face in her pillow, she wept. She thought of Nate and his lies, but also of how he'd saved her. She flashed on a collage of faces, many of them much like the one she'd just caressed, saw the fire overtaking them all in the hangar, the way the Antousians had howled and screamed, the sound like nothing she'd ever heard in her life. Those terrorized voices had mingled with the dying voices of her friends, of so many people she'd cared for and loved. Flinching, she could smell the intense smoke, the searing flesh, and her soft tears became absolute sobs.

Jake thought she was revolted by his appearance when what he couldn't possibly understand was that she desired him totally, in all his forms. But his Antousian one brought back so many painful, horrific memories that had nothing to do with him, and she wasn't sure she could ever get past those emotions.

"I want him to understand," she whimpered into her pillow, clutching it to ward off the incredible loneliness that she felt.

Jake closed the door that separated his room from Shelby's and slowly slid toward the carpeted floor. He roared his anguish, leaning against the door in an oversized heap of muscle and harsh skin. Burying his face within his palms, he felt tears sting his eyes. Again he threw his head back, bellowing his pain. He couldn't contain his shame and his rage, and with clutched hands he beat at the floor. He felt strangely relieved to find his Antousian voice—this part of him that could roar like the wild thing he truly was.

If this was what his captors had wanted to show him—that he wasn't any different than they, that the same blood coursed through his veins and defined his physical body as did theirs—then they'd won their battle. How many of these creatures, ones exactly as he now appeared, had he killed over the years? Hundreds, perhaps thousands. And yet here he was, forced to confront his true nature.

Hope had always been so blessedly kind to him, so accepting of his Antousian body the few times she'd seen it. But they'd never made love or been intimate, not like this; she'd never even glimpsed him naked in his original form, not like Shelby just had. More than that, Hope had come to him without any preconceived notions about what it meant to be Antousian, without a lifetime of memories of war—of bloodshed and loss and terror, like Shelby did. Oh, yes, it had been far simpler for Hope to accept his *vlksai* form; she'd come to him completely innocent of their war's menacing, brutal face.

With a glance across the room, he noticed the floor-length mirror. Slowly, he rose to his feet and with ungainly steps crossed to the silvery object, staring abjectly at the creature whose image confronted him. He filled the frame completely with his broad, hide-covered shoulders and chest, with his fathomless black eyes and permanently jutting erection that practically touched the mirror's surface, it extended so long. Planting one hand along the edge of the mirror frame, he reached with the other and enclosed his cock, slowly stroking it. Curious about its natural texture and feel. After all, he'd avoided his true form for his entire life.

The sensations that shot through his body caused his other hand to crush around the wooden frame. Gods, nothing could have prepared him. As sensual as he had always been, as much as he'd craved and sought sex, gods. Gods. *Nothing, nothing,* he thought, trembling with every tug he gave his thick, coarse length.

Shelby, he wanted to cry, pressing his face against the glass. *Shelby, please. Have mercy. Have mercy on me tonight.*

Newly purposed, he spun back toward the door that separated them. He'd never needed a woman's touch quite like he needed hers at this moment. Hope had taken him to nirvana and back, but what he needed tonight was to feel Shelby Tyler's acceptance. And by All, he needed the peace and release that only she could offer him.

The door that separated their two rooms opened gently, and Shelby bolted upright on her bed. Jake stood in the doorway, hesitating, a slip of moonlight limning his body beautifully. And he truly was beautiful to her in that moment.

"Come back over here, you big lug," she whispered, opening her arms to him. "Right now."

He kept his distance, tilting his head slightly to the side and studying her. "I don't want to hurt you, sweetheart. It's the last thing I want to do."

"I know that. Just come here," she practically begged, feeling tears burn her eyes once again. "Please come to me, Jakob."

Very slowly, he moved toward her, closing the distance between them. "I know all the memories going on in your head right now, when you look at me. I get that."

She swallowed, shaking her head. "They don't matter. Just come here."

When he stood unmoving, feet planted wide apart, she finally climbed out of bed. Taking his large hand in hers, she led him to lie down. She threaded her fingers together with his, feeling how the pads of his fingertips were calloused and harsh—yet his fingers themselves were long and elegant. Beautifully formed, like he might play a masterpiece on the *dulisthrama*. Or along the length of her body.

They settled beside each other on the edge of her bed. "I know I frighten you," he admitted in that thick vibrato of his, turning to face her.

She planted a palm against his chest, feeling the fast, uneasy tempo of his heartbeat. "I'm falling for you, Jakob," she admitted without even meaning to do so. "And that terrifies me."

"I won't hurt you," he promised softly, reaching his long fingers to stroke her cheek. The rough texture of his hands against her smooth skin aroused her intensely.

"We're gonna do this my way, okay?" she said. "I'm in control for once."

"Anything you ask of me." He gulped visibly, his long jaw twitching with emotion.

"Lie down on your back," she coached him. "Right there, just flat on your back. I'm gonna show you how this can work right."

Blinking his large black eyes, he nodded, unfolding his rangy body elegantly along the length of the bed. With both palms, she stroked his chest, feeling the tough skin, and smiling at the look of catlike pleasure that came over his face. Once again, the alien, rhythmic sound began in the back of his throat.

Without hesitating, she straddled him, planting her much smaller hips atop his. His long erection pushed against her belly, giving a jerk as she adjusted herself. Bending low, she kissed him gently on the lips, amazed by their satiny smoothness. On a breath, she whispered, "Your mouth's like velvet. So soft." Shockingly soft. With the tips of her fingers, she stroked his lips, and his purring sound grew much louder.

Lifting onto her knees, she reached between their hips and took his swollen erection within her palm. The moment her fingers folded about him, he arched wildly into the mattress, his full lips parting with an expression of ecstasy.

"Never," was all he could seem to moan, despite working his mouth and jaws to say more.

"Never what?" she teased, running her fingertips along his length.

"Never . . . this amazing," he gasped, turning his head to the side with a strangled cry of pleasure.

She slid her hand along his erection again, loving the play of brutal harshness that melded with the same softness of his lips. Again, he squirmed beneath her, helpless and gorgeous because of it.

He was hers completely, totally controlled, totally helpless, and she'd never been wetter for him.

"Take me inside of you," he half begged, thrusting his hips upward, trying to find her opening. She lifted out of reach.

"My rules, cowboy," she reminded him. "My timing."

When he opened his black eyes and stared up at her, the emotion in his expression was so leveling, so much more than she'd expected, she knew there'd be no waiting. She raised up slightly, bearing down atop him so that several inches of his hardness slipped into her.

He clutched at her hips, already almost to the edge, and wished like hell that he could get all the way inside of her. Her long blond hair loose and wild about her shoulders, the moon filtering in from the windows beyond them . . . well, she was the closest thing to heaven that he'd ever hoped to find again.

"More." He panted, jutting his hips upward, trying to get in deeper. "Please take more of me. I want you to have all of me."

Hell, he didn't care that she'd reduced him to begging. He didn't care if they both died in an hour. This moment was so beautiful, so perfect, he could live off the memories of it for the rest of his natural life.

Rotating her pelvis slightly, never taking her gaze off of his eyes, she managed to come down on him more securely, several more inches sliding up inside of her.

"Yeah, baby, yeah," he moaned greedily, right as she began to rock and move against him, gyrating like the sweet, wild thing he'd come to love.

Oh, gods in heaven, he did love her, he realized with a swelling feeling inside of his chest. Somehow, this woman had taken his heart completely.

"I love you," he blurted, falling into a frenzied pace that matched her own. "Shelby Tyler, I've fallen so hard for you, so deep. I . . . love . . . you!" he shouted, not caring how loud he was. Not caring who heard . . . and not even caring that she didn't say the words in return.

She cradled his naked form from behind, slowly stroking her fingertips along the ridge of his scalp. Tears flowed down her cheeks, and occasionally she would press a kiss against his bare head. Their lovemaking had been off the charts, beyond anything she had experienced with him before in his human form—and that had been amazing enough. Maybe the intensity was because of their desperation, their fears at being held captive; and maybe because they were finally baring their souls to each other fully.

His ragged, thick breaths caused his chest to rise unevenly as he slept, and she dared to run her fingertips across his hairless abdomen, trailing them along his muscular, defined pectorals. One thing was certain: He possessed an absolutely mythic body, defined by planes of muscle and tanned skin. If not for the hide-like texture, she would have considered him blessed by the gods. But even the rough quality of his skin electrified her body, gave him an edge of danger that drove her wild.

Mentally she compared the contours of his musculature with those of his humanized form. And, even oddly enough, of the man he'd once been, Scott Dillon. How many faces could this lover of hers show her? It was chilling, and she began to tremble against him. With a downward glance, she studied his thick shaft, the way it saluted skyward, the soft skin that covered one side, and the much harsher hide that encased the rest of it.

All Antousian men were permanently erect—she'd learned that one the first time she'd killed one of his kind, horrified to see a tenting bulge in his uniform pants even after she'd slit his throat. A fellow soldier had whispered vile things in her ear about how depraved the Antousians were, that they were forever saluting and ready to rape. Later she'd learned the real truth of it in a textbook. She'd also read, much to her chagrin, that it was a topic of great shyness and embarrassment for many Antousian males. They put a lot of effort into concealing their members, tying them down with a leather sling so the bulge wouldn't pop through their pants and wouldn't distract them from the tasks of their everyday lives.

Only then had she remembered that the Antousian she'd killed had been stabbed along the thigh, his uniform rent. Undoubtedly she'd forced the poor fool's cock to spring free, almost as if it were begging for some last moment of pleasure. She shivered, remembering the look of him that day, and again cast a tentative glance toward Jake's prominent, jutting erection.

Pressing her lips against the top of his head, she realized he didn't even know about those kinds of clothing rituals or how to treat his own body. He had no experience whatsoever with what he truly was—hence his overwhelming stimulation at having his Antousian cock stroked for the first time in his life. Even after he'd pumped up into her, throwing his head back with animal-like cries of pleasure, filling her with his thick alien semen, he'd remained taut as a fully cocked K-12—longer, she would have sworn, than when he'd first entered her.

She kept stroking the crown of his head, rubbing her fingers across the ridges, at once fascinated and repulsed by his body. With him sleeping, she could study it freely and let her gaze roam the length of him, touching, exploring. But flashes of memories warred for dominance in her mind: She saw the Texas warehouse going up in flames, heard the high shrieking screams of the Antousians who'd been caught in the explosion. Fell to her knees again, wailing at the knowledge that Nate was inside, dead . . . and that he'd betrayed all of them so mercilessly.

I cared for you, she heard Nate telling her a few hours earlier. Total *meshdki.* He'd ruined her, tapped her dry so that now, when she'd found the true love of her life, she had nothing left to give. Her heart was too damaged; Jake was too much a reminder of all the horrors she'd experienced.

If only . . . if only her past had been different, she thought, tears brimming in her eyes. If only her heart weren't so terribly broken.

He stirred slightly against her, and she wrapped both arms about him, closing her eyes. The thing that she couldn't admit—couldn't bear to confess, not to him or even to All—was that she'd found sex with this particular Antousian wildly arousing, even in his natural state. The form of her enemy.

Never again, she swore, reluctantly releasing her hold on him. *I can't love my enemy, even if his heart is pure. I can't want this Antousian body and the memories it brings back.*

As if hearing her thoughts, Jake moved, taking hold of her arms and wrapping them low across his abdomen. The lamplight bathed his body in a golden hue, causing his tanned skin to appear radiant. She heard the smile in his voice when he mumbled, "Hey, sweetheart. You awake?"

She kept herself still, closing her eyes and feigning sleep, letting her breathing assume a quiet, even rhythm. For a long moment, he kept his hands over hers, then blew out a contented sigh, drawing first one of her hands to his mouth and then the other. "You sleep, then, sweet Shelby."

Jake believed that she loved him, and gods help her, she did. Terribly, beautifully, she was just crazy in love with the man now lying in her arms. So much so that she was terrified of him. Totally frightened beyond reason because he had the capacity to destroy her even more thoroughly than Nate once had.

Jake believed that this was the beginning of a real future together for them, not what it actually was: the heartbreaking end of what might have been. If she were a braver soldier—at least on this emotional battlefield—she would tell him everything right now. After all, he of all people deserved the truth; it was the only fair thing to give a man whose heart had been battered and destroyed like this one's had. But she didn't want to be another person who hurt him—not yet, not until she absolutely had to. Perhaps that was the reason why she said nothing, but lay with her legs still wrapped about him and let him believe for just a little while longer that their hearts had melded as one.

Chapter Twenty-two

Shelby woke to find Jake on the far side of the room, already dressed. He'd covered her with a blanket, tucked it up neatly beneath her chin and around her body as if she was precious to him, priceless. The loving care such treatment displayed made her chest tighten.

She blinked her eyes, watching him drop into an intense set of push-ups, unaware that she was observing his maneuvers. His Antousian forearms rippled powerfully as, over and over, he dipped toward the floor, then lifted again. Clearly he was working to keep himself primed and ready for whatever might lie ahead of them. With a slight stretch, she turned in the bed and noticed that day was breaking outside the window.

Jake popped to his feet. "You're awake."

She smiled at him, yawning. "Barely."

He started moving toward her when a thunderous noise from the steps outside interrupted him. Someone was coming, and Jake dropped into a crouch beside the door while Shelby scrambled for her discarded clothing. But she didn't have time to so much as pull on her dress before the door opened loudly and several soldiers filed in.

The leader, a mahogany-haired woman, waved the others into the room. Jake's reaction to this woman's appearance surprised her: Instead of tensing up, he relaxed slightly, almost as though he knew her.

And then the last member of the group entered. At the sight of him, Shelby literally shrank back against the wall.

Not him, not again, she thought, beginning to tremble all over. She tugged the blanket protectively over her naked body, wishing like hell that the human Tierny wasn't back in her physical space again. A protective hand slid to her throat as she recalled the way he'd manacled her.

Why hadn't she dressed sooner? Why hadn't she been prepared, she thought, but all her fears dimmed to nothing the moment that *her* Jake laid eyes on his enemy. Before any of the gathered soldiers could stop him, Jake rushed Tierny and grabbed the bastard's neck with a strangehold.

"Why the fuck'd you do it?" Jakob snarled at the man, his Antousian biceps bulging with unrestrained power. "You tell me *why* right now!"

Tierny's human eyes bulged wide as he pried at the strong alien hands clasped about his throat. The dark-haired female barked a command, and the other soldiers began backing out of the door.

"Who . . . are . . . you?" Tierny rasped, and after a long moment, Jakob let him drop to the floor like dead weight. But he gave no quarter, squatting level with his crumpled foe.

"Who am I? I'm your enemy, that's who I am. I'm the man whose wife you murdered five years in the future." With a menacing, deadly snap of his Antousian jaws, he went on: "I am *Scott Dillon*. And now you will tell me why you were there, on that battlefield, and why you killed my mate. Otherwise"—Jakob curled back his upper lip, growling like a feral creature and eyeing Tierny's exposed neck—"I'll kill you now, you human freak."

Jake bore down on his prey. Years. Years he had waited for this moment of payback, but he'd be damned if he didn't find out the reason behind Hope's murder before finishing Tierny this second time. He needed answers, craved them almost as much as he did making the pathetic human before him suffer for his crimes. Like Hope had suffered, and baby Leisa had suffered.

Tierny rasped, sliding a hand over his throat as he tried to recover, his green eyes cold and menacing.

At last, the human spoke. "You're blaming me? For your wife's death?" He coughed, sputtered . . . and then, before Jake could anticipate it, he lunged against him, knocking him to the floor. Jake's large bald head hit with a crack, and Tierny was atop him in a flash.

Nothing could have prepared Jake for the words that the human snarled at him next. "You Antousian *nank*," he roared, slamming a fist against Jake's long jawbone. "You're the reason *my* wife died. You. I blame you! I've been hunting you down for three years."

Again, a fist slammed into Jakob's jaw with a cracking sound that caused bright spots to appear before his eyes. "Wh-what? I never hurt your wife. . . ."

"You slept with her! Just another one-night stand for you, but for me—" The human went wild, pummeling Jake's face harder and harder. From his violent outburst, Jake realized exactly how Tierny's wife had died—at the hands of her murderous, jealous husband. *Not my problem,* Jake thought, determined to regain control of his adversary. He had to protect Shelby, had to protect Hope in this time. In a roaring frenzy, Jake rose, thrusting the smaller man off of him.

The tables now turned, Jakob had his opponent pinned up beneath his massive, alien weight. "I slept with lots of women," he snarled, snapping his jaws against Tierny's face. "All over town. If your wife was one of 'em, that's your problem. But you killed my wife and my baby. In the future, you robbed me of everything." Jakob slid his rough hands about the man's throat, choking again. "Now you will pay."

"My wife . . . died," the human gurgled at him. Jake had to understand the truth and allowed his eyes to glow bright, soul-gazing his enemy. The waves of fury and hatred that radiated out of the man nearly caused Jake to pass out, the blackness of all the emotions were that terrible. It was true: The human had murdered his wife in a jealous rage. Not because of any particular one-night stand, but a whole string of them: The one with Scott had just been the one to finally send this killer over the edge. And he'd fixated on Scott as the cause.

"Your wife died because you killed her," Jake shot back at him, finally understanding the truth after so many years. "And so you killed mine to punish me . . . for your own crimes."

Jake allowed his hands to grow slack about the human's throat, shaking his head. But then his grip grew tight again as he said, "And what about my baby girl? What did she ever do to you? She was perfect, and you snuffed out her life before she even got to begin it."

With a roar from deep within his Antousian throat, Jakob closed in . . . and finished a killing that had begun on a battlefield five years earlier.

While the two men battled it out on the floor of the cabin, Kryn hurriedly explained to Shelby that she worked for Thea as her spy.

"You're helping us?" Shelby asked in wide-eyed surprise, sliding into her wraparound dress.

Kryn hesitated briefly, then bent her mouth to Shelby's ear. "Yes. Now, hurry. I can get you out of here." She cocked her luminator and tossed a familiar dagger onto the bed beside Shelby. "You'll want this back, I think."

Shelby took it in her hand, searching for her boots. Their stiletto heels would make another good weapon. With a glance toward Jakob, she saw that he'd accomplished his goal: Tierny lay slumped and lifeless on the floor. She barely had time to register that fact before several armed guards practically knocked the door off its hinges.

Wielding her dagger as first one, then a second, and a third Antousian soldier tried to attack her, Shelby barely had time to think. All her years of fury at Nate came roaring to the surface as she stabbed and kicked and flailed. Around her she heard grunting and panting, but there was another noise closer at hand: her own screaming.

Vengeance. She wanted her own taste of it—for all her friends who'd died, for what her enemies had done to her king, for all of it. Bodies fell about them, and she wouldn't be stopped. With a flick of her dagger, she went after the largest of her attackers, an Antousian in his natural form who was even taller than Jake. At least the other two were in their humanized forms, she thought, watching Kryn battle them single-handedly from the corner of her eye. Still, she was at least a foot and a half smaller than her attacker, and no matter how deftly she might wield her dagger, it would be no match for the looming figure coming at her.

With a flick of the alien's hand, she was on the floor, flattened. Her dagger had been kicked out of reach, too, leaving her gasping and vulnerable. She glanced toward Kryn, who had somehow—mercifully—gotten the upper hand with her two assailants, one of whom was now coldcocked and on the floor. Kryn never looked back at her, manning her K-12 expertly and focusing only on their attackers. Grabbing one of her boots, Shelby rose to her feet once more, unsteady but eager to face down her opponent. The man was massive, monumental, and he gave a brutal roar as he rushed her. Extending the stiletto heel of her boot, she catapulted against his beefy chest, closing her eyes and praying for the best.

Her attacker released an eerie exhalation, almost like a sigh, and sank to his knees. He cupped both hands over his eyes, muttering in Antousian until—after what seemed an eternity—he doubled over with a gurgling sigh.

When she was sure no one else would attack, Shelby dropped to the floor, gasping, sobbing. With a quick glance, she watched as Kryn finished off her own skirmish, holstering her weapon triumphantly. *Good,* she thought, *at least that's one battle we've won.* But she had no strength left inside of her, and curled against the floor.

After several moments, a large pair of hands drew up underneath Shelby's arms. "Shell, sweetheart, come on. It's done. Come on, we've got to roll."

She gave her head a stunned little shake. Jake got more urgent. "We're out of time, baby. Now or never, let's go!"

"I know where they're holding Jared," Kryn told them breathlessly, leading the way out of the door, but not before they'd armed themselves with the luminators the Antousians had dropped. Shelby kept her dagger in her hand, ignoring the blood that dripped from its sharp edge, and hoisted one of the luminators across her chest.

"Follow me," Kryn ordered. "Stay tight with me, and maybe we'll all make it out of here alive."

Shelby grabbed her hand. "Not yet. I can find out how we need to get out of here . . . but I need about five minutes."

Jake shook his head. "No way, Shelby. I'm not letting you try it."

"What do you have in mind?" Kryn asked, eyeing the door.

"I can time walk. It will tell us what we need to know."

Jake's large eyes slid shut. "It's too fucking dangerous for you—besides, there's not enough time."

"Time is all we have right now, Jakob," she told him softly. "Now, let me do my job."

Convulsing in Jake's arms, Shelby returned to consciousness, her mind riddled with images from her time walk. She'd followed the short thread, walking its length, seeing five, ten . . . maybe twenty minutes of what was to come in the immediate future. With a gasp, she lifted out of her fugue, and Jake clutched her tight within his arms.

She turned to face Kryn, who was crouched beside her on the floor, and addressed her. "I saw an aircraft. Antousian, midsized fighter." She sucked at the air, still shaking all over. "You're going to pilot us out of here, but there's a problem we have to avoid along the way."

Jake stroked her hair, trying to soothe her tremors. "Tell us what to do."

"Whatever they have Jared in, it's a containment system. . . ." She stared up into Jake's eyes. "I saw you failing to free him. Kryn gets the craft, but we don't get Jared. Not unless we can spring him from the glass prison he's in."

Kryn glanced back and forth between the door and Shelby. "I don't have the codes for dismantling the containment grid."

Shelby nodded, trying to breathe, aware that her body seemed to be fracturing crazily because of the visions in her mind. "But I saw another way," she finally managed to get out, still gasping. "Jake, it's you. You're the only one who can get him out. There was a second time thread, an alternate one. Kryn, you go after that craft, Jake and I free Jared."

"Tell me what to do," he said.

They moved slowly through the basement of the warehouse, back down the same dank hallways where they'd been captured the night before. The memories were hideous to Shelby as she passed the torture room where Jake had pinned her to the table, but lifting her luminator shoulder high, she crept ahead, taking the lead for Jakob.

Lifting a finger, she pointed toward the end of the hallway, and at last they reached the door. There was a keypad that required a security code, and Shelby closed her eyes, trying to configure the numbers from her vision. Taking a deep breath and hoping she was remembering correctly, she input the data. A moment later, the door sprang open.

Jake entered ahead of her, sweeping the room with

his weapon and his gaze, and waved her in. Dead ahead, suspended in the middle of the room, was the tall glass cell that she'd seen in her vision, and swirling in the center, his energy a dull yellow-gold, was the natural form of their leader and king. Long and narrow, the cell allowed only a few scant inches of width, not enough room to ever allow the man to change back into his physical body.

Jake turned to Shelby, black eyes swimming with painful emotion. "Now go to him," she explained in a whisper, "and soul-gaze him."

"I don't understand."

"His mental state will be devastating to you, but that's not the important thing. Be strong, battle past it . . . and use your gazing ability to rupture the glass shields."

Jake shrank back. "I don't possess that kind of power, Shell."

She reached high, taking hold of both his shoulders. "Today you do. Now go! We don't have much time."

Jake took several loping steps forward, his hulking Antousian frame glowing from the power captured within the cell. Hesitating, he reached out a hand and touched the surface of Jared's prison. Although Shelby couldn't see his face, the glass before him began to glow even brighter, a slight moaning sound coming from Jake's direction.

She'd foreseen this: his immense grief at Jared's pain.

"Press on," she encouraged, but she stayed back against the wall—not because she didn't want to support him, but because of what was about to happen. "You are the one, Jakob, but protect yourself. That glass is going to shatter with a huge amount of force."

Jake gave a nod, and then as if in reaction, the room all about them grew brighter and seemed to explode from the inside out. Shelby was thrown face-first to the floor, a massive roaring sound filling the entire area as thousands of glass shards flew in every direction. Then, as if they'd freed a bolt of supernatural lightning, Jared flung past them, down the hall, a loud, erratic noise following in his wake.

"He's out to destroy all of our enemies!" she shouted over the maelstrom.

Jake struggled to his feet. "But that's just putting him at risk of being captured all over again. I have to go after him."

Shelby rode out the heat wave, staying glued to the floor. "You're not going to stop him—not this time, Jake. He's simply not rational right now. He's spent too many hours in his natural form."

"Will he be all right?" Jake shouted over the wind and noise.

"I didn't see that far! But we've got to get going toward the craft."

"No!" Jake shouted, struggling to move into the hallway even though a gale-force wind battered the length of it. "I have to get Jared out of here safely. You go ahead. We'll meet you there!"

Shelby didn't like the plan, but it was clear she'd never convince Jake to do otherwise, so she started running.

Shelby tore across the open field, the early morning sun sparkling over the dewy grass. Barefoot, she ignored the slicing pain of rocks and other debris that cut into the soles of her feet, and made for the craft as Kryn lowered it unsteadily into the middle of the vast, open space. Behind her, she sensed soldiers, was aware that she was being pursued. But driven forward by the images from her time walk, she didn't dare slow down.

When she was only ten feet from the aircraft, a gangway lowered before the transport had solidly touched ground. She didn't look back, tried not to think about her king or about Jakob, and launched herself at the steps, catching hold with her forearms and dangling slightly above the earth below.

Suddenly, the aircraft opened fire, spattering the landscape with a hail of luminous shrapnel—nearly tossing Shelby back to the ground in the process. The wind kicked up all around her, blinding her and throwing her loose hair up into her eyes; still, she held to the plank, refusing to let go.

When the shooting stopped, she crawled up into the transport's belly, and only then did she glance back over her shoulder—just in time to witness the entire warehouse exploding into a giant fireball that threw her against the exposed floor of the cabin. The aircraft jolted, spun first in one direction, then another, by shockwaves from the blast, and for a moment she was certain that Kryn was going to lift off without waiting for Jared and Jake.

Wailing, Shelby watched as explosion after explosion rocked the warehouse. "Jakob!" she shrieked, hitching her arm through the accordion-like extension of the gangplank and holding tight for her life. "Oh, gods above, Jakob! My lord, my king!" She wailed and sobbed, inching backward until she sprawled on the floor of the transport.

Still Kryn kept the transport hovering low, as if she expected survivors, but Shelby knew differently. She'd already lived this moment once before, years ago, and the grief that overcame her was instantaneous. Huddling on her knees, pressing her face against the grooved floor, she folded herself into a ball. Into nothing. Because after today, there would be nothing left of her soul.

Then . . . after many long moments, a familiar vibrato sound startled her. "Go! Go! Go!" she heard Jake shout in his husky Antousian voice, and she felt his thunderous footsteps as he bounded onto the craft. Lifting her tear-stained face, she watched in shock as he lurched past her.

"Get down!" Jake urged. "Jared's behind me, and he'll scorch you alive." He launched himself atop her, burying her against the floor, and she felt a firestorm blaze past her. Still unable to believe what was happening, she glanced up just in time to see the glowing body of her commander hurl beyond her, toward the back of the craft. He'd made himself small and compact, even though he radiated enough energy to power a small nuclear arsenal.

She didn't even have time to react before the aircraft rapidly ascended, the gangway only halfway closed as they assumed full throttle.

Jake sank hard against the padded bench seat, not even bothering with buckling up. Shelby sat across the aisle from him, avoiding his gaze. He lifted his forearm to his nose; he hated the smoky smell that permeated his nostrils and had no doubt that the warehouse explosion had unlocked an unending litany of vicious memories for Shelby. He tried to catch her eye, shifted his legs uncomfortably, and finally quietly called out her name.

She trained her gaze on her bare feet. "I'm okay," was all she said.

"Come sit beside me," he prodded gently, patting the empty seat. "I want to talk to you."

She gave her head a slight shake, not looking up, and he shifted his long legs out into the aisle, bumping his left calf against hers. "Hey, you, get over here. Stat."

At last she lifted her gaze, and he saw such terror in the blue depths of her eyes, it nearly killed him. He didn't wait for her but rose to his feet and lurched unsteadily across the aisle. The craft definitely wasn't flying smooth and even, but he had to hand it to Kryn: For an inexperienced pilot, the woman was doing all right. They all owed her their lives, and it was a debt he figured they'd be paying for a long time to come.

He collapsed beside her, exhausted. "Look at me, baby," he said, turning to face Shelby. After a long moment, she finally tilted her face upward. "Are you all right?"

She wiped at her eyes, said nothing, and then finally whispered, "I thought you died. For a few minutes back there, I was sure you were gone."

He firmly grasped her by both shoulders. "I'm right here. We're out of that shit storm. We're all right. We've got Jared. Everything's going to be okay."

She gave a little nod. "Guess I just need to process that fact. That's all."

A curious burning began at the base of Jake's spine, but he tried to ignore it, shoving the sensation to the periphery of his consciousness. "You need rest. And to be held for a long, long time, Shell. Everything will feel normal again once we're home."

Again she nodded—but said nothing.

The achy burn along Jake's spine lifted higher, spreading upward into his shoulder blades and into the base of his ridged scalp. *Oh, shit. Not now. Any time but right now,* he thought, shifting uncomfortably. With a fast glance, he wondered if he could make it to the back of the craft where they were holding Jared. Staggering unsteadily to his feet, he started to make for that direction—anything so Shelby wouldn't see what had to be coming next—but it was too late.

"What's wrong?" she asked him in alarm, right as his entire body began to quake and tremor.

Not now, not now. Not like this.

"I—I . . . the serum is wearing off. . . . I'm gonna . . . Gods, Shelby!" He threw his head back and roared his anguish, dropping heavily to his large Antousian knees. And right then, his body began to splinter, to tear apart at its very axis, as if his backbone were shrinking and realigning. As if his skin was suddenly too big and his head too small.

As if he was going to die.

Shelby watched in horror as Jake collapsed face-first to the craft's floor, writhing and shifting in agony. His bones and flesh shrank, stretched a little, then shrank some more. His thick skin grew softer, moving over flesh and bone. He screamed in a voice that she'd hoped to never hear come out of his throat, and after a moment's hesitation, she fell atop him, holding him.

"It'll be over soon," she cried over his tormented

groans and shouts. "Hang on, Jakob. Just ride it out. Ride it out."

She buried her face against his rough shoulders, feeling the way his bulky body transformed and altered, knowing to the depths of her soul how he suffered.

It didn't seem fair that they'd done this to him, the way they'd forced him to shift, and now that he had to go through such agony to transform again.

Then a thought popped into her mind: What if he didn't live through it? She gripped him tighter, praying that he'd survive. At last, after an endless whirlwind of torment, his body fell, exhausted and still against the grooved floor of the craft, and she collapsed atop him.

"You got through it," she murmured against his much more familiar shoulders, relishing the smoothness of the humanized skin. "You're okay. You're almost home."

He mumbled something, groaning, clutching at the floor. "Shell, Shell."

"I've got you, big boy." She pressed her cheek against his sweaty shoulder. "I'm holding on tight."

"Don't leave me, please," he murmured, and she knew that he was talking about far more than this moment. He understood how spooked she was, what a toll all of this had taken.

"I'm here right now," she whispered in his ear. It was all she could promise; this moment, this time. "I'm holding you close, Scott," she whispered without thinking.

He groaned in reaction. "Don't call me that."

She stroked his brow. "You're still going to try and tell me that you're really Jake Tierny? Puhlease." She laughed softly, pressing a kiss against his cheek.

"Just don't leave." He sighed uneasily.

From the front of the craft, Kryn called out to them. "The base is rejecting my codes. They're interpreting our approach as a hostile one."

"I gave you the proper approach sequence," Shelby argued, panicked.

Jake leaned up on his knees. "But we're in an Antousian craft. They're going to shoot us down if we're not careful," he cautioned, standing unsteadily. "Put me on the comm."

Kryn was silent for a long moment, and Shelby could see her punching at the controls. "They won't accept the hail," she said after a moment, her voice unsteady. "We're flying in there blind."

Jake reached for Shelby's hand, dragging her to her feet. "You'd better buckle up tight," he said. "And prepare for a rough landing. This may get really ugly before we're in there."

"What about Jared?" she asked, glancing toward the rear of the craft. "We have to let them know he's on board. They can't shoot down the king of Refaria!"

Jake shoved her down onto the bench seat, thrusting the harness into her hands. "Buckle up," was all he said. "I'm going to try my best to get through to them."

Their craft cautiously approached what looked like just another stretch of mountainside, though in fact it concealed the lift door to a hangar. Jake offered quiet, urgent prayers to All. Everything rode on this moment, and so far, Base Ten hadn't accepted his hailing on the open frequency. Once again, he spoke into the comm, urgently calling out the code sequence, explaining that he was Lieutenant Scott Dillon, and their leader and king was on board.

No answer at all.

Kryn leveled the craft toward the door, and they all held their breath. Jake would be damned if he didn't do whatever he could to protect his best friend and king.

One last time, he issued an open hail across the frequency, explaining in code who they were, and the exact nature of their precious cargo.

"I can't keep holding steady like this," Kryn shouted, punching at the instruments. "Tailwinds are kicking in and I'm losing control." The craft made a horrible groaning sound, and Jake was just about to lose it totally when all at once the bay door cranked open, allowing them safe passage to the interior.

"Prepare to fire on my mark!" Thea commanded, waving three battalions closer to the Antousian craft. If the codes hadn't been current, they never would have allowed the transport entry, but they had guns ready to fire at the first sign of subterfuge. Two of her snipers took position right beside the craft's hatch, and as it slowly dropped down, the soldiers trained their weapons.

And then Jake's grimy face appeared in the portal, and she shouted, "Stand down! Stand down; hold your fire."

Jake looked like hell as he staggered down the platform. His clothes were falling off of him—oddly too big and in smoky tatters. Shelby came out behind him, looking stunned and equally smoke covered, her face smudged with ash. They'd obviously been through some sort of explosion. And then a willowy dark-haired woman that she'd never seen before popped into view, her eyes filled with anxiety as they darted about the deck. Kryn Zoltners, Thea thought with a smile.

"Kryn!" she called, giving a wave. At first the Antousian didn't know who'd shouted her name but took a hesitant step off the craft. Thea met her partway. "Kryn," she repeated, extending a hand. "I'm Lieutenant Thea Haven. Welcome."

Kryn's eyes widened, a faint smile on her lips. "And so we meet at last, Lieutenant."

Thea inclined her head. "We owe you our lives."

"No. So long as I can stay here, I think I owe you mine."

They exchanged a few more words until, catching sight of Thea, Jake called out to her, "We have Jared. I need help—we need help. . . ."

A twisting, powerless feeling began in Thea's gut. "He's on the craft?" she asked carefully.

Jake gave a nod. "I need to talk to you, Thea. Explain the situation."

At that precise moment, Thea noticed the sound of footsteps. It was one of those times when the sounds around you unfolded too slowly, when you wished you could kick time back by about three seconds. She knew the footsteps belonged to Kelsey, just as she knew that whatever the situation was with Jared, it couldn't be good.

"Is he here?" Kelsey blurted in a desperate voice, huffing and breathless as she pulled up beside them. She glanced between Thea and Jake, gasping and holding tight to her belly.

"My lady," Thea told her softly, "you were supposed to still be resting."

"I heard Jared might be here, and I got here as fast as I could." Kelsey pushed past them, started to walk up the gangway. "Is he still on board? Jared? Jareshk?"

Jake caught Thea's arm and gave his head a firm shake. *Stop her,* his eyes said.

Thea lunged for Kelsey, trying to halt her progress onto the craft, but was too late. Her queen had already rushed onboard and was searching for her mate.

"He's in his natural form still," Jake told her seriously. "I—I am worried about his ability to change back. We tried to get him to shift after we freed him. It was a wonder he followed us at all. . . . He's out of his mind right now, Thea. I soul-gazed him, and what I saw . . . what they did . . ."

"I understand," Thea whispered, emotion tightening her throat. "It's like before, after he was shot down."

Jake bowed his head but said nothing.

"I'll go talk to her . . . and try to link with him," she said, and boarded the craft.

Chapter Twenty-three

Halter tops, jeans, bras—Shelby crammed what little civilian clothing she owned into her open duffel, not bothering to fold any of it. Pausing, she struggled out of the soot-covered dress she'd been wearing when the warehouse exploded. The terrible odor suffused the room, was all over her body and clothing. The scent was downright nauseating, too similar to the way she'd smelled after the Texas fire.

There wasn't time for a shower, either. In a matter of moments, Jake would be busting down her door, splintering it if that's what it took to keep her within the compound. In fact, from what she'd seen, he'd realign the stars themselves if it meant making her understand how much he loved her.

Love would have been a simple issue. The sort of thing you could work your way through, fight your way past. But there just wasn't enough love in the universe to overcome the memories that had swamped Shelby—the burning warehouse, that maniacal, Antousian gleam in his large black eyes as he'd boarded the craft.

She jerked open another drawer, sending a pile of panties scattering into the air like silky snowflakes. Scooping them up, she dropped to her knees and stopped. Everything ground to a painful halt as she touched the pristine underwear, pure and white. Her own hands were filthy, grimy, just like she felt inside.

She was going to destroy Jake. Leaving him would

be the final act, the very thing that would take that man's gentle heart and demolish it once and for all. He'd already lived through enough pain for ten lifetimes, and yet she couldn't stop herself. Tears rolled down her cheeks, and still she knelt, stroking her dirty fingertips across the spotless lingerie. It was the pair Jake had left under her pillow their first night back on base, teasing her about going commando. On each side of the panties were delicate silver bows.

I want to unwrap you, sweetheart, the note had read. *I want to take what binds you and let it loose.*

Wiping at her tears, she wadded the panties into a ball and hurled them furiously at her duffel, missing by a *ketro*.

Get it together, girl. He's on his way now, has to be. That's not a battle you want to fight, so you better get your butt in gear.

She tucked the lingerie into a corner of the duffel, scooped the rest of her underwear in as well, then clamped the bag shut just in time to hear an urgent knock on the door.

Oh, holy hell.

Keeping her body perfectly still and holding her breath, she crouched and waited. No dice; he knocked again, louder and more frantically.

Through her nostrils she inhaled, forcing herself to breathe softly. Not that it mattered: The Antousian hybrid on the other side of the door had such refined senses he could scent her like he would a cold beer ten miles down the road. She buried her face in her hands, keeping silent as hot tears squeezed out of the corners of her eyes. There was no way out, nowhere to run, and definitely no way to avoid looking into Jake's eyes when she broke his heart.

"Pulling your best maneuver, I see."

Jake's voice speared the space between them before he'd fully materialized in front of her. Still, she jolted as his boots appeared practically eye level with where she sat on the floor.

Grabbing her duffel, she rose to her feet, but one

massive hand encircled her upper arm. "You don't go without us talking, Tyler. Evasive action is useless here." His gravelly voice was raw as sandpaper, filled with emotion. She could only imagine what his eyes looked like, so she hung her head, turning to look away from him.

"Can't." Her own voice sounded as rough as his.

For several long moments, they stood frozen in a strange, hypnotic dance, Jake with his hand choking her upper arm, neither speaking. Only the sound of heavy, erratic breathing.

"What do you want from me?" she finally asked.

Jake's other hand took hold of her chin, forcing her to turn and look at him. She resisted, yanking her head sideways, but no way could she stand up to his natural brute strength. He cupped her face again, and she found herself staring into those beautiful, haunting green eyes. Eyes that were practically electric, lit with something primal and alien that she had only just begun to understand.

"You won't leave me," he gritted out. "Not this time, you won't. Never again will you run from me, Shelby."

Tremors shook her whole body. "You don't get to call that shot, sir."

He took hold of her, pressing his lips over hers in a harsh, bitter kiss. Drawing her body flush with his own until she could feel his thick erection, pushing right against her abdomen. With his tongue, he worked at her lips, forcing her to open to him.

And how could she resist? She hadn't a hope or prayer of fighting, not with this man. Never with this man.

Run! You can still get out of here.

She sank her own tongue deep within his mouth, a sensation of reactive energy fanning throughout her entire body. One of his large hands curled around the back of her neck, sliding over her shoulders in a caress. His other snaked low across her back, pinning her tighter against his body.

I've got to leave. Got to run. Safe . . . must be.

Planting both hands against his thickly muscled chest, she gave him a forceful shove. Because he wasn't expecting it, he staggered slightly, but only for a moment.

She wiped her mouth with the back of her hand. "You need to go, right now. I'm leaving, and you should just go back up to the lodge or wherever it is you want to be. But not with me; you won't ever be with me."

He blinked at her, his eyes growing radiant and otherworldly. She spun away from him. "Don't you dare try and gaze me, Tierny."

She grabbed her duffel, heading toward the door.

"How else can I understand why you'd leave me . . . us?" The words, dropped like a prayer, were so quiet she almost missed them. "If I'm going to lose you, Shelby, please just help me get why."

Slowly she rotated to face him. His eyes no longer glowed, but instead were shimmering with dull, quiet emotion. He continued, "I love you, Shell. And it's not easy for me to admit it, not after all that I've lived through in the past ten years. I lost my wife, I lost my baby. But you"—he took a tentative step toward her—"you, I never pegged to be the losing kind."

Her heart wrenched within her, and with trembling lips she whispered, "I'm not losing. I'm leaving."

"I guess, in the end, it's the one thing you do best of all, isn't it?" The words weren't caustic; in fact, his expression was just deeply . . . mournful.

She hurled her duffel across the room, and it ricocheted right off her rack. "You don't know jack about me. Don't even try and go there."

He bent slightly to meet her eye, taking slow, almost menacing steps forward. "I know you very, very well, Shelby Tyler." He broke into a wicked, suggestive smile. "Much better than you could probably begin to guess."

"You've never soul-gazed me! I never let you," she

protested, staggering backward as he drew closer. His very body was a threat, with the broad, powerful shoulders and the smoldering heat and anger in his eyes.

"I never said I did, sweetheart." His voice grew gentle, wooing. "I'm only saying that I love you, and that I know this MO of yours front and back."

She shook her head, backing up again, only to bump right into the bunk bed behind her. Tears stung at her eyes, and she swiped at them. "I don't leave anyone. I don't even know what in hell you're talking about."

"I'm talking about *you*, Shelby. You and me. This thing between us."

"There is no 'us.' "

Jake startled her by tossing his head back and laughing loudly. "Whatever you say, Shell; whatever you say. But I'll tell you *this*." He had closed the distance between them completely, and she had no way to escape as he bore down on her. She clutched protectively at the bed frame behind her.

Jake continued, "I'll tell you the reason I know you so incredibly well, and know why it is you always wind up fleeing. Because I did it for *years*. For years and years I was the one doing the running." He threw his hands into the air. "Gods, I even ran ten years back in time. Know what I found?"

She squeezed her eyes shut, hands over both her ears. "Stop it! Please, shut up already." If he just wouldn't say it; if he'd just keep the truth in poisonous silence between them . . .

"You can't ever get away from the pain inside by running, sweetheart. You run, and it runs with you. Hell! You hide, and it hides, too. So . . . you just keep running and running and running some more. Nothing kills that burn. Nothing, Shell—nothing except one thing . . ."

"And you're going to tell me what that is."

"You have to open your godsdamned heart again." Jake squeezed both of her arms, his voice rising. "You have to stand still for a while. Stand still with me . . . will you, Shell? Here, somewhere else . . . hell, down in fucking Texas, I don't care."

She gaped up at him, searching for words, but the only thing she could conjure up was more and more tears. It was something about Jake staring down into her eyes, making himself so vulnerable and naked. Offering his soul to her like the prize jewel that it was, without wanting anything in return except . . . her.

"I thought you died," she managed to choke out. "I saw that building explode, and I knew you were in there. You were *in there*, Jake! Do you have any idea what I felt? My heart broke apart, my world . . ."

"Just like with Nate," he whispered, pulling her against his chest. She flailed, fighting him, but his strength advantage was too great.

"I saw you die."

"But I didn't die." He cupped her head against his chest. "I'm right here, holding you . . . right here, not letting you run away from me again. I can't watch you leave, any more than you can watch me die."

His fast heartbeat hammered beneath her ear. "Are you going to stop fighting in this godsforsaken war?"

"Never." He pulled her even closer.

"Are you going to stop pushing yourself, always taking such stupid, stubborn chances with your life?"

"No."

She squirmed against him, ducking out of his grasp. *He'll let me go if it's what I really want.* . . . "Then we've got nothing more to discuss." She retrieved her duffel from the floor. "I'm hiking right down to the highway and hitching a ride somewhere else."

"Texas? Oh, I'm sure you'll find your answers there." His words dripped with sarcasm.

"You won't find *me*; that's all you need to know. Wherever I am, it's going to be so far away that none of my people will ever know where I've gone."

"You came back last time, years ago. It took a while, but you did come back."

"Because I knew I was needed. Our forces have

tripled since then, and one less medic won't be missed."

His features hardened. "So it was all in the name of duty." Jake rearranged his pistol, shoving it into the waistband of his pants.

"Careful you don't shoot your dick off with that thing." Shelby gestured at the weapon. "I wouldn't want you to lose your best friend." She wanted to be cruel, wanted to wound, if it meant that he'd let her go.

Before she'd blinked, he had closed the distance that separated them again, taking hold of both her shoulders. "Don't think this is about me." His words were a hissing layer over the rhythmic drone of the cooling vent. "It's about you and me, Shelby, and about your fears of what I truly am." She tried to twist out of his grasp, but he rooted her there beneath his large hands, his eerie green gaze never leaving her own. "When you can accept that I share blood with your enemies and with Nate, then we might—*might*—have a future, sweetheart."

Words failed her. Not one smart-ass comment or parry came to mind as he peered down at her, the only sound between them that of their heavy breathing. Then he reached through the small distance that separated them, clasping her face between his large, rough hands, and pressed his mouth against hers, hard. For such a giant of a man, one with such abrasive ways, the kiss held the promise of lifetimes of gentleness. Of being held and cooed to, of being kissed from her toes to her earlobes. Of being worshipped.

But as he opened to her and thrust his tongue deep inside her mouth, hot and needy, she froze. She stiffened against him, and despite the overwhelming heat, she became ice. Because she remembered . . . everything that he was. She saw him as he'd been at the warehouse, emerging from the fire covered in fire. A monstrous Antousian, not the man she'd fallen in love with. Not the one who had his soft lips and delicious tongue coaxed up against hers.

He was every alien she'd ever feared, every enemy who'd ever taken one of her friend's lives. Jake Tierny was the embodiment of all that she reviled, and he knew it. One by one, his fingers uncurled about her shoulders, and he stepped away.

"Just what I thought." He gave her a sideways, melancholy smile. "This isn't about me almost dying in the fire or that I'm a soldier. You've seen exactly what I am, and there's no going back. Is there, Shelby?"

She blinked back hot tears. Never taking his gaze off of her, he pulled his T-shirt over the pistol he'd just holstered at his hip. "If only, huh?" He gave a rueful laugh.

She struggled to find her voice. "If only what?"

"All that time in the cabin, making love with me in my Antousian form, seeing what I really am in the depths of my soul. What a monster I truly am. If only none of it had happened, you might actually be mine—hell, you might be begging this bastard to stay and hold you in his arms."

With an angry gesture she wiped at her eyes. "You keep pushing me."

"Because years ago I made mistakes. More mistakes than I can count, and this time—just this once—I'm determined to get it right."

She winced, pressing her eyes shut as if he'd just slapped her across the face. "Maybe you should go." Her voice came out weak, sounding feeble, just like her objections.

"No problem there. I'm outta here." He brushed past her, but not without bending down to kiss her full on the lips one more time, an angry, aggressive gesture. "But that doesn't mean this is over between us. You'll run like hell, but you won't be able to shake it. Or me, Shelby. You won't ever shake me, no matter how far you go."

She kept her eyes closed, daring to open them only after her door slammed and she heard his booted footsteps retreating down the corridor. That was when she crumpled, slowly sliding to the floor, sobbing. She knelt there, rocking herself and crying long after she heard his deep voice bark across the comm, issuing angry orders.

And long after she'd realized he wasn't coming back.

Chapter Twenty-four

Thea was waiting for her outside the temple room, sitting on a spare wooden bench, its worn geometric design so intricate that it had to have come from Refaria. Kelsey's body burned with ungrounded heat, her face felt flushed, and she couldn't stop shaking.

"Here, sit down." Thea leapt up as Kelsey staggered toward the bench, weaving as if she'd just downed two bottles of wine. Or more.

With Thea's assistance, she made it to the seat, just barely, dropping heavily onto its smooth, polished surface. "Thanks for that time alone with him," she said. Jared still hadn't Changed back, not in the hours since his return, and Kelsey was struggling—seriously struggling—with his refusal to shift back.

"How did it go?" Thea didn't sound particularly optimistic, which only stoked Kelsey's fury and frustration even more.

"Don't ask it like that." Kelsey propped her head against the wall, using the surface for support. "Like you expected me to fail."

Thea folded her hands neatly in her lap, studying them intently. "If anyone could reach him, my lady, it would certainly be you."

"But you didn't think I would."

"No, I *knew* you couldn't." The words were like a poison arrow, ripping into Kelsey's marrow. Then, much more softly, "I'm sorry."

"Did your intuition show you that?" Kelsey felt

edgy and like she needed to move. She struggled to her feet but instantly buckled back onto the bench. "You've got to tell me, Thea," Kelsey pressed. "I need to know what you've seen."

"It's not what I've seen." The alien shifted uncomfortably beside her. "It's what I know from trying to link with him."

Kelsey gripped Thea's forearm, squeezing until the other woman yelped slightly. *"Tell me what you know."*

Thea lifted her eyes and met Kelsey's gaze. "He can't Change back."

"Of course he can!" Kelsey began to laugh hysterically, releasing her grip on Thea. "I've seen him make his Change at least six different times. And he always Changes back."

"But not this time."

Kelsey waved her hand between them. "It's just another Change, just another time when he needs to shift back—"

"They have separated his Refarian self from his D'Aravnian. Keeping him in his natural form for so long . . ." Thea shook her head, tears filling her pale eyes before she sat up taller. "He is a dual being, Kelsey, and I'm not sure you totally understand what that means."

For so long Kelsey had tried to wrap her mind around it but had never truly gotten to the heart of what his dual identity meant. That flaw within her suddenly became excruciatingly painful because now his very life depended on her understanding what and *who* he truly was. And she'd failed him. Dry heaves pulled at her stomach, but she battled them away.

Thea studied her for a long moment, her blue eyes alive with energy and something else . . . pity, Kelsey realized with another wave of crippling nausea.

"Tell me what you mean," Kelsey barely managed to choke out, gripping her full belly with both hands. "I need to understand what you're implying."

"He's not just a shape-shifter, capable of assuming

either form. He *is* both, to the very deepest layers of his being. He is both men, a dual entity. So when his enemies kept him from reassuming his physical body for such an extended period of time . . ." Thea's voice trailed off, and she bowed her head.

Kelsey's heart thundered, panic causing her whole body to shake. "Say it," she ground out. "Go on and tell me what you're *not* saying."

Thea stared at the wall opposite them, her jaw twitching. "His other self is dead, Kelsey. The fiery self, the D'Aravnian one, is all that remains."

"This happened before, when he was captured in Idaho. He told me all about it, and it was tough, but he did Change back."

"Kelsey, this situation is different. He was held longer this time, in a tighter containment cell. I've tried connecting with him—"

"No. No, that's not true. It can't be." Kelsey's eyes welled with tears, and she slumped in her seat. "He will Change back—he can. Eventually. I just have to keep trying to—to touch him, or talk to him—or maybe you can again. You will, won't you?"

"Even I find it difficult to communicate with him in this current state, Kelsey. It's not getting better—it's getting worse. He's"—Thea paused, studying her hands—"well, he's pure energy now. A very powerful being, a very vital force, but . . . an abstraction. And he's only going to grow more abstract and more powerful with every passing day. I don't know how we will even contain him. Soon he'll be too much for the temple."

"He's not a god, Thea. The temple isn't the right place for him anyway. If we could just get him into our quarters, let him stay there—"

Thea's hand shot out, gripping her arm. "He could kill you there."

"He'd never hurt me. Don't you understand?" Kelsey raked a trembling hand through her hair. "No matter who or what he is, Jared would never do anything to harm me."

"I promised him I'd protect you." The words were quiet, a guilty admission that caused Kelsey to sit up straight.

"What?"

"When he could still communicate with me, he made me promise that if it came to this, I'd keep him from destroying you and his child."

Kelsey's skin burned. Her eyes twitched. Every part of her body was coiled and ready for battle. "How dare you make a promise like that behind my back? I thought you were my friend."

"I am your friend." Thea dropped her gaze. "It's why I could make the promise. I love you as my sister—and I love Jared deeply. Not like you do, true, but I've loved him my entire life. First as king, then as cousin . . ." Thea swallowed hard, turning away. "I love you both, Kelsey. And I'll die before letting anything or anyone harm you . . . even Jared. Especially not Jared, and especially not after I swore to protect you with my life."

"If you truly love me," Kelsey answered slowly, "you'd do anything in your power to help me reach him."

Slowly Thea's clear blue eyes lifted. "If I thought you could still connect with him, I'd do anything in my power to make it happen. But he is completely lost—to all of us. I'm so sorry, my queen, but he's gone."

"You're wrong! I will reach him. He's my lifemate; I can do it. I'll be able to get through to him. You don't know him like I do."

Thea smiled sadly. "I know him differently, that's all."

"We are bonded mates." Kelsey whipped to her feet, pacing wildly in the small hallway. "You don't have the first clue what that means for us."

Thea's face fell, and Kelsey felt instantly guilty. Her friend might be madly in love with Marco, but for years she'd yearned for Jared.

"I have a mate of my own," Thea answered quietly.

"I do have an inkling of what you share with my cousin."

Kelsey dropped beside her again on the wooden bench. "I'm sorry." She buried her head in her hands, her whole body quaking with tremors. "God, Thea, I didn't mean it like that."

She felt Thea's arm around her shoulders. "I know you didn't."

"I just have to find a way to reach him. Please help me. Forget your promise to Jared and help me figure out how to do this."

Thea squeezed her shoulder, sliding closer. "I'll do whatever I can, so long as you don't die in the process."

Kelsey dropped her hands. "I don't care if I die. He's our king . . . my lover and and husband. And father to our daughter. Your people need him, Thea; it's not just me, it's what the Refarians so desperately need right now. My life doesn't matter, not when you figure those kinds of odds."

"What about Erica, then? What about risking her life? Is it really worth it?"

Kelsey shuddered. "I . . . can't go there. Just can't."

"You need to."

"Without Jared, our family is lost. I . . . I have to take this chance. I have to take it *for* Erica. She deserves to grow up with a father, and I'll do anything to make sure that happens."

Thea leaned back against the wall, still holding Kelsey against her side. For many long minutes they kept their silence, each lost in her own thoughts. Kelsey's mind ran rampant, testing theories, working at possibilities.

After a long time, Thea whispered, "There might be a way."

"Anything, just tell me." Kelsey grabbed Thea's hand. "I'll do whatever it takes."

"It could easily mean your life."

"I don't give a shit! Please, anything. Anything to bring him back."

"And it will hurt him . . . profoundly. It will mean a lot of pain for him, Kelsey. Are you really sure?"

"If it's the only way . . ."

Thea hesitated, cast her gaze at the ceiling, and then whispered under her breath, "We have to take you both to the mitres."

Jake paced his quarters—*Scott's quarters,* he corrected himself. No, even worse . . . Scott and Hope's quarters. For a moment he prepared to experience a deep wave of grief, that familiar onslaught of pain that he always experienced whenever he thought about them together.

Yet, surprisingly, nothing came.

His only emotion was a deep sense of missing not just Hope, but bizarrely enough, his younger self, too. And with that realization came another: Somewhere along the line he'd finally let Hope go. Not as a friend, and not as a beautiful memory of a life once shared with her, but as a mate and wife. The release had snuck up on him so stealthily, he wasn't even sure precisely when it had happened. But it remained the truth nonetheless. After so many years of wrenching pain and loss, he'd found his future; in joining his soul to Shelby's, he'd released his hold on Hope. Finally.

The fact only made Shelby's leaving him all the more confusing. He didn't have the first clue what to do about her, how to get her to stay when all she wanted was to run as far as she could from him. Before, he wouldn't have blamed her one bit. Even a few weeks ago, he'd have blessed her for hightailing it to the far side of his universe. But now? He wanted her, and badly enough to fight as hard as it took to have her in his life.

He sank onto Scott's plush leather sofa, staring at the wooden crossbeams overhead, wishing there were someone—hell, anyone—who could counsel him. His best friend would have had good advice for him, but Jared was so far gone Jake wasn't sure he'd ever be able to communicate with his lifelong friend again.

Kelsey would have been his backup, but she was far too distraught about her current situation to care about his love life at the moment, and he'd hardly expect her to become involved, anyway.

Hopelessly, he rotated through the possibilities because he wasn't such a stupid bastard as to think that he could figure out this mess on his own. Bolting to his feet, he began pacing the modest quarters, flipping through papers on the desk, picking up worship statues, pacing some more. He felt as caged and trapped as he had by his Antousian captors.

Damn it all, I have to get out of here, he thought, tightening his parka about his body. As he did so, his hand grazed the slim outline of his cell phone.

There was one other possibility, a friend—a brother, really, who might have advice for him. Flipping open the cell, he hit speed dial and held his breath.

When the acutely familiar voice answered after one ring, he was struck speechless. In fact, he was about to slam the phone shut when the husky male voice spoke his name. "Tierny? That you?" *Damned caller ID.*

He coughed. "Yeah. What's up?"

"You're the one calling me, man." Dillon released his typical dark laugh. But there was warmth in it as well—a strange kind of brotherhood, like having a twin you'd never known existed before. "But I guess you hit the wrong number, huh? Didn't you mean to call Hope?"

"No. I actually wanted to talk to you this time."

"Cool." His younger self's voice brightened, as if he were pleased that Jake was reaching out to him. "So what's going on?"

"I'm back on base," Jake offered lamely, avoiding the real reason for his call.

"So I heard. Heard a lot of shit happened, too, and you survived it. You sure you're all right?"

"I'm fine. . . ." He settled at Dillon's desk, rifling through the papers once again, his eyes searching for some clue as to what he should do. A lead he knew he wouldn't find in the documents stacked neatly on Dillon's desk. "You planning on coming back this way anytime soon? If so, I've got to clear out."

"Hope and I are staying here at Warren indefinitely. Working things from this angle."

"That's good . . . good."

"Why're you calling, man? Something's obviously on your mind."

Jake dragged a hand through his hair. "You could say that."

"So spill it already, because I'm supposed to be at a meeting in five."

"I need advice, brother." Then, in a rush, Jake unraveled the entire tale, from top to bottom.

When he was done, Dillon laughed softly into the phone. "What is it with you, Tierny? You've been in love before—really in love. Have you forgotten your moves? Forgotten what you've got to do when it comes to your woman?"

Jake bristled. "Fine. Whatever, man. I just thought you might be able to help."

A moment of silence. "I *am* helping. I'm reminding you of who you are, and that you know what to do." Once more, the voice on the other end of the line paused before going on. "Unless I'm mistaken, you've slept with a shitload of women, correct?"

"We share the same past in that regard." Ridiculous, but his face flushed, thinking that his younger self on the other end of the line knew all about his sordid sexual history, his youthful compulsions for bedding human women. "Only . . . she's not human."

"That surprises you?"

"Hell, yeah. I was always driven toward them . . . some sort of mating urge, I think. Another damned side effect of our hybrid DNA."

"But she's what you always want. Blond, has those curves that kill . . ." Dillon's voice trailed off, and there was muffled talking in the background; then Jake heard a quiet, "Come on, sweetheart, just helping Jake. You know you're it for me."

So Hope was listening in. "What does she think?" he blurted before he could stop himself.

"She wants you happy, Jake," Scott answered quietly. "We both do. So here's how you're going to proceed."

It had been good advice—damned good advice that Scott gave him—but unfortunately it had come too late. Jake stood in Shelby's quarters, staring at the open drawers, empty and pulled askew. At the open closet, a few barren hangers dangled from the bar. She was totally cleared out. Gone. In fact, the only personal item that remained in the whole room was her slim-line cell, dropped significantly in the middle of her neatly made bed.

And he had no way of tracking her without it. If she'd been Antousian, ironically enough, he could have followed her to the moon and back, going off her fresh trail. As it was, he loved a Refarian, which left him bereft of any leads. He'd have to rely on Thea or one of the other intuitives in the camp, which made him feel even more fucking out of control—and offered no guarantees that he'd be able to locate her. Jake kicked the bed frame with his boot in frustration, the wood splintering into a dozen shards at the impact.

Too godsdamned late. Jake placed his hands on his hips, breaking out in a sweat all over his body. His mind flooded with images, visions of himself running across the battlefield . . . Hope struggling so badly with her delivery of baby Leisa. How he'd run and run, praying his head off, begging All to save her. But he'd been too late.

Always too fucking late when it came to the women he loved.

At Scott's urging, he'd planned to all but beg Shelby to stay, to give them another shot, but now . . . it was truly over between them. His heart twisted inside his chest, a deep and hollow ache filling his soul. To have loved once had been a miracle; to have loved twice, well, it had been more than he'd ever thought All would grant him. Tears burned at his eyes. What was it about him, this curse inside that meant he was forever doomed to lose the people he loved most of all?

Jake dropped his head, pressing it against the top bunk that Shelby usually slept in. Dragging in long breaths, he drank in the faint remnant of her scent; familiar, like mountain air after a cleansing summer rain, it drenched him. His whole body tightened in reaction, just like it always did whenever he scented her. Inside his uniform, he felt himself tightening and lengthening. Shit, even now the smell of her had the power to make him harder than the barrel of a K-12.

"Oh, Shelby." He moaned and turned his cheek against the sheet, dampness touching his skin. The tears were coming harder than he'd realized, than he'd even allowed himself to feel. He pressed the crook of his arm against his face, blotting at his eyes.

All, what is it about me, this dreadful thing? Why have you cursed me like this? He prayed, still dragging her scent deep into his lungs. He hadn't felt this bitterly lonely in years, not since . . .

Gods, not since after Hope had died.

Please, Lord of All, just bring her back to me. I can't track her, but You can show her the way to me. I beg of you . . . make her understand how much I love her.

The words tumbled out of him, ardent prayers in his native Antousian—a language he almost never spoke except when he prayed. Wrapping both arms about himself, he began rocking back and forth, just standing beside her bed, murmuring to the One above who he'd always believed would protect him. Until he'd lost Hope. After that, he'd never truly had faith again. Had only believed the worst, that All had blighted him for some unknown reason. That All had turned his back on him forever, shunning him like the cursed, bitter man that he was.

Whatever I did, whatever is wrong inside this bastard's heart, I beg for her return.

And suddenly, unexpectedly, Jake began to tremble, warmth cocooning him from the crown of his head to his very toes. A force like a great golden whirlwind drove him to his knees, electrifying the room all about him. He kept praying, chanting in Antousian, begging, whispering . . . feeling the very wind of All about him. He didn't dare open his eyes. Heat overcame him, seeping into his bones, making the brittle places soft and pliable again . . . changing him. Transforming him.

"Wh-what is happening?" he murmured aloud, unable to stop the massive tremors jolting his huge body. It was as if All himself were touching him. A stream of Antousian prayers escaped his lips, hardly intelligible, but he couldn't contain the words. He might as well have tried to halt the sun's progression across the sky.

Then, just as suddenly, the whirling died down, until the room was empty. Devoid of the supernatural power that had occupied it just a moment before. Only a soft voice remained, whispering, *I have never left you.*

He glanced up, lifting a shaking hand to wipe the tears from his eyes. The words had been audible, a deep rumbling somewhere inside the room, only . . . not.

I have never left you. Was All telling him Shelby was still on base? Was it the sign he was seeking?

I will never leave you. The words chased across his spirit, electrifying his body, causing him to jolt and quiver until he fell to the floor. Even then he continued to spasm, his spine jerking and jackknifing off the hardwood, but he couldn't stop the flood of energy and healing seeping into his body any more than he could his physical reaction to it.

I will never leave you. . . . I will never leave you. . . . I will never leave you.

It was the last thing he heard before his whole world went black.

Chapter Twenty-five

Kelsey's back was pressed flat against the temple wall, barely out of reach from the spiraling cauldron of power in front of her. A force that still—somewhere deep in the middle of all that roaring and commotion—was her lifemate. Her eyes were completely shut, hands splayed at her sides. She listened as the Refarians attempted to maneuver Jared out of the temple and down to the hangar deck, but didn't dare look. God, she *couldn't* look—it was just too painful . . . no way she could look at all.

Marco stood beside her, leaning against the wall solidly. So resolutely, in fact, it was as if he intended to hold the very structure in place. She stole a glance at him, surprised that his dark eyes were wide open, missing nothing. He gave her arm a light squeeze, just letting her know he was watching over her. *And Jared.* Although there wasn't much a Madjin protector could do in a situation like this one. It had to be uncharted territory for Marco—and for the history of all Madjin before him.

Soldiers advanced on the glowing sphere of power that filled the entire temple . . . her husband. The sizzling smell of pulsar whips filled her nostrils, and she battled a wave of horrible nausea. Just knowing that they were putting those energized lashes against Jared's glowing body, knowing the deep physical pain it was causing him, was almost enough to have her call the whole plan off. And they would back off if she ordered it, a weird thought right there. She was the queen. She'd unleashed this plan, and she could end it, here and now.

This will be the ugliest part, she reminded herself. *But it's for him. Just remember, that this is the only way to bring him back.*

Without the ability to link or speak to him, they were reduced to wrangling him like a wild bull, slapping at his golden sides, urging him toward the chamber door.

Kelsey dared to open her eyes again; beside her Marco stiffened, almost as if he knew she'd chosen to watch. But he didn't look in her direction—his dark gaze was fixed squarely on Jared, his lips moving soundlessly. She still knew so little about how the ancient band of Madjin worked, but she guessed he was using his gifts somehow, trying to place a ring of protection around Jared.

Wincing, she remembered how empathic Marco was. "Is he hurting?" she barely managed to ask.

Marco's black eyebrows lowered, but he said nothing, a dark stain of emotion flooding his cheeks. It was the only answer she needed, even though she'd already known the truth. Tears filled her eyes.

Once more several soldiers advanced on Jared, spinning the vibrating whips toward him. Confused, he reared up in reaction, his energy growing greater and wider until a solid blast of power knocked the gathered soldiers against the walls of the room. There were curses and mutterings all around; two soldiers were even backing out the door, looking so visibly shaken, it was a wonder they didn't run at breakneck speed just to get away. A female lieutenant halted the departing men, saying something quiet that none of the rest could hear. One of the soldiers dropped his head, a terrible expression of grief on his face, but the commanding officer took him by the shoulder, guiding him back toward the room's interior. Then she took hold of her own rotating lasso, advancing toward Jared—

but not before hot tears began streaming down her face as she worked.

It wasn't easy duty putting a whip to the king, the one whom they all, to the very last man and woman within their corps, loved so completely.

The scent of smoldering power had Kelsey gripping her pregnant stomach, fighting waves of nausea because, in a very real sense, it was Jared himself whom she smelled burning. She pressed her eyes shut even tighter, haunted by the memory of what had been done to him by Veckus years ago. Frightened by the remembrance of the physical scars he bore all over his body from the Antousians whipping him.

They'd beaten him again during this most recent capture, too, brutally, and now his own people were treating him the same cruel way. Kelsey worked a hand at her belly, terrified of opening her eyes, but needing to see. She'd called this latest torture down on her mate and husband. The least she could do was watch as they tried to contain the out-of-control storm that he truly was.

At last, with a strange whirring sound, Jared grew far more compact, all the frantic rearing and spiraling finished. It was like being at the eye of the hurricane they'd been battling, which didn't exactly make Kelsey feel secure about his well-being—or their ability to corral him onto the transport.

Besides, what if he went wild on the craft? What if he suddenly grew confused or disoriented? What then? They wouldn't have a prayer of getting him under control, not thousands of feet in the air. Sure, he'd been compliant on the way back from the Antousian compound, but he'd still been stunned from being kept in that tight containment cell. In the past few hours, finally free from the walls of his prison, he'd expanded, had grown much less stable. His energy readings were off the charts according to the soldiers who were trying to rein him in right now.

"Got him," the female soldier in charge said, holstering her pulsar whip. Although her face was still streaked with dampness, it was perfectly resolved. She didn't reach to wipe her tears or even acknowledge them in any way.

Kelsey released a tight breath as she watched the soldiers guide Jared gently toward the door of the temple. She wondered whether he sensed her presence, whether he even knew she was right near him. Then again, maybe he didn't remember her at all, she thought in frantic despair.

The lead soldier paused at the threshold of the temple, turning her tear-reddened eyes on Kelsey. "My lady? You're joining us?" The lieutenant inclined her head respectfully.

"Oh. I—I . . . yes, of course I'm coming." Kelsey had been so paralyzed by the proceedings, so sickened at Jared's suffering, that she hadn't totally realized it was time for her to move.

"He needs you near him," the woman added, swiveling on her boot heels without lifting out of the bow. "He does know you're here, my lady. It's important that you stay right with him, no matter what happens during this procedure. Be strong because he is fully aware of you. You understand?"

Kelsey's body jerked in reaction to the words. *How do you know? Are you sure? God, please tell me you sense something of the man that he was. . . .* She wanted to blurt five thousand questions. Was the soldier an empath? Intuitive? But Kelsey didn't voice any of her doubts. She wasn't just a wife or mate today—she was her people's queen, and such questions would drive a wedge between the soldiers carrying out the difficult operation.

Kelsey stepped close to the soldier. "I won't leave our king's side," she whispered in a fierce voice. "This is where I belong."

"We need you, my lady. It's not just him—we need *you*, too." The woman rose from her half bow, pegging Kelsey with a steely, black-eyed stare that was so intense, she actually had to avert her eyes. Whoever this lieutenant was, she was definitely made of stern stuff.

As the soldiers wrestled with Jared's undulating form, Kelsey couldn't hold back a semihysterical laugh. Several of them glanced at her in shock, and she gave a small wave, letting them know she was all right. The thing was, she'd suddenly flashed on all those years of watching the Macy's Thanksgiving Day parade with her mother. She pictured the balloon handlers, how they battled the New York City winds to keep their overpowering cargo under control. That was exactly what this military procession looked like, with Jared hovering high in the air, encircled by the knot of soldiers who kept their whips at the ready. Then she felt suddenly grim: The last thing they needed was a Hindenburg-style accident.

"Surely he gets it now," Kelsey muttered to the lieutenant. "Surely he won't suddenly expand and—and . . ." *And we won't have to hurt him any more than we already have.*

"He's finally cooperating," the soldier agreed, reaching to wipe away her glistening tears. "That's a good sign."

Kelsey turned to Marco, who only shook his head. "I can't get a clear reading on his emotions." But the grief in his eyes told Kelsey everything the protector *wasn't* saying.

She glanced up, watching Jared's colors morph from pure gold to a slightly russet shade. She knew from experience that meant he was feeling—or expressing—some intense emotion, usually toward her. "He knows I'm here," she whispered in amazement.

"The change of color tells you that?" The female soldier cocked an eyebrow.

"Yes. Yes, that's exactly what it means." Kelsey pressed fingertips to her lips; she hadn't thought she'd actually said the words aloud. But she was totally rattled, shaking all over. "Thank you so much for this, uh . . ." She didn't know the soldier's name.

"I'm Lieutenant Mar Ariell." Another slight bow. "Well, it's Marley, but I go by Mar."

"Thank you for helping my husband . . . and me."

Again Lieutenant Ariell bowed, placing a fist over her heart. "I'm honored to serve you both, my lady."

Snapping back to her full height, the woman turned to the other soldiers. "Listen up! It's time to move out. Remember to be gentle. . . . Don't let anything go wrong on our watch, *soldiers*! This mission is critical. So is *respect*. This is your king and your commander," she barked. "This is the man we all love. Remember that . . . no matter what happens out there."

Kelsey filed out of the temple, barely allowing herself to breathe.

A steady vibration caused Jake to stir. His forehead was mashed against something hard, and whatever the constant buzzing was against his side, it was as annoying as hell. With a groan, he worked to move his limbs, dimly aware that he was face-first on a very hard surface. Rubbing his eyes, he rolled onto his side, and saw nothing but bare hardwood floor.

Damn, I was out cold. More vibrating, a jarring staccato along the floorboards. Only then did he notice his cell phone doing a little gyration beside his knee, moving a few inches every time the phone rang like some enraged beetle. *Must have fallen out of my pocket when I . . . When I what?* He wasn't exactly sure what had happened to him. But he felt renewed, and the bottomless hole inside his chest no longer ached so badly. Reaching for the phone, his heartbeat sped when he realized it was Kelsey.

"What's going on?" he nearly barked, unfolding the phone to his ear. Kelsey never called him unless it was serious business. Not in any timeline—past, future, or present.

"We're taking Jared to the mitres, Jake. Now. He needs you with him. . . . I need you. We all do."

"For what? What's at the mitres?" He gave his head a dull shake, struggling to his knees. Raking a hand through his hair, he tried to remember exactly how he'd wound up on the floor but couldn't seem to pinpoint what had led him there.

"I'll explain everything on the way, but the short version is that we plan to use the mitres to connect with Jared. Thea thinks the dimensional energy waves could help him stabilize enough so she can connect with him and . . . talk him down, so to speak."

"Shit. He hasn't shifted back?"

"He's still in his D'Aravnian form, and Thea says time is crucial. We do it now."

Jake rose to his feet, straightening his uniform jacket. "I'll meet you at the hangar deck."

"We're on the way there now. And Jake? Can you bring Shelby, too? We might need her time-walking ability while in the mitres. She might have some answers on how we can reach him."

Jake slumped. "Can't. She's gone."

"Gone where?"

Wouldn't he love to know. Gods, he'd do anything to be able to answer that question. "Long story, Kelsey. Let's just focus on Jared right now."

Kelsey and Thea made quick work of uploading the codes to the mitres chamber, the dimensional portal snapping open to allow their entry. They'd brought a skeleton crew inside the chamber, the other soldiers remaining on the transport. In Kelsey's mind, the fewer lives they risked, the better. Other than her, it was just Thea, Marco, and Jake . . . well, and Jared, who churned high overhead like an Old Testament cloud of glory.

Thea slipped a palm onto Kelsey's shoulder, guiding her toward the luminous tube in the center of the room. Two centuries earlier Jared's ancestor, Prince Arienn D'Aravni, had seeded part of his own energy inside the cylinder to power the mitres. From the moment they'd entered today, Arienn's vibrant essence had been reacting to Jared, glowing brighter and brighter with every passing moment.

"You know what to do," Thea coached Kelsey. True enough. She'd been down this path before, most recently when they'd used the weapon to defeat the Antousians over at Warren. Still, this was Jared's very life, their shared future, and Kelsey was far more terrified than she'd been that day months before.

Shaking, Kelsey approached the center point of the mitres, that large glowing cylinder that was the seat of its power. Capable of opening dimensions and warping time itself, the mitres would have its greatest victory today . . . or its greatest defeat. She bowed her head, slid both palms about the smooth, clear container, and allowed the mitres codes—locked within her mind since Jared had placed them there almost six months earlier—to unspool.

A jolt of supernatural energy drove Kelsey to her knees, the room all around them whipping with a blast of power more intense than anything Jared had been throwing off during the past few hours. But she kept a grip on the main unit, refusing to back down as a giant spiral began looping about them, a weaving thread of blue that blurred everything else.

"This isn't good," she thought Jake said, his words stretched like a rubber band. *This isn't goooooooood.*

"No other way!" Thea shouted behind her, her voice shrill above the powerful wind that whipped at them all. "Just hold on!" *Holllldddd onnnnnn.*

Inside her belly, Kelsey felt Erica gyrate, her own primal energy reacting to the onslaught of power that was unfurling around them. The blue circle expanded, became pure heavenly light. In backward narration she watched as Jared thrust inside of her, placing Erica's very life within her belly . . . then her mother was dying, so fragile and thin . . . and suddenly she was fourteen, kissing Jared for the very first time.

Backward and backward, time's footprints left their marks, voices bending about her. Arms pulling and dragging at her . . .

"Got . . . to . . . get . . . her . . . away," someone said, the words strung out and distorted.

Kelsey battled the rushing wind, focused her eyes on the image before her—it was that elder, wiping away her memories of Jared so many years ago. "Please, no!" she shouted, tightening her arms about the main cylinder, digging in for the duration. She'd be damned if any of her friends would pull her away now. Not now, when every instinct inside her said that if she couldn't link with Jared here in the mitres, he'd be lost to her forever.

Time spun on its axis, playing tricks: She was meeting her father's girlfriend at that fund-raiser, feeling awkward and angry. Jared was shot down over Idaho—only that was wrong—she hadn't been there then. Hadn't known his suffering . . .

Time halted and advanced, back and forth, forward and backward, until she felt something catch hold of her, a very real lasso wrapping about her chest. Laughing crazily, she looked up into the thundercloud and felt Jared sweep her into himself.

Thea rushed forward, but she was too late. Kelsey had vanished inside of Jared's rotating golden sphere. One minute their queen had been in a trance, Jared hovering over her like a funnel cloud of power—the next, she'd begun to levitate, hands extended as if reaching toward the gods themselves.

Jake shoved her aside, trying to take hold of Kelsey's booted feet, Marco grappling right beside him. Both men were more than a foot taller than she, but Thea still wanted in the battle herself, and kept trying to lay hold of Kelsey as she ascended high above them. *Still, too late. Far too late.*

Kelsey instantly became engulfed in the raging storm above them all.

Oh, my friend. Oh, dear, sweet sister, come back.

Then, as if in answer to her pleas, the ceiling above them opened—the mitres itself spun wide, a giant trail of power leading like a wormhole into the sky. Kelsey rotated upward, caught within Jared's essence and the interdimensional space weaving overhead.

"Marco! Gods, Marco, help them," Thea shouted, her voice nearly lost in the whipping wind.

Marco lifted both arms, trying to get a grasp on Kelsey, but she swiveled upward, lost in Jared's swirling hurricane. "Thea . . . I can't get her!"

"You've got to try," Thea insisted, actually jumping, trying to expand her small height enough that she might lay hold of her dear friend.

Jake pushed them both aside. "Let me," he thundered. "I've used this thing before. Maybe . . . maybe . . . I can get to her."

But try as he did, lifting his massive arms overhead, battling and warring, Kelsey was completely caught up in Jared's power. No longer standing straight, she lifted upward on her back, her belly glowing bright. Before Thea could so much as blink, her queen had vanished completely, lost in Jared's golden, radiant energy.

If Thea didn't do something soon, they would all die—or at the very least, Kelsey's human body would be obliterated by the sheer force of nature unfolding all about them, as well as the child within her. Cursing everything and everyone, Thea lifted upward, allowing herself to be swept into the rushing force. She had a shot at Kelsey's legs; even though the g-forces pulled at her face, Thea grabbed Kelsey's calves, determined to pull her queen back to the ground. She'd be damned if she'd lose her best friend and cousin on the same day.

Right as she laid hold of the human's legs, an electrified field shocked her, catapulting her sharply backward until she slammed hard against the mitres' floor. Thea shook her head, disbelieving. Somehow, some way, Kelsey had created a force field, blocking the rest of them out. Or was it Jared who'd created that perimeter? No, not Jared; every instinct told her that it was Kelsey herself who was shutting the rest of them out. Life or death, their queen was in this battle until the bitter end.

Chapter Twenty-six

Time drew to an awkward, jarring halt. Kelsey found herself face-to-face with her lifemate, knowing this was the very moment she'd spent years yearning for. At long last, she might actually touch him . . . and survive. The people below, whoever they were, didn't matter at all. Her impending death was nothing, an easy casualty when it came down to this—bonding with Jared in his natural state. Yet a thought teased at her awareness, something about the people below her, their identities. . . . Something wasn't quite right, but she couldn't be bothered with thinking why. The moment was only about Jared, about touching him. Nothing else mattered at all.

"I'm here, sweet love," she whispered into the golden wind roaring about her. "I won't hurt you."

A jolt of power yanked her higher into his flames, his massive force wrapping about her like the gentlest, wooing arms of a lover. Dimly, she was aware that she should be afraid, but this was Jared, and he couldn't hurt her. He'd never, not once, ever hurt her, no matter what form he took. Below her she could see only his fire, and a glance overhead revealed that the very mitres itself yawned like a great mouth to the beyond.

She might die here, and she was prepared to do so. There was no other purpose in her mind and spirit except reaching Jared. This was what everything, all the twining years between them, had come down to.

This one moment. God, all she wanted was to caress him, the ache so palpable within her that she could barely keep her hands off the tunnel of golden light encircling her.

But it wasn't enough: He had to return to her. *That* was the real reason she was here, she reminded herself. Suddenly she remembered Thea, Jake, and Marco down below. They were all counting on her to reach Jared; this was his only, absolutely only, chance at ever coming back. As if in reaction to those thoughts, a rush of his flowing power shot down her spine, convulsing her and making baby Erica react in kind. The tiny child in her belly grew warmer and warmer, and Kelsey trembled, realizing that their baby was shifting into her own D'Aravnian form. In a panic, Kelsey clutched at her stomach, and that's when it hit her: She was surrounded—within and without—by pure, blazing energy.

It didn't seem possible that she'd ever survive.

But she *would* connect with Jared; she'd be damned if she didn't, and for the first time, she forced her eyes open, blinking against her lover's beautiful essence.

"Jareshk!" she cried over the roaring, blinding rush. "I know you're still here with me. I know you understand. You have to Change back! You have to find your physical body again."

In response, a lurching grip took hold of her, bright fingers of power trailing across her abdomen, her chest . . . her face. He was touching her, truly touching her, yet she wasn't destroyed.

"You *know* it's me," she shouted into the blaze. "You won't hurt me, not ever. *Come back!*"

Then, the first miracle: Within her spirit she heard him. For the first time since he'd become lost in his captivity, she heard Jared whisper across her soul.

Love . . . touch.

His words electrified her to the very core of her being. Whipping at the fury around her, she tried desperately to reach him, but he retracted. He'd beckoned her closer only to pull away.

Grappling at air and wind, she flailed her arms, dimly aware that she floated high above the mitres chamber floor. "I'm trying to touch you, Jareshk. Let me!"

Destroy!

She shivered, gripping her belly, Erica blazing hotter within her with every passing second.

"Stop it, Jared!" she insisted. "Stop fighting me. . . . Stop fighting this. Come back, Jareshk. Come back to me! Come back to *us*!"

A desperate motion yanked her higher still, drawing her toward the gaping, roaring tunnel that led toward the heavens.

No . . . hurt . . . Kelsha!

After months of his pulling away, months of his warnings, something broke inside of her. A dam gave way, every emotion that she'd ever held back with him spilling outward, whipping wildly in the wind that tore at her very being. Too many times he'd retracted at the last moment, too many instances he'd been afraid of hurting her—and if she couldn't reach him now, everything inside her said that he'd be lost to them all forever.

With trembling hands, she fanned outward in a wide, tremulous arc that met nothing but stone-cold electricity. A shockwave of energy convulsed her entire body, but again she reached, this time touching what she could of Jared. Her fingers grew stiff as they met his power; electrified, her body jerked again in reaction.

"See?" she whispered into his storm, "I'm stroking you. You're not hurting me. I'm touching you . . . you're touching *me*." Then, it was as if he seeped into her very body, engulfing her. "You can't hurt me, Jareshk," she cried, free-falling into his core. In reaction, his otherworldly purring speared through her, sending a shiver down her spine. It coursed upward into her belly . . . and into Erica.

Shockwave after shockwave rent her, bone to skin, marrow to eternity. Her last conscious thought was of

Jared's shimmering body beneath her fingertips, the way his unearthly skin yielded and shivered at her human touch.

Help . . . me! His distant voice reverberated through her being. *Come back . . . you!*

Marco shielded his eyes, trying desperately to track the unfolding action overhead. His queen had vanished in a blaze of glory, swept upward in a supernatural cacophony of motion and wind. If not for Thea's frantic reaching, he might have kept his distance, mesmerized by the mating between his king and queen. For surely that's what this had to be, the purest union between human and Refarian.

Jake tugged at his arm. "Go after her!" he shouted over the rushing noise that filled the mitres' center. *"You're their Madjin!"*

Marco gazed upward, feeling his whole body grow hot. "I can't invade that . . . intimacy." The thing was, watching their union was causing a terrible, burning itch inside his own body, that utter compulsion to Change. He felt entranced, unable to move.

Thea grabbed hold of his torso, beating him back against the mitres wall. "Marco. *Marco!* You have to Change."

"Baby, no!" He couldn't reveal the truth. *Not here, not ever!* The itch inside his marrow increased, became louder and louder. . . . He became more and more compelled to Change into his D'Aravnian state.

Thea slapped him hard across the face, jerking him against the smooth wall of the mitres. "Don't you see what's happening?" Her blue eyes blazed furiously, bringing him back to reality. "Kelsey is dying up there. You are the one person . . . the only person who can possibly stop him from killing her."

Marco's heartbeat grew slow, sped up, flailed wildly inside his chest. "Why me?"

"Because you're his *brother*, his Madjin. . . . I've already tried connecting with him, but it didn't work.

With your empathy and your biological connection, you might be able to do it."

Dimly, Marco was aware of Jake having a reaction, of his surprise and shock. Shaking his head, he sank harder against the wall. "I could destroy him," he uttered, pressing his eyes tightly shut. "I can't control my gift, not here."

"Damn it all, Marco!" Thea slapped him harder, knocking his jaw against the wall again. Some dim part of his soul understood that she was reaching past gravity itself, struggling to connect with him. "You are the one. Will you do it or not? This is everything you trained for. . . . Save him! Save them, please!"

Marco steeled himself. Vaguely aware of his mate's angry gaze—and even more so of Jake's incredulous one—he struck out into the center of the chamber. Dropping onto his haunches, he folded inward, aware of his own D'Aravnian power, aware of his own quaking need to Change . . . and *turned.*

In a fluid motion, he was nothing more than pure power, shooting upward into the vast overhead spiral. Rational thought left him; verbal capacity vanished. In a shuddering instant he was everything that his own brother was . . . pure, unquestionable energy.

Speeding past Kelsey, only slightly aware of her human body, he undulated into the sphere of energy. Forsaking all pretense, disregarding all his lies, he came face-to-face with his king . . . and brother.

Connection was shockingly easy; he *felt* Jared more than communicated, bridging the gulf that should have separated them. His own sheer force imploded against his brother's, striving, battling . . . communicating. Without any real purpose, his empathy engaged—power to power. Golden energy to golden energy.

Come down, Marco urged wordlessly. *Change!* Unlike Jared, he'd spent only moments in his natural form, so communication remained almost effortless. Jared, on the other hand, had become utterly irrational after so many hours in Form.

Kelsey vibrated between them, her vulnerable human body still levitating within the mass of his brother's humming power. She jerked at his intrusion, spinning a strange, hypnotic circle, but Marco pushed right past her.

Jared! Must . . . return!

A startling wave of pain nearly sent Marco plummeting back to the floor, but he persevered, battling ahead. *My lord, transform! Release . . . queen!*

Jared's utter confusion assaulted him. His king didn't understand how he, his Madjin, had Changed.

Brother, follow me, Marco continued. *Release her. . . . Come with me. Return with us!*

He had nothing to offer, nothing spectacular or more convincing than Kelsey did . . . except one thing. His empathy. The link he forged with Jared began to quiver, came alive as if it were a vibrant power line. Jared was confused but responding for no other reason than Marco's simple ability to link with him—his empathy was as basic as Jared's form, honest and undeniable.

Brother! Marco murmured again, a shimmy across the thin emotional bond that linked them. *Return to us. . . . Release . . . queen.*

Gently, Kelsey began to lower back to the floor, spinning slowly downward—Marco sensed her descent more than saw it. Yet Jared remained swirling in the center, not Changing at all.

How?

Marco flinched at the question, retracted a bit; not that Jared was angry, just . . . confused.

It was now or never, now or never. . . . *Jareshk, Change!*

With an audible snap, the roaring being before him vanished, a hard thud sounding even above the din within the chamber. Only Marco remained, still in his natural state.

Jared collapsed face-first on the floor, his naked body heaving and shivering. Kelsey rushed forward, wrapping herself atop him.

"Get a jacket around him, hurry!" Thea pushed at

Kelsey, trying to pry her off of Jared. "He needs to be wrapped in this, right now. His body temperature is dropping fast."

Kelsey shoved Thea aside, yanking her shirt overhead. "No, he needs the warmth of my body. It's hypothermia, that's what you're telling me, and that means he needs my own body's heat."

Kelsey unsnapped her pants, yanked them low about her body, not worrying about Jake or anyone else in the chamber seeing her naked. Jared moaned low, practically convulsing with tremors, and Kelsey draped her whole body atop his, the pregnant mound of her belly pushing into his back.

"It's okay," she cooed gently in his ear, holding tight to him. Inside her stomach, Erica still burned intensely, and Kelsey hoped that maybe some of their baby's warmth was getting to him.

"I—I . . ." Jared's voice trailed off.

"Shh, it's okay. It's all right. You're here with us," she soothed, stroking his hair with one hand, holding tight to his waist with her other. "You're safe now. So safe, dear Jareshk."

Overhead a rushing wind pulled at her hair, her body, and then there was only stillness. A loud thud resounded beside them, the whole chamber growing quiet afterward. Kelsey opened her eyes and saw Marco collapsed right beside Jared, shivering and naked, too.

Thea covered Marco with her jacket, murmuring something in his ear, and Kelsey returned her full focus to Jared. For long, long moments he lay on the floor, trembling beneath her, saying nothing. Just shaking, and it was only after a few moments that she realized he was crying.

She rested her cheek against his shoulder. "You're all right; you know you are. You're back where you belong."

He reached a hand behind him, feeling for her, and rose. Only then did she see the harsh, brutal welts all across his back, and she shuddered.

"I'm so sorry. Gods, Jared, I'm sorry for what we had to do." Tears squeezed out of her eyes, and she reached a tender hand to touch one of his worst wounds. Even though he flinched, she pressed her lips to the mark, kissing him as gently as she could. "I just couldn't lose you. None of us could."

"Kelse . . ." Jared struggled to his knees. She knelt beside him, stroking his long hair, his face. A swollen gash ran from his forehead straight down his nose, a brutal ridge; his eyes were red with tears, but he was *with* her. Her king had returned.

For several long moments he worked his jaws, struggling to speak. "I—I was . . . so . . . lost," he finally managed to stammer. And then he reached for her, pulling her tight within his arms. "You . . . saved me, sweet love. Your love . . . found me."

"I'm right here, right here." She buried her face against his neck, drinking in his scent. Wrapping her arms tightly about his torso, she felt the sticky dampness of his fresh blood and cringed. What they'd been forced to do to save him made her shudder; the price had been almost too much to bear. But not when she imagined having lost him forever.

Jared reached a shaky hand to her hair, stroking, then pulled back suddenly. "Erica?" He gaped down at her glowing belly. "Our baby is safe?"

Kelsey couldn't help laughing, a tinkling, joyous sound that welled up from deep inside her soul. "She missed her daddy, that's all. She's perfectly fine."

Jared dropped his head, bending low . . . and planted a sweet kiss against her belly. She held his head against her bare stomach, stroking his thick, gleaming hair, and prayed silently, thanking the gods for his return.

"Where's Marco?" Jared jerked upright, his black gaze sweeping the room. For the first time in many moments Kelsey remembered their observers.

She glanced around and discovered that Marco was propped against the far wall, his face flushed and covered in a sheen of perspiration. Thea squatted beside him, pressing a bottle of water to his lips. Jake stood on the far side of the room, eyes shut, looking utterly exhausted.

Jared lifted his hand, gesturing toward Marco. "Come closer." His voice was thick and hoarse. "Come to me, Madjin, if you're able."

Marco had been in the whirlwind with them, she remembered suddenly. He had helped Jared. And he had been pure D'Aravni himself.

"My lord," was all the man whispered, slumping against the wall, a look of utter shame on his face.

Jared coughed, a whole spasm racking his brutalized body. "My *brother*," he said at last, "we must talk."

Marco glanced uncertainly at Thea, who stood, helping him to his feet. "Go on," she prompted, her voice gentle and filled with love. "It's time, Marco. Way past time that you told him the truth."

"I already know the truth." Jared wrapped both arms about his torso protectively, leveling Marco with his stare. "But I need to hear it from *you*, brother."

Marco gazed up at Thea, thousands of words seeming to pass between them, and then at last took her offered hand. He stumbled to his feet unsteadily, then crossed the small distance to Jared's side, dropping into a crouch. He kept Thea's uniform jacket around his waist, covering himself, and dipped into a low, reverent bow right against the floor.

Marco said nothing, waited. Kelsey watched the two men, the struggle evident on Jared's face. As confused as she was, she had no doubt that this moment would be etched within her mind for the rest of her life.

At last Jared reached a shaking hand, cupping the back of Marco's head with a tender gesture. "Why didn't you tell me?"

Marco's hands flattened against the floor of the chamber, his bow becoming more pronounced—but he said nothing.

"How long have you known?" Jared whispered, never moving his hand from atop Marco's bowed head.

"My lord, I beg of you . . ." Marco's voice broke.

"Tell me, Madjin. Are you truly my brother?"

Marco sighed. "Yes."

"Yet you kept this fact from me?"

Marco pressed his forehead against the floor, hesitating, then . . . "Yes."

Jared removed his hand from Marco's head, his voice assuming an angry timbre. "Why, in All's name, would you not have told me the truth?"

Marco didn't answer, and Kelsey sought out Thea across the room. Her friend's eyes were so deeply troubled, so melancholy, that she knew she had to intervene. "Jared, give him time. Okay? Just give him time. This has been a very big day for all of us."

"I don't want to give my brother time!" he roared, rearing back on his haunches. "My Madjin is a D'Aravni. . . . He just saved my life. I felt his love and respect for me, yet he chose to keep the truth from me? He chose not to tell me that he's my own brother?" Jared began to tremble. "You will answer me, Madjin. *Why* did you not *tell* me?"

Marco jolted upright, out of the bow, and clasped Jared by the shoulder. "Because of this! Because I knew you would cast me away. That you'd never trust me again."

"Because of this?" Jared repeated quietly. "I do not understand."

Marco buried his head in both hands. "I never knew, Jared. All my life I have been your bonded servant. I've trained as part of your Madjin circle . . . but no one ever told me who I truly was. I lived in ignorance until . . ." Marco shook his head, still averting his eyes.

Jared crawled closer to him, putting a hand on his brother's shoulder. "Until when?" he prompted in a gentle voice. "Tell me how you found out."

"I'm so ashamed," was all Marco whispered.

"Please, my lord, forgive me for my lowly station, for being your servant, for being . . . Gods, just forgive me for being your brother."

"Why would I forgive you when I'm so deeply grateful?" Jared asked, his eyes never leaving Marco. "You saved my life. . . . You saved Kelsey and Erica. And you"—Jared squeezed Marco's shoulder significantly—"you are the family I've always yearned for. I seek only to know why you've kept this fact from me."

Marco dropped both hands away from his face. "Because I feared you would not let me serve you. All I know is what I am." Marco extended his wrist, unfurling his protector's brand so that it glowed in the air just above his hand. "This is all that I've ever been. If I cannot serve my king . . . my brother, well, then I am nothing at all."

Jared reached out, skimming his hand across the undulating tattoo that hovered in the air between them. "Surely you trust me better than that, Marco."

"It isn't trust." He retracted the glowing emblem so that it disappeared again, and pulled his wrist against his chest. "It's who I am, what I am. I am not a D'Aravni, not in my heart."

"You certainly looked like one a few moments ago." Jared smiled thoughtfully, glancing toward Thea. "And you, dear cousin, you've kept this secret as well?"

Thea snorted gracelessly. "Please, Jared, don't blame me on that count. I've been begging him to tell you for months."

Jared rocked back on his heels. "So how long have you known—truly, Marco? When did you learn the truth?"

"From Sabrina. When I was ready to mate with Thea, she told me everything. . . ."

"We share the same parents?"

Marco's dark face blanched. "The same father. My mother was a Madjin in the palace. It's . . . a bit ugly, I'm afraid."

Jared stared at the floor. "I was never under any illusions about my parents' marriage, about it being a happy one."

Kelsey honestly thought that Marco might faint dead on the spot. "Truly?" was all he blurted out.

"Were you afraid the facts would hurt me?" Jared's voice was still deeply hoarse.

Marco nodded his head. "They were your parents. All you have are your memories of them."

"Not true." Jared rose slowly to his feet. "Not true at all . . . because now I have a beautiful miracle: I have a brother." Jared extended his large hand toward Kelsey. "And I have a family . . . a full, perfect family. All around me in this chamber are the ones I love most of all."

Kelsey burrowed against Jared's bare chest, still amazed that he had returned to her. Tears welled in her eyes, and she didn't blink them away. All she had ever dreamed or hoped for was right within her arms and belly. "If you hadn't come back to me," she whispered against him. "If you hadn't . . ."

Jared stroked her hair, winding his fingers through it in long, lingering waves. "I will always find my way back to you, sweet Kelsha."

"I just couldn't let you go." She felt the dampness of her tears touch his skin. "I'm sorry it had to be so harsh, getting you home."

"You're brave, sweetheart. So very brave." Jared shifted her in his embrace, calling out, "Jakob? It's your turn next."

"I'm here, J." Jake had held his distance for the past moments, obviously quiet inside his own head. He stood on the far side of the chamber, hands shoved deep in both pockets, staring at the floor.

"You are my other brother," Jared pronounced softly. "And I want to know why you're here and not with Medic Tyler."

"She's gone, J. That's all. Besides, where else would I be? Not when we were saving your sorry Refarian ass."

With that, they all began to laugh. The heady release was so palpable, the reality that they'd dodged a poison bullet from eternity so intense, what could they do but laugh?

They were together; that was the only thing that mattered. Their strange, ragtag little family was back together at last.

Chapter Twenty-seven

Shelby huddled on the bench, waiting for the bus that would take her from the square in downtown Jackson to . . . where? Gods only knew. The line just went in a fat circular arc, trekking from hotel to motel, resort to resort. She was in an idiotic loop that led to absolutely nowhere. The thing was, she could have practically been to Cheyenne by now, but she just couldn't summon up the nerve to really leave Jake.

His eyes haunted her, those electric green depths that forever seemed to sift right through her soul, to dive into the marrow of her very being.

You have to stand still for a while. Stand still with me.

That's what he'd said, and his urgent, loving words had only driven her farther away. Had only made her want to run, just like he'd accused her of doing. So if she really was a runner, why was she still riding circles around Jackson, just ten miles away from the one man who terrified her more than anyone else in the universe?

Because you can't leave him. And you can't stop loving him, either. . . . Running won't ever fix that one. You're a liar, but those lies can't keep you away from him.

She pulled her denim jacket tightly about her body, cursing Wyoming for being so godsdamned cold, even now in May. Whatever happened to global warming? Obviously someone in this part of the human realm hadn't gotten that memo, not with the light snow flurries currently falling from the sky. The snow itself seemed like nothing so much as one big, gargantuan lie. June was right around the corner, yet they had snow sifting down on them, as soft as a summer rain.

I'll call him. That's what I'll do! Just give him a little ring on his cell and make sure that he's all right. She felt within her jacket pocket but with sinking awareness remembered that she'd dropped the phone on her bed back at base. It had been meant as a *gesture*, one of those big, dramatic statements that indicated she was cutting all ties between the two of them. So much for melodrama, always better in theory than actual practice. What she wouldn't do just to have that little slim-line right back in her cozy pocket.

Gods, what she wouldn't do to hear Jake's throaty, deep voice just one more time.

You won't leave me. Not this time.

Clearly he hadn't thought her actually capable of it, hadn't believed the very worst of her nature. Tears burned her eyes, blurring her view of the square, of the bars and tourist shops lined all about her. Of the newly fallen snow dusting the elk-horn arch across the street.

From nowhere the urge to time walk overcame her. *I could just delve in, reach out . . . a little bit. I could know whether Jake and I are actually meant to have a future.* She bucked against the compulsion, knowing that whatever she might see, it would only doom her to fulfilling her vision's prophecy. Still, the impulse was there, that need to see what life might offer them if only she *could* stop running.

From around the corner, a bus lurched forward, hissing as it came to a stop in front of her. The door cranked open, the bus driver staring down at her expectantly. "Where you headed?" Shelby asked, stalling. The sign on the front said GREEN LINE.

"This is the In-Town, honey. That's what you've got."

"But your sign says it's the—"

"Doesn't matter what the sign says," the driver told her impatiently. "This is the In-Town line."

Lies and more godsdamned lies. Signs that claimed what wasn't the truth; snow when it should have been practically summer; men who went by names that didn't belong to them. *Lies and more lies,* she thought again, feeling suddenly furious.

Cars passed by, their headlights arcing through the nighttime that enfolded her. The driver continued to wait, her impatience so concrete she could almost smell the woman's irritation. "You gonna keep sitting there, or you gonna do something?"

Hell, yeah, she was going to do something. She rose slowly to her feet, tugging her denim jacket close about her body. The bus released another hissing sigh as if it were calling out to her, but she walked past its open door . . . and kept on walking. Then began running. Running and running and running; for her very life she ran, never planning to stop.

Because finally, at long last, she knew how she was going to fix the madness.

Shelby's feet slapped against the hardwood of the main lodge as she tore up the two flights of stairs that would take her to Jake's quarters. At the first landing, she nearly bowled over her queen, who was carrying several blankets in her arms.

"Whoa! Shelby, I thought you were . . ."

Breathlessly, she lowered into a half bow. "I'm back, my lady."

"And with a vengeance, I see." Kelsey gave her an insightful smile. "He went upstairs a while ago, so you should be in luck."

Shelby nodded, murmured a thank-you, and hit the next flight of stairs.

Arriving at Jake's door, she didn't wait to knock, didn't bother with any kind of formality—she just turned the knob and catapulted right through. Jake sat sprawled on the leather sofa in nothing but a pair of thin boxer shorts, a leather-bound novel in his hand. As she stumbled into the room, he jumped to his feet with a surprised shout.

"What *the* . . . Shell?" He looked past her at the open door as she kicked it shut without a backward glance. "I thought you'd left." His green eyes were bloodshot, tired, with dark smudges beneath them that betrayed his deep emotion and exhaustion.

"I did leave, but then . . ."

"You came back," he finished quietly.

She gave him a hesitant smile and took a few slow steps forward. "I hope that's all right."

He gave a vigorous nod. "Oh, yeah. Yeah, totally okay, of course. Do you want to . . . sit down or something?" He indicated the sofa, turning slightly so that the muscles of his bare chest rippled magnificently.

You are so very gorgeous. A true thing of beauty.

"You're not going commando," she observed flirtatiously.

Color rose to his face, and he gave the band of his boxers a little pop. "I—I, uh, I picked these up at the commissary. They're comfortable."

"Calvin Klein?" She took another step closer, struggling to breathe.

He stared down at the boxers as if he'd never noticed them before. "I dunno . . . I guess so? One of our purchasing agents has gotten way into the human realm, and I just thought . . . I dunno," he repeated, popping the waistband again. "I thought they were a good idea."

She bobbed her head, gasping, and staggered toward the sofa. "I . . . ran the . . . whole way here."

He planted one of his bearlike hands on her shoulder, pushing her onto the leather couch. "Sit down." Her body obeyed easily, folding downward. "Ran . . . from where?"

She pressed a trembling hand to her temple. "I think from town."

"Gods, Shell." He rummaged around on the sofa and then thrust a thick sweatshirt into her hands. "Put this on; you're shaking all over."

She did as he ordered, drinking in the heady scent of him that suffused the cotton pullover. If he hadn't been with her, she'd have curled up with the thing, holding it close against her body and sniffing it until the sun cracked the dawn.

As she settled back onto the sofa, finally catching her breath, he kept his hands self-consciously in front of his hips, and then after several awkward moments crossed the room, yanking a white T-shirt off the floor and over his head. As if that flimsy layer of clothing could hide the pure god that he was—could possibly contain his bulky muscles and his large, developed body.

"Do you need some water?" He gestured toward what she realized was a small kitchenette. "Or . . . food? I have a whole fridge full. I could make you a sandwich. Or soup . . . or not." He dipped his head, shuffling from foot to foot awkwardly. "Whatever. I can take care of you."

"I know you can, Scott."

His whole body gave an ungainly jerk, bright green eyes meeting hers in a flash. "Don't call me that. I've told you before," he said in a sharp tone.

She sank back into the sofa, barely able to lift her head. "I'm sick of all the dishonesty. In this war. And between us."

"There's no lies with you and me, Shell."

"Of course there are. Big, bad lies, the kind that can kill a relationship." She worked to lift her eyes to his, afraid of what she'd see. The white-hot pain in his gaze ripped at her very soul. "Every day I spend with you is a lie. Because you're Scott Dillon, and until you admit that fact—really admit it—then we got no future, you and me. You're still running, Scott. Your maneuver just looks a little bit different than mine. I had to accept who and what you are as an

Antousian; now you need to do the same thing and stop running from the truth of who you are."

He staggered backward, holding both hands up as if to shield himself. "I'm not the one running here; that's you."

She rose to her feet, feeling unsteady, but closing the distance between them easily. "So you've said, boy. So you've said. But I'm not the one hiding behind a name that's not my own. *Scott.*"

"Why does it matter?" he asked in a shockingly small voice. "Huh, Shelby? It shouldn't matter, not really."

"Because Jake still mourns Hope, still lives in the past, and he always will. That's why." She slapped her chest significantly. "But Scott? Well, Scott lives for me."

He shook his head, wincing as if she'd just shot him. "Please don't. Please just . . . really, just . . . don't."

"Why not, Scott? Does it hurt you for me to call you by name, Scott? Scott Dillon. *S'Skautsa.* Beautiful name, lovely Refarian name, plopped right down on an Antousian boy."

He lifted both hands against her, shielding himself. "Don't do this," he said, his voice almost pleading.

"Tell me why I shouldn't . . . S'Skautsa?"

"Because it is a Refarian name!" He screamed loud enough to rouse the entire compound. "I was given a Refarian name. . . ."

"Yes, that's right," she whispered, closing in on him, but still he stumbled backward. "You're Refarian."

"Antousian," he cried out in a plaintive voice. "A fucking hybrid freak. Everything you hate and despise. No wonder you run from me."

"I'm here, Scott," she whispered, reaching to touch his cheek. "And I'm not going anywhere. I don't despise what you are."

"I am a *vlksai*!" he spit out, clenching both her shoulders within his hands.

"Yet your parents gave you the name of a great

Refarian king from the very beginning. I wonder why that was."

He lifted his arm over his face, still backing up until he hit the solid wall of his room. "Stop, Shell. I beg of you."

She placed her hands squarely against his strong, muscular chest. "They gave you a Refarian name, Scott, for one reason and one reason only. Are you going to tell me why?"

He shook his head, clearly unwilling to lower his arm.

"Then I'm going to say it," she continued. "Because they knew your heart. They knew what and who you were going to be, right down to the marrow of your being, long before you even existed. You aren't a killer, and you're not a monster. . . . You're the gentlest, kindest man I've ever known. Of any species. *Any species.*"

Slowly, he lowered his arm, tears gleaming in his exotic eyes. "I can't accept that I'm Refarian."

"Scott does. I know him pretty well, you know, and he doesn't even consider himself Antousian at all."

He slumped heavily. "His life's been different than mine so far. Charmed."

"But you *are* Scott. Say it. Agree with me."

"No," he argued, shaking his head vigorously. "This is about you and your need to run."

"I won't confront that inside myself until you—you, Scott Dillon—stop running from me and the rest of the world. Tell me now. What is your name? *Tell me!*"

From the look on his dark face, she might as well have stabbed him with a dagger. "I don't mourn her anymore," he practically breathed.

"No, you're right. You don't. You only mourn the man you were before she died. So say it with me; tell me your name."

He heaved at the air between them, sucking in dry, desperate gasps of it—eyeing her so angrily, she almost decided to back down from this plan of hers. But the thing was, she knew it was the only way.

Every instinct inside of her said that he had to come clean with her, that they could have a future only if he would truly *be* himself.

One last time, she encouraged him; she pushed forward, wrapping her arms upward about his neck. Burrowing into him, planting her forehead against his thick, powerful chest, she nearly whimpered, "Tell me your name, soldier."

A long, long silence met her entreaty, and then he crumpled into her arms with a whisper. "I am S'Skautsa."

The need to claim her came roaring to life within his blood. He was so desperate to have that feminine, delicate body of hers pushed up beneath his that he began to tremble right down to his bare feet. With a bellowing growl, he spun her around until her back was up against the wall. Planting his palms on each side of her face, he framed her much smaller body with his own. His cock stiffened inside his boxers, lengthening until it pushed right out of the opening in front. Pressing his hips against her, he let her feel just how turned on he was.

"This is what Scott was always about," he said in a low voice. "He liked it rough."

"So make it rough for me." Her pale eyes sparkled with danger and seduction. "You take me however you want . . . Scott."

He rocked his hips, and she fell into the same rhythm. "You've been forewarned. Cause I can't hold back, not tonight." He pressed his mouth against her neck, nibbling so harshly it would leave a mark. This moment was all about claiming her.

She tilted her head upward. "Think I can't handle you, soldier? You already know I like it *just* like this."

He took her hands and planted them over her head, pinning them against the wall with his own, much larger palms. The position left her vulnerable, her large breasts jutting outward through the material of her turtleneck. Her nipples had beaded from arousal, looking like two fabulous pearls beneath the white material of her sweater.

"Arch for me," he commanded, and with a flick of her tongue, she complied.

The round fullness of each breast protruded even more dramatically, and he smiled, a low, dark growl of appreciation rumbling inside his chest. "Oh, yes, sweet thing. You are . . . stunning."

All her need for control had vanished; she was surrendering herself completely. Willingly. Still, her gaze traveled down his body, at least as much of it as she could see. He ground his hips against her, letting her feel the thickened length of his shaft.

"I know you want to touch me," he said as she flushed. "I sense it."

She raised her eyebrows, a coy smile on her lips. "Oh, you sense it, do you?"

"Do I have to soul-gaze you?"

She blinked up at him. "I want to feel you in my hands."

He growled in deep pleasure at her words. "Not just yet." He pressed his face against hers, scenting her. A long, sweet draft of her aroma filtered into his lungs, hitting his body like wildfire. "Oh . . . gods help me," he moaned, releasing her hands slowly until they dropped back to her sides.

And she was all over him the moment he set her free, nearly tackling him as she wrapped her body about his. His hands skimmed up and down her hips, around her back. Vaguely, she was aware that they were moving in a sort of circular motion, heading toward his bedroom as, piece by piece, he undressed her. Kissing her hotly, he tugged at her turtleneck, getting her loose from it, and only when he was ready to ditch the sweater did he break the kiss long enough to get it over her head.

Then he clamped his lips against hers once again, swirling his tongue inside her mouth, fumbling with her jeans. She slid her hands low about his waist, feeling the smooth warmth of his flesh as she began to work at his boxers, shoving them lower down his hips.

"Gotta have you out of these," she murmured, tugging them down until his cock sprang free with a heavy, joyous bounce.

She managed to untangle her feet from the crumpled jeans, and kicked them halfway across the room. They ricocheted off his coffee table with a soft thud, distracting her briefly, and when she turned back to him he was completely, gloriously naked. She sucked in a breath, staggering backward toward the fireplace.

He was so utterly beautiful to behold, his dusky skin glowing in the firelight, his feet planted slightly apart. That long, thick erection of his jutted outward, glistening with intense arousal and need. He stood bathed in the firelight without shame, his large shoulders defined by striations of muscle that roped down to his much narrower hips. She wanted to kneel at his feet, to treat him like the god he almost appeared to be.

"I can't talk," she finally squeaked out, her gaze traveling down his length one more time. "I mean, I've seen you before, plenty of times, but . . . not like this."

"Shelby Tyler? Speechless? This is a first." He laughed in a whiskey-rich voice, circling closer to her. There was an implied physical threat in his tone, the promise of intense, raw seduction as he neared her.

She reached a hand to the mantel, steadying herself. "It's you. I've never just . . . looked at you, not like this."

His lashes lowered as he tugged her flush against his naked body. Skin to skin, warmth to warmth, they stood before the fire. His erection pressed into her stomach, nudging at her belly button. "This body, Shell," he told her softly, sliding his palms underneath her bottom, "it belongs to you. I belong to you completely."

She grinned. "I promise to be kind."

"I know you will," he said, not dropping his serious tone.

She beamed suddenly, tilting her head back so she could stare into his eyes. "Question game," she purred softly, and rabid heat hit his face. The last time they'd gone that route . . .

"If you could have sex with me in any position right now, what would it be?"

He swallowed hard, his throat tightening. "I'd . . . be on top . . . so I could stare into your eyes the whole time."

"I like that answer," she whispered, her lashes fluttering coquettishly. Shelby Tyler definitely knew how to crank his engine to full throttle. That simple fluttering of her eyes and he couldn't hold back a needy growl. Hell, it was about the neediest growl he'd ever laid on her.

She planted her palm in the center of his chest, stroking him sensually for a moment, then whispered, "And where . . . where would you make love to me, staring me in the eyes the whole time?"

He eased her hands off of him, took one step back, and dropped right on his knees, falling into a worshipful posture that he hoped would reveal how totally he loved her. She deserved a little worshipping. Opening his arms to her, he fixed her with his gaze.

"Here," he said. "Right here, in front of the fire."

She launched herself into his arms, tumbling with him to the floor. He mounted her without another word, sliding into her slickness, and buried himself to the hilt. The floor was hard beneath his knees and forearms, but he didn't care.

There was only Shelby, looking up into his eyes with adoration. There was only the deepest realization inside of him: that he loved this woman. Completely, with absolute abandon. He, who had never believed he could fall in love again, was a total goner.

That thought sent his body into a frenzy; his hips went wild, pumping against hers, and she rose off the floor, meeting every single thrust. Then she took her muscular calves and wrapped them squarely about his lower back, and he sank even deeper into her core.

Faster he sped, feeling her quivering, grasping relief the moment it came. And he went off like a rocket grenade at the exact same moment, shooting hot spurts of his seed deep, deep inside of her.

Dimly he wondered if they'd just created a baby. The thought made him grin like a schoolboy as he pressed his sweaty forehead against hers. Yeah, he'd love a family with this woman. He'd love . . . a lifetime with her.

Chapter Twenty-eight

Kelsey walked with Jared into their bedroom, one large arm slung across her shoulders. He was still a little weak but otherwise seemed totally back to being himself, a genuine miracle when she thought of how he'd been locked in his D'Aravnian form only hours earlier. It had been one exhaustingly long day, no doubt about that, and she felt tired and achy throughout her body—especially around the middle of her very pregnant belly, but she tried to ignore that fact.

Jared had been examined at the medical complex immediately after returning from the mitres. His wounds had been treated, and the prognosis was good—he wouldn't have any significant scarring to speak of. The medics had poked and prodded at him until he'd grumbled impatiently, something quiet about needing time alone with his wife. They'd relented then, backing off with respectful murmurs that had made her grin. Everyone in the compound loved their king and would do whatever he wanted, including making sure he had time with his queen.

Closing the door to their quarters, he grumbled about the room temperature. "It's freaking frigid in here."

"Told you before." She laughed. "Please don't say 'freaking.' It's just too weird to me."

He laughed low, raking a hand through his long,

loose hair. "All right, then. I am cold, my mate. Our quarters seem quite chilled."

She handed him one of the extra blankets she'd fetched for him and sank wearily onto the end of their bed. "It's really not cold. You're still adjusting from your Change."

He nodded, looking awkward for a moment.

"What is it?" she asked.

He stared at the floor between them, and then cleared his throat uncomfortably.

"Spill it, Jareshk."

He nodded, still avoiding her eyes. "Thank you for not giving up on me when I was so . . . lost. So very, very lost."

"How could I ever give up on you?"

"I honestly didn't think I'd make it back to you. That was the worst part of . . . it. Of being unable to shift back. It was knowing that I'd never hold you again, never touch you again . . . never hold Erica in my arms." Tears gleamed in his eyes. "So, yes, uh . . . thank you."

"But you did Change back. You're here, right now with both of us," she told him softly.

His gaze lifted, boring into her very soul. "But I didn't think I would make it. Do you understand what that was like for me? Thinking I'd never touch you again?"

"I was scared, too," she admitted quietly.

"I know. I felt your fear."

She cringed. "I'm sorry. I tried to hide it—"

"No!" he thundered, stomping at the floor with his booted foot. "It kept me together. Knowing how desperately you needed me . . . still wanted me. I cursed your fear, but it kept me sane, kept me tethered to this world, Kelsey. Do you understand?"

"I felt your fear, too, and it kept me holding on."

He paced the room, clearly thinking. "Without you, I would have been utterly lost . . . forever."

"But we're both here now, and you're back. You're back for good."

"But my D'Aravnian side has had its way with me, love." He stopped in front of her, staring at her hard. "I'm different now, after being lost in my Change for so long. I'm not yet sure what that will mean."

Kelsey tamped down a fresh wave of fear, trying to ignore his dire warning. "Different . . . how?" she asked softly.

He turned his blazing black gaze right on her. "I feel more primal, much more on the verge of something. It's like I can almost touch my energy, like it's hovering right beyond my reach."

"It's only been a few hours, Jared! Jeez, give yourself some time."

He shook his head. "No. Something is altered inside of me. Only time will tell what this feeling means."

Kelsey just couldn't accept what he was saying, not now. Not with their baby so full inside her belly, not when she was so deeply grateful to have him back.

"You know what you need? A big, hot bath. With me."

He gave her a gentle smile. "That sounds like a fantastic plan." He cupped her cheek, kissing her on the lips. In reaction, Erica did a little shimmying movement inside of her belly. And then suddenly a sharp buckle of pain cinched about her waist. *Uh-oh.* Erica wasn't due for another week. But then, just as quickly, the pain faded.

She struggled up onto her feet, feeling more ungainly than she had at any point in the pregnancy. "Of course, you might have to call a battalion to get me out of the tub once I'm in there." She laughed.

"I'll sweep you into my arms."

She cocked an eyebrow. "Have you looked at me lately, sweetheart? I'm a bit round for arm sweeping."

He gave her a gallant smile. "Trust me, I will take care of you, sweet love."

* * *

"Cramps?" Jared jolted upright so fast that he sent bathwater sloshing over the sides of the claw-foot tub.

"Contractions," she amended, wincing as her belly grew hard and tight. She could have bounced a penny off the freaking thing. They'd been cuddled in the tub for almost an hour, until the warm water had finally grown tepid, and all the while her contractions had been growing more intense and frequent.

"It's time, Jared," she whispered softly. "Erica's coming . . . not this moment, but in the next few hours."

She leaned back between Jared's legs, holding him in place with the weight of her body so he wouldn't bolt right out of the tub.

"For the love of All." Jared's hands crushed down on her shoulders. "We need to get you to the medical complex right away." He slid a protective hand atop her belly. "She's so warm," he whispered hoarsely, and then looked at her. "Wh-what if we harmed her in the mitres chamber? What if *I* hurt her?"

Kelsey covered his hand with her own, rubbing it atop her belly. "Erica is fine, Jared. Perfectly, beautifully fine."

"You can't know that." The pained emotion in his voice tore at her heart. He'd already been through enough; the last thing he needed was to speculate that he'd harmed their baby girl in any way.

"I *do* know that, Jareshk. I'm her mother, and I sense it. Besides, while you've been running this revolution, I've been going to mothering classes with Anna."

"I never knew that." His hand, which had been stroking her belly, stilled. "Why didn't you tell me?"

She snorted with laughter, leaning into him right as the contraction finished. With a slight moan, she rode the wave of pain to completion. "Because I knew you'd want to be part of the classes. And too much info was just going to freak you out unnecessarily. You already worry too much about both of us as it is. So I saved this moment until . . . now."

"This moment?" He leaned forward in the tub so he could actually see her face. "This moment . . . You're having the baby now? Here in the *tub*? I don't understand."

"It's what the medical chief suggested. Said it was the most soothing way for Erica to enter the world, right here in the bathwater and in our own room. That if Erica should try to make her Change right after she pops out of me, well, the water would stop her."

"Erica can't Change the moment she enters this world. She's not prepared!"

"But apparently D'Aravnian babies do that. The doctor said you Changed right when you were born. It's in your medical records." She laughed softly. "Your poor mother; I can only imagine. It's also why I have to go natural with this birth, because it will reduce the likelihood of that happening."

Jared clunked back in the tub, his head making a loud crack against the tiled wall. Kelsey twisted, trying to make sure he was all right. "Jared?"

"I think I'm going to pass out."

"Don't you dare."

"Oh, I'm not. Don't worry, love, I'm right here. Right here." He leaned forward again, wrapping both arms about her. "But . . . you're going to allow me to call a medic, right?"

"Ha! So that's it. The king is terrified that he might actually have to deliver his own baby."

He growled at her, rising to his feet. "I'm going to contact the med complex right now. Get them to send a whole team up here."

"They're on alert and expecting it. But there's one more thing I need, Jared."

"Anything, sweet love." He swung a leg over the side of the tub.

"I want Shelby to be with me. I want her to help deliver the baby."

Jared placed one fist over his heart and bowed deeply, showing her the ancient, traditional gesture reserved for Refarian royals. "Yes, my lady. As you wish."

Jake lay atop Shelby, panting in her ear, trying to regain his equilibrium a little. Inside of her, his cock had softened, but he hadn't slipped out yet. He wanted to maintain the intimacy between them for as long as he could.

That plan was dashed, however, when his comm erupted from where he'd left it over on the sofa. And it was Jared, so there wasn't any dodging duty, not this time.

"Shit," he cursed, then for good measure tacked on *damn it* a few times.

"I'll be right here waiting," Shelby told him sleepily.

Jake walked backward toward the sofa, never taking his gaze off her. "I'm holding you to that."

Reaching for the comm, he barked into it without even thinking. "Dillon here."

Jared's voice crackled across the connection. "Scott?" His confusion was obvious, but more than that, he sounded . . . a little breathless.

"It's me. Long story, J. What's up?"

"Is Shelby with you?"

He coughed into the comm. "Uh, yeah, she's . . . uh, with me."

"Good, because I need her. I mean, Kelsey needs her. . . . Well, uh, we both . . . Oh, *meshdki*, Jakob, we're having a baby. It's princess time, and I need Shelby down here stat."

All the birthing and mothering classes didn't add up to zip, not when you were in the moment, ready to deliver. Kelsey glared at Jared across the bathroom. He'd propped himself against the door of the glass shower, his eyes assuming a glazed, stunned expression. It had been a big day for him, and it wasn't like there was room beside the tub, but freaking hell! The pain was like nothing—nothing—anyone could have explained to her.

With a scream, she glared at Jared again. "You bastard! You did this to me," she cursed, then began to laugh hysterically as another wave of crashing agony passed.

"I'm sorry." He looked sheepish as he grinned, muttering slowly, "I apologize for having given you baby Erica."

"You think I'm talking out of my ass? Just cause all of you can *see* my freaking ass? Huh, Jareshk? This freaking sucks!"

He inclined his head as the medics worked with her. "It's a beautiful bottom, sweet love."

"That doesn't make this better!"

Shelby kept massaging her belly, murmuring in Refarian. "And you!" Kelsey poked at Shelby's shoulder. "You're not helping at all."

"I know, sweetie," Shelby said soothingly, a strange smile on her lips. "But it's all gonna be over soon."

"That's what you say. You're not . . . oh!" Kelsey shouted, clamping her pelvis down.

Shelby held onto her. "You're doing great. Just hang on a little while longer, my queen. Ride it out."

"I don't want to ride it out." She shook her head wildly. "I want to yell some more."

"Then you just go right ahead." Shelby moved her hand to Kelsey's hair, stroking it away from her cheek. "You scream all you want. You let us all have it, okay? Let her rip."

Kelsey doubled over slightly, moaning. "Oh, God . . ."

Someone began running more water into the tub, and the warmth was soothing. "You're almost there. Almost there," Shelby promised her, continuing to comb her fingers through Kelsey's hair.

And then Kelsey's large belly began to glow. A radiant humming noise filled the room, emanating right out of her stomach.

"Here we go," Shelby told her. "When I tell you to, I want you to push. You hear me, my lady? You're gonna clamp down and just . . ."

"Push!" Kelsey screamed.

Chapter Twenty-nine

Jared stared at the tiny dark head that was nestled against his shoulder, feeling more than slightly in shock. He wasn't numb, not at all. No, it was as if every part of his being had come alive, as if every molecule of his dual self had been electrified in a wholly new way. These first few moments alone with Erica were a treasure he'd never forget, not if he lived one hundred years. Not if he traveled the universe and back, or jumped thousands of dimensions via the mitres. Nothing . . . nothing would ever compare to this one quiet, perfect moment.

Miracles were like that, he thought, nuzzling Erica closer. They were indelible, leaving a birthmark on time itself.

Kelsey lay sleeping beside him, down for the count, and he kept himself propped against the pillows, watching over his family. All the horror and blood of his past twenty years faded to nothing as he rested beside them, watching over them as they slept.

He couldn't stop kissing Erica's downy hair or sniffing the sweet newborn smell of her little body. Her scent was pristine, perfect, as if All himself had plucked her right from the heavens, delivering her into his arms. She slept with the deep slumber of the giants even though she was only slightly more than seven pounds.

Shifting on the bed, he held her tight against his shoulder, feeling uncertain and awkward. Surely someone so tiny would be irreparably damaged if you didn't handle her just right. Nonsense, of course, but he felt so inadequate, so unprepared to care for her—or even hold her—like she needed and deserved. She let out a soft gurgle as he adjusted himself against the pillows, but continued sleeping. After a moment, Jared released the breath he'd been holding tight inside his lungs.

"Erica Arianna B'net D'Aravni," he whispered against her head. "You are heir to the throne of your people. An awfully big job for such a tiny person."

Tears swam in his eyes, blurring his vision. After all the years of fighting, such a happy, joyful day seemed almost too much to believe. Why had he waited so long to hope for it?

A quiet knock sounded on their chamber door. He smiled. Although they weren't yet receiving visitors, he had summoned two particular people he wanted to be part of this moment.

"Come in," he called quietly, and after a moment, the knob turned. "It's all right—come on in," he repeated.

Marco's dark head appeared in the half-opened door, and Jared grinned, waving him in. Thea followed right behind, beaming as she practically knocked Marco out of the way.

As he moved so that Thea and Marco could get a better look, Jared was amazed that Erica didn't even stir.

"There she is," Thea whispered softly, bending close. "Oh, Jared, she's so incredibly beautiful."

Jared wanted to answer but found that he could do no more than smile and stare down at his gorgeous miracle.

"Can I touch her?" Thea asked, reaching a few tentative fingers toward the top of Erica's head. He smiled up at her. For all of Thea's soldier-hardened ways, he could see the yearning in her eyes that she, too, would one day a hold a baby of her own.

"Here," he said, easing sideways on the bed. "I'll give her to you."

Thea took a backward step. "Oh, no. I can't hold her. She might break."

Jared burst into quiet laughter. "I've been thinking the same thing, but so far, no damage done. Surely you can do at least as well as I, cousin."

Then he glanced past her at Marco, at his . . . brother. Still such a strange thought, but one that filled him with a rush of tenderness. "And, uncle, you may hold her next."

"Uncle," Marco repeated wondrously, blushing as he stared down at the bundle within Jared's arms. "Yes, I . . . I like that."

"It's who you are," Jared told him. "Just as you are my brother."

Marco swallowed visibly, nodding, but said nothing more.

After gently easing Erica into Thea's arms, Jared rose to his feet and extended a hand to Marco, a handshake that quickly melded into an embrace.

In an instant they pulled away from each other, clearly feeling awkward. "I'm proud to be your brother," Marco told him hoarsely. "And proud to be little Erica's uncle."

Jared smiled. "And you will always be my Madjin."

Relief filled Marco's eyes. "I'm counting on it, sir."

"No, I'm the one who's counting on it. I've come to rely on you far too much to have you back away now."

"I would never shirk my duties. You must know that, my lord." Marco stared at his boots, shifting from foot to foot, saying nothing for a long moment.

"I never had any doubt."

Jared eased a hand onto Marco's shoulder. "Look at me, brother," he whispered. Marco hesitated, then finally lifted his eyes. "You will be my Madjin, always, but you will also become much more. You are a prince, a D'Aravnian in your own right. I will expect much from you. So it's time that you expanded your view of yourself."

Marco shook his head vigorously. "I don't know that I can."

Jared tightened his grip on his brother's shoulder. "You will, because you are marked as a D'Aravni, same as I. Are you not?"

"I am, my lord."

"Show me your mark."

With a sigh, Marco extended his wrist and unfurled the vibrant, glowing tattoo that revealed his true heritage. This holographic brand was the one true proof that the man before him shared blood with him, that they were bound by far more than vows or tradition. They were family.

Without a word, Jared also revealed his royal mark, allowing it to spin out between them until their two swirling brands touched, joined, became one. "The blood that runs between us is the same, Marco," he said quietly. "You see it, right now. And now, my dear brother and Madjin . . . you will live it."

Marco nodded, whispering, "Thank you."

Behind them, Erica began to make soft sounds as if she were waking. "You two," Thea chided, "are making too much noise. Just hug each other again and come back over here. Marco, you need to meet your new niece."

And so they did embrace one more time, sealing their new relationship without words. Then Jared turned once more to gaze upon the beautiful faces of his wife and daughter.

Two hours later, and Jake had Shelby back in front of his fireplace. They'd made love again—several times—and he'd marveled at the way his body stayed on permanent red alert for her. Tangled as one, they were resting together in front of a roaring fire, propped up on several throw pillows, still and thoughtful. Outside the large windows of his living room, Jake could see heavy snowflakes swirling close to the panes, illuminated by the dim light filtering out through the glass.

Neither said a word, and for once the energy between them wasn't a sexual one. It was just the warm, humming comfort of knowing you were loved. Completely, front to back, up and down. Jake nestled her closer in the crook of his arm; she was lying right in front of him on her side, their two bodies a tangle of warmth and tenderness.

"I love you, Shell," he whispered against the top of her head. "With all my heart, I love you."

She said nothing, just gave a little bob of her head. Concerned, he leaned over her shoulder, wanting to see the expression on her face, and was shocked to see tears rolling down her cheeks.

"Sweetheart, why are you crying?" He reached with the pad of his thumb and stroked one of the big tears away.

She shook her head, leaning back into him, and he got the idea that she couldn't find her voice.

"You upset with me?" That couldn't be right. Couldn't even be close to accurate. He desperately ran through possible reasons for her tears. "Was it delivering the baby? What?" His voice rose in slight alarm.

"No," she finally croaked, exploding into sobs.

Damn it all, this wasn't the reaction he wanted or had anticipated. He'd thought they were blissfully happy here by the fire. Terror shot through him: What if she was having second thoughts? "Then what the hell's wrong?" He knew he sounded angry, but he could hardly help himself. "Tell me *now*."

She waved her hand back and forth in the air, shaking her head some more, then rolled onto her back. "Happy," she finally managed to gasp.

"You're *happy*?" He cursed low in Refarian, leaning over her. "Shelby . . . you scared the living shit out of me."

"I'm so, so happy," she repeated, gazing up into his eyes. "And I love you. I love you so much that my heart hurts with it."

He leaned down, brushing a loose strand of blond

hair away from her mouth, and kissed her slowly, teasing his tongue back and forth across her lips. "Will you bond with me?" he asked, surprised to realize he'd begun to tremble. This was terrifying terrain, especially knowing her personal history with Nate.

But she beamed, her blue eyes widening to the size of saucers, her eyebrows shooting up to her hairline. "Yes! Yes, yes."

He grinned, rubbing his fingertips lightly over her lips. "Cause if you're not sure . . ."

He was about to rib her some more, but she took hold of his face, yanked him down for a kiss, and murmured, "I'm completely yours . . . for life." With that promise, she silenced him totally by thrusting her tongue deep inside his mouth.

Yours for life, he thought, rolling her beneath him. Yes, he could live forever off that promise of hers.

"But there's something we need to do," she told him, pushing him off of her and sitting up.

"Anything you ask of me." He drew her hand to his lips, kissing her softly in the center of her palm. "I'm a fool for you, baby."

"I want to call Hope." She eyed him uncertainly, as if she expected him to buck against her request. "Is that okay? She's my friend, you know, and . . . well, I just want to share the news with her first."

He smiled, holding her palm against his cheek. "You know what? I like that plan a lot. With only one change."

Her eyebrows lowered slightly. "Okay."

"I want to call Scott first; then we'll get Hope on the line."

Her eyes grew wide. "Are you shitting me?"

"Your pal actually gave me some great advice earlier today."

She sat up on her knees, a look of incredulity on her face. "You are so not about to tell me that you—"

"I called him about you."

"No freaking way." She tossed a pillow at him.

He actually felt a little proud of himself. "See, I'm

not a total clod when it comes to dealing with my past. Or my future. There was no way I was letting you walk out on me like you did."

She bowed her head. "I'm sorry I hurt you. And I know that I did."

"I wasn't about to give up on you—especially not after talking to Scott."

"What did he say?"

Jake grinned, knowing how she'd love his next words. "He reminded me of who I am. Who I truly am."

"I always did like that Scott Dillon." She laughed, wrapping her arms about his neck and kissing him on the lips. "Such a wise man, too."

He growled despite himself. "Careful, Shell, or I'm gonna get all jealous on you."

She narrowed her eyes. "Maybe I like that."

"Save it for the bedroom," he told her hoarsely.

"I'll meet you there anytime." She slid halfway onto his lap, running her fingertips down his chest suggestively. His cock reacted with an enthusiastic salute, trying to pitch a serious tent right beneath her thigh.

Opening his cell phone, he muttered, "Let's get this call over with."

She pressed her mouth against his ear, and her scent rushed all over him, electrifying him. Awakening him. "The sooner the better." She slid a hand along his hard length, lingering at the thick tip of it as she added in a husky whisper, "Big boy. My *very* big boy."

He uttered a few curses, ready to get the call over with in about ten seconds flat. After he dialed out via the series of relays, his younger self answered on the first ring. "Shelby come back?" Scott barked into the phone.

Jake chuckled, adjusting Shelby on his lap. "Yeah, hey to you, too, buddy."

"I already talked to you earlier," the other man told him with a sarcastic laugh. "Who needs more of you? I just want to know if you got our girl back."

"*My* girl," Jake announced with a low, possessive

growl. Shelby giggled, listening in. Jake tilted the phone slightly outward so she could hear better.

Low, husky laughter crackled over the line. "Interesting. I'll take that as a yes."

"Look, this is a fast call," Jake said. "I've got some news for you."

"I'm listening."

Jake paused, staring deep into Shelby's eyes. She was so close up in his face, he could see all the tiny facets of color, the dark purple around her irises. "Beautiful," he murmured without meaning to.

"Whoa, Jakob. You're not really my type."

"That would be *Shelby*, not your hybrid ass." Jake cleared his throat. "So here's the big news. Shell and I are going to get married. She's agreed to be my bondmate."

The other end of the line exploded with a whooping noise that was so loud, he had to hold the phone away from his ear. Yeah, his younger self definitely liked this turn of events. He wasn't such a bad guy after all, he thought, with a strange laugh.

"Congratulations, man," Dillon told him once he'd stopped carrying on. "To both of you. Shelby's a great match for you."

"Just our type," Jake added, reaching to cup one of Shelby's fabulously large breasts.

Having Scott in his life was like having an identical twin, one you didn't remotely resemble, yet who had the entire universe in common with you.

Scott laughed low across the line. "Agreed completely. Possessing all the right attributes."

Jake squeezed Shelby's breast to underscore the point.

"I heard that, Dillon," Shelby said, leaning close to the phone.

"I meant for you to, Tyler," Scott replied.

Jake shook his head. "Whatever. Put Hope on the line, stat. Shelby wants to talk to her."

After some shuffling around, both couples had engaged their speaker phones, and Hope had shrieked joyously for both of them. Then, never taking her eyes off him, Shelby said, "So Hope, doll, I need a little advice since I'm marrying this guy."

"Anything."

Shelby cleared her throat. "You might want to take it off speaker phone for just a hot second. Girl talk, you know?"

"Uh-oh," Jake said as Shelby walked to the far side of the room. He heightened his hearing, determined not to be left out of this particular conversation.

As it turned out, he didn't need to enhance his senses at all because in an overly loud, overly exaggerated voice Shelby asked, "Well, if there's one thing—any one particular thing—that drives him crazy in bed, what would it be? You know, the sort of thing that you can use as bribery when you need it or to level the playing field if he's just too damned sexy to handle at any point."

Shelby's pale eyes grew wide and round. "Really? Now that I'd *never* have guessed. Uh-huh. Oh, trust me, I already know. I *know*! Yeah, it's insanely high. Just off the charts, but that's a great thing . . . yep. Got it. We'll let you know when the ceremony's going to be . . . not that Scott can actually attend, but we'll work out something."

They clicked off the phone, and Jake stared up at Shelby, his face burning hot. "Did you just tell her I have an insanely high libido? I swear to gods, if you did, I'm going to extract punishment from you in the bedroom."

"No, I didn't say that."

He lifted an eyebrow. "Sounded like it. . . ."

"Hope was the one who said it. I just agreed with her—and she gave me the Kama Sutra 411 that I was after."

He had a pretty good idea of what Hope had told her, but he braced himself nonetheless. "What did she say?"

"I think it's more a matter of demonstration, Jakob."

He groaned, hiding his face. Oh, gods. Hope *had* told her, he thought, his cock doing an urgent lift-and-jump maneuver inside his jeans. Which meant she'd just given his future wife the one sure way to keep him whipped for the rest of their natural lives.

With a roaring growl of anticipation, he leapt to his feet and almost knocked her flat in his eagerness to get at her. "To. The. Bedroom!" he roared, swinging her up into his arms. "Now!"

Shelby slid her thighs about his waist, locking tight around him with her calves. She was light and easy, both arms wrapped about his neck, her curvy little hips flat up against him. She even began a crazy rocking motion as he tightened his grip on her ass.

"She gave me another hint, too," Shelby murmured in his ear as he backed her toward his room. "A sort of runner-up."

He swallowed hard, pausing to kiss her throat, her collarbone, her ear. "Yeah?"

"Well, let's just put it this way. . . . Your wall or mine, cowboy?"

Oh, eternity wasn't going to be nearly enough time, not with this wild girl of his, he thought, pushing her up against his bedroom wall. That was okay because they'd already defied time itself in finding each other.

Surely All would help them a little bit more along the way.

Deidre Knight

Parallel Seduction

Warrior Jake Tierny travels back in time to stop a traitor in his beloved king's camp. But when a twist of fate proves the mission unnecessary, Jake is trapped in a time not his own, with friends who cannot learn his true identity.

Scott Dillon may be the king's trusted lieutenant, but he is also a man at war with himself, a human hybrid who refuses to succumb to the Antousian nature he abhors. The one that Jake Tierny embodies.

FBI linguist Hope Harper refuses to let near-blindness keep her from joining the Refarians in their war to defend mankind. Her attraction to both Scott and Jake forces all three to question the core of their beliefs. And as their enemies surround them, Hope knows she must choose one man for all time.

DEIDRE KNIGHT

Parallel Heat

An unforgettable alternate world of danger, seduction and the mysteries of time. Here Knight returns to that world as otherworldly warrior Marco McKinley is enlisted to personally protect the beautiful human solider Thea Haven. Now, as two sworn enemies are pitted against each other, their lives will be changed forever by the unpredictable perils of love, betrayal, vengeance and passion.

DEIDRE KNIGHT

Parallel Attraction

Exiled king Jared Bennett is fighting for his people's freedom. Now his otherworldly rebel force has the one weapon that can turn the tide against their enemy: the key to the secrets of time. With victory at hand, only one human, Kelsey Wells, has the power to change everything. Kelsey is unable to defend her fierce attraction to Jared Bennett, but is unaware of the truth: although Jared is exactly what he says, he hasn't told her everything. And when the future crashes into the present, Kelsey must decide if his deception will cost them the love that should have been their destiny.

"A fantastic and riveting new voice in paranormal fiction." —Karen Marie Moning, *New York Times* bestselling author of *Spell of the Highlander*